LINDA MITCHELMORE began w[...]
a late starter – when she lost her [...]
To begin with she buried herself [...]
then decided to have a go at writing. She found it a way of
communicating. And it paid! She has now had over 300 short
stories published, worldwide. Linda has had four full-length
novels and two novellas published with Choc Lit, *The Little B &
B at Cove End* is her third novel with HQ Digital, following
Summer at 23 The Strand and *Christmas at Strand House*.

Linda has lived in Devon, beside the sea, all her life and
wouldn't want to live anywhere else. She walks by the sea most
days, or up over the hill behind her house where she has fabulous
views out over Dartmoor. In summer she can be found on the
pillion of one of her husband, Roger's, vintage motorbikes, or
relaxing in the garden with a book and a glass of Prosecco. Life
couldn't be sweeter.

You can follow Linda on Twitter: @LindaMitchelmor

Readers love Linda Mitchelmore

'The perfect book to take on holiday.'

'It's inspired me to go on a little holiday of my own.'

'By the end of the book I wanted to sit on the veranda with a glass of wine, eat fish & chips and visit the local café.'

'A wonderful summer read.'

'Charming and uplifting.'

'Such a delightful, uplifting and heartwarming read.'

'A lovely book to read on holiday.'

'Fabulous.'

The Little B&B at Cove End

LINDA MITCHELMORE

HQ
An imprint of HarperCollins*Publishers* Ltd
1 London Bridge Street
London SE1 9GF

This edition 2019

1
First published in Great Britain by
HQ, an imprint of HarperCollins*Publishers* Ltd 2019

Copyright © Linda Mitchelmore 2019

Linda Mitchelmore asserts the moral right to be
identified as the author of this work.
A catalogue record for this book is
available from the British Library.

ISBN: PB: 978-0-00-833097-2
EB: 978-0-00-832774-3

MIX
Paper from
responsible sources
FSC
www.fsc.org   FSC® C007454

This book is produced from independently certified FSC™ paper
to ensure responsible forest management.

For more information visit: www.harpercollins.co.uk/green

Printed and bound in Great Britain by
CPI Group (UK) Ltd, Croydon CR0 4YY

Mike and Barbara Adams – for a lifetime of support, generosity, and love.

CHAPTER ONE

'But Mae, we have to eat!' Cara said, standing in the hallway, the flyer for the art festival in her hand: LARRACOMBE TO CHALLENGE ST IVES 3rd–7th AUGUST, it said in fancy script. There was a list of artists who would be showing their work and giving talks and workshops – Elisabeth James, Janey Cooper, Stella Murphy and Tom Gasson-Smith amongst others, although Cara hadn't heard of any of them. The festival was six weeks away, but she was thinking fast. She would have enough time to get her B&B up and running, and a bit of experience under her belt. August was high summer when high prices could be charged. There would be lots of people coming from further afield to the festival, people wanting somewhere to stay. There was even a number to ring for anyone able to host artists. Cara would ring just as soon as she had calmed Mae down a bit and reassured her that Cove End would still be very much their home, even though they'd need to take in paying guests to survive.

'Didn't Dad leave *anything*, Mum? Anything at *all*?'

Mae was practically screaming the words at her.

'Sssh. Don't shout, darling. We don't want everyone to know our business.'

1

'Huh. *You* tell Rosie everything.' Mae tossed her head of auburn curls and dragged her fingers through her hair, straightening and then tweaking the curls she loved and hated in equal measure, depending on her mood. Cara had a feeling she hated those curls at that moment.

'Keep your voice down. It's not nice to talk about people behind their backs. Rosie can probably hear you.'

Mae gave a couldn't-care-less shrug and Cara did her best to remember how it had been when she'd been on the cusp of womanhood herself – the moods, the angst, the lack of self-confidence sometimes.

Cara's friend, Rosie, was still in Cara's kitchen. She'd come over for Sunday lunch as she often had since Cara had been widowed, and the three of them – Cara, Mae and Rosie – had created a family of sorts. Yes, they were good friends and looked out for one another, but Cara did not tell Rosie *everything*.

'I do not tell Rosie everything,' Cara said, keeping her voice calm. 'But to answer your question, all your dad left us was the house.'

And that had always been in my name anyway in case of bankruptcy, but there was no need for Mae to know that.

'I want to believe you, Mum,' Mae said, screwing her eyes up tight, which Cara knew was just so the tears that were threatening didn't fall, 'I really do, but I can't quite. I mean, Dad loved us, right?'

In his way, Cara wanted to say. But just not enough to stop gambling; not enough that he didn't sell anything he could to fund his addiction; not enough that he wasn't open and honest with us both.

'He loved you very much, you know that.'

Cara hoped that would be the answer her daughter needed and wanted in that moment.

'Yeah,' Mae said, slowly, letting the word out like a sad sigh. And there was a tiny twitch at the corners of her mouth, the beginnings of a smile as though she was remembering the good times with her father and all they had been to one another. And then she took a deep breath and pulled herself up tall. 'Yeah, well, try and remember it's my house, too. I'm not moving out of my bedroom for any stupid B&B guests. Dad would never, ever, have wanted me to do that. Okay?'

'Of course I won't move you out of your room. Don't worry,' Cara said, weary of the fight she was having with her fifteen-year-old daughter over her new venture.

'Couldn't you get a job or something?' Mae asked, arms folded across her chest, a pout on her face. 'Go back to working in a bank or something, like you did before you had me?'

'No, I've been out of it too long for that. Things have changed so much in fifteen years I'd need too much training to even get in at the lowest level. I'm not computer-literate enough for a start.'

'Making stuff, then? Clothes. You're good at that. The vintage dresses Dad bought me and you copied when I'd worn them and worn them and they were falling apart in the end because I'd worn them so much and the material was, like, ancient anyway, or I'd grown out of them ... you always did that brilliantly. You could start a business – haute couture or something.'

'It's a lovely thought, darling,' Cara said, hugging her daughter's compliment to her because they came so rarely these days. But in her heart Cara knew it would be an impossible business to get into with just a now very ancient Singer sewing machine. She'd need a machine to do overlocking for a start and she just didn't have the money. Or, as she'd said a moment ago, the computer skills to sell her product online, although she could learn that if she had to. 'But I'm no Stella McCartney.'

'Duh!' Mae said, slapping her forehead theatrically. 'You don't need to *be* Stella McCartney, or anyone else, Mum. You just have to make good stuff that people want and ...'

'Enough, Mae,' Cara interrupted. Mae was making a very

decent argument about what she could do to get them out of the financial mess they were in, but Cara had already thought of all that; been awake night after night thinking those same things and if she could get any of them to work. 'Now go and meet Josh and have a lovely time.'

'I'm already gone,' Mae said, hurrying towards the door, not stopping to peck her mother's cheek as she usually did.

Cara followed more slowly, stepping out onto the terrace. She pressed her lips together, forcing a smile she didn't feel as Mae turned round for a brief moment before scurrying off. Mae was so pretty and never afraid to be different from her peer group. She was wearing the ballerina-length, black cabbage roses on a white ground, antique dress that had been her favourite since the day Mark had bought it for her from the vintage shop in Totnes. The fabric – starched to within an inch of its life – crackled as Mae walked. A black cardigan was draped over her shoulders, a simple, fine wool but faded.

'Don't be too late, Mae,' Cara called after her, stepping out onto the terrace. 'Please.' But the breeze off the sea snatched her words away, blew them back in her face.

But perhaps Mae had heard because she turned, teased some tendrils of hair down each side of her face – a habit of long-standing – and Cara resisted the urge to rush down the path and hold her daughter to her lest it be the last time she ever saw her. Mae pointed at the sign Cara had painted, clapped a hand over her mouth to indicate suppressed laughter, then disappeared from view.

The hastily made sign – COVE END B&B – that Cara had made using some old paints of Mae's she'd found in the toy cupboard, on a square of hardboard that had been propped up against the garage wall for as long as Cara could remember, swung back and forth, banging against the slim trunk of the lilac tree as Cara returned to the kitchen. She'd managed to find two hooks, screwing them into the bottom of the board on which hung a

4

strip of hardboard with VACANCIES on one side and NO VACANCIES on the other.

'Tea? Coffee? Something stronger?' Rosie asked.

'Tea, please. How sad would it be if I turned into a dipso widow-slash-single mother?'

'But you're not going to,' Rosie said. 'And you didn't have to let her go. She's only fifteen for goodness' sake. You could have said no, you know. Mae is way too young for Josh Maynard. Or Josh is way too old for her. Whichever way you want to look at it.'

'Not in Mae's opinion,' Cara said with a small sigh. 'Or Josh's, I suspect. If I forbade her to see him, she'd only find a way, behind my back, to meet him. Forbidden fruit and all that.'

'How long have they been seeing each other?' Rosie asked, arms folded across her chest and her hands tucked firmly under her armpits. Cara saw it for the gesture it was – disapproval. And Rosie wasn't going to be moved on her opinions either.

'Not long. Three months. Maybe four. Only at weekends because of school. Anyway, what is this? The Spanish Inquisition?'

Josh was good about bringing Mae home on time and Cara had to be thankful for that.

'It's only because I love you both,' Rosie said. 'I wouldn't want more angst and drama dropped on you. You know, young girl who thinks she knows it all but doesn't, and older man who knows it all and doesn't give a fig who he uses to get his own way and ...'

'Rosie, you are ...'

'I know.' Rosie thrust out an arm, traffic policeman-style, to halt Cara's objections. 'I'm out of order. Way out of order. But I've been that girl, done that, got the bloody T-shirt. It doesn't alter the fact that Josh is twenty. He gets through girls the way most lads his age get through hair gel or whatever the latest fad fashion is these days. Ask anybody in this place and they'd say the same about Josh.'

'Oh God,' Cara said. 'That's the trouble with this place: everyone knows everyone else. Mae's almost sixteen – she has to grow up sometime. If all I had to worry about was Mae seeing Josh Maynard, I'd be a happy woman.'

It was common knowledge in the village that Josh had been a bit of a rebel in his teenage years, railing against everything his father, a vicar, believed in. He'd left school in the middle of his A levels, stopped going to church on Sundays with his mother and sister, and loped from part-time job to part-time job with no real vision of his future. He was a regular at both village pubs and rumour had it he'd smoked pot for a while. Cara rather hoped he wasn't doing that any more, but was wary of asking Mae if he was. But Cara knew Josh wasn't the only one who had done these things. Hadn't Cara herself gone through life to date with no clear vision? She'd even smoked pot – just the once because it had made her very sick and frightened the life out of her. Time, she decided, to shift the focus from Josh Maynard in this conversation.

'Who else knows, do you think? About Mark, I mean, and his gambling.'

Cara bit the insides of her cheeks to stop her tears. She was sick of tears. Sick of the reason for them; Mark had spent every single penny of their savings on internet gambling, or down at the bookie's betting on horses or dogs or both. The dinghy Mark had bought for Mae, and which she loved with all her heart, had been sold. Cara's little Fiat 500 had been sold. Anything of any value had been sold so that Mark could gamble. Things disappeared – almost without Cara noticing sometimes – piece by piece. Mark had been crafty, taking a painting then regrouping the others so that it had taken Cara a while to notice it was missing. Amongst them had been three paintings she'd inherited from her great-grandmother, Emma. Two woodland scenes and a harbour scene. Emma's first husband, Seth Jago – a gifted but amateur artist, so family folklore had it – had painted them back

6

in the early 1900s. The only painting of Seth Jago's that Mark hadn't taken was a portrait of Emma that had been at the picture framer's in Sands Road having a repair done to the corner of the frame where Cara had knocked it off the wall when she'd been dusting. Thank God she still had that because on that fateful night, Mark's car had spun out of control at a roundabout and he'd been killed. Every other painting Cara had collected during their marriage – all fifteen of them – had been ruined beyond any hope of repair when the car had caught fire after Mark had been pulled free by the fire crew. Stuff in the boot had been saved, but not all the things on the back seat, the paintings amongst it. Cara often wondered where those other paintings of Seth Jago's might be, but in a strange way she was glad they hadn't become victims of Mark's fatal accident, because they'd vanished from Cove End a long time before that.

'Tell me, Rosie,' Cara said as she sipped the tea her friend had made her, 'is the whole village talking about me?'

'Well, yes. Of course they are. Not as much as when Mark died because that was a shock to everyone I expect, but you're probably still good gossip fodder.' Rosie's reply was swift and honest. 'You're only thirty-nine. You're a widow. They're sad for you, that's all.'

Cara studied Rosie's face as she spoke, trying to see lies in her friend's eyes, the way she'd known there were lies in Mark's eyes every time he'd said he hadn't gambled that day, nor the day before, and that he wouldn't gamble tomorrow. Whenever she'd challenged him, demanding to know where her silver, or her paintings, or her household goods had gone, Mark always said he'd replace everything just as soon as he'd won enough on the next throw of the dice. Always the next throw of the dice would sort everything. Except it never did. It was all lies, lies, lies. But Rosie's eyes were wide and clear as they focused on Cara's almost royal blue ones.

'But they know?'

7

'I think some of them do, yes. When a man starts selling his own household goods down the pub, people are going to know something's up. Andy Povey at the Beachcomber has a pretty good idea what Mark was up to because he bought Mark's watch off him. Amongst other things, no doubt.'

'Oh great. The pub landlord knows so now the whole village knows.'

Cara never went in the village pub, so at least she'd been saved from any knowing glances, and she felt oddly glad of that now.

'Not necessarily. A pub landlord's a bit like a priest at confessional but without the divine right to dish out Hail Marys. I expect with Andy, most of what he hears goes in one ear and out the other. He's a good bloke.'

'Did Andy tell you he knew about Mark?' Cara had to know. She was no shrinking violet, but now she'd need nerves of steel to walk down the street if Andy had told all his customers.

'He had a quiet word with me in Sainsbury's. Because he knows we've been friends forever, you and me.'

'In Sainsbury's? With the world and his wife listening in?'

'I'm not going to answer that,' Rosie said. 'I can do discreet, you know. As can Andy Povey when he sees a need.'

'Of course. I'm sorry,' Cara said. 'I don't know how you've put up with my outbursts at times.'

'Because I'm a saint,' Rosie laughed. Then she looked serious. 'No, I'm no saint, as you know. But you *are* my dearest friend, and I *am* Mae's godmother, and I care about you both. And I would, quite literally, give an arm for you not to be in this situation, but we both know that can't happen.'

Cara nodded.

'Thanks,' she said, 'for being there for me.'

'No worries. Now, if you don't need me to give you more advice on how to bring up your teenage daughter, I'd better buzz. I've got two eyebrow tints, a leg wax, then two Brazilians followed by a manicure on the books. And a thirty-minute drive to my salon, so ...'

Rosie had hit on the idea of opening her salon on Sunday evenings for women and girls who worked nine to five and couldn't make weekday or daytime appointments, and who – perhaps – didn't want to cut into their weekend time off by going to a beauty salon on a Saturday when they could be shopping or out with their mates. It was really taking off. But if she was honest, Cara was missing Rosie's company; needing it now more than ever. The first six months after Mark's death had been a mad scramble to sort the legal aspects that result from a sudden death, and Cara had got through it on automatic pilot almost. Then came the year of 'firsts' followed by a time of mourning for the good times she and Mark had shared, and a feeling of loss that they would now not have a future.

'No, I'm fine,' Cara said, feeling anything but. 'You go. I need to sort out bed linen and crockery and so on. Then I've got to think of something to send to the paper about putting in an ad for the B&B. With this art festival coming up, I can't fail to get guests, can I?'

Cara took a deep breath. *And I've got to try not to worry about Mae being with Josh Maynard and whether he is pushing Mae into having underage sex, and work out how many rooms I will need to fill to pay the rates and the supermarket and for Mae to go to Paris with her school in September,* she thought. Her head was a maelstrom of random thoughts, and she was starting to get a headache between her eyes.

'It's hardly St Ives here,' Rosie said. 'I mean, Larracombe? Two pubs, one church, a harbour that holds about a dozen boats, two gift shops and a handful of cottages. And a half hour drive to a decent supermarket. I don't know what all the fuss is about. It's all over the village that some famous painter is coming. I mean, now this house is denuded of paintings, do you really want an art festival thrown in your face?'

'I need the money,' Cara said quietly. Just as soon as she was alone she'd ring the number on the bottom of the flyer and register. 'And I thought you were in a hurry to go.'

Rosie laughed.

'Bugger off, you mean,' she said. Rosie reached for her bag, rifling through it for her keys. 'But think about it, eh? I wouldn't want you to have any more pain – emotionally that is – than you already have.'

'I have thought about it,' Cara told her. She glanced at the darker patches on the kitchen wall where her beloved paintings had been, knowing the walls in every other room in the house looked the same. 'Anyway, how hard can cooking bacon and eggs and a few rounds of toast be?'

Rosie had found her keys and jangled them at Cara.

'For me, my love, it would be akin to penal servitude – a fate worse than death. Oh God, sorry. I didn't mean death as in Mark, you know. I meant death as in the worst possible thing that could happen to a person and …'

'Stop! You're digging yourself in deeper. You'll need a sparrow's crane to get you out if you carry on. Go!' Cara laughed, feeling the ripple of the laugh ease her pain, and the tightness in her chest, just a little. Even the headachey worry lines between her eyes were smoothing out a little. She reached out and held onto her friend's hands, and for a moment the two women's eyes locked before Cara looked away, afraid that Rosie would notice Cara was hiding lies of her own. Because what she hadn't told anybody – not Rosie, the coroner, the police, or Mark's parents was that as well as all her paintings, Mark had also taken most of his clothes and his computer because Cara, unable to put up with Mark's gambling any more, had asked him to leave.

And would the guilt of that ever leave her? What if Mae were to even suspect that of her? What then?

CHAPTER TWO

'Great, Mae,' Josh said, giving Mae a quick kiss on the lips. 'Glad you made it.' He held out a hand and Mae slipped hers into it. How good it felt, her hand in his, especially knowing how half the girls in the village were greener than grass with envy that she was Josh Maynard's girlfriend and they'd been passed over.

'Course I made it,' Mae said.

Sometimes she had to pinch herself that he'd asked her out in the first place. She'd been shuffling along the breakwater, wrapped up against an early spring chill, looking out to sea, thinking about stuff, not really wanting to speak to anyone when Josh had come along and said, 'Hi'. She hadn't seen him around much since the time he'd come along to the funeral parlour with his dad, who was supporting her in her wish to see her dad one last time before he was buried in St Peter's Churchyard. Her mum hadn't wanted her to go. The funeral people wouldn't let her in without an adult so on a whim she'd gone to the vicarage to ask if the Reverend Maynard could help. She'd been so surprised when Josh had pitched up that day. His dad had said he thought it might be easier for her if someone younger was with her as well. But she'd only been thirteen then, and Josh a teenager. What a difference a couple of years made.

'So, here's the plan,' Josh said. He began walking away from the bandstand in the park, where they'd met, towards the gates. 'A little trip to Fairy Cove. Just you and me. I've borrowed my sister's car.'

'Cool,' Mae said.

'Parked up over there.' Josh pointed towards the car park.

Mae's mind fast-forwarded and she could already see them, kissing and cuddling in the car in the lane that went down to Fairy Cove.

'Love the frock, by the way,' Josh said. He held Mae out at arm's length. 'Give us a twirl.'

Mae obliged, doing a couple of spins as he twirled her round.

'Thanks. My dad bought me this one, you know, before he died.'

'Well, he'd hardly buy it after, would he?' Josh said. But he said it with a grin to show he was only joking. 'You've not told me much about your dad.'

'I thought you knew,' Mae said. Hands clasped, she and Josh were meandering slowly to wherever it was in the car park his sister's car was. 'You came with your dad that day …'

'He said I had to,' Josh said. His grin had dropped now. He looked more angry than sad that he'd been made to go with his dad and Mae to the funeral parlour.

'I'm glad you did come,' Mae said. 'But you could have said no.'

'No? To my dad? You have got to be kidding!'

'At least you've still gone one,' Mae said in a quiet little voice. Her dad hadn't been perfect and he got cross sometimes if she interrupted him when he was doing stuff on the computer, and almost never remembered to buy her mum a Valentine's card and stuff like that. But still she wished she could say, 'My dad's picking me up from school today,' or something.

'Yeah, but it's not easy,' Josh said. 'You should have heard the fallout when I *did* say no to him. About going to uni. He quoted, chapter and verse, how much he'd spent on private education for me and how I was an ungrateful so-and so. He wanted me to do theology like he had. And his father and his grandfather before him.'

'And you wanted to break the mould?'

'Yeah. Gardening's not his idea of a career move, although I think Monty Don would beg to differ.'

Mae had no idea who Monty Don might be, but she guessed he was a famous gardener or something. Mae often didn't know who or what Josh was talking about but wasn't so stupid as to ask because it would highlight the differences in their family backgrounds and their education. She didn't want to sound too much like a schoolgirl even though that was what she was.

'Mums and dads don't always know what's best for their kids, I shouldn't think.'

'*Your* mum? Does she give you grief about going out with me? Being older?'

'Yeah. Calls you Granddad!' Mae giggled.

'She doesn't?'

'No. I'm only joking. But she's been pretty cool about stuff since Dad died. Her friend, Rosie, was there when I was getting ready to meet you, huffing and shrugging and letting me know by her body language she didn't think I should go, but Mum's a right pushover at the moment. Doesn't want me to be hurt any more, you know. Anyway ...'

Mae let her words fade away. Some date this was turning out to be; her anger over her dad's death and now her mum wanting to turn Cove End into a B&B was threatening to bubble over. Josh was going to get pretty fed up of her in a minute.

'But you came anyway,' he said, giving her hand a squeeze. 'Like I said just now, I know your dad died, and how. My dad's version of it anyway. You can tell me if you want. I think you've got anger over your dad just under the surface the same as I have over mine. Yes?'

13

'Probably,' Mae agreed. 'But since you ask, just for the record, Dad made me angry a long ago before he went and got himself killed. He sold the dinghy without telling me and I loved going out in that with him. I don't know why he did that. And then he sold Mum's car and she couldn't drive me into Totnes for my Saturday dance class any more. Like he didn't care about me, you know. And there's not been much cash for Mum and me since, which is why she's got this stupid idea about turning the house into a B&B.' Mae sniffed back tears.

'If this was an old black and white movie, I'd whip out a pristine white handkerchief and offer it to you to mop up your tears.' Josh dangled an imaginary handkerchief in front of Mae's face.

'Idiot!' she laughed, pretending to take it. She felt a bit better having told Josh about her dad, although she doubted she would have if he hadn't slagged his off a bit. It felt good that she could do that – that they both could.

'I'm glad that's off your pretty little chest,' Josh said.

'Yeah, sorry. Didn't mean to be a drain.'

'You're not. But it must have been awful for your mum, too.'

Had Josh said that a few minutes ago, she might have snapped that he would say that, what with his dad being a vicar and everything – that he'd been brought up to say stuff like that whether he believed it or not. But now … well now she knew a little bit more about Josh, she could see the big house he lived in, the private education he'd had and the foreign holidays they went on meant nothing if he and his dad were at loggerheads all the time.

'Did you mean it?' Mae said. 'About me telling you about my dad?'

Mae hadn't had anyone to talk about it to really – what went before; before he'd died. There had been a couple of teachers who'd kept her back after a lesson when she'd been thinking about stuff and unable to concentrate who'd said if she needed

14

someone to talk to, then she only had to ask. But what could they do?

'Sure,' Josh said. 'Shall we sit for a bit?'

They were nearing a bench that was in the sunshine, a willow opposite dipping its frondy new growth almost to the grass.

'Yeah. Okay.' She took a deep breath and sat down, her hand still in Josh's. 'I don't know if your mum and dad row ...'

'Big time!' Josh interrupted. 'Language too. Some of it very Anglo-Saxon!'

'Really?' Mae said, stunned.

'The image of the benign reverend can be a myth!'

'Right. Okay. Well, mine rowed but not big time. No bad language as far as I could hear. Most of it was sort of theatrical whispering, in the dead of night. It went on and on sometimes although I couldn't hear what they were saying exactly. And sometimes I'd hear raised voices when I came in from school or something and they'd stop abruptly when they heard me shut the door, and it would be all false smiles and 'Hello, darling, good day?' and all that.'

'Same in our house,' Josh said. 'They'd be arguing for England about something, then there'd be a knock on the door and I'd answer it and shout through that it was old Mrs Ellis or someone come to talk about her husband's funeral and they'd appear in the hall, arms around one another, all smiles. I don't know if there's ever been a couple who hasn't had a row or ten.'

'No,' Mae said. She and Josh hadn't had one. Yet. She'd tackle that hurdle when she came to it. But right now, Mae thought that they'd exhausted the subject of rowing parents and how it affected their children. 'But I don't want to talk about it any more. Okay?'

'Okay,' Josh said.

He stood up, pulling Mae with him. He let go of her hand and put an arm around her shoulders instead. Mae snuggled into him, feeling loved. Feeling safe. They began to walk more quickly towards the park gates.

'What time have you got to be in?' Josh asked, which only served to make her feel less like Josh's girlfriend and more like a small child he was looking after. It knocked the wind right out of her sails for a moment.

'Eight,' she said.

'Right.'

They were navigating the car park now.

'Can we get a drink on the way?' Mae asked. She quite fancied a glass of chilled Pinot Grigio – Rosie always brought a bottle or two when she came to visit and her mum always let her have a glass with dinner when she did.

'Ah, Andy Povey won't serve me wine for you. But we can pick up a bottle of something and take it down to Fairy Cove.'

'Just the one bottle?' Mae giggled – already she could taste the Pinot Grigio she knew Josh would buy on her tongue. Rosie didn't like her mum letting her have a glass of wine and read her mum the riot act when she found out. Then Rosie gave Mae a lecture on the dangers of alcohol and how it altered your thinking, your rationale. Rosie used a lot of fancy words like that … rationale.

'Yes. For now. You're underage.'

'Oh God, not you as well!' Mae said, making a mock-cross face. 'You should have heard the lecture Rosie gave me when Mum went out of the room. "Having sex with a minor is a major offence, Mae, so best remind your boyfriend of that in case he gets ideas. And so is buying alcohol for the same minor. Which means you in this instance, Mae. Don't forget that will you, Mae? I know you're fifteen going on fifty-one, but I don't want you bringing any more worry on your mum's shoulders, okay? End of lecture, Mae.", Mae repeated, in a posh sing-song voice. 'And she said "Mae" that many times it was like I'd forgotten my own name or something. Just because she's my godmother doesn't mean she can rule my life!'

'She sounds like quite a woman, this Rosie,' Josh laughed. 'She's got you fired up anyway!'

'A force to be reckoned with,' Mae said, doing her best not to sound angry and bitter. She was failing miserably because all the hurt and anger had bubbled up again.

God, but this growing up lark was hard. No one in her class at school had a father who had died. No one had a mother who was going ahead with turning their home into a B&B against their wishes. No one knew just how horrid it was to go to sleep at night and dream about their dad and then wake up in the morning to realise he wasn't there any more. No one knew how it felt to have a sort of house brick sat permanently on their chest. It all singled Mae out as being different, although she was anyway through the clothes she wore. She smoothed down the skirt of her frock and bent to finger out the netting petticoat that peeped out from the hem of it. It had a sweetheart neckline and a band of black crepe around the waist. Like she'd told Josh just now, it was the last frock her dad had bought her before he died. She knew she was wearing it to death because the seams were beginning to look strained, but wearing it somehow made her feel closer to him. Anyway, anyone could wear ripped jeans and a T-shirt two sizes too small and most of the girls in her class did at the weekends, like they were in a team or something. Mae didn't know she wanted to be part of any sort of team.

'It's what godmothers are supposed to do – toe the moral line. That's the whole point of being one,' Josh said, dragging Mae's wandering mind back to the present. She thought she'd been thinking less about her dad lately, but somehow it was the other way round.

'Yeah, but I still think she was out of order. We're not even related. She's just Mum's friend from way back. And then there's the fact she's a bit of a slapper is Rosie. Two divorces, three live-in lovers – what sort of moral guidance is that?'

'It's life, Mae. And neither of the divorces might have been her fault. And has anyone ever told you that you're very beautiful when you're cross?'

'That line's got whiskers on it,' Mae said, but she was glad Josh had said it all the same. And she knew she was probably boring him to death carping on and on about Rosie, who Josh hadn't even met. She should stop. She'd try.

'Comes from being an old granddad,' Josh said, the skin at the corners of his eyes crinkling deliciously as he smiled. How dark his eyes were – 90% cocoa solids chocolate or something – and how Mae loved looking into them. 'Shall we go and get that wine?' Josh said as he unlocked the car door.

'Yeah,' Mae said, 'I might die of thirst if we don't!'

'A vicar's son, a murderer? That would never do!' Josh said. He opened the door for Mae to get in, handing her the seat-belt. God, but how chivalrous. How very grown up it made her feel.

Mae stood on tiptoe and lifted her face up to Josh for a kiss. When his lips came down on hers, she got a brief whiff of alcohol. Not beer. Not wine. Spirits maybe, definitely alcohol. Had he been drinking already? A glass of something with dinner, which she knew a lot of people were in the habit of having? Whatever, he was far from drunk, not even tipsy. But Mae thought it best not to ask as their lips met.

They were soon at the corner shop on the road out of the village. Josh took no time at all choosing a bottle of wine. Pinot Grigio. And a bag of crisps. They joined the end of a small queue, and Mae was amazed to see she knew no one in it. At least no one who would tell her mum she was buying wine with Josh Maynard.

But her relief was short-lived.

'Well, well, well,' a voice behind them said. 'If it isn't our local baby-snatcher.'

'Shove off, Bailey,' Mae said, not bothering to turn around.

She and Bailey Lucas had been at infant school together, and now at senior school as well, although Mae was in a higher tutor group. About six months ago, Mae and Bailey had gone out a couple of times: to the cinema once, and to drink endless glasses of coke in the Oystercatcher Café. They hadn't even got to the hand-holding stage, never mind kissing or anything else. And then Josh had asked her out and, well, she hadn't even bothered to tell Bailey she didn't want to go out with him again – she'd just stopped answering his texts and he'd got the message in the end. She wasn't proud of that now, but it was done and dusted. Josh had taken her to the cinema on their first date and they'd snogged their faces off in the back row. Her lips had been red raw when she got home, and she'd slathered on Savlon before she went to sleep in the hope her mother wouldn't notice in the morning. She'd moved on. She wished Bailey would too. He wasn't a bad bloke – just a bit boring, especially compared to Josh.

'You heard her, Lucas,' Josh said. 'Shove off.'

'When I'm ready,' Bailey said. 'And not before.'

A frisson of unease rippled, cold, across Mae's shoulders. Bailey took a step closer to Josh, squaring up to him. Josh was tall – just under six feet – but Bailey was taller by a good couple of inches. Thicker set too. He was easily the tallest boy in their year.

'You just mind how you treat her, Maynard,' Bailey said. 'That's all.'

'Explain yourself,' Josh said.

He let go of Mae's hand. Her right one. Surely he wasn't going to throw a punch at Bailey here? There were two people in the queue in front of them – chattering away for England so Mae didn't think they'd heard the threatening exchange. She glanced towards the counter where Meg Smythson was rapidly scanning the contents of a customer's basket.

'In case you need reminding,' Bailey said, 'you did the dirty on my sister, Xia. More than once from what I've heard.'

'None of your business,' Josh said. He turned to Mae. 'Ignore

19

him.' He put an arm around Mae's shoulder and swivelled her round to turn their backs to Bailey. He leaned in and whispered in her ear. 'He's just jealous.'

Mae hadn't told Josh she'd been out with Bailey a couple of times, but in this place she probably didn't need to – everyone seemed to know about everyone else or who knew someone who did.

'Jealousy is a totally useless trait,' Bailey said, coming closer – so close Mae felt his warm breath on her neck.

Mae turned around to face Bailey.

'Back off, Bailey,' she said. 'Please. I'm sorry I didn't answer your texts if that's what's troubling you. Okay?'

This was getting uncomfortable now and they were no nearer the counter than they were when they came in. Meg Smythson was looking their way now, forehead furrowed with puzzle lines as though she was sensing trouble brewing in her shop.

Bailey shrugged.

'You heard her,' Josh said, his voice low. 'Back off before I make you back off.'

Bailey stepped back a few paces.

'Let's just say, Mae, if you get any bother you know where to find me.'

'Your knight in shining armour, Mae,' Josh laughed, leaning closer to Mae.

'Who I won't need,' she said, catching a whiff of Josh's slightly alcoholic breath again.

This was all turning into some sort of old-fashioned film scenario, with two men fighting over her – it was sort of flattering really in a strange way. She felt a bit princessy. And there he was – her dad back again in her mind because he'd always called her his little princess.

Mae smoothed her hands down over the roses on the 1950s full-skirted dress, a lump in her throat … remembering.

'But if you do, Mae,' Bailey said, 'the offer still stands.'

Mae wondered what sort of terrible time Bailey's sister might have had with Josh. Two-timing wasn't the best way to go about things, but hadn't she done it herself when she'd been sort of going out with Bailey and not told him she didn't want to see him any more before starting to go out with Josh?

'Ignore him,' Josh whispered. 'He's not worth brain space.'

Mae nodded – too full up to speak.

It was their turn to be served.

'Sorry about the wait,' Meg Smython said.

Josh placed the bottle of wine on the counter and Meg Smythson reached for it, and the scanner beeped loudly as she ran it through. The crisps followed.

Josh reached for the wine, but Meg got there first, grabbing it firmly at the base and pulling it back towards her.

'Buying wine for a minor is an offence,' Meg said. 'But I don't need to tell you that, Josh, do I?'

'I'm fairly conversant with the law on that matter, Mrs Smythson,' Josh said.

Conversant? Mae suppressed a giggle – Josh sounded so much older than his twenty years saying that. It made her giggle.

'Something funny, Mae?' Meg Smythson asked.

'Not really,' Mae said. She pulled a mock-glum face.

'Well, lovie,' Meg said. 'I'll say the same to you in case you didn't hear the first time … buying wine for a minor is an offence. That is all. There are other people waiting to be served.'

Mae looked behind her and saw that three other people had come in, one was stood behind Bailey and the other two were filling up baskets with goods.

'In that case,' Josh said, 'I will part with the readies and we'll get out of here. And just for the record, this wine is for my old man and my ma. For later. Okay with that, Mrs Smythson? Honest. On the Bible.'

'You would say that!' Mrs Smythson said, laughing now. She blushed.

'I would. Oh, and that turquoise top you're wearing really suits you, by the way, Mrs Smythson.'

'Flatterer,' Meg Smythson said, as Josh turned to go. Mae started to turn, but Meg Smythson reached out for her, and held onto her wrist – just for a second – before letting it go again. 'You just watch it, Mae. I wouldn't want my licence taken away. Get my drift? About the wine?'

'Yes,' Mae said.

She turned to join Josh, who was already walking towards the door.

As she passed Bailey he said, *sotto voce*, 'He got my sister rat-arsed, which wasn't pretty. Then he did the dirty on her. Just saying. Just so you know.'

Mae couldn't think of a single thing to say to that, so didn't. She was so fed up of everyone telling her how to live her life. Fed up with being treated like a little kid, like she didn't know anything, anything at all. God but she needed that drink now.

CHAPTER THREE

The house was quiet now that both Mae and Rosie had gone and Cara was glad of something to do. She went into the hall, picked up the flyer for the art festival and rang the number.

'Hello, Cara Howard here,' she said quickly, the second it was answered. She felt nervous, stepping into the unknown as a landlady. Ought she not have rung on a Sunday and waited until the morning? Oh well, it was done now. She'd taken the first step towards her new venture – well, the second if you counted her handmade B&B sign – and there was no going back now. 'I live at Cove End. I'm interested in offering accommodation to people coming to the art festival. Am I speaking to the right person?' She knew her words were tumbling out like water over a weir, but that's what nervousness did for you.

'You are,' a friendly voice said. 'I'm Laura Pearse. What sort of accommodation do you have?'

Cara wondered if she knew anyone called Laura Pearse, but she didn't think so.

'Two doubles and a single. One en suite. All with basins. Two with sea views. Oh, and a breakfast room that would be exclusively for guests' use.'

'Lovely. Perfect actually. I'll just take your details. I'll have to get back to you nearer the date. Oh, hang on a minute. Actually I've had a couple of enquiries already from people thinking I'm the Information Bureau taking general bookings, and I'm not. One couple and a single male, wanting B&B accommodation in a few days' time. Would you be up for that?'

'I would,' Cara said with a confidence she didn't feel because she'd have a lot to do to get all the rooms ready.

'Great. I've still got their details so I'll get back to you and tell them they can give you a ring. Landline and mobile numbers. Okay with that?'

'Fine,' Cara said.

It had been as easy as that. The potential guests had got back to her within half an hour and Cara had booked them in. Three guests in three days' time. She was well on the way now!

She put the radio on low so as to have another voice in the house. She went upstairs, then down again, peering into all the rooms trying to see them with a stranger's eye. Cove End had five bedrooms – two en suite, and there were two other bathrooms. Three of the bedrooms had sea views and the other two looked out over fields. There were three reception rooms – one of which Cara had always used as a breakfast room because it faced east and got the morning sun. She thought she could squeeze a couple of small tables with chairs in there and the guests could use that rather than the formal dining room that Cara rarely used because the table in there seated at least eight. Even when Mark had been alive it had rarely been used because Cara always thought it felt too stilted to be eating there, and so cold somehow. The kitchen was large, with room for a table and chairs and a small couch. There was also a downstairs cloakroom. Cara's head was suddenly full of plans for her new venture. She'd need more tables and chairs for the breakfast room. And possibly some side tables and an easy chair or two for the bedrooms for guests. There was a homes section in one of the charity shops in Totnes that sold furniture cheaply. She'd ask Rosie to drive her over.

'How much will two tables and some second-hand easy chairs, and a couple of cans of paint eat into my meagre savings?' Cara said out loud, then clapped a hand across her face.

She was talking to herself now. A sure sign of madness. Or desperate loneliness. But at least she had the house. And she was going to make it earn its keep. One of Mark's perks as a bank manager had been a ridiculously low mortgage rate. When they'd first married, Mark had accepted every transfer posting he'd been given. They'd lived in just about every town in Devon that had a bank, and in each one they'd upgraded their properties. For one terrible moment after Mark had died, Cara had wondered if he'd embezzled money from the bank. The police had been one step ahead of her, of course, and had got into the hard drive of his computers – home and work. The extent of Mark's gambling – telephone number amounts – had stunned Cara. The WPC who had been assigned to her after the accident had been very kind and understanding.

'I knew he gambled,' Cara had said. 'I tried my best to get him to stop, but ...' Cara shrugged as if to show how hopeless it had been begging with him, arguing with him, threatening him to face up to his addiction.

'You couldn't?' the WPC said.

'No. Perhaps he thought he was doing it for the times he did win and he bought a new car, or changed the TV for one with a bigger screen or something, bought our daughter a whole load of new clothes – things to give us a better life.'

'You are in no way to blame,' she'd told Cara gently.

But Cara did blame herself because a bank manager's salary should have been more than enough to send Mae on school trips and she, Cara, ought to have challenged him about his gambling long before she had.

'These trips aren't supervised enough,' Mark had said once when Rosie had offered to pay for Mae to go on a trip to Amsterdam. 'I'm not allowing my daughter to roam about some

25

foreign city at night, un-chaperoned, while their teachers are in a bar somewhere drinking their heads off, whoever might be paying for it.'

And Cara had given in. But what do you do when you love someone as much as Cara had loved Mark? He'd been a good husband in other ways – a fantastic lover for a start. And on Cara's birthday there had always been another painting, or some other present that Mark knew Cara would love.

Now Cara knew different. Mark preferred to risk money that should have been spent on Mae in the hope of making more. And with that knowledge, her love for him had dimmed. And the original paintings had only been an investment, hadn't they? Mark had said as much, wanting her to sell a painting he'd bought for one of her birthdays once he realised the artist was on the up and her painting was making four times the amount he'd paid for it.

It was the car full of paintings, now smashed, and burned, beyond saving, in the back-seat area that had alerted the police to the fact that this was not just another sad, speed-induced accident. Mae had been at school and Cara, unable to bear seeing Mark leave, had walked down the hill to the harbour as he loaded his car with his clothes, his favourite CDs and his computer. She hadn't known he would be taking the paintings.

When she'd got back, she'd almost stopped breathing when she saw all the darker patches on the walls where her beloved paintings had been.

A knock at the front door jolted Cara back to the present, and glad in a way that it had. She raced down the hall, making a mental note to get the polisher out and give the parquet a thorough going over very soon. She could see the silhouettes of two people – a man and a woman at a guess – through the stained glass.

'Have you got a double room?' the woman asked the second Cara opened the door. 'Two nights?'

'Oh,' Cara said. She hadn't been expecting guests so soon. 'Well ...'

She had two nights with no bookings before the people she'd just spoken to arrived. A whole host of butterflies was doing a dance in her stomach – this was all happening so fast. What had been just the germ of an idea was being made a reality.

'Have you?' the man said. 'It does say B&B on your sign. And vacancies.'

'Yes, I know it does,' Cara said. 'But it was a try-out with the sign, and really I'm not quite ready for guests. I was just about to put the polisher over the parquet.' She opened the door wider so that the middle-aged couple could see the tatty state of the hall floor and her still-denuded walls. 'I'm in the middle of redecorating,' she lied.

'Well, it looks clean enough to me,' the woman said, 'so can we come in? We've tried the pub but they don't do rooms, and that place called...what was it, the Lookout? ... is fully booked, and the Information Office is closed. I know I sound desperate and really we would be so ...'

Cara took a deep breath. She hadn't really prepared herself for how it might feel to have strangers in her home. But she had to start her fledgling business some time. She hoped Mae wouldn't be too shocked – or cross – to find strangers in the house already when she got back from her date with Josh.

'A double,' the man said, as though to remind Cara of what she'd been asked.

'Yes, I've got a double room,' she said. 'Do come in, if you don't mind the fact the walls are less than perfect. My paintings are in storage while I redecorate ...'

'A bit of faded wall won't bother us, will it, Eddie?' the woman said.

Cara did a mental inventory of the linen cupboard. The best was an Egyptian cotton duvet cover and matching sheets and pillowcases, which was on her own bed – a luxurious treat to

27

herself, a bit of spoiling now that Mark was gone. But the lilac floral was clean and aired and would have to do. No matching towels, but she couldn't worry about that now.

'I'll get a room ready for you as quick as I can.' She opened the door wider and ushered them in. 'I'm Cara, by the way.'

She proffered her hand first to the woman, and then the man.

'Pam and Eddie Hine,' the woman said. 'Pleased to meet you, and I mean really pleased. We thought we were going to have to sleep in the car, didn't we, Ed?'

'Yes, love,' Eddie said, looking fondly at Pam as a flush reddened the side of his neck.

Well, well, well, Cara thought. *I'll bet my last £223.26 that these two aren't married, despite making a good display of being newly-weds.* She glanced at Pam's wedding finger where a wide gold band shone brightly in the lights from the hall. And that look, and that flush of Eddie's, brought a lump to Cara's throat that was threatening to choke her. She saw herself trapped, in limbo, between fifteen-year-old Mae's calf-love for Josh, and Eddie and Pam at the other end of the spectrum.

And her own love for Mark stripped bare, sucked from her by his gambling.

'Will you want the full English breakfast?' Cara croaked.

'Lovely,' Pam said. 'We don't usually have a fried breakfast when we're at home, do we, Ed?'

'No, love,' Eddie said. 'But we're not at home now, are we?'

'No, we're not,' Pam giggled, which made Cara's oneness more painful, and she felt herself invisible, a not-really-wanted witness to their coupledom.

'Right,' Cara said, battling to look like a real B&B hostess, 'I'll show you where the sitting room is and then I'll make you a cup of tea while I get your room ready. The downstairs cloakroom is over there,' she went on, pointing, and meta-phorically crossing her fingers it was as squeaky clean as it usually was. 'After that, I'll need to pop to the shop to get the wherewithal for a cooked breakfast because, as I said, I wasn't expecting guests so soon.'

At least the sitting room was nicely appointed. Mark hadn't had room to take the flat screen TV or what was left of the silver that had been Cara's grandmother's, although Mark had already squirreled a fair bit of that out of the house and sold it, much to Cara's annoyance at the time.

'You do that, Cara,' Pam said as Cara ushered them into the sitting room and urged them to make themselves comfortable. 'We'll be as happy in pigs in muck here while we wait.'

'I'll make you a cup of tea. Then ten minutes to sort your room, another fifteen or so while I pop to the shops and…'

'Don't panic, Cara,' Pam interrupted, laying a gentle hand on Cara's arm. 'We'll be just fine while you pop out or our names aren't Pam and Eddie Hine.'

'Lovely in here it is, Ed,' Cara heard Pam say as she walked towards the door that led into the hall. 'Quality. Lovely curtains and everything. Comfy cushions. Very high end, designer.'

A warm glow spread across Cara's shoulders. She'd made those curtains. And the cushion covers. Rosie was always telling her she should take up sewing and make a business of it … well, maybe if the B&B business didn't take off, she would. She left Pam and Eddie Hine cooing over her lovely sitting room and went to make the tea.

Cara ran along Higher Street praying she'd catch the corner shop before it closed for the night. The sky was beginning to darken, that lovely indigo shade shot through with fuchsia pink that Cara loved, and which usually meant that tomorrow would be a fine day. She speeded up as she saw Meg Smythson walk towards the door of her shop, as though she was about to lock up. But Meg had seen Cara and held the door open for her to go in.

'Well, fancy,' Meg said. 'I had your Mae in here earlier. Lovely girl, your Mae. Where does she get those dresses she wears?'

Mae had been to the shop? Cara wondered what for, and what she might have bought, not that she had a lot to buy anything with, but the bank was paying Cara a small widow's pension, even though it wasn't stretching very far and Cara liked to give Mae a bit of pocket money.

'Charity shops,' Cara said. 'And a stall in Totnes Market. And she's had some of it for ages, waiting to grow into it.'

'Well, she looks stunning in them,' Meg said. 'And is going to be more beautiful still once she's finished her growing. With that Josh Maynard, she was.'

Cara didn't like the way Meg had put the word 'that' in front of Josh's name, as though he was something best left in the gutter.

'I know. She's going out with him.'

'Bit of a disappointment to his dad is that Josh,' Meg said. 'Wanted university for his son, he did, but all that was in Josh's head was surfing and earning money and he was having none of it. Never going to get rich gardening, is he?'

Cara suddenly felt defensive of Josh. She didn't like his character being ripped to shreds by Meg, any more than she'd liked it when Mae had been dismissive of Rosie.

'Monty Don seems to do very well from gardening on TV,' Cara said. She had a 'bit of a thing' for Monty Don as she imagined many viewers did.

'Another world, that, TV,' Meg countered, her voice dripping with disdain. 'Hardly Larracombe, is it? A bit of lawn-mowing for the Thrupps at Barley Mead, and a quick strim around the edge of the graves up at St Peter's.'

Cara's blood seemed to chill in her veins at that last remark – Mark was buried in the graveyard at St Peter's. She hadn't been there for a while to lay flowers or just to stand there and talk to him, tell him how sorry she was for everything that had happened between them. She wondered if Mae had. She could ask, of course, but Mae thought questions like that were an intrusion so Cara tended to hold back. But right now Cara didn't really have the time or the inclination to be getting into any sort of philosophical argument with Meg about gardening and TV and she could only think that life wasn't too exciting amongst the prepackaged potatoes and the newspapers and the bars of Cadbury Milk, and that when Meg did manage to get an audience she liked to share an opinion or two.

'Have you ever asked Josh if he wants to be rich?' Cara asked. 'Or if, perhaps, he's happy working the soil, growing things?'

Meg Smythson bridled.

'Well, all I'm saying is,' Meg said, leaning closer towards Cara as though someone might overhear her even though there was no one else in her shop, 'I know I'm telling tales out of school, and that Josh can charm the birds from the trees, but it was alcohol he was buying.'

'And is legally able to do so,' Cara said. 'He's over eighteen.'

'Ah yes,' Meg said. 'I know that.' She tapped the side of her nose. 'And he assured me it was for his parents' consumption, if you know what I mean.'

Cara knew. Meg Smythson was implying that Mae would be given a share of the wine and none of it would be going back to the rectory.

'Eggs,' Cara said. 'I'd like half a dozen large eggs if you've got them. And a packet of best back bacon. Sausages – chipolatas if you have them. Oh, and a thick sliced loaf. Please.'

There were, Cara knew, a couple of tomatoes in the salad box of the fridge that had gone a bit soft but which would be perfect to go with a fried breakfast, and there was an unopened jar of marmalade in the cupboard, won at Mae's school winter fair, and neither of them liked marmalade, so that would have to do.

'And a dozen or so mushrooms,' Cara added, as she spied a basket on the counter with milky-white button mushrooms in it.

'Got guests, have you?' Meg said, taking a packet of bacon

31

from the fridge and handing it to Cara. 'I saw the sign. You've had the council people in, hygiene and that, I expect?'

'Er, yes. Of course,' Cara said, hoping Meg wouldn't realise the word 'yes' wasn't the answer to both questions. How had she completely overlooked the possibility that she might have to be registered to take in B&B guests and have her kitchen and bathrooms passed for hygiene?

Well, that's what widowhood did to you, wasn't it? It deprived you of rational thinking for a while at least. And widowhood, mixed with the terrible guilt that Mark wouldn't have died had she not asked him to leave, was threatening to overwhelm her now. She made a show of examining a tin of chicken curry on the shelf beside her, just for something to do – so she wouldn't have to look Meg Smythson in the eye and run the risk that Meg would know she was lying.

'Good,' Meg said. 'Because if you haven't had the hygiene people in *before* guests arrive, then they take a very dim view of the whole thing. A *very* dim view.'

Meg reached for the mushrooms to weigh them out. She sniffed, giving her head a shake and her shoulders a shudder as if envisaging the dire consequences for Cara if she'd failed to register with the council.

'And they take a very dim view of underage drinking around here as well,' Meg finished. 'No matter it might be the vicar's son what offered that drink.'

Oh dear, Cara thought, *Meg Smythson didn't like me stopping her telling tales about Josh and Mae, did she?*

'And that'll be four pounds and ninety-seven pence,' Meg said. 'Shocking the price of things today, isn't it? Money goes nowhere, does it? And I expect with you being a widow now it's even ...'

'Here's the money,' Cara said, certain that there had been knowing in Meg's voice and it was a crowing sort of knowing rather than a sympathetic one. She couldn't get out of the shop fast enough.

And if anyone from the council should turn up in the morning, she'd tell them that the Hines were personal friends and that she wasn't charging them. *There, stuff that in your pipe and smoke it, Meg Smythson!*

CHAPTER FOUR

'Josh, no!' Mae said. 'You can't drive. You've drunk almost the whole bottle.'

She lunged towards him and tried to snatch the car keys from him, but he jerked his hand away, held them over his head so that Mae couldn't reach. The car was parked at the bottom of a rough, narrow lane that led to a secluded rocky beach – a perfect place for courting couples although theirs was the only car there at the moment. How she was going to get herself out of this predicament she didn't know yet, but she'd think of something. Foremost in her mind was stopping Josh from driving.

'You want it all, you do,' Josh said, slurring his words slightly. 'Or don't want it in your case.'

Josh slid a hand between her knees, and began to slide it up her thigh, but Mae pushed it away.

'No, Josh. Don't. Please.'

Josh had never done that before and Mae wondered if it was the alcohol affecting his judgment – he knew she was underage for sex and she'd told him, right at the beginning, that she wasn't up for that and he said he understood. Mae shifted sideways on the car seat to put a bit more distance between her and Josh, wondering why alcohol seemed to change a person's personality the more they drank. They either became louder and funnier if they were cheerful people to begin with, but the flipside of that was that some people became nasty and mean. Where had the Josh, who was so kind and understanding when she'd been remembering her dad, gone? She was pretty certain now that Josh had been drinking before they'd met. Bailey's words flashed through her mind – *'He got my sister rat-arsed and it wasn't pretty'*. Well, she wasn't even tiddly. Perhaps what Bailey had warned her about had been in the back of her mind all the time.

'Teathe,' Josh slurred, leaning towards her, but she pushed him away. 'You're a teathe.'

'If you mean sex,' Mae said, 'it has to feel right for me and it would only be a drunken fumble at the moment, wouldn't it?' And against the law as Rosie had so recently advised her, she thought but didn't say. Josh knew that anyway. Best not to antagonise him by saying she didn't want to lose her virginity here in a secluded lane in the front seat of Josh's sister's car.

If she kept Josh talking, doing her best to stop him getting the key in the ignition while she did it, then Josh couldn't be driving, maybe killing someone because his reactions were reduced by alcohol. She was on the verge of tears now, thinking about her dad and how the last time she'd seen him alive he'd been sitting at the kitchen table, his head in his hands, not looking up as she'd said, 'Bye, Dad, see you tonight,' as she left for school. She'd assumed he was tired – yes, that would be it, he'd not slept well and he'd been too tired, lost concentration on the roundabout and …. mercifully he hadn't killed anyone else in the accident.

'I can fumble with the betht of them,' Josh said.

Which Mae took to mean that although she was a virgin, Josh probably wasn't.

'Give me the keys,' Mae said, but it only served to make Josh hold them higher over his head, jangling them noisily, teasingly out of reach for Mae.

Her dad had laid his car keys on the table in front of him that morning, and Mae had often wondered why. He normally kept them in his pocket, only taking them out as he reached the car before pressing the button to open the door automatically.

She wished now she'd asked why, or at least gone back and given her dad a hug, or kissed the top of his head or something. She'd heard her parents talking low – first her dad's voice, then her mum's – late into the night. She'd strained to hear what they were talking about, but they'd made a fine art of talking just quietly enough that Mae, in her bedroom, couldn't catch the words.

'Did you let Bailey Lucas do it?' Josh asked. He leaned sideways and tried to plant a kiss on Mae's cheek as she sat in the passenger seat beside him, but she jerked her head away from him.

'I'm not answering that.'

She didn't ask Josh, chapter and verse, what he'd got up to with previous girlfriends, so the same applied – he had no right to ask.

'Yeah, well, I have you down as having better taste than that anyway.'

She was going to have to make a decision about how she was going to get home in a minute. Let Josh drive back up the long lane to the main road, get out, and walk from there was an option. But would Josh stop the car to let her out?

Best keep him talking. Maybe talking would sober him up a bit.

'Bailey's only jealous I'm going out with you now,' Mae said.

Josh shrugged his shoulders. 'He made that pretty obvious! There's all sorts of rumours flying about the place.'

'What sort of rumours?' Mae asked.

'Shtuff.'

Josh jangled the keys high above his head again, and with his other hand began to caress Mae's knee.

Mae pushed his hand away.

'Come here, gorgeous,' Josh said.

'No!'

'You're nothing but a teathe, Mae Howard,' Josh said. 'You were up for it jutht now.'

He was well and truly over the legal limit for driving now, wasn't he? He couldn't say his s's properly.

'Just the kissing, Josh,' Mae whispered, suddenly frightened that if Josh, who was much bigger and stronger than she was, turned nasty down here, with no one to come to her rescue, she could be in real danger. It was the drink talking – she knew that. Josh wasn't a bit like this when he was sober. She wanted the Josh who had come to the funeral parlour with his dad so she'd have the support of someone nearer her own age as she bent to kiss her dad's cold, smooth forehead one last time. He'd come in with her, standing respectfully a step or two behind her even though they didn't really know one another then. The Reverend Maynard had stood beside her, his hand on her elbow. Mae wanted to remember that Josh, not the one who was frightening her. 'And your arms around me like my dad used to put his arms around me, loving and safe,' she finished.

'Well, I'm not your dad, am I?'

Josh turned away from her and began fumbling to get the key in the ignition.

'No, Josh! Don't drive, please. I wouldn't have agreed to come here with you if I'd known you'd drink the whole bottle.'

'You had some of it.'

'Nowhere near as much as you had.' Keep him talking. Perhaps he'd sober up a bit the longer he sat there. Mae reached for her bag in the foot well, and yanked it up onto her lap. Opening it she found a KitKat and a packet of mints. 'Eat these. They might sop up a bit of alcohol. Put you below the limit at least. Please, Josh.'

'Give over, Mae, it was only a few mouthfuls more than you had. I'm fine to drive. I'm used to it. I'm a big bloke. I can take more alcohol than that runt Bailey Lucas before it affects me. *The Leith police dismisseth me.* See, I said that without lisping.'

Runt? Bailey was taller than Josh was, not that that made a person better, or worse.

And then Mae realised Josh had said all of that without slurring his s's and she considered that perhaps he'd been playing games with her before, slurring his words, and he wasn't as drunk as she thought he was. Her mum and dad had often had a bottle of wine on the table in the evenings and at lunch on Sundays, but they only ever had a couple of glasses each, not a whole bottle. She couldn't remember either of them ever slurring their words. There were girls in her year at school who boasted on Mondays how out of their heads on gin or whatever they'd been, but she was never going to be one of them. She was too scared. What if too much drink turned her into another person, as it was turning Josh into someone she didn't know?

'I still say we should walk, Josh,' Mae said as calmly as she could even though her heart was hammering in her chest now. 'We can tell your sister the car wouldn't start. That you flooded the engine or something.'

Whatever that meant and however you did it, but she'd heard it said on a TV programme only a few nights ago. Maybe Josh would know.

'What? A good vicar's good son tell a lie? What are you asking of me, Mae?' Josh said, looking mock-outraged. 'I know, we could do a bit more kissing while I sober up. How would that be?'

'Hah! You've admitted it. You're drunk.' Mae had had enough now. She closed her bag, did up the buttons on her cardigan, ready to go. 'Well, if you won't walk back, then I will. Mum said not to be late and ...'

'You're listening to your mum?'

Josh made it sound as though Mae listening to her mum was a rare occurrence – rarer than hens' teeth.

'I might be,' Mae said. She opened the car door and tumbled

out, but Josh grabbed onto the fabric of her full skirt yanking her back. She heard a ripping sound. 'Josh, no! Let me go. Not my frock. It's the last one Dad bought me before …'

'Well, he's dead now, isn't he? He's not going to know if it's ripped or not.'

'Don't say that!' Mae yelled. She was a mixture of fear for the situation she was in and anger that Josh, who still had a clump of the material of her frock clasped in a fist, had just said what he had. Besides, there were times when Mae thought she could feel her dad's presence, smell his aftershave, knew that he was somewhere taking care of her, whatever scrapes she might get into.

'I jutth have,' Josh said, theatrically slurring the 's' again, which made Mae certain he was doing it on purpose to frighten her now. 'Oh, bugger off and let me sleep it off.'

Josh let go then and because Mae had been struggling to get away from him, the sudden release of tension made her fall against the door lock, the fabric of her frock catching in it, before she fell out onto the muddy, stony ground. Her knees hit the ground first and there was a searing pain as something sharp caught her below her left knee. She reached out a finger and found blood.

'You've hurt me!' she yelled. She wondered if she'd be able to get back up the lane now. 'Josh …?'

But there was no answer, so lifting the now-ripped skirt of her dress up over her knees, Mae half ran and half hobbled back up the lane, the heels of her shoes skidding this way and that on the rough, stony ground. If she ran really fast, she could be home in under ten minutes.

But would Josh still want to go out with her after this? Did she still want to go out with him?

CHAPTER FIVE

'Where the heck have you been, Mum?' Mae said. She was standing by the front door, arms folded. 'Honestly, you tell me not to be late and I wasn't, but you weren't here! And what did I find when I got here? The front door wide open, that's what!'

Mae's voice was angry, and if Cara wasn't mistaken, also a little afraid. One side of Mae's frock was hanging down a bit; the netting petticoat looked as though the stitching might have come undone. And was that a graze on her daughter's knee?

'Mae, what's happened? Your frock and ...'

'I'm fine,' Mae said. 'Really. I can't believe you went out leaving the front door open and unlocked. Where have you been?'

'To the corner shop,' Cara said. She held up her bag of provisions to show Mae. 'I'm sure I shut the door behind me. We've got guests. Can you believe that? We could be on our way to making money, Mae. But your knee ... Did you fall? I think ...'

'You don't want to know, Mum,' Mae interrupted. 'But what guests?'

'Pam and Eddie Hine,' Cara told her. 'I think you'd better wash that bloody knee off even if you don't want to tell me how you did it. There's Savlon in the cabinet in my bathroom. And then I'll introduce you to our guests. Okay?'

She ought not to be standing here talking to Mae with guests to see to, but she had an uneasy feeling in the pit of her stomach that something had gone badly wrong on her date with Josh. Cara made to walk past Mae, but Mae grabbed her arm.

'Eh?' she said. 'What guests? I've been in every single room in this house looking for you and there's no one here.'

'Oh my God!' Cara shrugged off Mae's hand and stumbled into her hallway. She leaned against the newel post at the bottom of the stairs for support. Perhaps Eddie and Pam Hine had changed their minds about stopping and had simply left? Mae had followed her in, so Cara put down her bag of shopping and put an arm around Mae's shoulders. 'They said they wanted a full English, but I didn't have the things for it so I went to shop. I was only gone a few minutes. Fifteen minutes at the most. I made them a pot of tea before I left and I ran all the way there and back. Perhaps they changed their minds?'

And then Cara realised that there had been no car parked outside when she'd left to go to the shop, and they'd had no luggage with them to speak of, only a tartan old-fashioned holdall thing. And she knew, beyond doubt, that if she hadn't given them the opportunity so recently to steal stuff, she would have found things missing in the morning.

'Just wait until you see what they've done to my room!' Mae yelled at her, running up the stairs.

Cara followed, her legs feeling like lead and her head pounding.

'Great idea not, Mum,' Mae said as Cara walked around the room as if on some sort of automatic pilot picking up Mae's clothes, which had been strewn all over the bedroom floor in haste by Pam and Eddie Hine – if that was what they were called – as they ransacked it.

Cara felt hot with rage one second and then cold with horror the next, just thinking about the Hines and how they'd touched all Mae's personal belongings.

'Your room's the same, Mum,' Mae said, as though reading

41

her mind. 'All the drawers pulled open or tipped out completely on the bed, like they do in TV dramas.'

'I'm sorry,' Cara said. 'I'd give anything for this not to have happened.'

She smoothed and folded Mae's clothes as carefully as she would had they been freshly laundered, with the scent of lavender fabric conditioner mixed with fresh sea air clinging to them. Although she knew, as she methodically piled Mae's school blouses and skirts and cardigans, that she would have to wash everything – everything! – because it was as if she could smell the Hines and the badness that was in them to have done such a thing.

'They looked perfectly respectable. Middle-aged,' Cara said.

Mae stared angrily at her.

'Huh!' Mae said. 'How stupid was that, to go out and leave strangers in the house?'

'Very stupid,' Cara admitted.

But this was a small place. There was hardly ever any crime and what there was only revolved around the pub when a bit of overdrinking got out of hand and a window got smashed, or someone's wing mirrors got trashed. Burglary just didn't happen in a place like Larracombe. Until now.

'It seems I no longer have a laptop,' Mae said. 'So perhaps you could tell me how I'm going to do my homework? We have to do it online, you know.'

'I know,' Cara said.

She thought fast. Perhaps Rosie would loan her the money? Or buy one in advance of Mae's birthday as her birthday present? Rosie was a good and generous present-giver to her goddaughter.

'That was the last thing Dad ever got me,' Mae said. 'I was the last in my class to get a laptop. And he only got it for me then because he wanted to use the computer at night when I wanted to use it for homework. And now you've let someone steal it.'

So, Dad good, me bad, Cara thought. She knew she would have

42

to tell Mae about Mark's gambling soon, but now didn't quite seem to be the time. While the robbery was making Cara feel uncomfortable, it was by no means as bad as Mark dying within hours of her asking him to leave the family home. Would she have the courage to tell Mae *that*?

'I'll get you a new laptop just as soon as I can,' Cara said. 'But perhaps Josh could loan you his in the meantime?'

'That waster,' Mae sniffed.

It was then that Cara noticed pins down one side of the skirt of Mae's dress, and that the netting petticoat was more than hanging off. Mae's knees had stopped bleeding – more bad grazes than deep cuts.

'What happened tonight, Mae? Your frock? Your knees?' Cara asked, suddenly cool and calm, her thoughts sharper and more focused. Whatever the Hines might have done was nothing compared to what she thought Josh might have done to Mae to get her into such a state. 'Between you and Josh?'

'You can't ask stuff like that,' Mae said. 'Not even because you're my mother.'

Yes, I bloody can if he's hurt you, Cara thought. She reached for Mae's hand.

'Let's sit down for a moment, Mae. On your bed. We've both had a bit of a shock.'

Much to Cara's surprise, Mae allowed herself to be led.

'He drank too much,' Mae said, still with her hand in Cara's. 'I'm certain he'd been drinking before then, although …'

'Meg Smythson told me he'd bought wine. And that you were with him.'

'Do you want to know what happened or not?' Mae said. 'Not that I think she had any right to tell you anything.'

'No, she didn't. Sorry. That wasn't meant to sound as though Josh shouldn't have been buying wine if he wanted to, or that I'm cross that he did. I let you drink wine sometimes. But I need to know, Mae … did Josh attack you?'

Did he try to rape you? was what she meant but couldn't bring herself to say the words.

'No. Not exactly. I only had one glass or maybe a bit more, but Josh had drunk the rest of the bottle and I knew he shouldn't drive so I tried to get his car keys off him. I wanted him to walk back with me and tell his sister the car had broken down or something, but he didn't want to. And my frock got ripped when he tried to stop me getting out of the car and ... it's the last frock Dad ever bought me and it's special and ...'

And then Mae dissolved into tears. Cara was full of questions, questions she couldn't ask like, where were you when this happened, were there no other people around, did you have sex?

'Time for a hug?' Cara said, opening her arms wide to her daughter.

'Not at the moment,' Mae said, her tears drying up rapidly as she reached for a corner of her quilt and swiped it across her eyes. 'I've been to hell and back, Mum, wondering what had happened to you when you weren't here and stuff was missing. Did you ever think of that?'

It was as though, in that moment, Mae was the adult, and she, Cara, the child.

'No, no I didn't,' Cara said. Whatever had she been thinking of going out and leaving people she didn't know in the house? Yes, she'd been desperate to start making some money for them both but, well ... 'We'd better phone the police.'

'I've already done it. I said I'd get you to ring when you got back.'

'In a minute,' Cara said. 'I'll tidy up a bit here first.'

She only had two vague descriptions of the Hines. Their accents could have been false, and there was no vehicle that she'd seen that could be traced.

'No, don't do that. The police will want to take fingerprints, won't they? Honestly, Mum, sometimes I wonder what planet you're on.'

'Of course. It's the shock. I won't touch another thing. Let's go downstairs. I'll make that call to the police to let them know I'm back and then make a cup of tea. And a bacon sandwich, now I've got the things to make one.'

The last thing Mae would want now was for her to bang on about washing her knees and putting antiseptic on, wasn't it?

'Surprising as it may seem,' Mae said, 'I seem to have lost my appetite.'

'Make that two of us,' Cara said. 'And your frock, Mae. I can mend it.'

'Whatever,' Mae said.

They stood up and together, mother and daughter went down the stairs.

In the kitchen, Cara rang the police to tell them she was home and then busied herself putting bacon and eggs in the fridge, and the bread in the breadbin. Mae sat and watched every movement her mother made around the kitchen as though she was afraid she might disappear again if she took her eyes off her, even for a second. Cara checked the time on the kitchen clock, wondering how long it would be before the police turned up. There was no resident policeman in the village and the nearest manned station about thirty miles away although, she supposed, there might be police nearer than that in a patrol car somewhere.

'Can I have that hug now?' Mae asked.

'Of course.' Cara opened her arms wide and Mae snuggled into them. Cara hugged her tight.

'I thought I was beginning to handle losing Dad,' Mae sniffed against Cara's shoulder.

'But now you find you can't?'

'It seems to be getting worse as I get older, not better. He keeps coming back to me in dreams and it's only in dreams I can remember his voice. And he's only been gone two years. Oh, Mum …'

'Me, too,' Cara said.

And the tears came for them both. They stood hugging and crying with loud and wracking sobs for ages, until Cara's arms ached with holding Mae to her. But for Cara, none of those tears were cleansing.

And then Cara became aware of someone watching her – that uneasy sort of feeling you get that makes you turn around.

'Evening, ladies.' A policeman with a policewoman standing beside him gave Cara and Mae a rather embarrassed, if kindly smile. 'We did knock, but …'

'We were making too much racket,' Cara said. 'Sorry …'

'Don't be,' the WPC said. 'A break in, is that right?'

'No,' Cara said. 'I very stupidly went out and left two people who came wanting B&B for a couple of nights alone while I went to get a few bits from Meg Smythson at the corner shop. Mae came home earlier than expected and found her room trashed – and mine, although I've not looked in there yet—…' Her throat began to close over with emotion again, and she couldn't get any more words out.

'Shall I make tea?' the WPC said.

Cara nodded. The evening was beginning to feel more surreal than ever, watching a strange woman – albeit a policewoman – searching for things in Cara's cupboards and drawers, filling the kettle at Cara's kitchen tap, while she felt herself unravel a bit emotionally, like a dropped stitch in knitting, she knew she could recover with patience and the right tool but couldn't at that moment.

'Have you touched anything?' the policeman asked when they were all seated around Cara's kitchen table.

'I haven't,' Cara said. 'Well, only the clothes strewn all over the place in Mae's room. Mae met me at the door and we went straight upstairs. 'I looked in the sitting room but didn't go in. There's silver missing. I could see that straight away.'

Silver that had been in my family for generations, she wanted to add, but didn't because it would add nothing to the investigation.

But it was the void that was hurting most – the family heirloom silver, which had had a grounding effect, anchoring her to her past in some way, had been snatched away.

'And you, Mae?' the policeman asked. 'Have you touched much?'

'Doors. I opened and closed every door. So my fingerprints will be on there, right?'

'They will,' the policewoman said. 'But we can eliminate all of yours in seconds once forensics get here. I've set that in motion. They shouldn't be long. It's a quiet night, apart from this.'

'How long will it take?' Cara asked.

'Forensics?' The policeman checked his mobile. 'ETA about ten minutes and then an hour or so.'

'Oh,' Cara said, unable to stifle a yawn.

'It's best done now,' the policewoman said. 'And it if helps, I know what this feels like because my mother's bungalow was burgled when she was in A&E having a broken wrist seen to. There was a feeling of …'

'Don't!' Mae interrupted. 'You were going to say evil, I know it. Miasma or something. We did a tutorial on it in psychology. Evil leaves a tangible presence, far more than good does. And these people were pure evil to do this.'

Mae shivered, hunched her shoulders up around her ears, and a lightning rod of guilt shot through Cara for putting her daughter through this. She struggled to find words of comfort or remorse or regret – apology even – but nothing would come. But Mae filled the gap.

'I just knew something bad had happened because the air wasn't right. I was afraid something had happened to Mum.'

'Oh, darling,' Cara managed to croak out. 'But perhaps we should be answering questions about the Hines?' She looked from one officer to the other.

'In a moment,' the policewoman said. 'Anything else, Mae?'

How kind this very young policewoman was being, how understanding; to allow Mae to talk about how the shock of the burglary had affected her.

'No, that's about it,' Mae said.

Cara told the police officers everything she could remember of Pam and Eddie Hine – what they'd been wearing, hair colour, accents, the small bag they'd brought in with them – from the few moments she'd spent in their company. She knew now she'd gifted them the opportunity to steal when she'd gone to the shop, but she had no doubt they'd have more than likely done a moonlight flit, and left without paying, taking stuff with them anyway.

'They can't have got much in the small bag they had,' she finished.

'Duh, Mum!' Mae said, slapping a hand to her forehead, cartoon comedy-style. 'They'd have had something else in that bag, like a roll of black sacks or something. They probably had a car parked around the corner as well.'

'Really?' Cara said, wondering how her daughter had become so streetwise all of a sudden.

'Really,' the policeman said, 'we need you to check where you kept jewellery, money, anything like family heirloom medals, that sort of thing. Small, portable things. To check what's missing. If you have photos of any valuables, that would be more than helpful. Ah, here's forensics now. Shall I let them in?'

'Do,' Cara said. 'I'll make a list of what I think is missing.'

And then the house became noisy with the organised bustle of people moving about and voices and the beep of phones as the police contacted colleagues at the station. Mae was practically glued to Cara's side as she went from room to room jotting things down, still afraid she'd find her mother missing again if she lost sight of her.

'All done,' the policewoman said, coming into the sitting room where there was still the evidence of forensics testing on all the furniture, and where Cara was sitting on the couch, with Mae beside her, snuggling in. They'd been at loggerheads more than a bit of late and Cara was finding it monumentally sad that a difficult moment with Josh and then the burglary had been the catalyst to the change in their relationship.

'Thank you,' Cara said. 'For being so kind and everything. I expect this is an everyday occurrence for you, but it's a whole new experience – and a salutary lesson not to leave strangers in my home – for me. For us.' She turned and smiled, somewhat guiltily, at Mae. 'Isn't it, darling?'

'Mmm,' Mae said and yawned.

'We'll leave you to get to bed, then,' the policeman laughed. 'We'll be in touch. We'll see ourselves out.'

Cara heard them talking in the hall. And then another voice joining them.

'Josh,' Mae said, with the hint of a question. 'That can't be Josh's voice.'

Cara got up to investigate. She heard the policewoman say 'Goodnight, Josh,' and then the door banged quite noisily in the frame, the wind getting up and blowing in from the east.

'What's he doing here?' Mae called after her mother.

'I don't know,' Cara said.

And then Josh was in the doorway. Cara hadn't met him before, although she knew who he was and had seen him about. Up close he looked well-built, muscled, with thick straw-coloured hair, and a fringe that looked as though he'd cut it himself with a Swiss Army knife. He looked every inch a man who worked physically for a living. He had his hands stuffed into the pockets of his jeans, and Cara noticed he was wearing trainers but no socks, and that his T-shirt stretched across a broad chest. He practically filled the doorway with his presence – rather the worse for drink – and Cara shuddered to think Mae had had to challenge him like this. Mae would have stood no chance against Josh had he pushed his case for whatever it was he'd had on his mind.

'What do you want, Josh?' Cara asked. She folded her arms

49

across her chest, doing her best to block Josh's view of Mae, although she realised she was being totally ineffective.

'I saw the police car outside. What've you been saying, Mae?' he asked.

'Nothing about you,' Mae said. 'Why would I waste my breath?'

'Some guests I thought were bona fide B&B guests were anything but,' Cara explained.

'Ah, right,' Josh said, sounding relieved that Mae hadn't called them to report him, although why he hadn't thought the police would have arrested him if she had, Cara couldn't think. The drink, probably, clouding his thinking.

'That sucks,' Josh said. 'Sorry. Anyway, I walked back should anyone be asking. You were right, Mae. I wasn't in a fit state to drive, but I've sobered up now. I don't know what Mae's told you, Mrs Howard, but I was properly out of order. I apologise for that, frightening her and that.'

'I appreciate that,' Cara said. 'But what with the burglary and the police being here, Mae and I haven't had chance to talk about … well, whatever it was that happened between you tonight. Apart from the fact you'd had too much to drink and she felt she had to get away.'

'Yeah, yeah,' Josh said, nodding. He looked more than a little embarrassed now, as though he was regretting coming. He ran his tongue around his lips as though he was nervous and they'd suddenly gone dry. 'I'm sorry about what happened to your frock and that, Mae.'

'You're not the only one!' Mae snapped.

Cara flinched at the vehemence in her daughter's words, but could understand her reason for it. This whole conversation was beginning to feel bizarre – as though they were all part of some stage play, a farce or something – and she considered inviting Josh to come on in, have a cup of coffee to sober up further before he went home, but it was getting late now and she was bone-tired.

'Actually,' Mae went on, 'I don't think the police should have let you just walk in here.'

'WPC Maynard? My cousin? Amy?' He said it as though he thought Mae ought to have known. 'Her dad – my dad's brother – is superintendent down Plymouth way. I told Amy we were going out, and I'd seen their car and thought I'd just pop in and see how things are. So, what's happened here? Just a straightforward burglary or …'

'Like burglaries are just normal, right?' Mae snapped.

'Darling …' Cara began. She was about to admonish Mae for being rude, snappy, but decided against it. Of *course* her daughter was angry about not just the burglary, but what Josh had done as well. She would allow her to express that anger, rather than have it fester inside.

'Have you been hurt, Mae? Mrs Howard?' Josh asked as though neither she nor Mae had spoken. He walked into the room without being asked. 'Has much been stolen?'

'A fair bit,' Cara said.

'Sorry,' Josh said. 'Looks a bit of a mess in here.'

'It does,' Cara said, and left it at that. There were gaps on the dresser where the silver had been and drawers had been left open, cushions scattered, and the seat pads of the couches pulled out as the Hines had riffled swiftly through her home. *They* were a mess – her and Mae. All she wanted in that moment was for Josh to leave so that she and Mae could take a shower and get to bed. She might suggest they share a room tonight because if Mae felt as shaky as she did, she probably wouldn't want to sleep alone. 'But it will get better.'

'Like I said, I saw the police car and well, I wasn't exactly a gent earlier to Mae, Mrs Howard, and I thought Mae might have made a complaint or something.'

'I guessed that might be the case,' Cara said.

'Well, now you know I didn't,' Mae said. 'Not as entirely altruistic as checking to see we were okay, but—'

51

'Mae,' Cara interrupted, 'can we just leave this? I'm tired, you're tired, and I think Josh has had as much of a shock as any of us.'

Cara knew Josh was popular with the girls and, if rumour had it, some older women too, and it can't have been easy for him having a fifteen-year-old squaring up to him, refusing to do his bidding, although why Cara was feeling sympathetic towards him she had no idea – tiredness probably.

'Yeah,' Josh said. He hung his head. 'Sorry. You know, for being a jerk earlier and also about the robbery. Hope they catch whoever did it. Have they cleaned you out?'

There wasn't a lot to be 'cleaned out' seeing as Mark had pretty much done that.

'Pretty much,' Cara said with a yawn – the last thing she wanted was to pursue this conversation, but poor Josh was looking genuinely contrite now, and concerned. 'Mae's laptop. Her jewellery. And a fair bit of my stuff's gone as well.'

'Look, Mrs Howard,' Josh said. 'I can see you want me to go. I can see you're both pretty shook up and tired by events. It's true I saw the police car and panicked a bit, wondering what it was Mae might have said about me earlier, but I was on my way here anyway. When I sobered up, I remembered stuff. So I've got something I have to tell you. Before Mae hears it in the village. Bailey Lucas is spreading rumours. Look, can I speak to you on your own, Mrs. Howard?'

'No!' Mae shrieked. 'Everyone treats me like a baby and I'm not. Anything you have to say to Mum you can say to me. Right, Mum?'

'What do you want to tell me?' Cara asked.

'Not in front of Mae,' Josh persisted.

'Oh, stuff it!' Mae said. 'That Bailey Lucas is just making trouble because I finished with him. I only went out with him a couple of times anyway so it's not like we were an item! Whatever he's saying it's probably nothing much, nothing even worth staying here to listen to anyway. I'm going to have a shower and wash my hair because the thought that strangers have been through my stuff is making me feel dirty. Get it? Let me know when I'm old enough to be in your company, Josh Maynard!'

Cara watched her daughter go, waited until she heard the shower running. Josh put his hands in the pockets of his jeans and took them out again at least half a dozen times.

'So?' Cara asked when the shower had been running for a good two minutes – Mae would be in there at least fifteen minutes.

'Bailey Lucas is saying that Mae's dad had a huge gambling habit and owed money and that half the goods from this house are in pawn shops all over Devon or sold to whoever would buy them. Pub landlords mostly.'

Cara put her hands to her mouth. What could she say? She'd kept Mark's gambling from Mae until now. But even she hadn't known about the selling of her household goods in pubs until Rosie had told her. But pawn shops? Cara didn't even know where there was one – or what you had to do to use one. But she didn't doubt what Josh was saying was true – Mark's addiction had been so great she'd often wondered if he'd sell his own body to fund it. Why, she wondered, was all this coming out now, two years after Mark's death? Respect, perhaps, for when she was newly widowed had stopped people saying anything before, but now time had passed, tongues were loosening up again?

'Do you have proof Bailey Lucas is saying these things?'

'Well, um …'

'You haven't, have you?'

'Must be him. We met him in Meg Smythson's earlier and he was, like, confrontational. His sister, Xia, works behind the bar …'

'That's not proof, Josh,' Cara said. 'And I think it would be a good idea not to spread that particular rumour yourself. But it is true my husband gambled.'

'But Mae doesn't know?'

'No. Not yet.'

'I won't say a word,' Josh said. 'But she needs to know. Soon.'

'Of course. But I have to find the right moment. Come with me.' Josh followed as she led the way into the kitchen. 'You probably noticed the patches on the walls that hadn't faded like the rest of it … where paintings had been. It's the same in here. Mark took the paintings, little by little, to sell them to fund his gambling. He left me – us, Mae and me – choosing gambling over his family. And it seems the Hines have taken what Mark left behind: my mother's silver, which was valuable.'

Cara knew she might be taking a risk telling Josh, but he seemed more man than boy. And he was the son of a vicar. He had to be used to his father being told things that would go no further.

'Lowlifes,' Josh said.

'More than,' Cara agreed. 'But I can't risk telling Mae any of that, Josh …'

But then Mae came back into the kitchen in the towelling robe that had been her dad's – her comfort robe she'd called it, wrapping it around her the night Cara had told her that her dad had been killed, and using it at every opportunity since; it drowned her, making her look so vulnerable, so small somehow, although she was already five feet six inches tall, almost as tall as Cara. Mae fiddled with the towel wound around her wet hair, loosening it then winding it tight again.

'Can't tell me what?' Mae said.

'That you're very beautiful when you're angry,' Josh said, grinning at them both. 'The biggest cliché of them all but hey, it's true at the moment. Forgive?' he finished, making a prayer gesture with his hands to Mae, and Cara remembered how Meg Smythson had said Josh could charm the birds from the trees. Was that a flutter of Mae's eyelashes?

'I might consider it,' Mae said.

54

'Another chance?' Josh asked.

'Try me?' Mae said, which served for Cara's heart to plummet to somewhere down around her feet that she hadn't given Mark another chance – all this wouldn't be happening if she had. 'As long as alcohol isn't involved.'

'Not a drop will pass my lips,' Josh said. 'That was one wake-up call tonight.'

'Yeah, but just remember,' Mae said, 'that actions speak louder than words. Right?'

Josh's eyes widened in surprise at Mae's words, which made Cara want to laugh. But how proud she was in that moment of her feisty daughter, coming back from her shock and commanding the situation.

'Indeed,' Josh said, pulling himself up tall, and looking directly at Mae. 'I was wondering if you fancy going sailing next weekend?'

Mae shrugged. I dunno, the shrug said, but Cara could tell by the light in Mae's eyes and knowing how she loved sailing with Mark that she was considering it.

It seemed Josh had come to that conclusion too because he said, 'If, you know, you haven't got any gear any more you can borrow a lifejacket from my sister. And even her Helly Hansen. She won't mind. That okay with you, Mrs Howard?'

'As long as Mae's comfortable with it,' Cara said. Rosie's voice came into her head asking her what the hell she was thinking agreeing to let her daughter go off with someone who was obviously a professional charmer, because hadn't he turned the situation around, barging in scared out of his wits about what Mae might have told the police about him, and when he found she'd said nothing at all and that Cove End had been robbed by the Hines, he'd come over all concerned for her and Mae to suit his own ends? 'Mae?'

'Yeah. Fine,' Mae said. 'Maybe I need the diversion? Text me, eh? Saturday or Sunday. Whichever's best for tides and weather.'

Cara let out an audible sigh of relief that Mae had water safety uppermost in her mind.

'Yeah, will do,' Josh said. 'Better let you get your beauty sleep, then. Not that you need it, Mae.'

'Oh give over, Maynard,' Mae laughed. 'I'm getting the drift. You're sorry. You're making amends, and I think you might be making my mother sick with all your smarmy charm, but it doesn't fool me. Any more and I'll change my mind about the weekend.'

Mae yawned theatrically and it was all Cara could do not to burst out laughing. Mae might not have a father around to look out for her any more, but she was learning how to stick up for herself and Cara had to be thankful for that.

'You're too kind,' Josh said, laughing. 'I'll see myself out.'

And then he was gone.

'You can change your mind if you want to, darling,' Cara said. 'You know, when you've had more time to think things through. If you think Josh might just be saying things he wants us to hear?'

Mae sighed heavily.

'Is this a lecture?' she asked.

'No, but a lot's happened here tonight, and I wouldn't want you to make a rash decision because of it.'

'I haven't. Okay?' Mae's eyebrows were practically meeting in the middle in indignation. And then she smiled at Cara, a broad beaming smile that lit up her face. 'Why would I not want to see him again? You saw him. He's like, lush!'

Cara couldn't think of a thing to say about that. Yes, Josh Maynard was a looker. And the word lush could mean more than drop-dead desirable – not that Cara was going to mention that right now.

'Okay,' Cara said. 'You've got school in the morning. Up the wooden hill?'

'When I've dried my hair.' Mae roughly rubbed the towel over her hair. 'And, Mum ... can I, like, sleep in your room tonight?'

'Of course,' Cara said, relieved that she wouldn't now need to ask that same question of Mae and get, perhaps, a flat refusal for the asking. Tonight had brought mother and daughter a little closer together. An ill wind and all that …

'Just tonight, you understand?'

'Of course,' Cara said again. Even the fact that the Hines had violated her space by searching through drawers and wardrobes, and even under the bed, couldn't take away her joy that she would have Mae lying close to her and could reach and give her reassurance in the night if she needed it.

CHAPTER SIX

In the cool light of day, with Mae now gone to school, and time to reflect on what had happened the night before, Cara set about getting the house back to how it had been before Hines had turned up. It was almost therapeutic finding a tin of paint and glossing over where skirting boards had been scuffed. She was glad she'd chosen matt white paint for all the walls in the house and it was just a matter of taking some cleansing cream to grubby bits and giving tired-looking patches a quick touch-up. The vacuum was put into overdrive – not that Cara ever let the house look too run-down. She got the polisher from the garage and mercifully there was a can of unopened polish so she waxed the parquet in the hall.

It felt good to be doing something physical and by lunchtime Cara was pleasantly tired but ridiculously pleased with her efforts.

She began to sing.

'I'm going to wash those Hines right out of my hair ...' She giggled as she paraphrased the famous line from *South Pacific*.

A quick tomato sandwich with lashings of black pepper for lunch and Cara was ready to tackle the soft furnishings. Cushion covers were whipped off and put through the washing machine, and were soon dry on the line and back on again. She even

58

vacuumed the curtains in the sitting room, before spray-polishing every surface to within an inch of its life.

Then she went outside, rang her own doorbell as though she were a guest, and came back in again.

She tried to see Cove End as a stranger might see it and decided it was more than okay – it was a very lovely home. A much-loved home. Lived in. And it would more than do for her next guests. The flowers in the garden – so many varieties – were coming into their own now and Cara made a mental note to put small posies in the bedrooms and a big display of whatever flowers and greenery she could find in the hall. It was the little touches, she told herself, that mattered. Chocolate. Yes, chocolates. She had a whole pile of glass dishes she'd saved from when she, Mark and Mae had had chocolate mousse or panna cotta or some other treat from the supermarket for pudding and she would use those to put a few chocolates on the bedside tables. A welcome.

Cara ran up the stairs, surprised but pleased beyond belief that a drama of sorts had made her more positive than ever to make a go of her B&B. She showered off the effort of her mad activity, changed into a pair of cropped leggings and a navy linen shirt and came back downstairs to ring Rosie.

'Rosie, have you got a moment?' Cara asked. She'd texted Rosie after breakfast but her text hadn't been answered, not that that was unusual if Rosie had a salon full of clients booked in. She was using the landline now.

'Half an hour before the next client. What's wrong? I can tell something is. You sound a bit breathy.'

'I've been all domestic goddess this morning.'

'Spare me!' Rosie laughed. 'But that's not all, is it?'

Cara sighed. She could never get anything past Rosie really – her friend knew her too well. It would take half an hour to tell Rosie everything – about the theft of her property, how Mae practically freaked out coming home to find Cara missing and her room trashed, and how things were now with her and Mae, and about Josh, and the police going all over the house and the fingerprinting and everything.

'Well, the précis is that I was an idiot last night and I left two strangers who knocked on the door asking for a bed for the night alone while I ran to the corner shop to get the wherewithal for breakfast ... and ...' Just talking about it all was making her hyperventilate.

'Shit, Cara, you didn't? No, don't answer that, 'cos you obviously did. What's missing?'

'Silver, a bit of cash I had in the back of a kitchen drawer for emergencies, Mae's laptop ... amongst other things. But the thing is, I can't be certain whether these lowlifes – they told me they were called Hine, but that's no doubt stretching the truth – took my jewellery, or if Mark did. Sold it down the pub or something. Mae's boyfriend told me that there's a rumour going around that Mark had sold stuff in the pub and other places so ...'

'Okay, okay. I'm getting the drift. Why didn't you ring me last night? I could have come over. No, scratch that, I *would* have come over. Look, Cara, I'm cross for you and could strangle these people with a length of barbed wire, but I've got a client coming soon, so shall I come over when I've dealt with that?'

'No, it's okay. But I was wondering if you know if there are any pawn shops in the area?'

'You want to know what?' Rosie yelled into the phone. She sounded shocked.

'Pawn shops,' Cara said. 'Do you know if there are any pawn shops in the area?'

'Cara, sweetheart, are you okay?' Rosie spoke slowly, her voice guarded. 'I don't know how that's going to help. I know this is an area we've not talked about now Mark's no longer with you – you know, sex and the lack of it – but, well, looking at porn won't help, I don't think. Not really. It would be a bit like someone holding an open bottle of Bollinger in front of you and then ramming the cork back in without giving you any. It's the emotional side of things you need. And yes, I know this is a woman talking who puts physical before emotional every time, but I'm not you, or you me. Lecture over.'

'Oh my God,' Cara said. 'I need to sort my diction. I meant p-a-w-n, not p-o-r-n.' Trust Rosie to get the wrong end of the stick. Cara knew that Rosie would often say something ridiculous just to make Cara laugh, lift her spirits, but she wasn't laughing now because the thought of both sex and Bollinger weren't thrilling her as once they had. Would she ever get back to them?

'That's all right, then,' Rosie said. 'But you do know pawn shops are a bit Victorian, don't you? You know, the downtrodden wife with six kids and a husband who spent his wages in the pub before coming on home on payday, so she had to take her wedding present linen down the pawn shop, yet again, so she could put a bowl of broth on the table for her family.'

'Thanks for the history lesson,' Cara laughed, and glad of it. 'Haven't you got a client to see to soon?'

'Yeah, yeah,' Rosie said. 'But I want to help …'

'Well, you can. If you know about pawn shops. I know my engagement ring is missing, but I also know I put it in the back of my knicker drawer long before Mark left so he wouldn't take it to sell, so I don't know if he found it and put it in hock or something, or if the Hines took it or what. I thought with you running a business you might know about things like pawn shops.'

Rosie sighed heavily on the other end of the line.

'Sorry, I'm rabbiting and you've probably got things to prepare. Sorry …'

'It's not that,' Rosie interrupted, her voice kind. 'But I could kill Mark for what he's put you through. Sorry, I didn't mean kill as in snuff the light out of him … oh God, I'm digging myself in deeper again, aren't I?'

'Yes,' Cara laughed. 'But don't worry. We all do it. Yesterday I said to Mae, "Your dad would have died rather than have guests in the house." Since the Hine fiasco, I've wised up a bit, but I'm

61

sailing by the seat of my pants because the hygiene people haven't been yet. I'll ring them when I've finished speaking to you. Mark would turn in his grave if he knew....Oh no, *I've* said it now!'

Rosie laughed nervously. 'I know, it's not funny, but death is a bit like meeting the vicar and then finding yourself swearing and blaspheming when you don't do either normally – you just can't help yourself, can you? Anyway, I'm rabbiting now and I really will have to go in about fifteen – seconds, that is. Yellow Pages or the internet should tell you all you need to know about where to find pawn shops. Torquay used to have one. Probably still has. I could get Ellie to do my clients on Thursday if you like and we could go on a pawn trail. That's p a w n, not p o r n. Okay?'

Cara laughed, the laugh making her cough. When she recovered, she said, 'I'm so glad you're my friend, Rosie.'

'Phew! Thought you'd snuffed it then. Oh, whoops ... there I go again. See you Thursday, ten o' clock? Can you get the bus into Torquay and I'll drive over from Cockington and meet you there? It'll save me coming all the way over to fetch you. I'll drive you back.'

'Yeah. Sure. No problem. Looking forward to it,' Cara said, even though the thought that she might find her engagement ring in a pawn shop was making her feel sick.

She flicked through the local telephone directory and found the number she needed and dialled. Cara had to sit through a few minutes of canned music and 'your call is important to us' but she found she wasn't nearly as irritated by this as she usually was. It was a little lull in the mad activity that had been her day already.

'Health and Hygiene, how can I help?' someone said.

Cara explained why she was calling, gave all the details asked of her, and was told to hold the line for a few moments.

But the person on the other end was soon back to her.

'This could be your lucky day,' the woman at the other end

said. 'We've just had a cancellation. One of our officers will be in your area on Thursday and can fit you in.'

Lucky day? Cara was tempted to ask the woman to define lucky because it had hardly come in spades so far ... 'Fortunate' might have been a better word. And she'd just said she'd see Rosie on Thursday.

'Er, what sort of time?'

She knew she could re-schedule with Rosie although she'd prefer not to have to.

'Say, nine o' clock?'

'Great,' Cara said.

Perhaps luck was on her side after all?

After school – and what a shock that had been coming home to a house that smelled like a hotel or something, a bit bleachy and polishy, with echoes of fresh paint, like her mum had gone mad with the cleaning products – Mae sat on her bed, leaning against the wall, her knees bent. She knew every single thing in her room had been washed and dried with scented sachets, but still she felt as though there were fingers creeping over her, touching where they shouldn't. Her mum must have used a whole bottle of Cif cleaning every surface and had even shampooed the carpet – it wasn't as though she hadn't tried to make things right.

She took her mobile from the pocket of her jeans and scrolled down to Josh's number.

'Hello, beautiful,' Josh said before she'd even spoken.

'I bet you say that to all the girls,' Mae said, attempting a joke, even though she didn't feel in the least like joking.

'Nope. What's up?'

'What do you mean – what's up?'

'I can tell by your voice that something is.'

'Oh, that's a nice thing to say,' Mae said. 'Like you care.' And in that moment it felt like there was some sort of invisible cashmere blanket wrapping her up safely, keeping her snug. She was glad now she was giving Josh a second chance after the wine incident down in the cove.

'Well, I do care. I was a total tit yesterday and want to make amends. So give. What's up?'

'Mum's got three guests booked in. She says she's putting the whole Hine incident behind her. How do I know it won't happen again?'

'Well, my guess is your mum won't leave the guests alone in the house. I'd also chance my arm and say she'll probably check on names and addresses before she lets them over the doorstep. And deposits for their stay and stuff like that. And you could ask for a lock and key for your room so you can lock it when you go out.'

'That's a good idea.'

'I'm full of them,' Josh laughed. 'Oops, sorry.'

'For what?' Mae said.

'Not you,' Josh said, his voice suddenly much quieter than it had been. 'I'm trimming hedges for old Bert Godfrey and it seems I've just snipped off the best of his roses while I was doing it.'

'You're working?'

'Yes.'

'But it's way past working time.'

'Not for self-employed gardeners, it isn't. Not at this time of year when everything grows like crazy. Look, Mae, I'd better go. Bert Godfrey's standing at his back door watching me now.'

'Okay. And, Josh ...?'

'What?'

'Thanks for the chat. And caring.'

'No probs. Try not to worry, Mae. Your mum's only trying to make a better life for you, more financially secure you know, since your dad, you know, messed up and didn't. Anyway, got to go.' Josh made kissy noises down the phone. 'Bye.'

Didn't? Messed up? What did Josh mean by that? Did he know more than she did? What hadn't her mum told her?

'Bye,' Mae said, comforted in one way by the chat with Josh and yet discomfited by what it was he hadn't said. He had a job that brought in a bit of cash if not a lot. Mae knew Josh's dad gave him money as well. Mae knew her mum's balance in her bank account was going down and down because she'd taken a sneak look at the latest bank statement on the kitchen table when her mum had turned her back for a second. Less than three hundred pounds at the last sneak look. Not having money of her own made Mae reliant on Josh when they went anywhere, beholden to him, which was a vicar-ish sort of word to use, but appropriate with Josh's dad being a vicar; like she was a charity case or something. Well, she could change that, couldn't she? She could get a job. She'd ask Meg Smythson in the corner shop if she needed any help in the evenings or for a few hours on Sunday morning or something. Or there was the ice-cream kiosk down by the harbour that was opening up more and more now the weather was turning warmer and more summery. She could try the information office, too, to see if they knew of anyone needing help. And then a well of emotion threatened to overwhelm her. She could do all that on the internet if her dad hadn't taken the computer and if it hadn't been wrecked beyond repair in the accident and if her phone was so ancient she couldn't access the internet on it. And if her stupid mother hadn't left the stupid Hines people alone so they'd had the opportunity to take her laptop. Mae grabbed a tissue and wiped her eyes to stop stupid, stupid tears from falling. Crying wasn't going to help, was it? And life existed before computers and laptops and mobile phones.

And then there was her frock that had got ripped when she'd struggled to get away from Josh. It had always been her favourite, that frock, though it was getting a bit tight for her now. When her dad had bought it for her, it had been a bit big and he'd said, 'You'll grow into it, honeybun.' But her dad hadn't lived long enough to see her grow into it and now she was growing out of it, especially the bust bit seeing as her boobs were now two sizes larger than they'd been back then. 'Hand-reared,' Josh had joked when she'd mentioned it. She loved Josh fondling her boobs, kissing them, nibbling them, sucking on them – it made her feel more grown up and it made her body want to go the whole way but she was holding out for the moment – just! Her mum would probably go ape if she knew. That thought made the corners of Mae's mouth turn up, almost involuntarily, into the beginnings of a smile and it felt good. Not because she had a secret from her mum, but that she did have a life still, even if her dad wasn't in it. He'd have probably killed Josh for touching her boobs. Mae reached for her now sad-looking frock and held it to her for a second. Then she leapt off the bed and decided to start putting her getting-a-job idea into reality.

Her mum was sitting on the bottom stair, her mobile clamped to her ear, as Mae ran down the stairs.

'Hang on,' her mum said to whoever it was she was talking to. She leapt up off the stair and reached out an arm to Mae. 'Is something the matter, Mae …?'

'Just going for a walk for a bit,' Mae said. 'It's like asphyxiating me up there, all the cleaning products.' She did a mock-faint to show her mum it was a joke really. 'Who're you talking to anyway?'

'Rosie. Just checking a few details about something.'

'Right.' Mae didn't think there was any point in asking what and her mum would probably fob her off with something anyway, like she was a kid in primary school.

Mae glanced at the hall clock, a huge thing that looked as though it should have been on a railway station platform or something. Twenty- five to four. She'd have to get a shift on.

'I'll let you get back to Rosie,' Mae said. Sometimes she was jealous of Rosie and how close she and her mum were, like they were sisters or something. 'Okay?'

'Supper in an hour, Mae.'

'Okay,' Mae said again but without the hint of question in the word this time. Then she was out the door and running down the hill.

'Well, well, well,' Meg Smythson said when Mae burst through the door just before the shop was about to shut up for a couple of hours so Meg Smythson could eat her tea and watch Corrie before opening again for the evening trade for those people who forgot milk on their online Tesco shop or whatever. 'Without the boyfriend tonight, Mae?'

'Am I?' Mae said, looking behind her theatrically. 'Oh yeah, seems so.'

'Come for some more bacon and eggs, have you? Saw the B&B sign up. New venture there, is it?'

'No to the first question, yes to the second,' Mae said, struggling to retain the good manners her mum would want her to have when speaking to an elder … another vicar-ish word that, elder.

'The police were up at your place last night, so I heard.'

'You heard right,' Mae said.

'Everything all right?'

'Yep,' Mae said. 'Just a social visit. The lady copper is a cousin of Josh's, just thought she'd stop by.' Mae knew she'd failed miserably to keep sarcasm out of her voice. That was the trouble with small village living – people knew all your business within minutes of it happening, and sometimes even before it. 'That was a lie, obviously, about the social visit. The WPC *is* Josh Maynard's cousin. A couple of old people took advantage of being alone in our house while Mum was here buying bacon and eggs from you. Helped themselves to stuff and scarpered. That's the official version, Mrs Smythson. Ignore anything anyone else tells you.'

'Really? Good grief. In Larracombe? Nothing much ever happens here. Did they take much?'

'Enough.' And that, Mae decided, was more than Meg Smythson needed to know. And then she bit the bullet. 'Could you give me a few hours in the shop? I'm old enough to work and I'm honest. You wouldn't have to worry about me helping myself to money from the till or anything. I could get references. My mum's friend, Rosie, runs a business of her own and I expect the Reverend Maynard would speak for me as well. I know you close for a couple of hours in the early evening and I was wondering if I could step in so you still get the trade. I could come every weekday, and maybe on Sunday mornings. Five pounds an hour seems reasonable.'

Phew! Mae hadn't realised how asking for a job could make her so nervous. She'd rabbited on there a bit and it had made her blush, she knew it had – the sides of her neck had gone all hot.

'Well, I like your cheek, Mae Howard – five pounds an hour seems reasonable! But there's a little problem. You're not eighteen yet and around that time of day the biggest sales are beer and wine and you wouldn't be able to serve those, being underage, now would you? Or drink it. If you get my meaning.' Meg Smythson tapped one side of her nose and Mae wanted to laugh because she thought people only did that in old black and white films but she managed not to.

'I get your meaning, Mrs Smythson,' Mae said. 'And just for the record my mum lets me have a drink with lunch on Sundays sometimes. And the law says she can do that so … actually, I don't know that I want to work here now anyway. Thank you for your time,' Mae finished, remembering her manners.

She didn't want to work for such a sanctimonious old cow anyway, Mae decided, as she rushed out of the shop twice as fast as she'd rushed in.

Hmm, maybe finding a part-time job was going to be harder than she'd thought.

CHAPTER SEVEN

'Well, Mrs Howard, everything seems fine to me.'

Thursday morning, and after a very busy few days touching up yet more paintwork, moving furniture around, washing the bedroom curtains, weeding and mowing the back lawn, trimming shrubs, and all the other things she thought it would necessary to get right for paying guests, Cara exhaled audibly as the man from the hygiene department at the council delivered his verdict. She was glad now that she'd insisted on a new kitchen with granite worktops when Mark received a back-dated pay rise, although the row with him at the time about the expense of it all had been hurtful and damaging. If she hadn't stood firm, it would have all been gambled away and she'd have been left now without the opportunity to earn money through a B&B.

'Thank you,' Cara said, glad now that she'd worked her fingers to the bone getting Cove End as pristine as she possibly could. She'd still been at it past midnight, giving the banister rail a quick coat of paint in the hope it would be dry by the morning. It had been. She and Mae had a habit of running their hands along it every time they went up and down, and a rather grubby and worn banister rail would not do for guests – first impressions count, she knew that. And she also knew she should have done it before, but grief, guilt and worry had made her tired 24/7. Mark's pension money had gone on paying back massive debts, and the little the bank had let her have before paying those debts was fast running out. She'd been holding her breath that Mae wouldn't ask if the paintings had been valued yet and when they would be coming back. Rosie had said that teenagers don't really notice their surroundings unless it's the pile of junk in their bedrooms, the exact position of it hotwired in their brains. Cara had laughed at the time, and she hoped now that Rosie was right and that Mae believed her story about them being taken away for valuation.

'You're VAT-registered, of course,' the man from the council said – a statement rather than a question.

'VAT,' Cara said, thinking fast. 'Of course.' This was the first time those three very important letters had entered her mind. But VAT was something Rosie would know all about so she'd ask her to explain. 'I'm getting it all sorted.'

'Good, good.' The council inspector closed his files and put them back in his briefcase, although he made no attempt to leave. 'Lovely place you have here. Great views.'

'Yes, it is,' Cara replied, glancing out towards the sea just as a small dinghy edged its way around the harbour wall. Should she have been firmer about Mae going sailing with Josh at the weekend? Ought she have insisted that Mae get a proficiency certificate or two under her belt? And how experienced with boats was Josh really? Although Mae had been sailing with Mark quite a lot when she was younger, it didn't make her an experienced sailor, did it? Cara felt her heart rate go up a beat or two per second at the thought something bad might happen to Mae. Gosh but there were just so many things to be thinking about at the moment – so many compartments in her brain with so many different issues in them. She took a deep breath and held it there before letting it out again.

'Mrs Howard? Are you okay? Only you went a bit pale there.'

'I'm fine. Fine,' Cara said, pulling herself together mentally. 'I'm a little anxious about the B&B business, to be honest. Cooking for my family was one thing, but for people who may have higher expectations, higher standards …'

'You'll be fine. For the record I only check on hygiene issues and some of the places I see are palaces, but the food … well, what some people do with bacon and eggs should be a hanging offence!'

Cara laughed. She'd only given him coffee and two digestives from a new packet – he was yet to know whether or not she could cook.

'But that's out of your jurisdiction?'

'Unfortunately, yes.'

He still seemed reluctant to go, his briefcase clutched to him now like a hot water bottle for comfort.

'But I'm sure you are a veritable Nigella in the kitchen department.'

Goodness! Cara thought, *I do believe I'm being flirted with.* The year of firsts was long gone. Being flirted with wasn't one of the issues she'd thought about. She must remember to tell Rosie – she'd get great mileage out of that! And here it was in the guise of the man from the council's hygiene department. She was so relieved when her telephone rang because it meant she wouldn't have to comment on the conversation.

'Right, I'll be off,' the man said. 'I'll see myself out.'

Cara waved at his retreating figure and picked up the phone.

'Cove End,' she said, cheerily, into the mouthpiece.

'Ah, good.' A man's voice with no discernible accent. But deep. Fruity even. Gosh, what was getting into her today – one man had flirted with her and now she was seeing, or hearing, flirts everywhere. 'First question – is it quiet at Cove End?'

'Very,' Cara said. 'The last road out of the village – well, just a lane really.'

'Good. Good. With views?'

71

'Beautiful views. From all the front-facing rooms you can see down over the hill to the harbour and out to sea as far as the horizon,' Cara told him, slightly bemused. A woman would have asked about the bedrooms and if there was an en suite and about the food.

'Great. So do you have a room free with this far-reaching view? Available, um, soon?'

'Just the one night?' Cara asked, grateful that she could now offer accommodation complete with a licence to operate.

'Well, no. More than that. A couple of weeks, possibly more. A month, maybe six weeks would be good, if you can manage it. The thing is, I won't be able to get to you until ten o' clock on Saturday evening, at the earliest. Is that too late? You see I've got an exhibition on and it might overrun. I'm Tom Gasson-Smith, by the way.'

'That's fine. I rarely go to bed before then, so ...'

She left the rest of her sentence unsaid – he would know by that she was happy to wait up until he arrived. The guests she had booked in for just the one night the following day would be gone by Saturday evening. She was going to have to keep very accurate records if she was to avoid double-booking rooms if things were always going to happen at this pace.

There was no response and Cara wondered if, perhaps, Tom whoever-he-was – she'd forgotten for a moment – had changed his mind.

'Er, no problem,' she said, encouragingly, hoping her voice would stir him into confirming the booking. A long one would be good.

And now she thought about it, she remembered seeing the name Tom something-Smith on the list of artists who would be exhibiting at the art festival, although she'd never heard of him before and had no idea what he painted, or sculpted, or potted – all sorts of artists would be exhibiting, so the flyer had said. So it would seem Tom double-barrelled-whatsit was bona fide.

Unlike the Hines. And she also remembered she ought to be down on the harbourside waiting for the bus to take her to Torquay to meet up with Rosie. 'I'll book you in, Mr Smith.'

'Tom Gasson-hyphen-Smith. You might have heard of me.'

'Of course. You're here for the art festival. I'll look forward to seeing you. But I really do have to go now. A bus to catch. Bye for now, Mr Gasson-hyphen-Smith,' Cara said, and a giggle of sorts escaped that surprised, thrilled and embarrassed her in equal measure. What on earth was she thinking, flirting over the telephone with a complete stranger? But then she heard Tom Gasson-Smith laugh in return and it was a sort of rounded, treacly sort of laugh that made her catch her breath for a second.

'The feeling's likewise. Looking forward to meeting you that is, not having a bus to catch.'

And then the line went dead as he obviously replaced the receiver. Such old-fashioned things, landlines. How strange that she and Tom Gasson-Smith should both have been using one.

Cara replaced the receiver and stood still for a moment. She was on the way to making money. For a split second she wondered just how famous Tom Gasson-Smith was. It would probably give her a brownie point or two if she were able to talk about his landscapes or his abstracts or whatever – a diving-off point for a conversation between them because she'd got the feeling Tom Gasson-Smith was happy to chat. But how was she going to find out who he was, and what he painted? Mae, who might have helped her, had had her laptop stolen, and the police hadn't yet returned Mark's computer, not that she wanted it back. But if she was going to be running a B&B business, she'd need to get online soon and have some sort of website prepared – although with the expense of all that, maybe not just yet.

Cara made a decision. She'd give Tom Gasson-Smith one of the bedrooms with a dormer window that provided views out to sea and also north and south should he want them. She didn't know a lot about art, apart from knowing she liked what she liked, but she knew that light from different directions made a difference to how things looked. When she got back from seeing Rosie, she'd make sure that room was as comfortable as it could be for what she hoped would be a long, and lucratively pleasing, stay.

'Mae! Hey!'

Mae turned at the sound of her school friend, Abby's, voice. She lifted a hand in greeting but didn't really want to stop and chat. They both had the afternoon off school for study leave before exams – Mathematics and English literature – in a couple of weeks' time, but it was obvious neither of them was studying. Not that it would matter much to Mae because she'd inherited her father's aptitude for maths – a subject you either got or you didn't was what her dad had said when he was alive – and her mother brought her back books from the library on a regular basis, so she'd read more than most.

'Escaped study leave, then?' Mae said. 'Like me.'

'Yeah,' Abby said, hurrying to fall in step with Mae.

Mae wished she hadn't spoken now, just waved and moved on. Abby would only want to boast about something she'd just been bought, or was about to be bought, and how much it all cost. Mae was sick at the thought of the price of things.

'Where're you going?' Abby asked.

'Around,' Mae said. 'You?'

'Just escaping my mother!' Abby let out a loud sigh. 'As well as the home study, obviously!'

'You and me both, then,' Mae said.

Her mother only let her go out with Josh at weekends. On Saturdays they often went to the Boathouse because there was usually live music of some sort. Tribute bands mostly. On Sundays it depended on the weather. If it was fine, they'd go somewhere they could be sure of a bit of privacy for a necking session, but if it was wet they had to hole up in a café or something because the Boathouse was full of people having Sunday lunches – such an OAP thing to be doing. She knew there was no point in trying to see Josh today because he was working two villages away and besides, her mother would kill her if she did. But she hadn't wanted to stay in the house on her own seeing as her mother was going to Torquay to see Rosie. She wouldn't have minded going actually … there had to be charity shops in Torquay she could trawl for something interesting to wear but two's company, three's a crowd and all that, and her mum and Rosie would only have bored her to death with their conversation. Mae had told a porkie when her mum had asked why she was going out when she was supposed to be on home study and said she was going to get the bus into Churston to do a bit of research at the library.

'Where'd you tell your mother you were going?' Abby asked.

'Library. Research.' She wanted to be shot of Abby's company now because she was wanted to catch the information office to see if they knew about any part-time jobs going in the area – anywhere she didn't need transport to get there.

'I guess it's a bit different for you now,' Abby said, 'I heard you aren't online at the moment. What with your dad dying and that, I expect your mum is less than cheerful these days.'

I'm not exactly over the moon about it myself either. She wondered how Abby knew about her being unable to access the internet at the moment but decided not to ask. It was probably common knowledge at school anyway.

'Mum's not so bad. It's just that she's full of the B&B business she's starting and I so do not want a house full of strangers cluttering up the bathrooms and stuff.'

'Nah,' Abby said. 'Could be some hot hunk coming to stay, though!'

It was no secret that Abby had done it with at least three different boys in their class.

'Not looking,' Mae said.

'You still seeing Josh Maynard?'

'Of course.'

'When you've finished with him, pass him my way,' Abby said. 'I could probably teach him a thing or two!'

It was Mae's turn to sigh heavily. She was so over this conversation. Her mother, her now-dead dad, and Josh were not up as topics for conversation.

'Got to go,' Mae said.

And off she hurried. Alone again. Would the ache around her heart after losing her dad ever go?

On the way to the information office, Mae paused to look in shop windows to see if any of them were advertising vacant positions. None were. She pushed open the door and walked up to the desk.

'Hi,' she said, plastering on a smile she didn't really feel. She didn't recognise the man behind the desk. 'I'm Mae Howard and I live up the top of the hill.' She turned and waved an arm in the general direction. 'I need a job I can do for a few hours after school and one day at the weekend. I'll be able to do more hours when school breaks up, but I need something now. Do you know if there's anything going?'

'Hi, Mae Howard,' the man said. 'I don't keep that sort of information here, I'm afraid. I'm more for places of entertainment and accommodation, churches, that sort of thing. Sorry.'

'Oh, right,' Mae said, feeling stupid that she'd come to the wrong place looking for work but how was she to know – she'd never been out looking for a job before. And now a stupid, stupid blush was spreading up the sides of her neck so the man would know how stupid she felt.

'Look,' he said, kindly. 'My girls all got jobs in catering of some sort in the school holidays – cafés and that. They did chambermaiding for a bit as well – always a call for that around here in the hotels and the B&B trade. Does that help?'

Not really, Mae wanted to say, because hadn't she just come here from a B&B place ... not home any more, but a business?

Having people in the house would change things. Her mum would put on her posh voice and fall over herself to make sure the guests were comfortable and had enough coffee and stuff. And what if she and her mum had one of their spats? No doubt her mum would give her a look that said, *Don't you dare start that now, there are people here. They don't want to hear our disagreements!*

'Yeah, great,' Mae said, her heart heavy.

And then her heart skipped a bit – would she be expected to do all the chambermaiding stuff for free at home? Would her mum expect her to serve breakfast and make tea and coffee when guests arrived? And would she have to strip beds and load the washing machine, and put her book away when she'd finished reading instead of leaving it open over the arm of a couch, which she usually did? Well, she wasn't going to ask in case it put ideas in her mum's head.

The bell on the door clanged then and someone else came in. Her cue to go.

'Thanks, you know, for your help,' Mae said to the man behind the desk.

'Good luck then, Mae Howard,' he said, before turning his attention to the new arrivals with a welcoming grin.

Mae stepped out into the street. Where next? She'd try the ice-cream kiosk on the quay, see if that was open. The day was sunny enough for ice-cream so it should be.

'Well, no one can say I'm not trying to get a job,' Mae grumbled at a seagull picking at the leftovers of a polystyrene takeaway box on the harbour wall. 'Now the flipping ice-cream kiosk is closed. Oh ...' She'd just noticed a handwritten sign stuck on the window. She rushed over.

'WEEKEND HELP NEEDED. WOULD SUIT STUDENT. JULY START. SATURDAYS AND SUNDAYS. MIDDAY – 4 PM. RING 528421'

'That's me, then,' Mae said out loud as she logged the details in her phone. 'I'm a student.' She'd ring later. It was still June so no rush really. Not that she wanted to work Saturdays and Sundays because that would mean both days were out for seeing Josh instead of just the one, but it was a start. *If* she got the job.

What now? Her mum would still be with Rosie and what a flipping secret her mum had made about what they were going to Torquay for. 'Oh, just a girlie outing,' her mum had said when she'd asked, but Mae didn't believe a word – she hadn't been able to hold Mae's gaze while she said it. 'Things to chat about. You know Rosie, always some man drama or other going on. You wouldn't want to listen to all that!' Oh yeah ... Mae hadn't even asked if she could go along but it was pretty obvious her mum didn't want her to know what she was doing.

As though she was on some sort of automatic pilot, Mae walked down the slope into the harbour. When the tide was out, as it was now, there was a little beach of light terracotta-coloured sand, studded with a few small shells. How many times had she and her dad launched the dinghy from this slope, and then pulled it out of the water again afterwards? Loads.

She pulled off her ballet pumps and stepped down onto the sand. Who could resist a bit of pristine, virgin sand? Mae always thought it was almost magical to be the first person to step on the beach after the tide had gone out when there were no foot-prints and no scuffy patches where dogs had been digging for imaginary bones or something. Abby and the other girls at school would probably consider her a saddo for even thinking that, but they thought that anyway, making snide comments when they thought she couldn't hear about her fifties frocks and the fact she wore ballet pumps instead of Converse trainers or whatever was in fashion at the time. Not that she cared – why be like everyone else? Her dad getting killed had made her different from all her friends anyway so what difference did a vintage frock and a pair of ballet pumps make?

Mae stood there remembering ... or trying to. How had her

dad's voice sounded? What was his aftershave like? How much taller than her would he be now if he were still alive, or would she be almost the same height?

The sand was firm but damp and Mae's feet began to sink down into it, as though it was sucking her down. Little worms of cold, coarse sand were pushing up between her toes – at least *that* was the same as when she'd been on this same little beach with her dad after a day's sailing.

'A job, Dad,' she whispered, expecting there to be a heavy weight around her heart and a lump in her chest that would bring tears to her eyes thinking about her dad, but there wasn't. She felt calm for the first time in a while. Maybe it was because she'd made her own decision about not wanting to be in the house all the time if it was going to be a stupid B&B, and she'd started to do something about it. She hoped she'd get the ice-cream kiosk job. Everyone would be in a good mood buying ice cream, wouldn't they?

'I'm going to get a job, Dad. What do you think of that?'

CHAPTER EIGHT

It was Rosie who was late arriving in Torquay. Despite the fact that Cara had had to run all the way down the hill after taking the phone call from Tom Gasson-Smith, and wave like mad at the bus to get the driver to wait before pulling out because he'd already had his indicator going, she'd been on time.

'You're late,' Cara said, a little pleat of lines forming crossly between her eyes as Rosie arrived, cheeks pink from running from wherever it was she'd parked her car.

'And I'm pleased to see you, too!' Rosie rebuked her. 'Car park was full actually, so I've had to park halfway up the hill to Babbacombe. Coffee first? Something sugary to sweeten you up?'

'Sorry. I'm being a grump, aren't I?'

'Just a bit.'

'Good news or bad news first?

'Bad. Get it out of the way.'

'I'm not VAT-registered and I've fibbed a bit and told the man from the hygiene department at the council who came around to snoop in every crevice looking for rats and bugs, that I'm looking into it.'

'Ah. I'll give you a crash course. But not now. Good news?'

'I've actually passed the hygiene test. And I've got some bookings – three people coming tomorrow night and then a longer one arriving on Saturday. Quite late he said, because he's an artist and has some sort of exhibition to be at. He's coming early for the festival.'

'Who?'

'Tom Gasson-Smith. He didn't sound best pleased when I called him plain Mr Smith.'

'You are joking! Tom Gasson-Smith?'

'Oh, do you know him? He said I might know his name but I don't. Only that it's on the flyer for the festival.'

'Sometimes, Cara Howard, I despair of you. You were the purchaser of original paintings – none of this print stuff for you, not even limited-edition ones – and you've not heard of Tom Gasson-Smith. Tut-tut.'

What was Rosie going on about? Why couldn't she just spit it out?

'Should I have? I certainly never bought anything with his name in the corner. I buy paintings I like, not to own some sort of status symbol – you know, collecting the *right* artist and all that. Maybe he paints stuff I don't like much.'

'He's all over the glossy mags at the moment. You know, the ones that come with the Sunday papers, that sort of thing. Supplements.'

Cara swallowed. She gave up buying the Sunday papers – or indeed any paper – months ago. It was money she could ill afford.

'Oh, is he? I haven't bought a newspaper in ages,' she said quietly.

'Oh God. Sorry. Me and my big mouth again. But there was never much left over for things like that with Mark anyway, was there?'

'No. So what does this Tom Whatsit paint, then?'

'Figurative,' Rosie said. 'Mostly.' She slid her hands down over her hips emphasising the shape of them. 'But tasteful. As far removed from Page Three as the Pope is from marriage troubles. But nudes to you.'

'And nudes to anyone else with half an eye I expect,' Cara

laughed. 'As I'm female and know what women look like nude, I've never had the urge to buy a painting of one. Now come on, coffee and then let's hit this pawn trail.' Cara dismissed Tom Gasson-Smith and his artwork.

'I can't believe this,' Cara said as she stood making a visor of her hands as she peered in the window of a pawnbroker's in Higher Union Street.

'What?' Rosie said. 'That so many people pawn their stuff? I mean, the window's stuffed.'

'Well that, yes,' Cara said. 'But I mean one ring in particular. Over there. The display stand in the middle, third row from the top, second ring in. The square emerald edged with diamonds.'

Rosie put an around her shoulders, which brought tears to Cara's eyes – the closeness and the caring after so long being untouched by anyone, was making her soul ache. She knew she shouldn't be surprised that her ring had turned up here because Mark had often been seconded to another branch to step in if a manager was ill or on holiday, and the branch just up the road from where she was standing had been one of those. Cara swallowed – that and a betting shop.

'Are you sure? I mean, I've got vague memories of your engagement party and the fact your ring was an emerald but well, we were all looking at things through the bottom of a glass all night, weren't we?'

'We were,' Cara managed to croak out.

She knew Rosie was just trying to make her laugh, trying to remember the positives, but it wasn't helping. Not really. Of course Cara knew her engagement ring. But she was grateful to Rosie – she couldn't have come here alone. And she could hardly have brought Mae with her, could she? She wasn't yet ready for the conversation she knew she would have to have with her daughter about Mark and had Mae been with her, that would have been right now, outside a pawnbroker's.

'It will have C and M linked by a heart on the inside at the bottom of the shank. If it's mine.'

'Right. Action needed,' Rosie said. 'Here's what we'll do. We'll go in and see who brought it in. Man or woman. And when. You do realise those bogus guests might have lifted it if you'd left it in a drawer and not worn it for ages, although I doubt they'd have got it here so quickly if they had. But if it was them, then the police will have to be involved.'

'I know. Can we cross that bridge when we come to it? I've got a hunch about this.' A shiver rippled across Cara's shoulders and snaked its way down her spine – someone walking on her grave, her grandma Rachel would have said. It was her ring and she knew it, like she'd known her own baby in a roomful of newborns at the hospital when Mae had been born.

'Okay. Next part of the plan is to see if we can get a name out of the old boy running this place.' Rosie jerked a finger towards a chap who looked about eighty, perched on a stool reading a paper at the end of the counter. 'Shouldn't be difficult. I'll just unbutton my blouse a button or two …'

'Rosie!'

'Do you want to know or not?'

'Of course. But could you go? On your own? Please. I don't think I can. I mean, if it was Mark who pawned it … how could he?'

'Mark did a lot of things neither of us could understand, sweetie,' Rosie said. 'How he could have been so cavalier with his cash when he had a beautiful and loving wife at home, and a daughter anyone would be proud of – with or without a boyfriend of whom I don't approve, it has to be said – beggars belief really.'

'Oh, Rosie,' Cara said, 'that was a bit double-edged with the reference to Josh. But I'll leave that bit out of it and say thanks for the lovely things you said.'

'Only stating the truth – well, my truth,' Rosie said. 'If Mark were here, he'd say the same. About Josh.'

'But he's not,' Cara said, her voice firm.

'But I am, and I'm being a bit bossy but I'm only psyching myself for going in there and sealing the deal, if that is indeed your ring.'

Cara laughed. So sometimes Rosie wasn't as confident inside as she looked on the outside? She dressed to impress, always, and today was no different. Monochrome from head to toe today, with earrings like liquorice allsorts – the white round ones with the black centre – and a black and white-striped shirtwaister dress cinched in tight with a black patent belt about six inches wide. Black strappy sandals with a huge white fabric bow on the toes.

'Psych away,' Cara said. 'And, you know, thanks. In advance. For what you're doing for me.'

'Sure you don't want to come in?'

Cara nodded, tears suddenly springing to her eyes that she had such a good friend to whom she could say just about anything and who returned the compliment, even though it might not be what Cara wanted to hear sometimes.

'Okay. I understand. Stay there. Close your eyes if you don't want to see it being taken out of the window. I won't be a tick.'

Cara squeezed her eyes tight, which only served to make her slightly dizzy as the traffic roared past sounding louder than normal. Her mouth went dry with nerves and she thought she might faint, although she'd never fainted in her life before. She remembered reading somewhere that if you clench your buttocks alternately it will stop you fainting. Clench, clench. Breathe in, hold for four counts, exhale slowly. And repeat. And repeat.

'Sorry,' Rosie said, touching Cara gently on the arm, startling her. 'The good news first. It's your ring. The bad news is it was Mark who brought it in.'

'Oh my God,' Cara said.

'But,' Rosie said, 'the even better news is that the time for claiming back has come and gone. I told the old boy that Mark's no longer able to come and collect it himself anyway, and he said he'd heard of his death as there's a bank just up the road and the staff were full of it at the time because most of them knew him. Anyway, be that as it may, I'm now the proud owner of a rather beautiful emerald and diamond ring. But seeing as emeralds aren't my thing, it's all yours.' She grabbed Cara's hand, placed the ring in her palm and then closed her fingers for her tightly over it.

'You can't. I won't let you.'

'I already have. If you're going to be all prissie about it, sell the thing and use the money to start a new collection of paintings.'

'No, I need to keep it. Mark bought it for me and I think I should leave it to Mae.'

'If we're going to start talking funeral plans, this is where I make my exit.'

'Very funny,' Cara said, unable to stop a chuckle rising. 'Not yet, I hope, for the funeral plan. But I will pay you back. Just as soon as …'

'No need,' Rosie stopped her. 'Now, did I hear you say you fancied lunch? With wine? At Hoopers? Do posh now we've got something to celebrate?'

'You might have,' Cara said, although she knew she'd said no such thing.

'My treat,' Rosie said.

'You …'

'I know,' Rosie said, putting a hand up to stop Cara finishing her sentence. 'I'm too good for my own good.'

'You are so. But if I were to tell you that, your head might swell.'

Arm in arm the women hurried back down the main street to the harbour and Hoopers, and lunch.

'Scrambled egg with smoked salmon, please,' Cara said when the waitress came to take their order.

'Make that two,' Rosie said. 'With a glass of Prosecco,' she added. 'For my friend here. Water with lemon, no ice, for me, saint that I am, seeing as I'm driving. No! No! Scratch the water. I'll push the boat out and go for tonic water, with lemon, no ice. My brain will tell me I'm drinking gin and tonic.'

Cara and the waitress laughed in unison.

'I'll remember that little trick!' the waitress said, grinning, as she went off with their order.

'I don't know how you do it,' Cara said, settling herself into her chair by the window, Torquay Harbour looking glorious in the sunshine with yachts at anchor, the ferry just coming in from Brixham with a full load of tourists, and a long snake of passengers waiting on the quayside ready for the trip in the other direction. It could, Cara thought, almost be the Med here today, with the light and the colours and the atmosphere. 'You're always so cheerful, and I'm sure you must get down sometimes and I want to say I'm sorry if I've not asked you about you for ages, and I'm sorry if I've been a bit, well, self-indulgent about things and ...'

'Stop! Enough!' Rosie wagged a mock-cross finger at her. 'I'm out of here if you're going to get all maudlin on me. Seriously.'

The waitress came back with their drinks. And a bowl of olives – green ones, black ones, and some the colour of mashed blackberries that Cara hadn't seen before. She couldn't remember anyone ordering those.

'On the house,' the waitress said, placing the dish carefully on the table between them. 'For the tonic water trick. Your meal won't be long,' she finished, and walked away.

Rosie took Cara's drink from the tray and handed it to her. 'Now, drink up like a good girl, and there's more where that came from. Seeing as you're not driving, and seeing as we're celebrating.'

'Yes, Miss!' Cara said. She sipped cautiously at the Prosecco but still the bubbles managed to tickle up her throat into the back of her nose as they always did.

'This is a lovely surprise. You know, lunch, the Prosecco, the waitress being so kind with the olives, finding the ring, getting it back. And it being such a ...'

'Eat!' Rosie said, holding out the dish of olives for Cara to take one. 'You're straying dangerously into maudlin territory again! Besides, I've got another little surprise for you when you get back to yours.'

And a surprise it was. Cara had asked if Rosie minded stopping off at the supermarket on the way back so she could stock up a bit on things for the freezer for future guests. Rosie had hesitated for a moment, checked the time on her phone and said, yes, if you're quick. Cara understood the reason for that hesitation now. A computer. Seeing as she was upgrading all her IT equipment at the salon, so Rosie said, she had no use for her old one, and insisted Cara accept it as a gift. The new one would be all tax-deductible expenses so Cara wasn't to even think about paying her back for it. She'd even arranged for her IT man, Ian, to install it for her. He'd arrived before the engine on Rosie's car had cooled down from the journey from Torquay to Larracombe. Quick introductions were made and then Rosie was out the door again.

'The schemer!' Cara said as Ian carried his box of tricks into the house. The computer was on the table in the kitchen, not that that could be its permanent location. 'She had this all set up. She knew I'd object.'

'Sounds like Rosie,' Ian said. 'So, where do you want it all set up?'

'God, I don't know,' Cara said. 'I haven't had time to think about it yet. It's all been a bit of a whirlwind really. I wasn't expecting her to give me a computer. I doubt it's as ancient as she says it is.'

'Got it in one,' Ian smiled at her. 'I do stuff for her a lot. Her and some of her staff, and a couple of clients who, well, need a bit of help. Random acts of kindness I call it. You're not the first.'

'No, no,' Cara said, a lump in her throat now.

'So, where's it going to live?' Ian asked, taking his mobile from his trouser pocket and checking the time.

'Sorry,' Cara said. 'I'm sure you're more than busy.'

But where should it go? In the corner of the breakfast room? In her bedroom? If she chose her bedroom, she'd need a desk of some sort up there. Maybe she could use Mae's old desk that now no longer had a laptop on it, but in her room, not Mae's.

And then a thought hit her, like a punch to the stomach. How much an hour did IT experts charge? How was she going to pay for his time, and how long was all this going to take anyway?

'Um, before you start,' Cara said, 'we need to talk finance. I don't know how much Rosie's told you but, well, I'm no Kardashian at the moment. I ...'

'All dealt with,' Ian said. 'I'll bill her as arranged.'

'I might have guessed as much,' Cara said, wondering how she could recompense Rosie for her kindness and her generosity. 'So, in the breakfast room, I think.'

'Great. I'll get it all hooked up to the internet first, then we'll sort a password and I'll need to take some photos to upload so punters can see what you're offering. We can get views of the area off the internet, but I'll take a few of the garden as well. Lovely terrace you've got out front, I noticed on the way in.'

Cara gulped. She could quite see how Rosie and Ian might have a great working relationship because they both thought fast, and both talked fast – no doubt this job would be finished in no time.

'Yes, the terrace is a lovely feature. It's what sold Mark and me the house really. The view. Mark being my late husband ...'

'I know. Rosie said. I'm sorry for your loss. Breakfast room is which way? Desk? Table?'

Of course, he would need to get on and here she was rabbiting.

Cara showed him the way, then left him to it as she raced around the house at breakneck speed plumping up cushions and tidying away anything that needed to be tidied away, like towels airing on the edge of the bath, the book she was reading, and the tubs of cream she put on her face and body every morning so she didn't turn into a wrinkled old woman before her time. Now she was almost up and running as a B&B landlady, she'd need to do this on a daily basis.

It wasn't long before Ian called up the stairs that it was all up and running and he was ready to take photographs.

Cara came scurrying down the stairs.

'Gosh, that was quick!' she said.

'Yeah. Your pal's very generous, but she's also a business-woman. Flat fee and all that. Very focusing is a flat fee!' Ian laughed. 'I'll take five or six photos of each room and then upload them. The basics are on the website already, like "home", "loca-tion", "local facilities". I'll leave you to work out what you're going to charge, but I'll show you how to add that before I leave. You can find out what's reasonable by googling other B&Bs in the area. Any problems, here's my card.'

'Thank you,' Cara said, taking his card. Ian looked, to her, as though he should have still been in sixth-form college but then, all children were more than computer-literate these days and Ian prob-ably knew more when he was seven years old than she did now.

And then Mae came in. Cara had assumed she'd been upstairs in her room still studying when she'd got back because the door was closed. Obviously not so. Where, she wondered, had Mae been? Oh yes, the library, Cara remembered now. Back via the beach by the look of it. Mae stood in the doorway of the break-fast room, her ballet pumps swinging from one hand, and leaving little trails of sand on the parquet. Her hair was blown every which way, but she had rosy cheeks and looked happier than Cara had seen her look in a long while. And then the smile faded from her daughter's face.

'Who's this?' Mae asked. She folded her arms across her chest – a shutting-out gesture that told Cara she didn't like coming home to find a stranger in the breakfast room one little bit.

'Ian,' Cara said. 'This is my daughter, Mae. Mae, darling, this is Ian, who's come to set up the computer Rosie gave me earlier, and build us a website for the B&B business. Is that the right word? Build?'

'Or create,' Ian said. 'But either will do. Hello, Mae.'

'So this stupid idea is going ahead, then?' Mae said, a pouty sulk making her look about five years old, not fifteen.

Cara was on the cusp of telling Mae to mind her manners and at least acknowledge Ian's polite and friendly 'hello', but Mae turned round sharply and raced down the hallway before thumping her way, very noisily, up to her room.

'Good luck with that, then!' Ian said, jerking his head in the direction Mae had disappeared. 'I've got three sisters. All younger than I am. Teenage girls, eh? I take it Mae's room is off limits for photos?'

'Very off limits,' Cara said. 'And I'm sorry you had to be on the receiving end of that.'

'No worries. The sisters, remember! I'll get on with the photos, upload them, and then scarper. It won't take long.'

'Take as long as you need,' Cara said.

Clearly Mae hadn't come around to the idea of Cove End being a B&B, but Cara had no other option – it had to be done. And besides, there was a little fizz of excitement underneath Cara's breastbone that she'd come up with the idea. Aided now by the very generous Rosie, she couldn't afford for it to fail.

CHAPTER NINE

'Mum, I'm sorry,' Mae said next morning at breakfast.

Cara noticed that Mae's eyes were pink as though she'd been crying very recently, although she hadn't heard her when she got up. She'd heard her in the night, though. To go to her or not? Cara had decided not. Mae was growing up and she must let her. Mae knew she could come to Cara at any time – day or night – about anything, and Cara hoped she would.

'For?' Cara said.

'Flouncing off yesterday. Missing supper. Being a pain. I should be grateful, right, that we've got a computer now?'

'Apology accepted,' Cara said. There would be no point going over old ground. She could see Mae was genuinely contrite about her bad manners and that was enough. 'And yes, we must be grateful for Rosie's generosity, yet again. I don't know what we'd have done without her, you know …'

Cara let her sentence trail away. But Mae finished it for her.

'Since Dad died. It's been, like, two years now and it seems like yesterday sometimes, and when I got back from the library, expecting Rosie to be here, and found a strange man in the kitchen, it sort of threw me all over again. I'm not doing very well with this B&B stuff, Mum, really I'm not. So … so, I'm going to ring about a job later. Weekends for the moment but I might get more once school's broken up. In the ice-cream kiosk on the harbour. It said "would suit student" on the notice in the window so seeing as that's what I am, I'm going to ring and see if I suit.' She waggled her phone at Cara. 'The number's in here.'

'Oh,' Cara said. She hadn't quite been expecting that. 'That's … that's great.'

'Once more with feeling,' Mae said, unable to stop a grin lighting up the seriousness of her pretty face.

'I know. Sorry. It's a surprise, that's all. I was going to ask if you'd like to help with the B&B guests. A bit of vacuuming, and sorting the laundry, that sort of thing.'

'Thanks, but no thanks,' Mae said. 'That's your little enterprise. Actually, I think I'll ring now.'

Mae waggled the phone at Cara again.

'It's a bit early. It's only just gone eight. And you've got to get to school.'

Mae shrugged her shoulders.

'Either they want my brilliant help or they don't.' Mae pulled herself up tall, ran a hand through her hair. But she put her phone back in her pocket. 'I'll do it on the way to school. That's a joke, by the way, about my brilliant help. Although it can't be hard selling ice-cream. It isn't astrophysics, is it? Anyway, if I don't get it, I'll try for something else. In a café or something. Just … you know, so you know.'

And just so you're out of the house when we have guests here, Cara wanted to add but didn't.

'Okay. And to paraphrase, just so you know, you know, I'm proud of your enterprise in doing this.'

'Yeah sure,' Mae said, giving Cara an awkward hug.

They hadn't done enough hugging lately – each in their own little bubble of grief and loss at the change in their lives, no doubt.

Cara hugged her back.

'There should be guests here when you get back. Three. Just for the one night,' she said quickly, now she and Mae were so physically close. She didn't want Mae to get back from school and give the guests the same welcome she'd given Ian because she was surprised to find them there.

But Mae pulled away.

'Right,' she said.

How, Cara wondered, did Mae manage to use the word 'right' and yet imbue it with the absolute opposite meaning? This was all anything but right for Mae. But it had to be done.

'Okay to pop in your room and get the black and white dress?' Cara said as an idea popped into her head that might make Mae feel better about things. 'I'll have a go at mending it.'

'Not sure it's worth repairing,' Mae said. 'It's lost its happy memories for me. And, well, I'm growing out of it anyway. It's a bit short in the waist now, and everything. Once I've earned a bit of money selling ice-cream or whatever, I can cadge a lift off Rosie and go into Totnes and look for another in the vintage shop.'

Ah, so Rosie's got her uses, then? Not just the interfering godmother Mae often said she was.

Cara smiled. 'Good idea.'

'Right,' Mae said. 'Actually I've changed my mind. I'll ring about the job now. I might not get a chance if Abby or someone tags along with me on the way to the bus. In my room.'

And suddenly she didn't look as confident as she had a few moments ago as she headed for the door.

'Mum,' Mae said, coming out of her room a few minutes later, as Cara crossed the landing, 'I've got an interview! After school. Just as soon as I can get down to the harbour.'

'Wow! That was quick. Well done.'

Mae was holding her damaged frock in her arms, all bundled up like a pile of old rags, which made Cara feel sad because Mae had always taken the greatest care of all her clothes but especially of that dress. She thrust the frock at Cara. 'Does this go for recycling, or what? It's not good enough now for a charity shop.' She sighed. 'Anyway, I'm wasting time. Gotta go.'

Cara held out her hands to take the frock. Whilst Mae had accepted Josh's apology and was still seeing him, it seemed the frock would only serve to remind her of a bad time.

'It's lovely material, Mae,' Cara said. 'Maybe I could turn it into something else?'

'Cleaning rags?' Mae said. She leaned in to kiss Cara goodbye.

'Cleaning rags?'

'Don't look so cross, Mum! That was a joke! Yours to do with whatever.' Mae planted a noisy kiss on Cara's cheek, Cara returning the gesture with a gentler one. Getting a job interview had certainly lifted her daughter's mood.

'Good luck,' Cara said. 'With the job.'

And then Mae was hurtling down the stairs, dressed in a cerise sundress with a scooped neckline and a full skirt, all cinched in with a fabric belt. Dress down Friday. Mae's hair was tied back in a high ponytail with a cerise ribbon and Cara couldn't help thinking she looked like an extra from *Dirty Dancing* – young and vibrant and full of hope. Mae got a lot of stick over her clothes choice, Cara knew that. All the other girls in Mae's year would be in jeans or leggings and whatever top was the fashion of the moment, and Cara was just so proud of her daughter for sticking to her choices.

'Oh, Mark,' Cara whispered to herself as she watched Mae leave, 'you would have been so proud of your little girl.'

She cradled the old, discarded, frock in her arms like a baby, and knew exactly what she would do with it now. The memory of the dress might have turned sour for Mae at the moment, but there would come a time when her daughter would remember it with love.

CHAPTER TEN

The morning passed quickly, Cara making a full inventory of the linen cupboard and all her crockery. She managed to get a small round table that had been in her bedroom for ages and which she didn't use much down into the breakfast room. It would be big enough for a couple to sit at and there'd be enough room to go with the table that was already there. There were half a dozen fold-up wooden garden chairs in the garage that would be fine for people to sit on for the short time it took to eat breakfast. She got them out and gave them a good scrub, and put them outside on the back terrace to dry off in the sunshine. Then she remembered that there was also a folding wooden garden table at the back of the garage under a tarpaulin. With a cloth on it, that would make a table to seat four at a push. It was a huge effort half carrying, half dragging it into the house, but she managed.

After lunch she checked on the bedrooms her guests would be using, opening the windows to air them a little. They were due to arrive at about four o' clock, leaving plenty of time to get other things done like iron tablecloths and put posies of flowers on the bedside tables.

'There,' Cara said, as she put the finishing touches to the tables in the breakfast room, the cloths now ironed to within an inch of their lives. She'd never usually been one for using tablecloths, but hadn't felt able to throw out what had been well-meaning wedding presents from neighbours when she and Mark had got married – one of them had never been taken out of its cellophane wrapping. She was glad she'd kept them all now. 'Table mats next. Drinks' coasters.' More unused wedding presents being put to good use.

Suddenly Cara was looking forward to having people around, someone new to talk to, with stories to tell perhaps. Things that would put a stop to her talking to herself out of loneliness anyway!

And then the doorbell rang. Only three o' clock. They were early. She hurried to the door.

'Hello,' she said, opening the door, a smile pinned to her face, which she hoped would mask the nervousness she was feeling inside. 'I thought there was three of you?'

A very well-dressed couple stood on Cara's doorstep.

'I'm sorry?' the woman said. 'I don't think you're expecting us. We've just called on spec. Do you have a room free by any chance?' the man asked.

'Well, um,' Cara began. There was the room she'd got ready for Tom Gasson-Smith. If they only wanted to stop the one night, they could use that, and she'd have to have a quick turnaround for Tom. 'How long for?'

'Just the one night if it's not too much trouble,' the woman said. She didn't look best pleased at Cara's less than effusive welcome.

'It's no trouble,' Cara said quickly. 'I was just thrown for a moment because I've got three guests booked in for tonight. But, please, do come in.' She would have to get used to this sort of thing – people calling 'on spec' as the saying had it – whatever that meant. She threw the door open wider. 'Welcome to Cove End. I'm Cara.'

'Kate and Andrew,' the young woman said. 'We can bring our luggage in in a minute, now we know you can put us up.'

'Hi Kate. Hi Andrew.'

There was an awkward moment of handshakes – to whom did she offer her hand first, Andrew or Kate? Was there etiquette for all this? There was a flutter of butterflies in her stomach, probably because she felt that she hadn't prepared properly for this venture, but then she chided herself that this was hardly Buckingham Palace and Kate and Andrew weren't visiting dignitaries, were they?

'I'll show you to your room, and then make tea. You can come down and join me when you're ready.' Cara was aware her voice sounded stiff and stilted, as though she'd rehearsed her one line for an infant school play and just delivered it. 'Follow me.'

'Oh, this is lovely,' Kate said. She ran a long, slim hand with exquisitely manicured nails over the pristine white duvet with its broderie anglais trim. 'I love white. You can see that it's clean, if you get my meaning.'

Cara thought the young woman sounded nervous. She thought about asking why they'd arrived on spec for just the one night but decided not to. There could be a million reasons and Cara's mind went into overdrive thinking about them: two lovers, escaped from their marriages for a night of love; one of them had been given bad news and they'd come away from home to digest it and plan how to tell their families; they'd started a course of IVF and come away to relax so it had its best chance of success.

'Um, come and look at the view,' Cara said, suddenly aware there was a silence in the room and she ought to fill it. She hoped neither Andrew nor Kate were mind readers. She strode to the window and pulled the curtains back as far as she could.

Kate and Andrew were right behind her.

'Lovely indeed,' Kate said. 'Will you mind if we take photos? The room? The garden.'

'Nothing invasive,' Andrew said. 'For our vlog.'

Vlog? Cara had heard of vlogs although she'd never looked at

97

one, and the fact that this couple might have one hadn't been one of the scenarios she'd thought of.

'Are you from Trip Advisor?' she asked, not that she'd object if they were because she knew that recommendations and reviews were the way forward for this sort of business.

'No,' Andrew laughed. 'Not quite in that league, but we do have followers.'

Andrew didn't offer figures so Cara didn't ask. She was feeling uneasy and excited in equal measure at the thought of maybe thousands of people seeing her B&B on Kate and Andrew's vlog and wanting to come and stay.

'My daughter,' she said. 'She's not here at the moment, but I'd appreciate it if you don't take any photos of her, not even in the distance coming up the path or anything.' Cara couldn't be sure if Mae would welcome the idea of a vlog with open arms as she was the generation brought up on technology, or whether she would hate the intrusion.

'Of course not,' Kate assured her. 'Don't worry. It's not just Cove End we've come to see and take videos of. We're promoting the area for the visitor trade. I hear there's an art festival coming up. Have I got that right?'

'There is. In August. I've got a flyer for it somewhere.'

'Great!' Kate said.

'I'll find it and you can do whatever you want with it when you come down for your tea.'

'Ah yes, tea,' Kate said. She looked around the room as though searching for something. 'I think we'd rather have tea here. What do you think, Andrew?' Andrew gave a sort of shrug as if to say he didn't mind, but it was up to Kate. 'Hospitality tray?' she went on. 'Have you got it hidden in a closet somewhere?'

Oh God! Cara hadn't given hospitality trays a thought. She'd assumed her guests would be happy to use the breakfast room, which had a couch in it and a view of the side garden. She thought fast. What went on a hospitality tray? Tea, coffee, cocoa. Possibly decaffeinated varieties and some herbal teas. Sachets of sugar. Those silly little pots of milk that ripped your nails off trying to open them. Where would she source those? Meg Smythson certainly didn't stock them in the corner shop. Biscuits. Kettle.

'I'll bring it right up,' she said. But best to come clean. 'There's nothing decaffeinated at the moment, but I could run to the corner shop and get whatever you want.' What was she saying! She'd already been caught out once doing that, although she didn't think this couple were anything like the Hines had been.

'No need,' Kate said. 'A caffeine fix is what we both need after the journey.'

'Great,' Cara said.

'But that's something you'll need to address for future guests,' Kate said, smiling, not appearing to judge it as a bad mark against Cara. 'Just a tip.'

'Thanks for that.'

Cara scurried from the room.

In the kitchen she quickly found a tray, some dishes in which to put sugar and biscuits, and a small jug for the milk. She put tea bags into a pretty tin she'd not had the heart to throw away but had had no use for until now. A jar of coffee granules would have to do for the moment.

'Phew!' she said to herself, as she carried it all back up to her guests. 'Learning on the job or what?'

Half an hour later and Kate and Andrew were on their way out again, taking advantage, they said, of the lovely day and the light evenings. They'd have a mooch about and find a pub some- where for supper. Cara gave them a spare key so they could let themselves in later, and then they were gone.

Cara checked her phone to see if Mae had texted to say if she'd got the job or not. And then the doorbell rang again.

Of course. Her expected guests. She hurried to let them in.

'Welcome to Cove End,' she said, opening the door.

Three people. She'd got it right this time. Two men and a

woman, and all carrying backpacks and dressed in serious walking gear, not exactly camouflage but not far off. All had binoculars around their necks. She had a stab at guessing their ages and came up with early retired. Sixties anyway.

'Thank you,' the taller of the two men said. 'I'm Eric and this is my wife, Sheila. And this bundle of trouble is my brother, Frank.'

More handshakes, more entreaties to come in; they were welcome; she would make tea after she'd shown them to their rooms. She was getting good at this.

She'd even had time to put hospitality trays in their rooms this time. Decaffeinated anything would have to wait until she had time to nip down to Meg Smythson's and see what might be available. Thank goodness she'd asked Rosie to stop off at a supermarket because she did at least have enough bread and breakfast essentials.

'No need,' Eric said. 'We'll just drop our gear in our rooms, if that's all right with you, and then we'll be off out again. This time of day is perfect for seeing peregrine falcons returning to their roosts and apparently there are at least three nesting pairs on Elberry cliffs.'

Ah, twitchers.

'Perfectly fine,' Cara said. 'There's a short cut to the coastal path,' she told them. 'There's a slipway between the two end houses.' She pointed in the direction they needed to go.

'Perfect,' Sheila said.

'Your key,' Cara said, taking the second, and last, spare key from the hook beside the front door. She'd have to get more cut at this rate.

'Ideally, we'd like breakfast at seven,' Frank said. 'Wouldn't we?' He turned questioningly to his brother and sister-in-law.

'Told you he was a bundle of trouble,' Eric laughed. 'But if you could oblige, Cara?'

She could. She would. Cara was used to being up early to get

Mae off to school, although she wasn't in the habit of cooking a full English breakfast.

'No problem,' Cara said.

She'd be the perfect landlady if it killed her!

But first, once these twitchers had gone back out again, she rushed to finish the project she'd started with the fabric of Mae's dress. She ought to be back by now, but at least it was giving her a bit of time to put her daughter at the forefront of what she was doing instead of looking after B&B guests. Ah, the front door, and Mae coming in dropping her school bag with a thud in the hall as usual.

'Mum!'

'In here, darling,' Cara called back. She'd have to ask Mae not to do that when guests were around – leave her stuff lying about all over the place for people to trip over.

'Mum, I ...' Mae began. 'What the heck is that?'

'Your old frock.' She held up the pieces of fabric she'd been stitching together. 'Now a cushion cover. It's been a bit of a rush to get it done because, well, wait for it, but we've got not just three guests but five now. Can you believe it? Kate and Andrew arrived on spec. They're doing some sort of vlog. Then there's Eric and Sheila and Eric's brother, Frank. Three twitchers – quirky, but nice with it. They want breakfast at seven so a bit of an early start, but hey, it has to be done now we're in business. All five have gone out. I'm going to have to catch Kate and Andrew when they get back and ask what time they want to eat. Oh, and I'm going to have to ask you not to dump your stuff in the hall when you come in, darling. Not when we've got guests anyway.' Cara turned the cushion cover the right way out, checked the zip worked. She teased out the frill she'd made, then reached for the cushion pad and put the cover on. Perfect. Yes, she was pretty pleased with that. She looked up. 'What do you think?'

'I think,' Mae said, 'none of this would be happening if Dad hadn't died. He would so hate this – a house full of people. Not

101

being able to, like, relax in his own home. And just for the record, so do I!'

And then Mae ran from the room.

'I'll take my offensive stuff up with me, don't worry!' she yelled back over her shoulder.

'Mae ...' Cara began, wanting to rush to her. Deciding against it, she flumped back down on the chair.

Cara's heart plummeted. No, Mae had got that wrong. It still might have happened because Mark would have been living somewhere else by now if he hadn't died and she would have had to find a way to earn a living so they could stay at Cove End. She hadn't expected running a business to be easy, but she hadn't expected it to be this hard either. It was going to take more of a juggling act to be both mother and landlady than she'd given any thought to.

She held the cushion to her, smelt the perfume – Victoria Beckham, which Mae always drenched herself in – still in the fabric. Mark had bought her that first bottle and then every birthday afterwards, Cara had bought it for Mae in his memory.

How had she got it so badly wrong, thinking Mae would welcome a cushion as some sort of substitute for having to share the house with strangers?

And she hadn't even asked Mae if she'd got the job at the ice-cream kiosk either. She'd make spaghetti carbonara for supper – Mae's favourite. A peace offering of sorts for her thoughtlessness.

CHAPTER ELEVEN

'Well, darling,' Cara said the next morning when Mae came down to the kitchen for breakfast. 'That wasn't so bad was it?'

It wasn't ten o' clock yet and already she'd cooked breakfast for five, done toast for five, made coffee for five, and served it all. Eric, Sheila and Frank had left the breakfast room just as Kate and Andrew had come in. There had been a series of quick hellos and goodbyes in the doorway. If all guests from now on were like this lot, she wouldn't have much to worry about, would she? She'd have to get her skates on and change all the linen on the bed that was to be Tom Gasson-Smith's, vacuum and polish, and clean the en suite but it was, thank goodness, another glorious day and everything would soon be dry on the line. Far from being thrown by the extra work the on-spec guests had made for her, Cara was fired up with enthusiasm for her new venture. For life. They could put the bad experience of the Hines behind them once and for all.

Mae shrugged, which brought Cara right back down to earth.

'The early start didn't wake you?'

'No,' Mae said.

'They all seemed to like what I did in the breakfast room anyway.'

Cara had thought to pick a few flowers – some Zepherine Drouhin roses in bud, the leaves of Lady's Mantle, which always reminded Cara of water lilies, rather frilly ones, and some ox-eye daisies – to make posies for the breakfast tables. Kate had said she loved the gesture and had got Andrew to take photographs. But now they were all gone and she had one hundred and sixty pounds in cash in her hand. Getting a card machine would be a priority because not everyone would want to pay cash, she knew that. Cara waggled the notes at Mae.

'Good, eh?'

'I suppose,' Mae said.

'Well it is! If we get fully booked like that throughout the season then we should be able to save a tidy sum to see us through the winter. Maybe something else will come up. A job of some sort I can do.'

'I've got one of those,' Mae said. 'A job. Not that ...'

'Oh, darling, I'm so sorry. I forgot to ask. What with the first guests – well, the first bona fide ones – arriving all at once, and trying to make that cushion cover against the clock, and ... well, no excuses, I should have remembered. Tell me about it.'

Cara was contrite now. Mae was probably beyond irritated that her mother had been so wrapped up in her first foray into being a landlady that she'd forgotten to ask how she'd got on at the job interview. Mae had come down at supper time, but had taken her meal to her room, not giving Cara a chance to ask.

'I got the job. Thursdays and Fridays after school until we break up, then two full days, plus Saturdays. I had a little practice run for half an hour. Dead easy. I got paid as well.'

'How much? I don't want you being exploited.'

'Seven pounds an hour. Seems okay to me.'

'It seems okay to me too, darling,' Cara told her. 'The Paris trip will be coming up ...'

'Like pay for my own trip?' Mae said, looking beyond hurt.

'Of course not. I was thinking you could save some for a bit of spending money.' Oh God, whatever Cara said, she seemed to be putting her foot further in the muck. 'I'll pay for the trip like I promised I would.'

'Right. Okay. Thanks,' Mae said. 'Just so it's clear. I'm going out later. Josh texted at silly o clock to say the forecast is good and our sailing trip is on.'

She didn't sound very enthusiastic and Cara wondered if it was all a bit too quick after the ripped frock episode. But Cara knew how it felt to cling to what you know because the thought of casting yourself off, alone, in the hope of finding someone else better suited to you was beyond scary – it was how she'd felt with Mark.

'You don't have to go just because Josh has asked you, if you don't want to.'

Mae sighed theatrically. 'I want to,' she said. 'Okay?'

'Okay.' Cara knew how much Mae had loved to sail with Mark, and perhaps she'd agreed to this to get that same feeling of freedom she'd had with her dad out on the water. She thought about asking what Mae was going to be wearing because Mark had sold just about all the sailing gear – even their lifejackets – when he'd sold Mae's dinghy. 'What sort of boat has Josh got?'

'Laser.'

'Ah,' Cara said. She knew lasers were sleeker and faster than Mae's old vintage Mirror dinghy had been. 'Well ...'

'Don't even think about trying to put me off going, Mum,' Mae said. She put her arms behind her back and Cara knew her hands would be linked – Mark had had that same gesture when he'd felt challenged. 'Please,' she added in a tiny voice.

'Not for a moment,' Cara said.

'Good. Well, best get going.'

Mae was wearing the navy jeggings she wore for cross-country runs at school and a lime green and white striped top that came down over her bottom. Seeing her dressed like that seemed rather alien to Cara now, used to seeing Mae dressed either in school uniform or one of her vintage frocks. But she was glad Mae was dressing for the occasion. If she was surprised Mae was going so soon after breakfast, she did her best to hide it.

'I can read your mind there, Mum,' Mae said, the beginnings of a smile tweaking up the sides of her mouth. 'You're thinking why this early, right?'

'Might have been,' Cara said, pleased that mother and daughter did still have that connection despite the current problems over the house being turned into a B&B.

'We're going cove-hopping. Got to catch the tide, you know.'

'Of course.' Cara knew all about tides and how people could get caught out sometimes if it came in or went out more quickly than they'd expected it to. It had happened to Mark and a sailing buddy from the yacht club a couple of times.

'I can make some sandwiches to take, okay?'

'Of course,' Cara said again.

Despite the fact there would be work to do now her guests had gone, Cara felt suddenly bereft; one minute the house was full of people and now she was alone. She'd rather hoped that she and Mae could search the internet for places of interest to add to the Cove End website, and maybe have lunch together outside on the terrace in the sunshine. Just chilling, as common parlance had it. She would find something to do because sitting and fretting was not her way – and Tom Gasson-Smith wasn't due until ten o' clock.

The something to do was sewing, or rather sewing-related. When she'd taken Mae's ripped frock apart to reuse some of the material, she'd done it very carefully. She could use the pieces to make a pattern. Her plan was to see if she could find some vintage fabric on the internet that was similar and then make Mae a new frock, using the old one as a template, but a couple of sizes larger because Mae had filled out since Mark had bought her that frock. And while she was on the internet, she'd see if there were any dressmakers in the area. Thanks to the genes Cara had inherited from her great-grandmother, Emma, she was gifted with a needle, something she hadn't realised until Mae had been born and, unable to find dresses and jackets she liked for her baby daughter that weren't pink, or twee, or patterned with butterflies, she'd begun to make her own. She had some old black and white photos of Emma in a box in the loft, and in some of them she was standing beside mannequins that showed wonderful wedding dresses of the 1930s, and costumes with dropped waists and fancy collars. Cara could do fancy collars because she'd practised and practised until she'd got them to sit just so. But she didn't want to step on anyone's toes if they had a decent dressmaking business going so she'd check first, but dressmaking might be something she could do in the winter months.

The morning sped by, Cara pleased to be unable to find any local dressmakers on the internet. She also managed to find a site selling both vintage patterns and fabric – all at very reasonable prices – so she bought six yards of fabric and two patterns. It felt good planning for the future at last, after a couple of years just floating in the here and now but not really knowing where she was going.

And then, on a whim, Cara decided to google Tom Gasson-Smith. Well! If the photos that came up when she clicked on 'image' were of him then, wow! A slightly older version of Aidan Turner perhaps? Cara wondered if there was a very lucky Mrs Gasson-Smith somewhere. There were rather a lot of photos of his art work – as Rosie had told her, mostly figurative – which to Cara's untrained eye did look very professional in their execution. Tasteful too. A giggle bubbled its way up into Cara's throat, wondering if Larracombe was ready for Tom Gasson-Smith and his art.

'Cove End Guest House/Larracombe,' Cara said out loud as she typed it into the search box, and was startled when a link popped up immediately. She clicked on it and there was her hallway with the highly polished parquet, and her chandelier. And there was the terrace with Kate sitting at the patio table, a glass in her hand, and there was the bedroom she'd let to Kate and Andrew, Kate leaning against the windowsill admiring the view. Five stars. Kate and Andrew had given her five stars and they must have done it before leaving earlier, or en route to wherever it was they were going next. What a great start to her venture.

Cara still had the rest of the day to fill until Mae got back and Tom Gasson-Smith arrived. She walked all over the house, checking bedrooms, straightening towels in the bathrooms, re-doing the posy of flowers on Tom's bedside table. Then she did one for Mae. And herself. Yes, it all looked good, and all by her own efforts.

By four o' clock all the laundry had dried, been ironed, and put away. Time, then, to chill. Cara searched out the book Rosie had bought her for her birthday back in April that she hadn't even opened yet. She took it out onto the terrace and sat down to read. The sun was warm on her shoulders, but she was in no danger of getting sunburnt. Things couldn't get better – life was beginning to taste very sweet again.

CHAPTER TWELVE

'It's a bit tight,' Mae said as she fastened the locks on her buoy-ancy aid. She'd tried putting a waterproof jacket underneath it, but there hadn't been room. 'And what is this wetsuit like!'

'Um, tight would sum it up nicely,' Josh said.

'I didn't mean that,' Mae said. 'I meant the ankle cuffs are halfway up my calves. You'd never get any of the girls in my class rigged up like this!'

The second the words were out of her mouth she knew she ought not to have said that – about the girls in her class. It would only serve to remind Josh he was going out with a schoolgirl – it showed up the age difference.

'You're not *any of the girls*,' Josh said. 'I've gone past only seeing what you look like. And actually you look fine to me. With or without the fancy frock you usually wear. Sorry, you know, for what happened the other night. That frock ...'

'Forget the frock. It's past tense now anyway. Mum made me a big cushion for my room from the fabric.'

'Cool,' Josh said.

'Which is more than I feel in this already,' Mae said.

They hadn't been able to set off as early as Josh had hoped because he'd read the tide tables wrongly. They'd had to spend the morning mooching about the harbour, drinking coffee and eating pizza for lunch. Josh had said he fancied a pint, but Mae said there was no way she was going out in a boat with him if he'd had a drink, and he'd laughed and called her the hooch police.

It was four o'clock now – or so it said on the clock of St Peter's church tower. But they were on their way at last, now the tide was right. Mae's tummy was a tangle of excited knots just thinking about it. They'd be able to get a good three or four hours sailing in before they'd have to turn back. They wouldn't be able to do as much cove-hopping as they'd hoped because they'd need to get back before dark, but that wouldn't be for ages yet.

It was a hot day, and getting hotter still. Wriggling into the wetsuit had made her body temperature climb even higher. She'd cool down once they were out on the water though.

Mae glanced back at the clock on St Peter's tower. Her dad was buried there.

First trip without you, Dad.

For Mae everything was a first at the moment. The first open evening at her school when he hadn't been there to be proud as anything that Mae was good at maths as he had been. The first time she'd come home from school knowing he wouldn't be coming in from work, going up on the computer in the spare room for hours. All the other firsts – her birthday and Christmas. And not being able to tell him she had a boyfriend, although he'd probably have been less than pleased to know who it was. She bit her lip to stop her thoughts manifesting themselves as tears.

'In you jump,' Josh said, steadying the boat so Mae could step from the quay into it. 'We could sail around to Seal Cove. Are you up for that?'

'And drop anchor and swim to the beach? I love doing that.'

'Me too. We should be able to do a couple of coves if we watch the tide and make good headway. Sorry about the mess up with the tide tables.'

Josh loosened the mooring rope and dropped gently into the boat, pushing them away from the harbour wall in one swift movement.

'It's okay,' Mae said. Just being with Josh today had been good, what with her mother forgetting to ask about the job and everything, and being so thrilled that the house had been full of people – like they and their needs were more important than she was.

'I've got biscuits and coke in my dry bag by way of compensation. No wine this time, though. Honest.'

Josh grinned at her. He was being kind and his kindness was overwhelming Mae a bit.

'Thanks for coming round to see Mum. Apologising about me having to walk back because of the drink, and that.'

'No worries. Right, grab the tiller a moment, I'll just sort the sails a bit.'

Mae did as she was told, excited to be sailing again because she'd always loved it. And yet her life had been going so wrong lately, and she was anxious, too.

'The wind won't get up, will it?' she asked. There seemed to be a bit of a breeze now they were out of the shelter of the harbour at last.

'Nah,' Josh said.

And then the old thrill of sailing, being as one with the boat and the sea, came back for Mae. She hadn't forgotten a thing since she'd sailed with her dad. Josh didn't have to remind her to duck under the boom, she just knew she had to. She knew when to flick the tiller to port, or to starboard. She knew when to lean with the boat and when it was best to maintain her position.

'This is great!' she called out to Josh. She was just so happy in that moment, enjoying the sound of water slapping on the hull, and gulls screeching overhead, and breathing in that salty smell, almost metallic as it hit the back of her nose.

Berry Head seemed to be swarming with people and dogs enjoying the sunshine although they looked like toy figures from

111

where Mae was, a hundred feet or so below them and zipping along now. Someone waved and Mae waved back. She often wondered why people did that – waved to sailors. People did it with trains as well. There was a heritage line running along the coast and try as she might not to wave back when passengers waved at her, she never could resist. Ah, there was the train now, steam pluming from the funnel. Mae closed her eyes for a moment and she could have sworn she heard the clack of wheels on the rails.

'Crystal Cove for a first stop alright with you?' Josh asked. 'Seal Cove after if we've got time?'

'Very alright,' Mae said. She knew that with the tide the way it was, the path down from the headland would be covered in water. Anyone in the cove would have to stay there until the tide receded a bit – there were big notices up on the headland and down in the cove reminding people of the dangers, and the tide times, which were changed weekly. With luck no one would be in the cove at the moment. It would just be her and Josh, and they could get back to how they'd been before the wine in the car incident, and her ripped frock, and well ... they hadn't kissed since and she hoped that would be rectified soon. Mae liked kissing. Or liked the way Josh kissed, having only ever been kissed at school discos against her will by a couple of boys in her class when Mr Rutherford dimmed the lights and they took advantage of a quick lunge for her lips which had been, like, yuk. Bailey hadn't tried to kiss her – not once. She was glad of that now – it made her a virgin kisser if she discounted the school disco gropes.

'Penny for them,' Josh laughed. 'You looked far away then.'

'Nope,' Mae laughed. 'I was right in the moment!'

'That's my girl,' Josh said. 'Here we go, anchor's away!'

His girl? He'd really said that – his girl! Mae was more than glad she'd given him a second chance now.

CHAPTER THIRTEEN

Cara rang Rosie. When the answerphone cut in, she hesitated for a moment – to leave a message or not? Struggling to keep panic from her voice she said, 'Rosie, please can you come over? Just as soon as you pick up this message. I may need to go out for a short while. Mae's not back and she should be. The key's in the usual place.'

Cara always left a key in case she lost her own while out, and also so Rosie could get in if she needed to – underneath a garden gnome, a joke present from Rosie. 'This gnome's got no home,' she'd said, laughing when she'd given it to Cara one Christmas.

But Rosie would know something was wrong when she heard Cara's message. All through the bad times with Mark and his gambling, Rosie had known what was going on, but Cara had never asked for her help before. She would be there just as soon as she could, Cara knew it.

Then, just before nine o' clock, when the light was beginning to go, and she was feeling more scared than she'd ever felt in her life, she rang the Reverend David Maynard.

'David Maynard. St Peter's.'

Cara took a deep, steadying, breath. She'd not spoken to the Reverend Maynard since Mark's funeral and she felt bad about that now. He'd been very kind to both her and Mae back then. But wasn't that the way most people behaved – asking for a vicar's help at the worst time in their lives and then when they were back on track just sort of moving away physically and emotionally? But she needed him again now.

'Hello, it's Cara Howard. I'm Mae's mum. Is Mae there?'

'Mae? No. Not as far as I know. Were you expecting her to be?'

She took another deep breath, trying to slow down her quickening heartbeat and banish worst-case scenarios from her head. The phone propped between her shoulder and her ear, she turned her now-returned engagement ring round and round on her finger. It was a bit loose now she'd lost a fair bit of weight – more due to stress than any sort of diet.

'Mae left here just after ten this morning to meet Josh. I was expecting her back around tea-time. They've gone sailing. In the Laser.'

'What?' David Maynard shouted, and Cara had to yank the receiver away from her ear. 'He promised me he wouldn't take Mae out in it. I said she was too young and inexperienced for the Laser. Just wait until … Have you've tried Mae's mobile?'

'Yes, but it's switched off. I know it's still light – just – but it's fading fast and …'

'And we're wasting time,' the Reverend Maynard cut in, but kindly. 'Now, what I think we should do is, you stay where you are in case Mae rings your landline on Josh's mobile to say they're becalmed or something, and I'll nip down to the harbour to see if they've moored up and have gone to the pub or wherever. I'll take my mobile, give Josh a call as I go and then I can ring you as soon as I locate them. I'm sure they're just being typical unthinking young people and all will be well.'

'I'm sure you're right,' Cara said, although she wasn't entirely sure that he was. Her mouth was as dry as ash, but her palms were sticky with nerves. She felt an almost overwhelming gratitude to him that he was taking over. They exchanged mobile numbers and rang off. Then needing to do something, she picked it up again – thank goodness for cordless telephones – and went upstairs. Some sort of invisible thread drew her towards Mae's room. How tidy it all was. Cara had often commented on it. 'Yeah, but is it normal,' Rosie or her mother or Mark would ask, 'for a teenager to be so tidy?' But they always laughed it off and told Cara to be grateful for small mercies.

Cara walked over to the bookcase – everything arranged in alphabetical order by author, and then within genres, also in alphabetical order, and every book standing straight. Had Mae read them all? She knew since Mark's death that Mae had retreated to her room more than she'd ever done before. Perhaps she'd been reading. Mae turned away from the bookcase and saw the polka dot frock – turquoise with white spots – Mae had bought only recently from a charity shop in Totnes and not worn yet. It hung from a padded hanger, freshly washed and ironed. Cara gulped – what if she never came home to wear it. Again, Cara twirled her engagement ring around her finger. And the ring – what if she never got to say, 'Daddy bought this for me the very same day he asked me to marry him. We were so in love.' And they had been for a very long time. It wasn't that she'd fallen out of love with Mark, just that she'd lost the respect she'd had for him over his gambling. Telling him to leave had been a desperate measure – something she hoped would give him a wake-up call. Except it had been anything but that. 'This is who I am, take it or leave it, Cara,' was what he'd said. And she'd said just the one word – leave.

And then Cara saw it – Mae's mobile. She picked it up. Hugged it to her.

'Oh, Mae,' she said out loud, 'how stupid not to take this.'

CHAPTER FOURTEEN

Mae writhed and wriggled deliciously in Josh's arms, his kisses transporting her to somewhere else entirely – she wasn't even minding the aroma of wet rubber and a faint fishy smell from the rotting seaweed at the tide-line. They hadn't got any further than Crystal Cove once the kissing had started, taking advantage of being alone with no one likely to access the cove before the tide turned. Not that they'd only kissed. They'd talked too – about their families, about what the future might hold for them both, although Mae wasn't so stupid as to think she would be in Josh's life forever. She'd opened up and told Josh how hard it was being without a dad and Josh had listened and nodded but not offered any sort of platitudes, which pleased Mae. And then he'd said she could have his dad if she liked because he was always on his back wanting him to go to university, to get a better job, to be the son he wanted him to be and not who he was. She'd heard rumours that Josh had been seen with Alice Morrell in the Port Light over in Paignton, but why spoil the moment by asking him about that now? They were only rumours, and it was her who Josh was with at that moment, not Alice. They were lying side by side, their hands clasped, when Josh threw an arm across her and reached for her again.

'Come here, gorgeous,' he said.

Mae rolled over towards him and their lips touched, just lightly at first, before Josh's tongue began to explore her mouth and she thought she might die of pleasure at how it made her feel inside. He tasted of coca cola and ... alcohol? Josh had offered Mae a drink from the bottles of coke he'd brought with him, but she'd declined because she didn't like it – it always gave her terrible indigestion. But she was in danger of becoming paranoid if she started thinking every time Josh had a drink of something there'd be alcohol in it, wasn't she? But still ... Mae kissed him back long and hard, trying to banish the thought.

'What time is it?' she asked after breaking away from him reluctantly. She looked up at the faint outline of what was going to be a crescent moon.

'Time we got back probably.'

'No. Not yet,' Mae said. She tugged on the zip of her wetsuit so that Josh could slide his hand inside. Touch her skin. Make her writhe in ecstasy.

'As contraceptives go,' Josh laughed, 'wetsuits are pretty effective!'

'I'll go to the doctor soon,' Mae said. 'Get fixed up. The pill.'

But how soon was soon? And did she want to really? What if, once she'd let him do it, Josh moved on to his next conquest? Or Alice Morrell...

'Actually ...' Josh began, fumbling in the pocket of his buoyancy aid that he'd taken off and dropped onto the sand. 'Oh God, no! Where the hell's my phone? I put it in here.'

'I left mine at home,' Mae told him. 'It was the last present Dad gave me and I didn't want to lose it and it hasn't got much credit on it anyway.'

'You can't get a signal down here anyway.' Josh reached for a bottle of coke and took a long swig.

Mae's heart flipped. There was more than just coca cola in there. Josh was on his second bottle now.

117

'You've been here before?' she asked.

'Well, of course I have. I was born here. I've been sailing since, like, forever.' Josh took another swig from his bottle.

'I didn't mean that. I meant I'm not the first girlfriend you've brought here, am I?'

'I didn't have you down as totally naïve, Mae,' Josh said. 'Just because my old man's a vicar, it doesn't make me a saint.'

Mae felt her heart almost stop in her chest – he was changing again before her very eyes. It had to be the drink. He was an alcoholic, wasn't he? She was getting scared now.

'I can't believe you've been so stupid as to leave your phone at home,' Josh said. He sat up now and began scrabbling about in the sand beside him looking for his phone.

'Hey! Watch who you're calling stupid,' Mae said. 'You seem to have lost your phone so …'

She left her sentence unfinished, feeling frightened now as to how the mood between them had suddenly changed, just like before. They had to get out of here. And before Josh drank even more. There was a steep and very basic path up the side of the cliff, but now the light was beginning to drop Mae knew they'd be stupid to attempt that in the dark. She stood up and walked towards a set of roughly hewn steps that led up to a grassy area where there had been a lookout post during the Second World War. They could leave the boat moored, walk up the steps and on through the housing estate and maybe hitch a lift or call Josh's dad from there. And then she saw it – a warning sign at the top of what was now very obviously broken steps with a gap about twelve feet wide that they'd never get over. And another one, smaller, leaning against the cliff face. No wonder no one had attempted to come down onto the beach as the tide went out.

She walked back to Josh to tell him what she'd seen, but it was as though he'd read her mind.

'It looks like we're stuck, Mae. The tide has gone out at a fair pace. Let's hope we can get the boat afloat.'

Mae looked towards the boat they'd anchored when they'd swum in and it was obvious by the way it tilted that it was on some sort of sandbank. She dropped onto the sand and sat hugging her knees as though that gesture might give her inspiration.

'And if we can't?'

'Then we'll have to shack up here for the night, or until there's enough light at dawn to climb the cliff, or the tide has come back in far enough to float the boat and we've got enough light to sail by. Honestly, Mae, do I have to explain everything to you, chapter and verse?'

'Flares?' Mae said, her voice shaky. Josh seemed like a totally different person now. 'Have you got some in the boat?'

'Nope.'

'How stupid was that – to come out without a flare?' Fear was, she knew, making her sound very confrontational.

'Did you check, then?' Josh snapped back at her.

'Of course not, it's not my boat,' Mae said. And then she added, even though she'd probably have come anyway if he'd told her there wasn't one, 'But I ought to have asked you if you had some. Dad would …'

'Oh for God's sake, Mae, can you give over being Daddy's girl, just for a moment.' Josh leapt to his feet.

Mae was too shocked at his words and the fact he was now looming over her.

'Right! Someone has to be the grown up around here!' Josh's voice was so loud Mae put her hands over her ears. And she could feel his angry breath ruffling her hair. 'I don't think we're going to be able to get the boat off that sandbank for a while. I'll wade in and take the sails off and we can wrap ourselves in them and it'll be …'

'No, we can't! We *can't*!' Everyone would assume they'd really done it then, wouldn't they? It was against the law – Rosie had said. 'We've got to get out of here. We can't stop here! We just can't!'

'Actually, Mae,' Josh said, his voice suddenly serious. He turned away from Mae. 'I'm beginning to think the age gap between us is just too wide. I'm getting a bit fed up with this on/off, off/on stuff from you.'

'You mean the sex, I suppose,' Mae said. She knew they were wasting time talking when they should have been doing something practical about getting back to the harbour, and she knew Josh was probably as scared as she was, but he was being bully man not macho man and she wasn't going to stand for it. 'I said I'd go to the doctor and I …'

'Forget it,' Josh said. 'It's going to be too much hassle. Doctor Green is bound to tell your mum, with you being underage. He and your dad played golf together.'

'I know,' Mae said. There was only one doctor in the village and everyone went to him. She didn't really want to be reminded of what her dad used to do, and with whom either. But Josh was right – Doctor Green would split on her, more than likely, seeing as she was underage for sex.

'Right, I'm making a run for it,' Josh said. 'Stay here if you want.'

'What!'

Mae couldn't believe what she was hearing. He was running out on her!

Josh was running towards the sea in a rather wobbly fashion. It could have been because he was running on sand, but Mae knew now that whatever had been in the bottles with the coke wasn't helping. The boat now looked a lot further away from them than it had been when they'd been lying on the sand kissing.

'Hey!' Mae called after him. 'Don't forget your buoyancy aid! Wait for me!'

She picked up both buoyancy aids and ran after him, her heart hammering like crazy in her chest, making her take quick gasps of breath, like she was having an asthma attack or something, not that she'd ever had one.

Struggling to get into her buoyancy aid, she reached the boat, which Josh was trying to pull from the sandbank into the sea now.

'Put this on!' she yelled at him, tossing his buoyancy aid into the boat. Josh ignored her and carried on tugging on the boat, but it was making little headway.

'Pull for God's sake, Mae,' Josh yelled at her.

Mae pulled, adrenalin taking over now. She wondered if her mum had missed her and whether she might have called the coastguard or something. She hoped so, even though she knew she'd get read the riot act for getting herself into this position – she couldn't blame Josh entirely for that, it had taken two and she'd been a willing participant just a short while ago.

The bow was in the water now, and then came a little surge of incoming tide and the whole boat was more or less afloat.

Josh jumped in.

'Keep pulling!' he yelled at her. 'We're nearly off.'

Mae had no option but to do as she was told, despite being shocked at Josh's lack of grace in jumping in first, leaving her to do the donkey work.

But the dinghy was going nowhere fast. Josh – still refusing to put on his buoyancy aid – began to raise a sail, which scared Mae because the wind was getting up now. Sailing in the dark was never a good idea, although visibility was still okay for the moment.

'Is there a torch?' she asked.

'What do you think?' Josh said.

Mae didn't even bother to answer. Perhaps she should have agreed to spend the night on the beach wrapped in the sail after all?

Each time there was a surge of incoming tide, Mae pulled the boat and then, at last, it moved freely on the water. Mae hauled herself over the side.

Please, please, Dad, she prayed, looking up to the fast-darkening sky – there were millions of stars out already – *please look after me.* Then she amended *me* to *us* because she didn't want Josh to die, even if she knew beyond doubt now that she didn't want to go out with him any more.

Please, Dad, guide us back safely.

'Shit, Mae,' Josh snapped at her. 'What did you do that for? We're stuck again now with your added weight. You're going to have to get out again.'

'No, I'm not! You get out. You're bigger and heavier than I am.'

And then she looked at Josh's face – he looked terrified, white, as though he was about to pass out.

'Oh my God,' Mae said. 'Josh …'

'You'll have to get out,' he said, not sounding forceful any more. He was beginning to shake, and although Mae felt chilly, she wasn't cold and began to wonder if Josh had hypothermia beginning to set in.

She knew she ought not to leave him.

'I think what we'll do is both sit tight a while longer. The tide's coming in faster and it won't be long before we're properly afloat and then …'

'For fuck's sake, Mae, just get out and pull us off, will you?'

'Put your buoyancy aid on,' Mae said, taking charge of the situation. Fear and cold – and alcohol – were clouding Josh's judgement now and she knew it, even if he didn't. 'Then I'll get out.'

Josh sighed heavily but reached for it in the bottom of the boat anyway.

Mae considered telling him to do up the buoyancy aid, but he'd probably object and then there'd be an argument about that and they'd waste even more time.

She stepped gingerly over the edge of the boat and found purchase when the water came up to her waist. With one almighty pull on a tidal surge she had the boat well afloat now.

Josh leaned over the edge of the boat, reached an arm out over Mae and grabbed her backside, hauling her none-too-gently back on, where she landed with a thud.

'Can you get the sails up?' Josh asked, his teeth chattering, and his whole body beginning to judder now. 'I don't think I can.'

Mae did as she was told.

She noticed that the houses along the cliff edge had their lights on so that she could just about make out the shape of the coast-line. She thought she saw a torch flashing on and off or it could, perhaps, have been the intermittent beam from the lighthouse reflecting off something.

'Help!' she yelled into the darkness, just in case it was someone up on the headland and the predicament they were in had been spotted.

'You're wasting time yelling, Mae. Who's going to hear us anyway? Just get the sails up,' Josh said, his voice cracking now.

The light had almost gone by the time Mae had the sails up.

'Are you okay to hold the tiller?' she asked, worried now because Josh seemed to be swaying, and not with the rhythm of the boat on what was beginning to turn into a much more turbulent sea than it had been when they'd set out.

'Yeah,' Josh said. He manoeuvred himself into position while Mae shouted instructions.

A blast of wind came from out of nowhere and while Mae knew this happened sometimes when you were sailing, and her dad had taught her how to cope with it, her orientation had gone now in the darkness. Fear crept over her, cold and all-enveloping.

And then it happened – what Mae had feared might happen: they caught the keel on something … something hard that gave a sickening crunch, so loud it hurt her ears.

And then, almost in slow motion, the boat tipped and Mae knew she had no hope of righting it, and they were both in the water.

'Mae! Help!' Josh yelled. 'I can't swim!'

CHAPTER FIFTEEN

Cara took the phone into the bathroom. Fear had made her clothes stick uncomfortably to her, her skin oily and slick with sweat. She could shower in two minutes flat she knew that, and she knew two minutes wouldn't make a lot of difference if David Maynard rang to say Mae and Josh were safely back in the harbour, or if Mae herself were to ring and say they hadn't gone sailing after all and were holed up in the Boathouse at a music gig with friends. A shower – the cold side of warm – would sharpen her mind, stop the woolly thinking that was pervading it right now. It was something to do and Cara had to do something to escape her thoughts if only for a moment.

She stripped faster than she ever had in her life and turned on the shower. She counted the seconds out loud, not allowing herself longer than two minutes.

And then she heard it – the boom of the lifeboat siren going off. And within seconds the phone rang. She yanked it from the bathroom windowsill.

'Yes?' she said, her voice a jelly-wobble of fear.

'Mrs Howard? It's David Maynard. They've been sighted.'

'Thank God! I'll get down to the harbour,' Cara said. She

grabbed a towel from the pile on the bathroom chair and began flacking it on her damp body.

'Um, not yet. You heard the boom I take it?'

'What's happened? Tell me what's happened!' Cara could barely get the words out as fear was making sandpaper of her throat.

'A man walking his dog along the clifftop heard a bang and then a splash. Fortunately he had a torch so was able to spot them in the water. He rang the emergency services. The inshore lifeboat is on the way. Couldn't you just murder them for putting us to all this trouble?'

Well, actually …no. And David Maynard had only said the inshore lifeboat was on its way, not that it had reached them and got them aboard wrapped in warm blankets and drinking cocoa. All she wanted to do was hold Mae to her, get her warm and dry and tucked up in bed.

'Where are you calling from?'

'The lifeboat station. I'll ring you again as soon as I have them in my sights.'

'No. I want to be there when …' Cara felt her voice cracking. She'd never been a drama queen, but she knew she was getting dangerously close to being one now. 'I want …'

'Ssh, a moment. Please,' David Maynard said. 'I'm listening to the shortwave …'

Cara could hear muffled sounds in the background – voices not clear enough for her to hear properly, a bang or two, something hissing like a tap being turned on and then off again. Pressing her lips so tightly together that they began to hurt, Cara curbed her urge to get into the first clothes she could find and race down to the harbour – she could make it in fifteen minutes if she ran.

'Right, Mrs Howard,' David Maynard said, his voice – after minutes of silence and only her rapidly beating heart for company – startling Cara. 'They've got a firm sighting. Both in the water, both moving. ETA at the harbour is now fifteen minutes. I'll keep you posted.'

'I'll stay here, then,' Cara said. She wriggled the towel around her shoulders and instantly felt a little warmer, calmer.

'Good idea,' David Maynard said.

'They might need to go to hospital for a check-up. I don't have a …'

Cara stopped. The line had gone dead. But what would she do if Mae was taken to hospital? The nearest A&E was over twenty miles away. It was night time, no buses, and she didn't have a car any more. And then she remembered she'd rung Rosie and left a message. If Rosie had picked up, she'd be here soon and then at least the transport problem would be over.

Cara slid her feet into an old pair of mule-type sandals, not smart enough for wearing out, but fine for the house. She finished towelling herself dry, walked through to her bedroom and grabbed her old but much-loved trench-coat and slipped it on – it would be warmer than her dressing gown. The emotion of the last half hour had drained her, made her feel almost too weak to struggle into clothes, but there would be time for that in a minute, when she'd grounded herself better, and her thoughts had stopped flying about like butterflies caught in a storm. Holding the banister rail for support, Cara went downstairs. She opened the front door and stood on the terrace. She could just make out lights on a moored naval ship far out on the horizon. And something closer, moving rapidly, which she guessed was the inshore lifeboat. The scent of the roses that grew untidily over the arch by the front gate wafted its musky perfume around her. A car was turning at the end of the cul-de-sac and the driver suddenly stepped on the throttle and sped, far too fast, towards the junction, not stopping before it careered off down the hill towards the harbour. A boy racer, Cara decided, because lads often raced up the hill at speed as though they were in some sort of speed trial hill-climb, before racing back down again. Harbour to Cove End in four minutes or something like that was the benchmark, she'd heard someone say in Meg Smythson's shop. Suddenly music filled the air – 'Maria' from *West Side Story* being sung in a deep voice, the orchestra reaching a crescendo now – from a neighbour's open window somewhere further along the road.

How normal it all was for everyone else, and how very abnormal this moment was for her. How sounds and smells were exaggerated in the night air. How almost overpowering, over-whelming, they seemed to Cara as she stood alone on the terrace staring out to sea. Her damp hair was drying in wispy tendrils around the edges of her face, as water slid down her neck and formed a rivulet between her breasts. She loosened the tie belt of her coat a little because it was making her feel stifled, suffo-cated, claustrophobic.

She would have to get dressed soon, but she was loath to move in case she missed the lights of the lifeboat coming back into harbour with Mae and Josh on board, although she knew she didn't have a whisper of a hope of seeing them. Not yet. But they were on the way back and her breathing had returned to some-thing like normal now.

She stayed listening, her hearing sharpened by the stillness of the night – the click of a gate somewhere, the scent of lavender and night stocks. A dog barked close by, and an aeroplane droned high overhead in the blackness.

And then a voice saying, 'Don't move. Just don't move.' A man's voice followed by the flash of a camera.

'I can't hold out much longer, Josh,' Mae said, struggling for breath. Her fingers were almost numb with cold as she clung to the hull of the upturned dinghy, with nothing much to cling onto anyway. She'd threaded her free arm behind Josh's back and under his armpit and was just about keeping him afloat too. She hadn't been able to believe it when he'd said he couldn't swim. She'd never have gone out sailing with him if she'd known that. And he still didn't have his buoyancy aid done up, and there was no way now that he was going to. She just had to keep them both afloat somehow. She'd heard the boom at the lifeboat station go up and she knew help was on its way. 'Josh?' she said again.

Still no answer. The moon disappeared behind a cloud and Mae felt real fear, real loneliness, in that moment, even more lonely than she'd felt when she'd realised her dad was never coming back. If only her mum had protested more about her going out with Josh, this wouldn't be happening. If she'd put her foot down and said, 'No, Mae, I don't think it's a good idea to go sailing with Josh. Lasers are faster than what you were used to with your dad.' But Mae knew in her heart that she would have gone anyway.

'Dear God,' she whispered, fearful that Josh would hear her and pour scorn on her words, call her a convenient Christian or something. 'I'll work hard at school, get a good job, not be any trouble to my mum ever again if you'll let me live. I'll even be nice to Rosie.' Then she added, 'And let Josh live, too.'

She could see a torchlight flashing on and off on the clifftop. And a dog barked from time to time.

'Help!' she yelled, but her voice echoed back at her in the curve of the cove.

'Mae?' Josh's voice. It sounded far away and even more frightened, if that were possible, than Mae felt.

'I'm here,' she said. They were drifting slightly, but not much. Clinging on.

'I feel sick. And faint.'

'Breathe in slowly, hold it, then breathe out even more slowly. Help's on the way. I heard the lifeboat boom. Did you?'

'No. Must have passed out or something. Mae …'

'Sssh. Save your strength.'

'Mae …' Josh said again, his voice weaker this time.

'I said sssh. I can hear something. A motor. The inshore life-boat, I hope. Can you hear it?'

Mae stopped speaking and just for the briefest of seconds there was silence, save for the drone of the boat engine. Then a frantic splashing as Josh, caught in a beam of sudden moonlight, began thrashing wildly in the water.

'Stop it!' Mae yelled. 'I can't hang onto you if you do that!'

'I'm sinking!'

'No, you're not. I'm hanging onto you.'

'I can't feel you. I can't feel anything. I ...'

'Shut up!' Mae yelled at him. 'You're wasting energy. If you could reach up and hang onto the hull that would help.'

'Can't,' Josh said. 'My arms ...'

And then Josh stopped thrashing and lapsed into silence again.

The sea was getting choppy now, the water splashing into Mae's face and she knew she had to do all she could to stop swallowing salt water. Josh too. With a strength she didn't know she had, Mae pulled Josh higher. If he was unconscious, he wouldn't be able to stop himself swallowing water. And then, the lights of the inshore lifeboat pierced the darkness, shining in their direction.

'Over here!' she yelled with the last ounce of her strength. A beam from the inshore lifeboat scanned an arc of light across the top of the upturned dinghy, before its glare blinded Mae. She felt Josh's inert body twist and turn on the current. 'Help! I'm losing him!'

CHAPTER SIXTEEN

'Just who the hell are you?' Cara said with a bravado she didn't feel, knowing how vulnerable she was naked underneath her raincoat, and with her nerves shot to pieces because of her worry over Mae. The flash of the camera was still making little circles of light float before her eyes. She tried to turn and run back to the safety of the house, slam the door, but her feet, still wet, slipped on the leather insoles of her mules and she felt herself falling.

'Tom Gasson-Smith. You're expecting me. Although I wasn't expecting the welcome you're giving me.' There was humour in his voice, unthreatening, although Cara still felt unnerved and conscious of the fact her raincoat was slipping over her shoulders, exposing more and more flesh.

She felt herself grabbed by strong hands. *Tom Gasson-Smith – the artist.* Of *course* she was expecting him.

'Yes, of course. Look, I'm sorry but there's been a problem. My daughter. She's out there in a boat somewhere and although I know the lifeboat's been launched and the crew know her exact location and …'

And all Cara's cool melted and she began to sob noisily and very copiously before pulling herself – now that she was no longer at risk from falling – from Tom's restraining hands, and heading for the front door. 'You'd better come in. If you still want to, that is.'

'I do. But is there anything I can do to help? Nip down to the harbour to see if the lifeboat is back yet with your daughter? Although I imagine someone will ring you when it is. But if ...'

His words were stopped as the phone rang. Cara grabbed it, and before she could say her name Josh's father was telling her the inshore lifeboat had just arrived on the quay and that Mae was okay, but that Josh had been taken to hospital – mild hypothermia and shock, but he was in no real danger. A police car would be bringing Mae home very soon.

'Thank you. Thank you for ringing,' Cara said but David Maynard had already killed the call.

Tom raised his eyebrows questioningly.

'Mae's being brought back soon and Josh – that's her boyfriend – has mild hypothermia and shock. He's going to be okay, though.'

'Kids, eh,' Tom said. 'Don't they give you grief?'

'Experience speaking?' Cara asked, relieved that this man whom she hardly knew understood. Tom was tallish with loosely curled medium-length dark hair, greying slightly at the side – looking older in the flesh than in the pictures of him that Cara had googled – more Aidan Turner's father than his twin brother, perhaps. Not that she thought for a moment he'd been trying to deceive anyone. Eyes that were almost coal black in this light. Rosie would love him!

'No.'

Rosie was going to love him even more – a man roughly her own age and with no baggage. Then Cara realised how ridiculous the situation was with her standing there in the hall with nothing on underneath her old raincoat, her hair all over the place, with a man dressed in expensive-looking chinos and shirt with a tiny YSL logo on the pocket.

'Tea?' Cara asked. 'Coffee? I'm being a lousy landlady.'

'Not at all,' Tom said. 'You're the best I've met so far. And sorry about the flash from my camera. I use it all the time to take photos of settings for my paintings. I was taking shots of the lovely proportions of your house with the terrace lit by moonlight when you opened the door, and there you were with the light behind you, framing you – it was just too good an opportunity to miss.'

'Oh,' Cara said, part of her listening to Tom, another part straining to hear a police car's engine pulling up the hill, turning into the cul-de-sac. 'So, was that tea or coffee? Or something stronger?'

She noticed her hands were shaking and her legs weren't feeling too strong either. She ought to go upstairs right this minute and get dressed, but she had a sudden urge to sit down before she fell down and made a run for the sitting room and the couch, but her legs buckled under her and suddenly she was being lifted by strong arms as Tom carried her to the sofa, placing her as gently as if she'd been the finest of bone china, and plumping up the cushions around her. She leaned back into them.

'I need a good shake.' Cara laughed nervously. She was embarrassed now at how she'd coped – or maybe that should be not coped – with events over Mae.

'Happy to oblige,' Tom said, leaning forward to place his hands either side of Cara's shoulders. He gave them a little squeeze and then a mock shake.

'Well, what was I supposed to think?' Rosie cradled a mug of tea in her hands, forehead furrowed with disapproval. 'There you were on the sofa with the most delicious man, wearing nothing at all underneath that wreck of a raincoat you love so much, revealing lots of flesh. He was shaking you, so I hit him.'

Cara shuddered, remembering the sound of her bud vase, complete with water and rose, hitting the side of Tom's face.

133

'You might have asked what was going on first. I'd almost fainted – he was just trying to rouse me.'

'Oh, yes? And give him chance to wangle out of the fact he was assaulting you and leg it? The message you left on my answerphone was full of fear, you know. And I broke every single speed limit between my place and here. I believe I even went through the lights when they were on red. Twice.'

'I know. I know. You're a brilliant friend. Thank you. And thanks for running a bath for Mae, seeing to her. Shock, mixed with relief that Mae is okay, overwhelmed me. Is she asleep yet? No, no, don't answer that. My legs are losing the jelly feeling, I'll go up to see her in a minute. Oh God, I hope Tom doesn't get a shiner from when you hit him.'

'Of course he will,' Rosie giggled. 'I connected fair and square with his rather beautiful cheekbone.'

Cara eased herself up from the sofa. While Mae was being supervised by Rosie, and after Cara had shown Tom to his room – of which he thoroughly approved – she'd hastily thrown on some leggings and a pink shirt that had once been Mark's. She hardly looked her best and she wondered why she'd chosen that particular shirt – to connect them in the ether perhaps, after the safe arrival of their daughter after her ordeal? Who knows why what we do what we do sometimes? She'd come back down to find Rosie in charge, having drawn all the curtains to shut out the night, lit the gas faux wood-burner – to create a feeling of well-being, so she'd told Cara – and made tea and dug out the biscuit tin.

'Feeling better?' Rosie asked.

'Lots. Thanks. The relief, you know, of having Mae back safely. I knew Tom would be arriving tonight, but I lost all track of time. I can't believe, in the middle of it all waiting to know if Mae was alive or … well, you know but I'm not saying it, that I took time out to have a shower.'

'Some other force takes over sometimes,' Rosie said. 'A safety valve for our brains or something.'

'Yeah, maybe. It was pretty embarrassing though, welcoming Tom the way I did. You know …'

'I know. Half dressed and looking damned sexy, if I might say so, and don't take that the wrong way. Although, if I were a betting woman – which I'm not – I'd put money on the fact Tom Gasson-whatsit doesn't think you're rat-ugly.'

'I'll take that as a compliment,' Cara laughed.

'Meant as one, sort of. It's time you started thinking about it again, sweetie,' Rosie said.

'What?'

'Feeling sexy. Being sexy.'

Cara didn't think this was really the moment for this sort of conversation, but that was Rosie all over – sort one problem, onto the next. Not that Cara had considered feeling sexy or not a problem.

'Rosie, I …'

'Stop! No excuses!' Rosie held a hand out, palm forward, traffic-policeman style. 'And you can start with that chap upstairs.'

'I don't think so …'

'If you don't want him, I'll have him.'

'Hey, hang on. I only said I didn't think so, not that I wouldn't – not the same thing. But maybe not tonight,' Cara said. She grinned at Rosie.

'But you're thinking about it?'

'I could be,' Cara told her. She twisted her rings round and round her finger.

'Not with those still on your finger, you couldn't. Did Tom double-barrelled Whatsit notice?'

'He didn't bring it into the conversation, no,' Cara said. She yawned, monumentally tired now.

'Ah, my cue to go,' Rosie said. 'Or I could stay if you want me to. In case you have the vapours in the night or something.'

'No, I'll be fine,' Cara said, unable to stifle yet another yawn.

'Oh yes, quite forgot. You've got your very own knight in shining armour upstairs.' Rosie affected an over-the-top pouty pose and performed a sexy wriggle.

'Stop it. I doubt he'll want to stay more than the one night now. He must think this is a madhouse. First you clock him one, then a policeman walks in with Mae looking white with shock and soaking wet. This B&B hasn't got off to a good start, has it? And I need the money, I really do.'

'Right. There's only one way to do that then, isn't there? Get some shut-eye, then get to work on getting more bookings and earning it. You don't think I like doing Brazilians on women who, well, let's say, should be spending more on personal hygiene, for heaven's sake! No, don't say anything. I'm off, sweetie.' She reached for Cara and gave her one of her massive, rocking, bear hugs. 'As that lightweight Scarlett O'Hara would have said, tomorrow is another day.'

Mae lay shivering in the darkness despite the hot bath that Rosie had run for her. *Honestly, did Rosie really think I wanted her to sit and watch me?* Mae was outraged at the thought. But Rosie had stayed, citing the fact that shock was dangerous and that Mae might faint in the bath from the contrast of going from cold sea to warm scented bath water. The paramedics had already given her a going over in the back of the ambulance and pronounced her okay to go home and not to hospital, so how come Rosie thought better than them? What was Rosie doing here anyway? She could hear her mother and Rosie trying to talk quietly in the room below, but since being in the water and listening hard for sounds of the lifeboat, her hearing seemed to have taken on radar-like properties. Ah, the front door was being opened and then closed again – well banged shut – that would be Rosie, who never did things by halves. And then Mae heard her mother's footfalls on the stairs; the way she stepped on the outsides of the treads so as not to make the loose boards creak – it sounded to

Mae like a large and loping creature coming slowly to get her.

'Mae?' Her mother's whisper, not far from her ear.

Mae opened her eyes a little and her mum was there, silhouetted in the light coming in from the table lamp on the landing, a bit spooky really.

'I was nearly asleep then,' Mae grumbled. She didn't want to talk now. Didn't want to have to say that it was all over between her and Josh, even though she'd probably saved his life. The scumbag hadn't even said thank you. And as for his father, well, the Reverend David Maynard had had the cheek to suggest it was *her* fault for making Josh take the Laser out! As if!

'We'll talk in the morning, then.'

'Like who was that bloke on the sofa with you? You practically had no clothes on, Mum. And I'd been out there in danger, and you knew!'

Oh God, why had she said that? She was only prolonging the conversation, wasn't she?

'Shock and fear makes you do funny things, Mae. I knew there was nothing I could physically do to save you, and that all I could do was sit and wait. But I had to do something, so I had a shower. And ...'

'Yeah, yeah,' Mae interrupted. She knew all about shock and fear now. She'd been shocked at how quickly Josh seemed to give in when they were in danger and did nothing to save her. Fear had made her try to keep him afloat in the darkness – keep him alive because the thought of being with a dead body had terrified her. And then there was the fact he had been drinking again, sneakily putting something in his coke bottles, changing his personality – the Jekyll and Hyde effect, so Mr Trimble had told them all in a Social Studies tutorial.

'And I was wearing a raincoat,' her mother said.

'But it's beyond terrible, that raincoat!'

'I don't suppose he noticed. And anyway, he's a B&B guest, not a friend or anything.'

'Keep him that way then, Mum. Okay?'

'I thought you didn't want to talk.'

'I don't. So who is he?'

'Tom Gasson-Smith. He's an artist. He's our new B&B guest. I thought I'd told you?'

'I dunno, did you?'

Mae glanced at the photograph of her dad on her bedside table. The light from the ridiculously low-wattage bulb her mum insisted on made it look as though he had a halo. Whatever ... he was a million times better than that Tom Gasson-Whatsit and if her mum thought for a minute...

'He could be here until the ...'

'In the morning, Mum,' Mae interrupted. 'Please.' She snatched at the switch on the bedside lamp. She turned away from her mother and pulled the duvet up over her head. *Oh, Dad, none of this would have happened if you hadn't gone and got yourself killed. Nothing's been the same since. I don't want all these strangers sharing the bathroom, sitting in the kitchen eating toast and drinking coffee. And I want to know why it's taking so long to value a few paintings.* Mae yawned – she must remember to ask her mum about the paintings and when they would be coming back. Or, if they were worth thousands, she could sell them and then they wouldn't have to have stupid B&B guests, would they?

She felt the weight of her mum's hand, pressing the duvet onto the top of her shoulders. Although she didn't really want it to, the gesture brought tears to her eyes. Her mum hadn't said one word about the accident with the dinghy. When she got back home, she'd just hugged her tight like she'd never let her go, as wet as Mae had been and wrapped in a scratchy, smelly old blanket the policeman who'd brought her home had got out of the boot of the police car.

But now she was going to have to face the whole village as the ex-girlfriend of Josh Maynard, wasn't she?

I'm not going to cry. I'm not. I'm not...

CHAPTER SEVENTEEN

'Cocoa,' Cara whispered to herself, closing Mae's bedroom door gently behind her. 'I need cocoa.' She knew she wouldn't sleep yet, so there was no point in trying.

She crept back down the stairs, doing her best not to step on the loose boards and make them creak. Tom might be asleep – and probably nursing a black eye by now.

But no, there he was, as though thinking about him had made him materialise in front of her. Tom stood facing the door, hands deep in the pockets of his chinos, glancing back now and then at a pan of milk beginning to bubble on the stove. The cocoa tin, and two mugs with spoons in them, were on the table.

'How's your daughter?' he asked.

'Cross, I think. Probably embarrassed.'

'About?'

Cara shrugged. What could she say? The fuss she'd caused? The worry she'd given her mother? The fact her dad had died and wasn't there to protect her? Cara knew in her heart that Mark would never have let Mae go sailing with Josh. And then there was the fact Mae had read all the wrong things into the fact she'd come home to find her mother on the sofa with Tom, showing more flesh than she ought? No, she couldn't say that.

'Mothers and daughters. Never an easy ride,' Tom said when Cara was slow to respond, helping her fill the conversational gap. 'My mother and my sister were at one another's necks for years. Still are at times. And don't get me on the subject of fathers and sons.'

He smiled sadly at Cara. Now wasn't the time to ask what sort of a rotten time of it he might have had with his father. And anyway, wasn't he just being kind, saying all that – trying to make Cara feel better about things?

'Ah! Milk!' Tom said. He yanked the saucepan from the flames just before it boiled over. 'Hot chocolate? I thought you might be able to use one. Forgive me for taking liberties when I've only been here, what, a couple of hours, but cocoa's my cure-all.'

'Mine, too,' Cara said.

'You're not going to throw me out, then?'

'For making cocoa?' Cara said, a smile creeping to the corners of her mouth. 'No.'

'Phew! Tom said, wiping the back of a hand across his forehead. 'You'll find I'm fairly house-trained.' He scanned the room as though looking for something. 'Sugar?' he asked.

'Middle cupboard, top right,' Cara told him.

'Oh, I've found that. I meant, do you take sugar?'

Cara waited for it to feel strange, having a man in her kitchen again, and a stranger at that, but it didn't.

'Two, please. I think I might need a sugar fix after tonight's drama.'

'Make that two of us,' Tom laughed. He put a hand to his eye, which was now beginning to close, the skin around it taking on the start of a bruise. There was a strip of drying blood on his left cheek where Rosie had hit him. 'Your friend packs a punch.'

Cara winced.

'I'm so sorry about that. Rosie's been overprotective of me ever since ...' No, she wouldn't go there, wouldn't even think about evoking sympathy from Tom for her situation.

Cara waited while Tom finished making the cocoa.

'I've got some hobnobs in a tin on the dresser.'

Tom put a hand to his mouth and brushed away imaginary crumbs.

'Already found them as well,' he laughed.

'Have another.'

Suddenly, Cara didn't want to be alone. But could she reasonably expect to keep Tom chatting? It was getting late. And he had a bruiser of a black eye in the making.

'Not now,' he said. And then he yawned. 'Right, I don't know about you, but I'm more than ready for a bit of shut-eye. And I'm not talking about the one Rosie shut for me.' He stirred sugar into Cara's cocoa for her, found a tray and put her mug on it. 'Up you go.'

'Your room's on the second floor. I could show you.'

'You did. Earlier.'

'God, yes,' Cara said. 'Sorry. It's been a long day. I think I remembered to put a hospitality tray in there, didn't I?'

'Yep. But no cocoa. Hence the field trip to find some.'

Cara picked up her mug of cocoa from the tray and wrapped her hands around it – such a simple gesture to have a hot drink made for her, but a very profound one from Tom to know what she needed at that moment.

'I'll see you in the morning,' Cara said. 'Breakfast room is just down the corridor. You can't miss it.'

'I'll find it,' Tom said. 'Not for nothing did I get an A level in geography. Now up you go. I'll turn off the lights.'

Cara went. Closing her bedroom door behind her, she put the cocoa down on the bedside table, and without taking off her clothes, crawled into bed.

She heard Tom moving about downstairs, shutting the fanlight windows, locking the door. Ought she to be more wary that he was doing that? After all, the Hines hadn't felt threatening and look what they did! But there was something about Tom that

141

told Cara he was to be trusted – the sort of man who would always do more good than harm. She must remember to ask him how long he would be staying, just so she could let his room if he decided to go. He might or might not want to stay more than the one night now, and really it didn't matter if he didn't, but Cara hoped he would.

CHAPTER EIGHTEEN

Tom Gasson-Smith didn't disappear in the night. Cara took tea and toast to Mae in bed and came back down to find Tom leaning against the counter-top by the sink in the kitchen.

'I don't suppose,' Tom said, 'that you have that old American movie remedy for a black eye lurking in your freezer, have you?'

'Steak?' Cara laughed. 'Afraid not. Half a pound of streaky bacon is the nearest I can get. Sorry. And I'm sorry I laughed. That eye doesn't look funny at all.'

Tom's eye had completely closed up and was very swollen, the skin around it all shades of blue and yellowing at the edges, and there was a deep ridge of the same colours on his cheekbone.

'Let's just say,' Tom said, 'that it's probably fortunate Rosie is your friend. I wouldn't want her as an enemy.'

'That's what Mae says. She can be a bit bossy sometimes. She's Mae's godmother, and lays down the law a bit.'

'So, what does the handy-with-her-fists Rosie do?'

'Beauty therapist.'

And the irony is not lost on me, looking such a wreck this morning – and my best friend a beauty therapist.

Cara ran her hands through her dishevelled hair, ran her tongue around lips she knew ought to have had at least a slick of lip gloss. But since Mark's death she simply hadn't bothered to do her make-up first thing, only bothering to put a bit of mascara and lipstick on before leaving the house.

With Tom standing in front of her, she didn't wonder why she was now bothered about looking good, wanting to look better than she knew she did in her second-best jeans and a T-shirt that had gone out of shape with age. At least she'd had a shower – first hot, then cold to wake her up and get her circulation going – and rubbed some face cream in.

'I didn't expect you to be up so early, Tom,' Cara said.

A lousy excuse for slapdash habits, she knew.

'The artist in me,' Tom said. 'Dawn light is quite marvellous to paint and there are few distractions. Um …' He was looking embarrassed now. 'Cara?'

'Yes. Cara Howard.'

'Phew! I know you told me but, well, with everything that went on last night I lay awake for ages trying to remember your name. I went through the whole alphabet at least a dozen times before I decided it had begun with a 'c'. Lovely name, by the way.'

'Thank you. I've always liked it. My mother always told the story that she was reading a romantic novel when she was pregnant with me and the heroine was called Cara and so here I am!'

'Mrs Cara Howard?' Tom asked.

'Officially,' Cara said. 'I'm a widow.' Widow. The word sounded so old – something that normally came with a pension and married children there to have you over for Sunday lunch and Christmas Day. Not someone who was yet to have their fortieth birthday. And then, because she hadn't intended to play the sympathy card and she was afraid that was how it might have come out, she went on, 'That's why I asked Rosie to come over when Mae went missing. Being on your own is scary, and the thought of something terrible happening to Mae was just too much. And I didn't want to be here on my own if it had.'

'No. No, I can understand that. I'm sorry, Cara,' Tom said softly. 'That you've had the sadness of widowhood to deal with.' He pressed his lips together as though he wanted to say something else on the subject, but wasn't going to. Then he smiled warmly. 'Shall I cook the bacon and rustle us up breakfast, or will you?'

'I will, of course,' Cara told him, already beginning to find bowls and plates and cutlery – things that didn't match but which would have to do. She opened the door of the fridge and found a box of eggs, and two tomatoes.

'I'm easy to feed,' Tom said. 'In fact, if you show me where everything is, I'll do it myself for the rest of my stay. I need to be up and out very early to catch the light, and then I'll be in my room painting, maybe start a few canvases if that's okay with you.'

'What do you paint?' Cara asked, knowing she was being rather unrefined if Tom was indeed as well known for painting nudes as Rosie said he was. She'd looked him up on Google but hadn't looked at any of his artwork, only him.

'I've got a reputation for figurative art. That's, um ...' Tom laced his fingers, making his knuckles crack. Choosing his words?

'Nudes,' Cara finished for him. 'Rosie said.'

'Ah, I thought she might. My reputation has come before me.'

'She was full of compliments.'

'Phew!' Tom said, running the back of his hand across his forehead in mock-relief. 'But nudes aren't all I can do. I've got to the stage where I feel my work needs to move on, hence this art festival. I might have a stab at portrait painting, too. Watercolours and oils, but I'm straying into acrylics now as well. The view from your front door is amazing, so I may want to take some photos from there after breakfast, do a few quick sketches. I won't get in your way. Don't worry if you hear the click of my camera at odd times.'

Tom was sounding as though he was reading Cara his CV – almost as though he was nervous.

'Yes,' she said smiling, and doing the best she could to make him feel at home in her house, 'the view is amazing, and no, you won't get in my way.'

She looked at the wall opposite the window where once had hung two small but beautiful watercolours of woodland scenes – different styles but both wonderful in their own ways. Both had disappeared long before Mark had had his fatal crash. Cara could still see the little holes where the hooks had been and the darker patches where the pictures had hung and the paint had faded slightly around them. She glanced away from those tell-tale pinpricks in the paint, but not quickly enough because Tom's gaze was still on them.

'What happened?' he asked.

'About what?'

'Something used to hang there,' he said, pointing directly at the bare wall. 'Something I think you liked and wish was still there.'

'Well, you think wrong,' Cara said, suddenly feeling very exposed – naked and vulnerable that Tom had guessed so quickly that the paintings had been very dear to her. But although Tom had homed in exactly on how she felt about those patches, she had no intention of telling him the intimate details of what had happened. She hardly knew him, or he her. Yes, she liked him, and she had a feeling he liked her, and she did feel safe with him. And, yes, he had asked if she was Mrs Howard and at a guess that was because he wanted to know if there was a Mr Howard about to put in an appearance and perhaps wonder what he was doing so early in the morning in her kitchen. And Cara had been quick to tell him she was a widow, not a single mother or a divorcée. They were laying their cards out, slowly, one by one, to one another, weren't they? 'Now, if you'd like to go through to the breakfast room, I'll bring you some coffee and then cook your bacon and eggs.'

Tom placed his hands together, prayer fashion. 'I've overstepped the mark, haven't I? Taken liberties. Forget what I said about seeing to myself during my stay. I'll be the perfect guest from now on. Forgive?'

'Nothing to forgive,' Cara said, suddenly contrite that she might have come across as dismissive. 'I'm a bit washed out after yesterday.'

And very touchy about my missing paintings. But she certainly didn't want Tom Gasson-Smith's sympathy about them. One day she'd replace them. But not just yet – she was seriously beginning to realise that being a B&B landlady wasn't going to earn her enough to do that, even with a long-stay guest as Tom had just hinted he would be.

'You look fine to me,' Tom said quietly as he made for the door.

Cara gulped. There'd been truth and tenderness in his voice and she didn't know she could trust herself to speak without welling up. She took a deep breath.

'Thank you. For the compliment. And it's fine by me if you want to overstep the mark, take liberties – to paraphrase – in my kitchen. Really. Which you won't be, I might add.' A grin was spreading across her face, threatening to crack it. She was doing her best to make a joke, and she hoped Tom would see it.

Tom turned back to look at her, his grin mirroring her own.

'I hoped you might say that,' he said. Then he turned and made for the breakfast room, and it was with shaking hands and a heart that was dancing with delight and hope that Cara set about making his breakfast.

'Has he gone?' Mae asked when she came downstairs to the sitting room where her mum was sitting in the big chair by the window, reading. The the whole house was eerily quiet now – such a contrast to the night before when the police had brought her home and Rosie had been here and the new guest had arrived. Tom something. It was almost midday. She was still feeling a bit shaky from the events of the day before. She was glad it was a Sunday and she didn't have to go to school, didn't have to concentrate on anything. She wondered if any of her friends had heard about what had happened to her and Josh the day before.

'Who? Tom?'

'Yeah. If that's his name,' Mae said.

'It is. And he's gone out looking for venues to paint. He's got a key so he'll let himself in later. He'll probably be here for a while now.'

'Like how long?' Mae said.

'A month or so.'

'Oh.'

Mae had got a glimpse of Tom the night before but hadn't met him properly yet. She didn't know that she wanted to. Already her mum was looking different somehow. She'd heard her and Tom talking and laughing earlier. It wasn't right. Her mum should be in mourning still, shouldn't she?

'How are you feeling?' her mum asked.

Her mother did that – changed the subject if the conversation was getting a bit difficult.

'I dunno,' Mae said. She'd told her mum a bit about what had happened but not everything – not the heavy petting session on the beach, which had made her and Josh forget the time. It was the policeman who'd told her mum that she'd been instrumental – his words – in saving Josh's life. But she didn't see it like that. It was what sailors did when they were in the same boat if things went wrong. Her dad had told her that. She'd been brought home in the wetsuit Josh had loaned her – she'd have to arrange to give it back, but she didn't want to see him. 'Sorry, you know, for the worry and that.'

'I'm proud of you, Mae, for being so brave. Saving Josh.' Her mum put down her book and stood up. 'Come here,' she said, and opened her arms wide. 'I'm just so, so pleased you're safe. That you both are.'

Mae moved into the circle of her mother's arms and slipped her arms behind her mum's waist.

'It'll be all over the village, won't it? What happened.'

'I expect so.'

'Josh's version anyway.'

'He's okay,' her mum told her. 'I rang his father earlier. He'll be home now.'

Mae pulled away from her mother's hug.

'I'll check my phone. See if he's texted or anything. To see if I'm okay. Not that I'm going out with him ever again.' She pulled her phone from the pocket of her frock. Her new one. Well, her new old one – the turquoise one with white polka dots. She might go out later. Or she might not. Just as she thought – no text and no voicemail from Josh.

'Nothing?' her mum asked.

Mae shrugged. She was feeling a bit shaky now. Delayed reaction or something because she'd been quite calm the night before.

'Nothing. He's probably hungover. He had something in the bottles of coke he brought with him. He started off all nice and kind and considerate and everything and then he, like, just flipped.'

'Oh Mae,' her mum said. 'I'm sorry you've had to find out like that. It's what drink does to people sometimes. Addictions are like that. All sorts of addiction, not just drink. People promise they'll give up when they're found out, but they rarely do.'

'Yeah,' Mae said. 'Fags and computer games, and burgers for every meal and stuff like that. Willow Tucker in my class has got a polo mint addiction, big time. She stinks!' She tried to laugh, but a laugh wouldn't come. 'Is there anything to eat?'

It would be good to get back to some sort of normality – just her and her mum having lunch on a Sunday. No Rosie today. The painter bloke out somewhere. She'd now told her mum as much as she wanted to about yesterday.

'There is. Come on.' Her mum linked her arm through Mae's

and together they walked towards the kitchen. 'We'll eat in the garden, shall we? I can rustle up some salmon and spinach pasta in no time and there's a new tub of Hagen Das in the freezer – almond and caramel – for pudding.'

'Great,' Mae said.

She'd been expecting to be read the riot act for being so stupid as to get herself almost drowned. But it hadn't happened. Her mum had sounded more understanding of Josh and his problem, than cross.

As Mae watched her mother gather the ingredients for lunch, she thought how almost perfect it was again – just her and her mum.

CHAPTER NINETEEN

On the Monday morning after Mae's sailing incident, Cara had registered with the Information Office, offering Cove End as a B&B venue, surprised to discover that people came down to Devon on holiday without booking accommodation – on spec as Kate and Andrew had. But three weeks on in her venture, it had been to Cara's advantage a few times now. She was hardly fully booked, but it was a better start than she could have hoped for. Now she had a computer she'd registered for internet shopping and once a week a Sainsbury's orange van pulled up outside. She'd hit on the idea of providing Continental breakfasts as well as the full English and it was a 50/50 split what guests chose. Not Tom, though – he always went for something cooked: scrambled eggs or a sausage bap, if not the full English. And then he'd be off out somewhere, dressed in shorts or jeans, depending on how warm it was, a bag containing his sketching things slung across one shoulder. He was almost always back by mid-afternoon. Usually he came in and went straight up to his room, coming back down around eight o'clock to go to the pub for supper. But some days he'd search Cara out to say hello and ask how she was and how was Mae now after her ordeal before going upstairs to paint. Cara enjoyed those times, wished he'd stop to chat for longer really, but the last thing she wanted was to come across as needy. Besides, he was busy. The art festival was just over a fortnight away now. She had no idea how many paintings Tom would have on show or how long it took him to paint one, but there had been a couple of times when Cara had woken in the night and seen the light from his room shining out into the darkness, so presumably he'd been hard at work still.

Ah, there he was now.

Cara stepped out from the kitchen where she'd been making a quiche for her and Mae to eat later with some salad.

'Off out?' she asked.

'As ever,' Tom smiled. 'Exhibitions don't paint themselves, alas.'

'No,' Cara agreed. 'Well, I'll let you get on.' And then on a whim she said, 'If you'd like to join us for supper later, we'd love that.' She didn't think for a second Mae would love it because she seemed to have made an art form of not being in the same air space as Tom, but Cara would love it. So why shouldn't she ask him? 'Quiche Lorraine. With pancetta instead of streaky bacon. Although I know ...'

'... real men don't eat quiche!' Tom finished for her.

Oh God, had she got it terribly wrong and he was a closet gay or something? She didn't know what to say now.

Tom filled the conversational gap.

'Sorry, that's an old joke. Sorry if it came across a bit rude. I love quiche actually. And I'd love to say I'll join you, but I'm a bit behind schedule so ...'

'I could leave some on a plate for you in the fridge maybe? There's some *pain de campagne* in the bread bin. Save you a bit of time if you don't have to eat in one of the pubs. More time for your painting ...'

Cara's train of thought trickled out. God but she was sounding needy with a capital N, wasn't she?

'Cara, I'd love that normally. Really I would. But not tonight. Tonight I'm meeting Louise for supper in the Beachcomber. Sorry. Look, can we talk about this later? Tomorrow if I don't see you when I get back?'

'Louise?' was all Cara could find to say.

'Yes. Louise. She's my ex-wife.'

'Mae!'

Bailey Lucas was coming out of the paper shop down by the harbour. He ran across the road towards her.

'I'm going to work,' Mae said. Now school had broken up, from tomorrow onwards she'd have more hours at the ice-cream kiosk, and the village would be filling up with visitors.

'Yeah, I guessed as much. Just wondered how you are.' Bailey stuffed his hands down hard into the pockets of his jeans He looked, Mae thought, a bit anxious about something.

'Fine, thanks,' Mae said. 'You?'

'Trying to find a job of some sort for the holidays, but it's not easy. Anyway, I was wondering, now Josh Maynard isn't on your radar ...'

'How do you know that?' Mae asked, then instantly realised she'd given herself away.

'A bloke has ways of finding out,' Bailey said.

'Oh, shove off, Bailey. Like I said, I've got to get to work.' Mae still had plenty of time before she had to be there, but Bailey didn't need to know that. She went to skirt around him, but he dodged sideways and stepped in front of her. He reached out and gripped her wrist.

'Hey!' Mae said, trying to wriggle out of his grasp, but his hand was huge and his fingers wrapped easily around her small wrist.

'Mae, I've got something to tell you I think you need to know.'

'What?' Mae said. Bailey was still holding her wrist but not tightly. Mae stood there and gave in to the inevitable – Bailey

153

Lucas was going to say what he wanted to say, so she'd just tough it out. 'Tell it, then.'

'I think you need to know what's being said around here. About your dad.'

'What about him? He's dead. Can't everyone just let him rest in peace?'

'Seems not. Been in any of the pubs around here lately?'

'What's it to you?' She'd been to live music gigs in the Boathouse but not since the sailing incident. 'Anyway, what are you talking about? And could you let me go?'

'Sorry.' Bailey let go her wrist. 'It won't take long. Have you got time? You know, if you've got to be at work, I could meet you after.'

'I've got time,' Mae said. She had to know now. There was something in the way Bailey was looking at her that told her he wasn't making trouble and he was concerned about something.

'Great,' Bailey said. 'Shall we walk out along the breakwater – there's hardly anyone about. It'll be more private.'

The breakwater wasn't far – Mae would have time to walk there, listen to whatever it was Bailey had to tell her, and then walk back to the ice-cream kiosk and still be in time for her shift.

'Okay. As long as you're not just trying to trick me into something?'

'No. Why would I? Trust me.'

'Let's get a move on then,' Mae said, beginning to walk in the direction of the breakwater.

They hurried along without saying much apart from general stuff like wasn't it great school was out, and Bailey asked what subjects Mae was going to choose for A levels and she told him she hadn't decided yet. Strangely, it felt comfortable to be walking along with Bailey – different from when he'd asked her out and their relationship back then hadn't come to anything, just fizzled out.

They were there in no time. They walked halfway along until they came to a bench and sat down. The tripper boat to Torquay was just leaving the quay, full to the brim with passengers. An old lady further along the breakwater was throwing bread to the gulls despite the fact there were notices all over the place telling people not to.

'This place is in a time warp,' Bailey said, grinning at Mae. 'All those shops selling rock that rots your teeth, and leery postcards we had to walk past to get here. And parrots on sticks. I mean, who needs a parrot on a stick?'

'Or a neon pink, Day-Glo, crocheted loo roll cover?' Mae giggled. 'And kiss-me-quick hats. Do you think they wear them to do the school run or whatever when they get back to Birmingham or Manchester or wherever it is they live?'

'Not unless they want to get sectioned,' Bailey said.

'Probably not then,' Mae laughed. She hadn't realised Bailey could be so funny. But then she'd not given him a chance to show her he was, had she? 'But we haven't come here to talk about holidaymakers and their dubious choice of holiday gear, have we?'

'No.' Bailey stuffed his hands down into the pockets of his jeans again. 'That was a preamble, to psych myself up. For what I want to say. The thing is, Mae, I'm not liking how Josh has behaved since the sailing incident. I know you saved his life because my Uncle Jack was lifeboat crew that night and he told my dad, who told me.'

'This is all about Josh?' Mae said.

'Not all. A bit …'

'Just tell me!' Mae snapped. 'You're making me nervous now.'

'Okay. I'm not trying to make trouble or anything but … did you know your dad gambled?'

'Gambled? Like on the slot machines?'

'Well, there's that, I suppose, but I didn't mean them. I meant on the horses and the dogs and other stuff. Online.'

'Everyone does the lottery now and then, Bailey,' Mae said defensively.

'I didn't mean that either,' Bailey told her. 'I meant things like betting on chess games and the other things I've just mentioned. Serious stuff that takes a lot of cash.'

'What are you trying to say?' Mae said. Cash was something she and her mum didn't have much of any more, now her dad was dead and there was no pay coming in from the bank. Scales were starting to fall from Mae's eyes – her dad had sold her dinghy and all her kit, all the paintings had vanished from the walls, and he'd taken the computer the night he'd been killed and ... oh my God, had he done all that to fund a gambling habit? Could Bailey be telling the truth, as much as she didn't want him to be?

'I think you know, Mae, right? I can tell by your face. But the short version is your dad was forever in the pubs selling off stuff so he could gamble. My old man bought a bit of silver off him once 'cos my mum loves silver stuff and your dad was selling it off cheap. He knew what horse was going to win the Derby so he said, except he got that wrong.'

'Stop!' Mae said. 'I'm getting the drift.'

Even though she didn't like what she was hearing one little bit, she knew Bailey wasn't lying. She felt sick.

'You believe me?' Bailey said.

Mae nodded.

'And Josh is spreading rumours?'

'Yeah. Did your mum never say? About your dad's gambling?'

'No.'

'Maybe she didn't know,' Bailey said. 'That's what my mum said. That the wife is often the last to know.'

'That's about their husbands having affairs,' Mae said, knowing exactly how stupid that remark was. 'So your mum knows about this as well?'

'Only in our house,' Bailey said. 'She doesn't blab, my mum.

156

Nor me. It's why I'm telling you now because my dad's not the only one who goes down the pub and he's probably not the only one your dad tried to sell stuff to.'

'Oh God,' Mae said.

'And I don't trust that Josh Maynard not to spread more stuff now he's been outed as a non-swimmer who got in a bit of a panic and had to be rescued by a girl.'

'Yeah, well,' Mae said. 'Thanks, you know, for letting me know. Although how I'm going to get through my shift now, I don't know.'

All she wanted to do was go back home and confront her mum. And if she was honest, she wanted her mum to deny everything Bailey had told her, but she didn't think that was going to happen. She knew silver had disappeared from the dresser in the sitting room – perhaps she ought to have asked at the time where it had gone? Her dad had sold the dinghy without asking her and other stuff so … oh God, she felt sick with the weight of all this.

'You'll be fine, Mae. You're strong. Really strong. But I could meet you afterwards if you like. We could get a coffee or something …'

'No, it's okay, but thanks,' Mae interrupted him. 'I'll be okay.'

'Yeah,' Bailey said, as instinctively they both got up and began walking back the way they'd come. 'Sure you will.'

CHAPTER TWENTY

'In here, darling,' Cara called from the sitting room where she'd just managed to grab half an hour to read, doing her best to put the embarrassing scene she'd had with Tom earlier out of her mind. But it kept creeping back in. She glanced at the clock on the wall beside the fireplace – a huge railway-style clock that she'd loved and bought from a stall in the market at Totnes. It was perfect for checking the time when sitting down. That would be Mae who had just come in, letting the door bang noisily. She was back later than Cara had expected.

'Now there's an offer I ought not to refuse,' Tom said, suddenly appearing in the doorway, leaning against one side of it, arms folded, legs crossed at the ankles.

'Oh, oh ....' Oh my bloody God! What had she said? Just a few hours ago he'd told her he was going to be having supper with his ex-wife and the wind had been knocked right out of her sails, and she'd squirmed with embarrassment for ages after he'd left at how forward and needy and downright bloody sad she must have sounded. It wasn't helping now, either, that Tom was looking so downright, well, shaggable was a word Rosie would have used.

'My guess is you were expecting someone else,' Tom said. 'Can I come in?'

'Yes. Double yes. I was expecting it to be Mae around now, but come in. I thought you were meeting, um …'

'Louise,' Tom said. 'I will be later. Just come back to dump some sketches I did today and pick up some paperwork.'

'Okay. Fine. Right,' Cara said. Her mouth seemed to be going ahead of her brain. She couldn't be making it more obvious she'd been thrown that Tom's ex-wife was still in the equation, could she? It was just sod's flipping law that she was beginning to fall for Tom and now his ex-wife had put in an appearance. Couples did divorce and then realise they'd made a massive mistake and then remarried. Perhaps that was how it was going to be for Tom and Louise.

'You made those three words sound as though they're anything but, Cara,' Tom laughed. 'Can I sit down?'

Cara couldn't trust herself to say anything coherent so she merely waved an arm towards the chair opposite her. Tom sat down.

'Explanation needed, I think,' he said. 'Louise and I have been divorced for four years now. She was my muse. Still has been a few times between then and now. You understand what I'm saying?'

So Louise had been his model. And still was sometimes, post-divorce. None of her business.

'Yes?' Tom prompted her.

Cara nodded.

'We're still business partners, Louise and I,' Tom said. 'We hold joint copyright on some of my work that's gone to limited edition prints. All part of the divorce settlement. I know I don't have to tell you any of this, but I want to. I'm feeling a bit of a heel that I've had to refuse your offer of supper tonight. I had no idea Louise was thinking of coming down today until she texted me after breakfast. I like it here, Cara.' Tom leaned forward

159

in his chair, placing his hands on his knees. 'I've been happier here than I've been in a long time. I've loved hearing you pottering about in the kitchen, singing snatches of old Beatles songs. Not our era but I love Beatles songs too. And I've loved watching you in the garden hanging out the bed linen between guests, stopping on the way back in to pull up dandelions or some other weed. Do you understand?'

Was she supposed to be reading between the lines? When he'd said he'd loved – past tense – listening to her pottering around, and being in the garden, he was trying to tell her he was leaving, wasn't he?

Cara nodded again, her hands clasped tightly together. She really, really didn't want him to go, and it wasn't just the very generous money he was paying her each week.

'There's a calmness about it here, Cara, if you ignore the drama going on when I arrived. I never had calmness in my marriage.'

Nor me for a long time. Cara had been permanently on edge around Mark from the moment she'd found out he was a compulsive gambler.

'Hmm,' Cara said, lips pressed firmly together to stop any other inane comments pouring out, but she couldn't just keep on nodding to everything Tom said, could she?

'Tongue out,' Tom said. He poked his own out to show her how it should be done, grinning at her. 'Only I'm beginning to think you've lost yours.'

Cara obliged with a wobbly smile. Just the tip of it. God, but she was going to miss him. She glanced at the clock again. Where was Mae? She was more than hour overdue now.

But Tom must have seen the glance because he said, 'I'm keeping you from something. Sorry.'

'No, no. It's just that I thought Mae would be here by now and she isn't.'

'Phew!' Tom laughed. 'She speaks! That's a relief. I don't think I've ever rendered a woman speechless before. But she'll be back

160

soon. Perhaps she's met up with a friend or something. It happens. Especially when you're a teenager and live by a different clock to the rest of society.'

'Yes, there's that,' Cara agreed.

Tom stood up, and on rather wobbly legs because she hadn't allowed for just how much she was falling for Tom, Cara stood up too.

'One more thing before I go and fetch my paperwork,' Tom said. 'Just so you know how sorry I am about not being able to take up your invite. My guess is my dinner with Louise isn't going to be the restful scenario I imagined when you asked me to join you later. My second guess is Louise will arrive with another list of demands, mostly monetary, and she isn't going to be best pleased when I tell her I'm changing genre. And my third guess is she's going to be very less than thrilled when I put her right back on the train again afterwards. Wish me luck.'

He stepped towards Cara and leaned in for a kiss on the cheek.

It's me that's going to need the luck that you don't get sucked in by Louise and her wiles and whatever it was that made you fall in love with her for the first time, Cara thought, as she watched Tom hurry from the room, and take the stairs three at a time. And another dose of luck that Tom hadn't been letting her down gently about leaving soon, and that he would stay.

She put a hand to her cheek where Tom had kissed it – his lips warm and dry against her skin. If she were a teenager, she would have vowed never to wash that cheek again, but she wasn't. No harm in not washing it until the morning though, was there? And then the door opened again, and Mae came flying in, slamming it so hard that the stained glass rattled in its frame.

'Mae …' Cara began. She could see by Mae's face that something terrible had happened.

'You, you …!' Mae shouted, her face red, her hands in tight fists.

'Sssh, sssh. Don't shout, darling. What's happened? Oh my God, not Josh again?'

She hurried to Mae and reached for her arm to pull her to somewhere they could talk. But Mae shrugged her off.

'Not here,' Cara said. 'Tom's upstairs and ...'

'I don't care if Michelangelo is upstairs and can hear me. I want the truth, Mum! Did Dad gamble? Did he pay off his debts by selling stuff down the pub? Bailey Lucas had to practically drag me into the Beachcomber to show me. He told me about Dad's gambling and him selling stuff before I did my shift at work and he said he'd meet me afterwards and even though I told him not to he was there. He said he thought I needed to see the evidence, just in case his dad hadn't got the facts right about it being Dad who'd sold the painting to Andy Povey. I nearly died of shame to see the picture that used to be over the fireplace in our sitting room in one of the alcoves. The frame was all dusty. Apparently, there are two more of our paintings in the Boathouse and I'm afraid to go and see what state they're in. So tell me the truth, Mum. Please.'

Mae was rightfully angry, and Cara knew she was to blame for that. Josh had told her much the same as Bailey had now told Mae – some sort of brinkmanship going on between the two boys?

'In the sitting room,' Cara said, knowing Mae would follow. 'Now sit down.'

'Why must I sit? I can hear just as well standing up, you know.'

'It's more dignified. We look like boxers squaring up for a fight.'

'So? It's how I feel right now. Anyway, what's so dignified about you not telling me about Dad? *If* it's true, which I don't want to believe.'

'I'll tell you if you sit down, and not otherwise,' Cara said firmly.

With a huge sigh, Mae sat – in the chair Tom had occupied

so very recently when the atmosphere in the room had been totally different.

'Okay,' Cara said. 'The truth is your father did have a gambling habit. A big one. The internet mostly, but also betting shops. Totnes. Torquay. Dartmouth – places where he didn't think he would be seen by customers of his bank, or neighbours. He took things to pawn shops, too. And sold them in the village pubs – you've just seen the evidence and I'm sorry you had to find out that way.'

'Me, too,' Mae said. 'It would have been nice if you could have told me.'

I couldn't find the words to tell you the father you adored thought so little of your future and how we were going to fund it.

'I regret that I didn't now. It must have come as a shock.'

'Yes, well. Anything else I should know about?'

'How do you mean?'

'Bailey said he'd heard rumours that Dad was leaving you because he had most of his clothes in the car when it crashed. You were always nagging him about money. That's what he told the barmaid in the Beachcomber when he sold the picture. The barmaid is Bailey's sister, Xia. I don't suppose you know that.'

'No, I didn't know that, about Bailey's sister being the barmaid, I mean. I knew he sold things, but not where until Josh told me.'

'Huh! Him! *He* never told me!'

'Perhaps he thought he was protecting you,' Cara said.

'Stand up for him, why don't you?' Mae shouted.

'I can understand your anger, Mae, but you don't have to be rude. And we don't need Tom hearing our private business, which if you shout like that he will do. And I know I'm instrumental in that anger, and I'm sorry. Truly sorry.'

Cara had heard Mae mention Bailey once or twice before. Mae had been to the cinema with him if Cara's memory served her right. But if there was the rumour going around, via Bailey's barmaid sister, that Mark had been leaving her because she nagged

163

him, maybe it would be a good idea for Cara to leave it like that. But keeping secrets was doing Mae more harm than good, wasn't it?

'So, was Dad leaving us, Mum?'

'Yes,' Cara said. She got up and walked over to Mae's chair, sat on its wide arm beside her daughter. She reached for Mae's hand, expecting Mae to whip it away, but she didn't. Cara took a deep breath and said, very slowly, 'I'd asked him to go. I gave him an ultimatum to sort his gambling, but he chose gambling over, well, us.'

Mae breathed in sharply and Cara feared for a moment she would never let the breath out again.

'Well,' Mae said, after what seemed an eternity of silence, when all sort of scenarios went through Cara's head, 'at least you're not a liar.'

'Sorry?'

'That's what Bailey said Xia had told him – that you had asked Dad to leave. Because of his gambling. I made the nagging bit up to test you.'

Glad now that she'd told Mae the truth, Cara said, 'I'd come to the end of my tether, darling. I'd begged and begged him to sort himself out with the gambling. Little by little our home was disappearing as he took ever more stuff to sell. It was fast becoming a shell, not a home any more and I didn't want that for you. For us. I thought it would be a wake-up call for him. Do you understand?'

'Sort of,' Mae said.

'And your dad had cashed in insurance policies so there was nothing to come to us after the accident. That's why it's been so hard financially, and it's why we have to make this B&B thing work. If we don't, we'll have to sell the house and move somewhere much smaller.'

'But it's not working, is it?' Mae said.

'It's early days.'

164

'Well, I *hate* it. You can't say you like it, Mum. All the washing and the fried breakfasts stinking the house out and the vacuum cleaner going all the time.'

'I'm enjoying bits of it. The company. After that fiasco with the Hines, the guests have been okay, hardly any trouble really. They arrive late afternoon and are out after breakfast. Aren't they?'

'Apart from Michelangelo up there!' Mae pointed to the ceiling and Tom's bedroom two floors above it. 'It smells in there. I can smell it through the door. Something chemical anyway. I'm not sure he's a painter at all, to be honest. I mean, we haven't seen any paintings, have we? I'm always having to tell him to put used coffee mugs *in* the dishwasher and not leave them sitting in the sink. Dad ...' Mae's eyes welled with tears and she swiped them away with the back of a hand. 'Dad used to do that. Leave his mugs in the sink.'

Cara gulped. Yes, Mark had always done that although it had never bothered her much.

'And...and,' Mae went on, 'he leaves the toilet seat up. He's got an en suite for goodness' sake, but he uses the downstairs cloakroom and he *always* leaves the toilet seat up.'

'It must be a man thing,' Cara said, trying to lighten the mood. 'Men do that. And the not putting things in the dishwasher thing.'

'I hope that wasn't meant to be funny,' Mae said.

'No. Just an observation. Men don't put the caps back on toothpaste either. Or hang their flannels up to dry, and they don't put the soap back in the rack but leave it to go all slimy on the edge of the basin. Well, all of the men I've ever known do all of those things.'

'And another thing,' Mae said. 'Michelangelo never lets you go in his room. He keeps it locked and you have to leave his clean bed linen and towels outside on the landing. He could have a pet orangutan in there for all we know.'

'Oh, Mae,' Cara said, unable not to laugh. 'You say the funniest things.'

Yes, Tom had asked that he be responsible for his own room and Cara had respected that. He'd have all sorts of things laid out for his artwork, she imagined, and it would be impossible not to touch things she ought not if she were to go in there and clean. The vacuum made regular trips up the stairs anyway so he was keeping to his side of the bargain too.

And how come your rant at me about not telling me the truth about your dad has turned into a litany of Tom's misdemeanours?

'So,' Cara went on, bringing Mae back to what they'd originally been talking about, 'how do you feel about things now you know the truth about your dad's gambling?'

'Hurt. Hurt that you didn't tell me. If Bailey Lucas knows, then everyone knows. Anyone else who was in the pub when Dad sold the paintings and other stuff could have spread the rumour, couldn't they? Bailey hasn't blabbed and he says his family aren't blabbers either and I want to believe him. I think I can because it would have got back to me before if they had, don't you think?'

'Yes,' Cara said. If what Mae was saying was true, she was surprised she hadn't heard the rumour before. Perhaps Mark hadn't sold things openly and had known who he could trust, people like Andy Povey and the Lucas family. Perhaps no one else but them did know. She'd never know now though, would she? 'Did Bailey tell you why he was telling you all this now?'

'Yeah. He said he'd heard Josh was telling people Dad gambled. And he said it was spite because Josh wouldn't be liking it one little bit that he'd been a big wimp and I'd had to save him from drowning and, like, I said I didn't want to go out with him any more because he was going to leave me in the cove and just rescue himself, and he .... Oh God, I don't know ... revenge or something.'

166

'Oh Mae, I'm so sorry that this has happened and …'

'But not sorry enough to think it would have been better to tell me yourself!' Mae's voice rose a few octaves and she had angry furrows of lines between her eyes, squinting at Cara as though she didn't really want to be looking at her. 'It was much easier believing Dad had just been driving too fast and had an accident. I feel sad all over again – like he's only just died and we haven't had the funeral yet, but I know we have because bits of that come back to me in dreams sometimes. Well, nightmares really. I worshipped Dad. He was my hero.'

Mae began to cry silently, the tears sliding down her face. She did nothing to wipe them away.

Gathering her daughter into her arms, Cara said, 'You can still worship him. He loved you, Mae. You were his little princess.'

'I know,' Mae said huskily. 'It's why I do the old-fashioned flowery frocks – I wanted to live up to his image of me. I don't want to wear jeans that are ripped to shreds up the front or crop tops that show muffin tops, or look like a mini Beyoncé or something. You should hear some of the stick I get because I always say frocks and not dresses.'

'Frock is a much nicer word than dress, I think, because dress is also a verb and frock, well, frock conjures up a more glamorous, more dignified time somehow.'

'Yeah. You get it, Mum, don't you?'

'I do. I haven't got the sort of figure that wears a frock well, though. But you have. We should all have the courage to be who we want to be and to wear what we want to wear, and I'm very proud of you, Mae, that you've got the courage to do that.'

'Bailey said that. About my frocks and that. I think he fancies me.' Mae disentangled herself from Cara's arms. 'Bailey's okay. I like that he doesn't swear every other word like most of the boys at school do. He's got an old-fashioned way of talking as well, like he's a lot older than fifteen. He sort of speaks the way his dad probably does. I never realised that before, but then I never gave him the chance because Josh came on the scene and sort of dazzled me.' She laughed nervously.

'Some men are like that,' Cara said. 'Dazzlers. Like sparklers, Rosie always says; all fizz for a very short while and then they're duds.'

She listened hard to see if she could hear Tom moving about, coming down the stairs maybe. He'd need to be off out again soon. Tom definitely wasn't a dazzler, a sparkler, Cara decided – he was never going to be a dud.

'What is Rosie like!' Mae laughed.

'A bit of a dazzler and sparkler herself really, I think,' Cara said. 'But there's room in all our lives for that at times, eh?'

'Yeah,' Mae said.

'So, back to Bailey. If he asks you out again, will you go?'

'Today, he sort of hinted we could start going out together again, but I don't know ...'

'If he asks again, maybe you could give him a chance now?' Cara said.

'Yes, well,' Mae said, 'I've got all this gambling thing to think about now, haven't I?' She stood up. 'Is it still quiche for tea? I'm starving!'

'Me, too,' Cara said.

And perhaps some Prosecco with it. Not that they were celebrating anything, but things had moved on for them both now Mae knew about Mark's gambling and Cara had told her the truth about his leaving.

'In the garden?' Mae asked. 'The sun's still on the top terrace by the apple trees.'

'You're on,' Cara said, surprised how easily Mae seemed to have accepted the situation.

'I might change for supper,' Mae said. 'This dress feels a bit skanky now. What with me wearing it at work all day, and all the angst when Bailey was telling me what he did, and then now ...' Mae shrugged.

'Do that,' Cara said. 'Half an hour?'

'Perfect.'

'But you still look lovely, Mae, whatever's been going on.'

'Yeah,' Mae said, taking a sneak look at herself in the huge mirror over the fireplace. 'I'll pass.'

And then she skipped out of the room, turning to give Cara a twirl in the doorway, before running to her room.

'And I feel like a dishrag full of holes,' Cara said, flopping down into the chair again, her head in her hands.

'You're too tough on yourself.' Tom's voice. Tom's voice very close, close enough that his hand had now reached out and squeezed Cara's shoulder. She flinched. 'Sorry. Didn't mean to startle you. Do you want to talk about it?'

'Yes. No. What's the time? I thought you were going out?'

Please, please, say you've cancelled dinner with Louise.

'I am. But I got trapped when Mae came in. I couldn't go past the sitting-room door without being seen. I didn't want Mae to know I'd heard so I just stopped there, just managing to nip into the downstairs cloakroom when she went upstairs. I promise to put the toilet seat down from now on and for evermore, by the way ...'

'Oh God, you heard everything.'

'Just about. Flattered beyond belief that she compared me to Michelangelo. In my dreams!'

'It wasn't all bad, then?' Cara said.

'Far from it. But I'll say my pennyworth and then you can tell me to mind my own business. I can see it must have hurt Mae like hell to have only just found that out about her dad. But I also think it must have hurt you more to have been shielding her from that, and having to live with it all before asking Mark to leave.'

'And my paintings that Bailey told Mae are in the village pubs. I'll have to go and see if that's true.'

'It sounds as though it might be,' Tom said. 'Do you need a hand to hold when you do it?'

169

A metaphorical hand or a physical one?

'Company would be good,' Cara said. 'If you're offering.'

'I am. But I've got to go. Louise should be there by now. She won't like being kept waiting.'

'Then I'll let you get off,' Cara said, her thoughts all over the place now. Tom was making it sound as though he really would like to go with her to see if the paintings really were hers or not, and yet his ex-wife still seemed to be featuring very heavily in his life.

'I might be late back. I'll be as quiet as I can coming in. Wish me luck.'

'Good luck,' Cara said, crossing her fingers on both hands.

CHAPTER TWENTY-ONE

'Sorry I'm late for breakfast,' Tom said the next morning, suddenly appearing in the kitchen doorway. 'If there still is some.'

Cara glanced at the clock. Not quite ten. She'd been looking at that clock at ten-minute intervals since eight. Mae had had breakfast and gone off to her job. Cara had taken a call from the Information Office and now had a lady – a Miss Horsham – due to arrive at about four o' clock and booked in for two nights. She'd then made soup, some cheese scones, and cleaned the worktops to within an inch of their lives. Something to do while she waited for Tom. She'd stayed awake until at least one o' clock waiting to hear him come back but had eventually fallen asleep.

'But you're here now,' Cara said. 'And of course you can have breakfast. What would you like?'

Cara was aware she had come over all landlady and not a woman who the day before had been, perhaps, on the cusp of having a relationship with the man standing in her kitchen, looking so damned desirable.

'Scrambled egg? A rasher of bacon? Coffee? That'll do me.'

'I'll bring it …'

'To the breakfast room? I've been thinking, Cara, that I'd like to have breakfast here from now on, if that's okay. I don't feel like a guest any more. Besides, I get dragged into conversations with other guests in the breakfast room that keep me from getting on with my work. So …' Tom looked, pleadingly, at Cara.

Cara hadn't been expecting that. She walked over to the fridge and took out the bacon, found the butter and the milk.

'I can get it myself. I don't want to put you out more than I already do. And you can tell Mae I promise to put my coffee mugs straight in the dishwasher from now on instead of leaving them in the sink. I am a man reformed!'

'Will do!' Cara laughed. 'And of course it'll be okay for you to have breakfast here.' And then, as Cara took three eggs from the rack and cracked them into a bowl, she asked, because she needed to know, 'How was dinner last night?'

'Ah, I was going to ask *you* that. I kept thinking about you and Mae eating quiche and salad while I was listening to Louise's demands. How did it go?'

'Surprisingly good,' Cara said, smiling. Tom had very neatly turned that question around, hadn't he? 'She sort of understands why I had to ask her dad to go. Well, to try and sort himself out really. And we talked about relationships. Making them, breaking them, then making new ones again.'

'Yeah, never easy that, is it?'

'No.'

'Has there been anyone since Mark?' Tom asked. 'No, no, don't answer that, I shouldn't have asked. Sorry.'

'It's okay. Violin time,' Cara laughed, playing air violin. Tom had asked as though he really was interested. 'I haven't, no. Not even a drink with anyone. No one's asked me.'

'Well, if you want my opinion, there are probably more than a few men around here who need to go to Specsavers.'

Was that his way of asking her out for a drink?

'I'll take that as a compliment!' Cara laughed. She lit the gas and put butter in the pan ready to scramble the eggs. Then she put three rashers of bacon under the grill. 'You?'

'Ah. I can't claim to be so saintly,' Tom said. 'Post-divorce, that is. Before that I was faithful, which is more than I can say for Louise. Which is probably more than you need to know but I learned a lot about you last night when I was unintentionally eavesdropping, so it's only fair I offer you some info in return. Well, I think so. Tell me if I'm out of order.'

'No, no,' Cara said quickly. 'Carry on.'

'It took me years to figure out that she was being unfaithful. The saying has it the wife is the last to know, but in my case it was the husband. My turn for the violin.'

What he'd told her wasn't exactly funny, but as Tom played air violin with a hang-dog expression it made her laugh.

They were laying out a bit more of their pasts to one another, weren't they?

'And dinner last night with Louise?' Cara asked, reaching for a plate from the rack on the wall. 'Don't think you can get out of telling me!'

'I tried,' Tom said. 'The thing is she wants to come down for the art festival. She wants to share my venue to show her own work ...'

'Louise is an artist?' Cara asked. The delicious banter she and Tom had been sharing had suddenly soured. What was he trying to tell her?

'Potter.'

'And will she? Be sharing your venue?'

'No. She wasn't best pleased when I told her that. Or when I drove her back to the railway station to pick up the night sleeper back to London. Louise – as ever – is between lovers. She got as mad as hell when I wouldn't tell her where exactly in Larracombe I'm staying. We share an agent, Louise and I, and that's how she found out I was down here.' Tom reached for the wooden tub of cutlery Cara always kept on the kitchen table. He placed a knife and fork either side of the table mat. How very comfortable he looked doing that despite the conversation they were having. And how good it felt to Cara watching him.

But she was itching to know if Louise had been someone with whom Tom had been less than saintly *after* their divorce. But she couldn't ask that, could she? Tom would tell her in his own time – if he wanted to. It was none of her business anyway, and what they'd both been, and to whom, was in the past.

Tom's breakfast now plated up, she set it down in front of him.

'Coffee in a tick,' she said, flicking the switch on the kettle. 'Croissant? I've got some in the freezer.'

'Only if you'll join me,' Tom said.

Cara reached for another mug, then took two croissants from the freezer and put them in the microwave on defrost. It ought to have felt strange being invited to drink coffee and eat croissants in her own kitchen but somehow it didn't.

'The paintings,' Tom said. 'The ones Mae's been told are in the village pubs? When do you want to go and see if they're there?'

'Now?' Cara said. 'I've got a guest booked in for tonight, but she won't be here until mid-afternoon.' Cara spooned ground coffee into a cafétière and then poured on the hot water. Maybe they could do lunch as well, her and Tom? Perhaps, over *moules marinières* or something, and a glass of wine to loosen their tongues, there'd be a bit more unravelling of one another's pasts, paving the way for a new future for them both?

'Ah, not right now,' Tom said. 'Back to the coalface for me when I've eaten this. Tonight maybe? And if there's any of that quiche left over from yesterday, I'm sure I could find it a good home.'

'There is,' Cara said. 'I'll put a slice on a plate for you in the fridge.'

She ought to go, sooner rather than later, to see if they were her paintings in the pubs but didn't want to go on her own; Tom had offered her a hand to hold yesterday, and he'd brought the subject up again now. She'd just have to patient, wouldn't she?

174

'When you've got a moment,' Cara said, sitting down opposite Tom, and cradling her mug of coffee in her hands. 'To go and look at the paintings, I mean. It's been a while since I've seen them … I can wait a bit longer.'

Miss Horsham – Sylvia – was late arriving. Very late. Mid-afternoon came and went. It was well after eight o'clock when she turned up.

'The traffic around here is horrendous!' Sylvia Horsham snapped the moment Cara opened the door. 'And this place wasn't easy to find. Hilly. And it's raining.'

Cara had urged her to come in, given her a choice of teas from which to choose, regular and decaffeinated coffee, then shown her to her room.

'My bags,' Miss Horsham had said. 'They're in the boot of my car.' She'd jangled her keys at Cara, held them out towards her. 'My wrists, you know. I can't lift heavy things. Oh, and I can't stand flowers in a bedroom. All that pollen.'

'Right.' Cara took the offending flowers in one hand and Miss Horsham's car keys in the other, too stunned to say or do anything else.

Miss Horsham's stay went from bad to worse after that. The rain didn't let up and Miss Horsham refused to venture outside.

'I've got plenty to read,' she told Cara.

So that was why her case had been so damned heavy to carry in.

Miss Horsham rang out for takeaways. Fish and chips. Curry. Chinese. She didn't seem to have regular mealtimes. The first morning she'd turned up at gone eleven expecting breakfast.

'Breakfast finished at nine,' Cara had told her. 'But seeing as you had a horrid journey yesterday, I'll make an exception this morning.'

Miss Horsham had merely harrumphed.

The first time the takeaway delivery lad from the fish and chip shop in Quay Street had arrived on Cara's doorstep, she told him he must have got the wrong address. Miss Horsham then appeared on the landing.

'He has not!' she called down the stairs. 'I'll take delivery of it in the breakfast room.'

In two days, Miss Horsham seemed to have cancelled out all the good experiences Cara had had with the guests who had come before her. Cara wrote a list of rules to be posted in the guest rooms. *No takeaways permitted on the premises. Breakfast served 7 – 9 a.m. Rooms must be vacated by 10 a.m. on day of leaving.*

Tom had been mildly amused at Miss Horsham and her antics. At breakfast on the second morning of her visit, he'd joked that if she got any worse or overstayed her booking, he'd nip down the Beachcomber and round up a few burly fisherman to come and turf her out. But Tom had hardly left his room during Miss Horsham's stay. Cara had heard him talking to someone on his phone quite a lot. Sometimes quite late. Cara didn't want to think about who it might be.

But now the rain had stopped and the sun was out again in full force and Miss Horsham had gone – as well as two of Cara's best Egyptian cotton towels and the little dish Cara had placed on the bedside table in the room to hold coins or keys or whatever else her guest might use it for. Ah well, she'd put it down to experience.

Cara set about cleaning the room, sorting the bedlinen. She opened the window to rid the room of the lingering food smell. She wondered just what Miss Horsham might have got from her stay, apart from reading a lot of books that she'd left at the bottom of her bed – her idea of payment for the towels and dish she'd taken, perhaps.

'Has she gone?' Mae asked, suddenly appearing in the doorway.

'At last!' Cara said.

'I don't know why you didn't just chuck her out,' Mae grumbled, leaning against the door jamb, dressed today in a deep cerise and white gingham boat-necked dress with a wide white cumber band.

'I considered it,' Cara said. 'Tom offered to round up some heavies from the Beachcomber if she overstayed her booking!'

'Huh!' Mae said. 'Did you know he had breakfast in our kitchen this morning?'

'Yes,' Cara said. 'I said he could. I mean, would you want to have breakfasted with Miss Horsham?'

'*And* I caught him putting a portion of cottage pie in the microwave last night,' Mae said, ignoring Cara's question.

'I told him he could do that as well,' Cara said.

'Huh!' Mae said again. 'Anyway, back to the Beachcomber, seeing as you mentioned it. Are you going to go in and see the painting? And the others in the Boathouse?'

'Of course,' Cara said. 'I would have gone before but, well, with Miss Horsham here I didn't want to leave the house. I wouldn't have put it past her to go exploring, and make herself more at home than she already had if I wasn't here.'

She could tell Mae was put out that she hadn't been before. Cara considered telling Mae that Tom had said he'd go with her when he had a moment. She could hear him upstairs, dragging something across the wooden floor in his room. An easel probably. Or maybe a chair.

'Yeah, there's that,' Mae said. 'Anyway, I'm off in a minute.'

'To work?'

Despite the fact it had been raining fairly heavily for the past two days Mae had been in the ice-cream kiosk, coming back to report that 'stupid people eat freezing cold lollies even when it's wet and freezing cold! Losers!'

'Nope, not today.' Mae grabbed the hem of her dress on either side and made figure-of-eight movements with it – a coy gesture, Cara thought. 'I'm, like, seeing Bailey.'

'Ah,' Cara said.

'Josh came by yesterday and the day before. Gardeners don't work in the rain, I suppose. Well, *he* wasn't anyway. He was with Alice Morrell. Came right up to the kiosk he did and bought two pina colada lollies. All over her he was, like a dose of hives or something, slobbering on her neck when he fished the money from his pocket. Like I cared. Lollies, Mum, when it was so cold I wore my jacket all day at work.'

Ah, so that was where the comment about people eating lollies on freezing cold days – losers! – had come from!

Cara smiled. Mae was still learning about making and breaking relationships, still finding it a bit difficult to move on from Josh, if Cara was reading between the lines correctly. But now she had Bailey to help her do that perhaps.

'The paintings, Mum,' Mae said, standing up straight. 'Do you want them back or not? Or what?' She'd raised her voice an octave or two.

'Of course I do. But they're not mine any more if your dad sold them, so ...'

'Oh, forget it,' Mae said. 'All this B&B stuff takes precedence now, doesn't it? I ...

'Mae,' Cara said, keeping her voice low. 'You don't have to be rude. I've explained.'

Mae shrugged. 'I'm off,' she said. 'I'm a bit late anyway.'

'Okay. Be safe. Love you,' Cara said, not expecting Mae to respond, expecting another shrug. Yes, she ought to have made it her business to go and see if the paintings were hers after Mae had told her they were. She couldn't be sure Mae would be positive they were her paintings because she knew that at that age, she'd never really taken in anything that had been hanging on the walls of her childhood home.

'Yeah,' Mae said, blowing Cara a kiss before running down the stairs.

'Oh!' Cara said, seconds later, as she stepped out onto the landing, the bundle of dirty linen in her arms. Tom had chosen that moment to step out onto the landing too. 'I expect you heard some of that. About the paintings?'

'Yes.'

'Fancy a pub crawl?' Cara said, laughing. She didn't feel so alone with this now that Tom was here. 'The Beachcomber first and then the Boathouse?'

'Well, I make it a rule to never drink before the sun is below the yardarm, but I'll break my rule for once. I've had a very productive two days. Rain is very conducive to productivity for a painter. Of course, I had the charms of the delectable Miss Horsham to avoid, but I was strong, and resisted.'

'Awful woman,' Cara said. 'She's lifted two towels and a trinket dish.'

'Well worth the loss she's gone, then,' Tom laughed. 'I promise to leave my room in exactly the same state I found it in.'

Cara's little bubble of happiness deflated a little – Tom was still intending to leave. Sometime. Just not yet. Not until the art festival was over.

But he was here now.

'Say half an hour?' Cara said. 'I'll just get this lot through the washing machine.'

'Perfect,' Tom said. 'Thanks for the food parcels by the way. You've saved this artist from starving in his garret.'

'My pleasure,' Cara told him. 'I still can't get out of the habit of making too much. Meals for three like I did for years and now there's only Mae and me.'

'Ah yes, Mae,' Tom said. 'My money's on her wishing I'd left with Miss Horsham this morning. She turned up as I was putting the cottage pie you left in the microwave. I made my starving artist in his garret joke and she just looked at me, lips pressed together so tight I thought she'd super-glued them. Mae can make silence sound so loud!' Tom put his hands over his ears and pulled a pained expression that made Cara laugh.

179

'Oh, I've just remembered. I'll need to leave about half past three. Train to catch.'

'Oh,' Cara said. 'A date?'

'Grown-ups do have them sometimes, Cara,' Tom said, grinning. 'But this one is more of a business deal. Louise is becoming difficult. She's misunderstanding the terms of our settlement – God forbid that I should say deliberately, but I think that's the case. It's patently clear that she's only entitled to share profits of any paintings she features in, and she thinks she's entitled to a share of anything I do from now on. So it's a meeting with our agent, and then a solicitor practised in this sort of agreement.'

Louise. Again. Still in the picture.

Perhaps it would be best if I backed off?

'If you'd rather go now,' Cara said. 'I won't hold you to any offers.'

'I'd rather not go at all,' Tom said. 'But thanks for the offer. You can't get rid of me that easily!'

'Right,' Cara said. 'Our half an hour is now just over twenty minutes.'

'Then we won't waste another second!'

Tom disappeared back into his room, which made Cara think he'd intentionally come out onto the landing when he had, so she'd know he'd heard everything and he still wanted to help.

180

CHAPTER TWENTY-TWO

Leaving the house, Tom reached for Cara's hand – initially, she thought, to guide her in a gentlemanly fashion down her steep steps to the road – but then he hadn't let it go again. How deliciously comforted, how cared for, that made her feel.

Nothing could have prepared Cara for how she'd feel when she saw the seascape painting that had once been hers hanging in an alcove in the Beachcomber. The alcove was all dark wood and maroon furnishings, and the lighting dim, but she knew in a second it was hers. She loved that painting – one of the those she'd been left in her grandmother's will. She loved the deep turquoise of the sea with just a few petticoat frill tops to the small waves, and the pink thrift in the grass on the headland where the artist must have stood, or sat, to paint it.

She couldn't take her eyes off the painting now. She stood in front of it, mesmerized. How much had Mark sold it to the landlord for? Would the landlord let her buy it back for the same amount he had paid for it? People were chatting around Cara, glasses clinking, but it was as though they were miles away. Cara turned as Tom touched her shoulder to let her know he was back.

'Five minutes for the coffee,' he said. 'Machine's just gone down. Won't take a tick to sort it so the barman said.' Tom pulled Cara gently away and guided her into a battered Windsor chair. 'Fifty quid.'

'For coffee? Fifty pounds for two coffees?'

'With biscuits. Homemade.' Tom laughed. 'No, silly. I meant the landlord gave your husband fifty pounds for the painting.' He walked over to the wall and lifted the painting from its hook. Cradling it like a baby in his arms he brought it back to Cara and held it out towards her. 'So I've reimbursed him.'

'But you can't! You can't just buy my painting. I don't want you to. I hardly know you ...'

'I think you know me well enough to know I mean you no harm,' Tom said, a thoughtful expression on his face.

'I'm sorry. Yes. You've been very kind. A gentleman, in fact. But I was going to ask the landlord if I could pay him back in instalments for however much he wanted.' Cara looked anxiously at Tom. She'd insulted him by what she'd said, hadn't she? But to her relief he was smiling now. 'I need to do it by myself, Tom. Do you understand?'

'I understand but ... no ... I won't say it. I'd lose my "gentleman" tag if I did.'

And what does he mean by that? That I'm stubborn? Wearing sackcloth and ashes over the situation?

'I'm not in the habit of buying fifty-pound presents on a whim, not even for those who leave me a portion of cottage pie with a little note to say, *I made too much. Do eat it if you would like to.*'

'It would have been a shame to waste it,' Cara said.

'Indeed,' Tom said. 'So, perhaps when we know one another a little better we can come to some arrangement – a few more of your delicious leftovers would go some way towards the painting.'

Cara couldn't tell whether or not he was serious, but she wasn't going to ask.

'I really don't mind sharing food,' Cara said. 'But I honestly haven't got fifty pounds to spare just at the moment,' she said. The bank was being very tardy in releasing funds from Mark's pension; she'd heard of the 'widow's year', but for Cara it was turning into a very elastic year – almost two now. She was worried that Mark had stopped making payments into the fund, in favour of the gambling tables and the bookmaker. Until she did get whatever little pension of Mark's was due to her, she was only just about keeping the proverbial wolf from the proverbial door with her B&B lettings. 'So, maybe we could compromise?'

'We could. And I think we should.'

The barman came over with their coffee and biscuits, setting the tray down carefully in front of them. Cara wondered if this was the man who had bought her painting or if he just worked there. She wasn't going to ask.

'I'm still not comfortable letting you do this. Paying for the painting, even though I'll pay you back as soon as I can,' Cara said as firmly as she could when she and Tom were alone again. 'Can you give the landlord back the money and I'll sort it with him? To pay by instalments. And don't tell Rosie any of this or she'll want to buy it back.'

'Rosie? She of the hefty punch?'

'Your bruises have gone down,' Cara said. 'But yes, *that* Rosie.' Cara twirled her engagement ring round and round her finger. She was feeling guilty she hadn't been in touch with Rosie for well over a fortnight now. It wasn't unusual for Rosie not to get in touch if she was busy or off on some romantic trip to Paris or Barcelona with a new man – it was, more often than not, Cara who made the running anyway, but she was happy to do so. 'She bought something back for me when I didn't really want her to.'

'The something you're winding round and round your finger and which you're in danger of rubbing away?'

Cara stilled her fingers and looked at her engagement ring as though seeing it for the first time. *How observant Tom was.*

'Yes. When the two potential B&B guests looted my place

while I went to the shop for bacon and eggs, I thought they'd taken my engagement ring. But I also wondered if Mark might have pawned it because there were rumours going around that he had done that – without my knowledge, of course.'

'And had he?'

'Yes.'

'And Rosie bought it back for you because the time for collection had passed?'

'Yes.'

'So Rosie's got her gentler side, then,' Tom said, laughing. 'I can't imagine, though, that Rosie would have shown the restraint you have in not coming into my room to snoop – it's your room, after all, and you'd have every right to.'

'You've got Rosie in one!' Cara said. 'But I don't snoop. Did I tell you Mae said she doesn't think you're an artist at all and for all we know you've got an orangutan in there?'

'Oh, she's rumbled me!' Tom laughed.

'Very funny,' Cara said. 'She'll be proved right or wrong soon, though, won't she? It's not long to the festival.'

Tom threw back his head and laughed.

'And then she'll be shot of me?'

'She didn't say that – not in as many words.'

'Actions speak louder than words sometimes, Cara.'

'They do indeed.'

Tom had just proved that by making the decision to buy Cara's painting back for her.

'And is that how you feel? You can't wait to see the back of me?'

'No, it's not that,' Cara said.

'What is it then?'

It's the way you made me feel when you grabbed my hand and pulled me out of my own front door to come painting-hunting. It's the way it felt to have my hand held after years of Mark stuffing his hands in his pockets when we were walking anywhere together.

184

It's … it's because I don't want to lose my heart to you if Louise is always going to be around. And I'm not liking it one little bit that you'll be away overnight when anything might happen with your ex-wife.

Cara had been sleeping better since Tom had turned up. She felt safer with another adult in the house – someone else to listen out for burglars or the smoke alarm … things that had kept her awake for so many hours in the night before.

Cara shrugged. She couldn't tell him any of that, could she?

Tom studied her, his head cocked to one side.

'Tell me to mind my own business, but I hope you're not thinking of selling that ring to realise a mere fifty quid so you can buy the painting back yourself, fair and square, no exchange of leftovers?'

Cara hadn't been thinking that at all, but now the idea was in her head, why not?

'Thought so.' Tom reached out and touched Cara's hand briefly before taking it away again. 'Gagging's too good for me, but I'll say it anyway – you might regret it if you do.'

Yes, Cara thought, *I probably will.*

But all she could think of to say was, 'Hmmm.'

'There must have been good times,' Tom said. 'When you were given the ring.'

'Oh, there were,' Cara whispered. 'There were.'

'And I'm probably overstepping the mark here with personal remarks like that. Forget I said that.' Tom pulled a mock-sorry face that made Cara smile despite herself. 'But just for the record, this painting is going back to Cove End with you and if you need any help to re-hang it, I'm your man. Come on, we've got more paintings to track down. And then I've got a train to catch.' Then Tom picked up the painting and stood up, and began to walk towards the door. Cara had no option but to follow.

'*I'm your man.*' She knew it was just an expression, but she couldn't help liking how it sounded.

'Don't look now,' Mae hissed at Bailey. 'But that's my mum. She'll go ape if she knows what I've done.' She glanced at two hooks in the wall now bereft of the paintings that had been hanging on them a short while ago. The two small watercolours of woodland scenes were propped up against the table leg. 'Oh, my God! And she's with Michelangelo.' Mae ducked down behind the back of the high settle.

'As in the Sistine Chapel?' Bailey said.

Mae looked at him sharply.

'See,' Bailey laughed, 'just because I don't live in a posh house like yours or Josh Maynard's, it doesn't mean I don't know anything.'

'Okay. Lecture over. But what is Mum doing with *him*?'

He'd been getting his feet under the table rather a lot, Mae realised now. She'd seen the note her mum had written sitting on top of a leftover portion of cottage pie. It wouldn't be long before she was signing notes 'Cara xxx' and not just 'Cara', would it?

'Coming for lunch?' Bailey said, dragging Mae's thoughts back to the present.

'As *if*. Can't she see he's just going to take advantage of her being a widow? We haven't seen any of his art yet.'

Seeing her mother with a man who wasn't her dad was making all sorts of emotions swirl around inside Mae. She felt anger that her mum had asked her dad to leave home over the gambling. Like, hadn't she heard of counselling? But another part of her was pleased her mother fessed up about the gambling once she'd been asked. And there was fear in the pit of Mae's stomach now, too, wondering what would happen if her mum and this Tom Gasson-Smith bloke were to get together.

'Have we?' Mae insisted, looking straight at Bailey as though expecting him to know the answer although she knew he couldn't possibly. 'Seen any of his art?'

'Calm it, Mae,' Bailey said. 'From where I'm sitting it looks as though they've bought back the painting from the Beachcomber.'

'Oh God, have they? Well, *he* might have done, and that can only mean one thing ... Mum will owe him, and then he'll never go.'

'Mae, I ...' Bailey began but Mae stopped him. He was only going to tell her off for being mean, wasn't he? Or try and reason with her or something. Bailey hadn't lost his dad and he had no idea how this was making her feel.

'Do you think I could just slip out to the Ladies and escape?'

'Chill, Mae.'

Bailey reached for Mae's hands and held onto them tightly. He gave Mae the sweetest of smiles.

Mae smiled back, a very watery smile, but a smile.

Then she turned towards her mother who had just been handed a bottle of Evian and a glass by Michelangelo. 'Mum! Over here!' she called.

Her mum came rushing over and before she could say anything, Mae said, 'It's okay. This is a bistro, not a pub, so I'm allowed in the bar area. Food, you know.'

'A bistro?' her mum said. 'I didn't know.' She looked around the room, her eyes finally settling on the two watercolours propped up on the table leg. 'My pictures?'

'Correction,' Mae said. 'They're mine now. I've offered to come in and wash up at lunchtimes on the days I'm doing the late afternoon/early evening shift at the ice-cream kiosk. Mondays, Tuesdays and Fridays. Starting next Monday. A business arrangement.'

'Oh, darling,' her mum said, her eyes all glassy with tears. She turned to Bailey and said, 'Thank you so much, Bailey, for letting us know. For being so supportive to Mae.'

''s all right,' Bailey said.

'What are you doing with *him*?' Mae jerked her head towards Tom who was handing the money over for the drinks. She was all churned up inside. Seeing her mother with Michelangelo and the fact they'd already been to the Beachcomber where Mae and

187

Bailey had been going to go next had spoiled the surprise she'd been planning for her mum.

'Tom? We've been buying back my painting from the Beachcomber. It was Tom's idea, because we ...'

'We?' Mae interrupted. That was twice in as many seconds that her mother had said 'we'. Like they were a couple already. Damn it – tears were threatening to make a right drip of her again. Tom Gasson-Smith was far too sure of himself. Famous artist indeed – where were all the paintings then?

'Tom's paid for now, and I'm going to pay him back just as soon as I can.'

'Right,' Mae said.

'Aren't you going to introduce me?' Bailey butted in.

'Oh, yeah. Sorry,' Mae said. 'Mum, this is Bailey. Bailey, this is my mum, Cara.'

'Hi, Mrs Howard,' Bailey said.

'And I'm Tom,' Tom said, putting his glass of wine down on the table, and handing her mum a glass of something fizzy – champagne or Prosecco or something.

'Handshakes all round then,' Bailey said.

Now Bailey seemed to have broken the ice, they all chatted easily enough for a while. Mae found it strange sitting in a pub with her mother and a man who wasn't her dad. She couldn't help noticing that he touched her mother's arm to emphasise a point, or draw her attention to something on the walls of the pub that interested him – art stuff mostly. There were loads of paintings of yachts and schooners on the walls. Well, it was a seaside pub, Mae supposed. But if he was touching her mother's arm, what else had he touched? If they were an item, why the hell hadn't she been told?

'Right,' Tom said. 'I'm afraid I'm going to have to leave you lovely people now. The train to London, and Louise, await. Neither will wait for a mere mortal like me.'

Louise? So Michelangelo already had a woman in his life.

And then, Michelangelo leaned down and kissed her mother on the cheek. What was he like? Going off to meet this Louise woman, and kissing her mother before he went?

'Be safe,' her mother said.

Be safe? That's what her mother always said to her when they parted company, even for a little while.

If … if … if she adds *'love you'* Mae was going to be sick!

CHAPTER TWENTY-THREE

'Are you going to put them back up?' Mae asked.

'Tom said he'd do it,' Cara told her.

She still couldn't quite believe she had three of her paintings back, or how close they'd been to Cove End for years and she'd had no idea. No wonder Mark had always brought a bottle of wine home, or some beers, some champagne sometimes, saying he'd rather enjoy a glass of something in his own home and not in some noisy bar somewhere. Cara knew the reason for that now – so she wouldn't see her paintings on the pub walls.

'Muuum,' Mae said. She sighed. 'You can handle a power tool, right?'

Could she? She'd never tried. Mark hadn't been much into DIY and they'd always paid someone to do anything that needed doing. There was a drill in the utility room, she knew that. And some boxes of screws and hooks and things.

'Of course I can,' Cara said. 'But I might not need to because there are still little holes in the wall where the screws were taken out.'

She fervently hoped that was the case because although she might not have had much experience of this sort of thing, she did know there could be wires inside the plastering and if you hit them with a drill bit, well …

'Let's do it then,' Mae said.

She raced off to the utility room and Cara was reminded of the six-year-old Mae who used to race around the house on Christmas Day following the treasure hunt clues Cara and Mark had left for her to find her presents. She had that same excitement about her now. Cara followed rather more slowly.

Mae was riffling through a drawer when Cara caught up with her. She came and stood behind her daughter and put her arms around her shoulders, pulled her gently towards her and kissed the top of her head – she smelled of the apple shampoo that was her current favourite.

'I'm very proud of you, Mae,' she said, 'for doing what you did, taking control and getting the paintings back once you'd been told where they were. And for how you're going to pay for them.'

''s all right,' Mae said. 'When Bailey told me I was, like, what? I thought he was winding me up at first. Glad they were somewhere we could buy them back.'

Mae turned in her mother's arms and put her arms around her, clasping her hands together behind Cara's waist. She snuggled in.

'What time's he coming back?' Mae asked.

'Tom?'

'Yeah, him,' Mae said. She wriggled out of Cara's embrace, turned back towards the drawer and began noisily sorting through the screws and hooks. She pulled out a handful and showed them to Cara. 'Will these do?'

'I expect so,' Cara said, her voice weary now.

Mae wasn't any closer to accepting Tom in the house after three weeks than she had been on the day he arrived, was she? Was now the time, though, to take her to task over her attitude, given the wonderful hug they'd just had and what Mae had done in getting the paintings back?

'Goodo,' Mae said. 'So, what time?'

'Tom won't be back until tomorrow sometime. He's stopping at his house in London tonight. He's got meetings tomorrow.' Cara had put extra stress on the word 'Tom'.

'Great,' Mae said, grinning. 'It means we can get the job done before he gets back. Women don't have to rely on men any more, Mum, the way you always relied on Dad for everything. If you start relying on him to do everything, like hang a few pictures or something, then he might never want to leave.'

Cara considered reminding Mae she'd not had anyone to rely on for two years now and she was managing just fine. *They* were managing just fine. Mae had grown up in front of Cara's eyes earlier when she'd organised getting the paintings back and getting a job to pay for them – it had been heart-warming to see.

'I expect Tom will want to leave at some stage,' Cara said.

'Good,' Mae said. 'Then we can have our house back. He's like always in the kitchen now.'

'I know. I told him he could.'

'Why?' Mae hunched her shoulders up and let them drop again.

'Because if he goes in the breakfast room when we have other guests he gets drawn into conversations and that takes time away from his painting. There's only a fortnight to the exhibition now. Time's running out.'

'Not long,' Mae said. 'Then he'll leave.'

Cara bit her lip to stop her telling Mae she'd like a bit more respect from her for Tom – that she wanted her to use his name and not 'him' or 'he' every time she spoke about him. But uppermost in her mind was the fact she, Cara, was getting very used to having Tom around the house. She liked the fact he didn't impose on her time or her space but was always friendly and funny when they did get to spend time in one another's company, albeit those times were short and often just in passing. She liked the solid safety of his presence. But did she want him to leave? No. Not yet anyway.

Mae jiggled the screws and hooks in her hand.

'Are we going to get these paintings back up or what? You know, before he's finished kissing this Louise person or whatever else they might be doing.'

And that, my darling daughter, Cara thought, is what you are hoping might be happening so that Tom and I don't go on to that stage ourselves and become an item.

'Louise is Tom's ex-wife. He's gone to London to sort out some sort of business problem.'

'Yeah, right,' Mae said, making it sound as though she didn't believe a word Cara had said.

Couples did sometimes get back together again, realising they'd made a terrible mistake getting divorced, Cara knew that. The thought chilled her and she shivered.

'So are we getting these pictures back up or what?' Mae prompted.

'Yep,' Cara said. 'We are. Of course we are. Women rule, right?' She held out her hands for the screws and hooks, hoping that amongst them would be the right thing for the job. Mae tipped it all into Cara's hand, then linked her arm through her mother's and together they went back to the kitchen to hang the first two pictures.

'Cara?' Tom said, looking from one woodland scene painting to the other. 'Seth Jago? You've got two Seth Jago paintings? How …'

'I know.' Cara came to stand beside Tom. It was late afternoon the next day and he'd been back from London about twenty minutes, Mae stomping off to her room the second he got in. 'I inherited those from my grandmother, Rachel. Seth Jago was Rachel's mother Emma's first husband. There's no name on them, I thought …'

'There!' Tom said, pointing. 'Do you see? Down the side of the tree on the far left on this one, and along that bottom branch that dips to the ground on the other one. Almost as though he didn't want anyone to know he'd painted them.'

'I've never noticed,' Cara said. 'Was he famous?'

'Not in his lifetime,' Tom said. 'But he's become very collectable. I suspect I might have to die before I become really famous.'

'Oh, don't die,' Cara laughed, pulling a mock-sad face.

'I'll do my best not to. These could be quite valuable, you know. Worth far, far more than the fifty quid the pub landlord wanted for them. Technically, I suppose, they're Mae's now she's agreed to work in lieu of payment for them.' He shook his head as though trying to clear it of jumbled thinking. 'I'm finding it hard to take in that you're related to Seth Jago.'

'Only by marriage,' Cara said. 'Not blood. Alas. Or I might be able to paint.'

'And these two, being slight abstracted, will fetch more than his photographic studies. See how the trees are slightly out of proportion to the leaves on the ground? And how the leaf shapes aren't botanically correct in any way – more a representation? And how that bird on the branch there isn't anatomically correct either? And the sky? It reaches far nearer the ground in these than it would in reality. A bit of artistic licence. He's known for painting the Rockies where I think these might have been done.'

'That fits. The Rockies, I mean. I remember my grandma telling me Seth and Emma emigrated to Canada about a hundred years ago.'

'God, I love them!' Tom said.

'Me, too,' Cara said. And especially because they'd been done by her step-great-grandfather and Tom seemed to be rating them so highly. She'd had no idea Seth Jago was so famous. She was feeling slightly giddy with the knowledge of it all. It was a mercy that Mark hadn't sold them further afield. 'I felt sad when they disappeared off my walls, but told myself they were only paint-ings, if you know what I mean?'

'Only paintings?' Tom said, looking mock-offended. 'I'll have you know paintings are good for the soul – to paint and to admire. It would be like a spear through my heart if anyone was to call my work "only paintings"!'

'I'll try and remember not to, then,' Cara laughed. 'Not, of course, that I've seen any proof that you're painting anything.'

'Ah, but you will,' Tom said. 'All in good time you will.'

Tom's voice was full of warmth and ... well, what? Hope of some sort?

'I'll remember to be fulsome in my praise,' Cara said. 'I've hung the other one, too. Do you want to look?'

'Lead me to it,' Tom said.

So Cara led the way to the room she'd set aside for herself and Mae, a room not to be used by guests. It had been the old TV room when Mark was alive, but the TV had been sold off and Cara hadn't replaced it. A small room. Intimate. And feeling more intimate now with Tom standing so close to her as they looked at the seascape Mae had helped her to hang on the wall behind the wood-burner.

'Blimey,' Tom said. 'How did I not notice that when I lifted it off the wall in the Beachcomber? This is definitely a Seth Jago as well. This one is more obviously signed. Very tiny writing. I'd say he used a brush with about three hairs on it to do it. And an earlier work, I'd say, although I'm no expert on him.'

'It was a bit dim in there,' Cara said. 'Even for summer. All that dark wood and artificial light struggling to get through those dingy maroon lampshades.'

'You're too kind,' Tom laughed. 'Call myself an artist and I didn't recognise a Seth Jago when I had one in my hands! Perhaps I was distracted by other things?'

Other things? And then a thought struck her, like a bowl of cold porridge tipped over her head. Louise. She was cross with herself now for letting jealousy dance between them like the Northern Lights, but nowhere near as beautiful.

'How did London go?'

Had he, as Mae had suggested, ended up kissing Louise, and other things, for old times' sake? She had no right to be jealous and yet, there it was, spoiling the moment.

'Difficult would sum it up, Cara,' Tom said. 'Louise is like a dog with a bone when she gets an idea in her head, and especially one I don't agree with. I'll spare you the details. The short version is, well, I'm glad I'm back. Can I leave it at that?'

'I'm glad you're back too,' Cara said, almost a whisper.

'Good, good,' Tom said, his eyes still on the seascape as though he hadn't really been heard what Cara had said. 'God, but this is good. I'll be a happy man if I can get as much soul and feeling in my seascapes.'

'Seascapes?' Cara said. 'Rosie said you did nudes.'

'Rosie's right,' Tom said, 'except in the art world they're known as figurative paintings. Art should be like gardens, as my mother is always telling me – shouldn't stand still. That said, it's still come as a surprise to find how easily I've been able to change artistic direction stopping here. Move on.'

'I see,' Cara said. Tom had told her that Louise only had rights to any paintings she'd posed for. So was changing genre Tom's way of moving on? Putting distance in more ways than one between him and Louise? 'And Louise wants a share in these paintings as well?'

'Got it in one,' Tom said. 'She went ballistic when my solicitor told her she'd no rights whatsoever to my new work. I doubt I've heard the last of it.'

'No,' Cara said.

Louise would always be in the background for Tom the way Mark always would be for her. It was just how it was, and something neither of them could do anything about.

'Anyway, Louise is now off my conversational menu! And I'm

not going to let her spoil my surprise at finding Seth Jago paintings hanging on your walls. It's been so good being here, Cara, in so many ways. Cove End is growing on me. Despite the fact Mae can't stand the sight of me still. Hates me being here.' Tom laughed nervously.

'I know. Sorry,' Cara said. 'Although I think hate is too strong a word. She's uncomfortable with a man in the house all the time who isn't her father, I think.'

There he was, Mark, back in the conversation again, just as Louise had crept back into Tom's.

'Do you want me to go? I can. I ...'

'No!' Cara said quickly.

There'd be a gaping hole in her life if Tom were to go now.

'Well, that's a very positive reaction!' Tom said.

He reached for Cara's hands and she let him pull them towards him. He held them gently but firmly against his chest and smiled at her.

'Would a positive reaction from me too, be too much?' he asked.

Cara could see her reflection in Tom's eyes. She could smell whatever fragrance it was he used. She could hear her own breath escaping in nervous excitement at what was about to happen. She could feel the beat of his heart – quite fast now as though he were anxious of her reply. She knew what was coming.

Cara lifted her face to his and Tom leaned forward and kissed her tenderly on the lips, lingering a little but not too much. A sweet kiss. A pure kiss. Cara couldn't remember ever having been kissed like that before.

'Is that the first time?' he asked. 'That you've been kissed since your husband died, I mean?'

'Yes,' Cara said. And for a long time before it as her marriage had deteriorated, but there was no need to tell Tom that – that was the past, and Tom could be her future. 'That felt good. Special.'

'For me, too,' Tom said. 'Sometimes, for some people, these things – death and divorce – are meant to be so that they can become someone different with someone different.' Tom put his arms around Cara and hugged her to him. 'I think you know, Cara, how I'm beginning to feel about you,' he said, his breath warming the side of her neck. 'I don't think I'd get a C- if I said I'm pretty sure you feel the same. But there's Mae in the equation and while I don't have children, I know they come first for parents, mothers and fathers. Right?'

'Right,' Cara agreed. In a few short sentences Tom had brought her up to date with his life, and shown understanding over Mae. Who wouldn't love a man like that?

'However,' Tom said, with a mock downturn of his mouth, 'I might need to keep a low profile for the next couple of weeks. The art festival date is getting closer and I've got work to do. So …'

'Of course,' Cara said, disappointment wrapping itself around her like a damp dishcloth. She didn't think for a second Tom was saying that because he'd instantly regretted kissing her. But still … she might have to wait a bit before they could kiss again, was what he was perhaps saying. 'I'll be getting supper shortly. Panzanella. In fact I'll need to get on with it right away actually. Mae will be back soon. You can come and chat to me while I make it if you want.'

She walked briskly towards the kitchen and Tom followed.

'Panzanella?' Tom said. He perched himself on the high stool by the counter top as Cara took tomatoes from the fridge, and some peppers, and lifted the pot of basil off the windowsill. 'Which is? My Italian – I'm guessing it's something Italian – is the pits.'

'Right first time,' Cara said. 'Basically it's tomatoes and peppers and basil and olive oil and bread … lots of tomatoes, baby ones for preference. Will you join us? At the table tonight instead of me leaving you a portion in the fridge?'

Cara walked briskly to the plate rack and took down three plates, placing them on the table. She put the pot with the cutlery in the centre.

Mae might have something to say about that. She might insist on eating in her room, but Cara would insist she didn't, and that she minded her manners.

'Um, maybe not,' Tom said. 'Not that I don't want to because I do, but I don't think it would be a good idea at this precise moment. You wouldn't have to have Hercule Poirot's powers of detection to work out that Mae would probably rather gouge her eyes out with bent paperclips than sit at a table with me.'

'Ouch!' Cara said.

'So, off I go. You might hear me moving about up there for a while. I've got a couple of things I want to finish tonight. I'll pop back for the panzanella later. Okay?'

'Okay.'

They were still standing so close and to Cara it seemed as though Tom really was reluctant to go, but had decided not to invade Mae's space at the moment.

'Goodnight, then,' Cara said. 'And thanks, you know, for …'

Tom placed his free hand under Cara's chin and lifted it so she was facing him. Then he kissed her lips – a gentle pressure, warm and dry.

'The thanks are all mine,' Tom said, 'for letting me into your life a little more.'

And then he was gone, and Cara stood for a few minutes feeling bereft but not without hope. She set to, preparing supper.

'Not hungry, darling?' Cara asked.

Mae had only picked at her supper, spearing a few olive oil-soaked pieces of bread and cutting the already small tomatoes into even smaller portions, popping just a forkful in her mouth and taking an age to eat them.

'You had three plates out, Mum,' Mae said. She pointed to the plate Cara had hoped Tom would use that she'd taken from the table and put on the counter top. 'Is there something you haven't told me? About you and ... and Tom,' she finished in a quiet voice.

'Yes and no,' Cara said. 'But can I ask you what would have been so awful if he'd joined us? It must be lonely eating on your own all the time, which he often does when he brings back takeaways and eats in his room, or in one of the pubs.'

'His choice,' Mae said. 'I would have got that other painting as well, you know. Bailey said it was in the Beachcomber. He ... Tom didn't have to do it.'

'I know, but he did.'

Cara had rather hoped that Tom would have told Mae over supper that the paintings they'd managed to recover were now valuable, and not just the family duty heirlooms Cara had always thought they were.

'We know nothing about him,' Mae said.

'No, not a lot,' Cara agreed. 'Divorced. No children. Very knowledgeable about art and artists. He really rates Seth's paintings.'

'Really?' Mae said. 'I thought you said Seth was only an amateur artist. You sure Tom's not making it up? You know, just to get you on his side or something.'

Cara took a deep breath. There was no need for Mae to know she and Tom had shared a kiss, but she wasn't going to pretend they didn't like one another.

'We'll look him up, shall we? Now? We can google him.'

'Who? Seth Jago or ... Tom?'

Oh dear, poor Mae – she was struggling to even say his name.

'Both. Come on.'

Cara leapt from her chair, almost knocking it over in her haste. Mae got up more slowly with much huffing and puffing and deep sighs.

'Here we go,' Cara said, clicking search. 'Seth Jago coming up.'

Although she was doing it to prove Tom had told the truth, she was also curious to know just who her step great-grandfather had been.

'Blimey, there's loads of stuff,' Mae said. 'Do "images".'

Cara scanned the brief information panels. Fishing smack owner, Brixham. Emigrated to Canada 1912, died from complications after saving a would-be suicide from Vancouver Harbour. Posthumous bravery award. Married Emma Le Goff aboard the RMS *Royal Edward* during its crossing from Bristol to Halifax. Gosh, so much she didn't know. She could read more of that another time and it was the paintings that were the important thing here at the moment. She clicked on 'images' and the screen filled with painting after painting. None were of her own paintings, but the style was more than recognisable. She came to the conclusion Tom had been right about her paintings being of the Rockies because most of the ones here were and the styles were similar.

'Now galleries or something,' Mae said. 'To see what they're worth.'

Cara clicked. It seemed there were galleries in London, Vancouver and New York with paintings for sale.

Mae leaned towards the screen checking the prices.

'How much? That's five figures, Mum,' she said. She pulled her chair closer to Cara's and leaned her head on Cara's shoulder.

I want to stay in this moment,Cara thought, just Mae and me, how we were before Mark died.

Mae was trembling now. Shock and surprise probably. And to her own shock and surprise, Cara was a bit shaky too.

'See,' she said. 'Tom was telling the truth. And the two woodland scenes are now technically yours, seeing as you will have paid for them by the time your washing-up job has earned the wherewithal.'

'Really? You don't want to sell them? You know, use the money for us to live on so we don't have to have any more B&B guests?'

'I don't want to sell them, no,' Cara said. 'Even that sort of money would soon go. We could only spend it once. We need more regular income.'

'Yeah, I suppose,' Mae said, and Cara dared to hope that Mae was taking a more mature attitude to it all now.

'Anyway,' Cara said, 'the seascape one is now technically Tom's, but I know he wouldn't dream of selling it over my head.'

'Yeah,' Mae said. 'I mean no ... he could have done that already after he bought it, and he didn't, did he?'

'No,' Cara said. 'Tom next? Shall we google him?'

Cara had googled Tom before but only to check he was a bona fide artist after the fiasco she'd experienced with the Hines.

Mae typed Tom Gasson-Smith into the search box.

'This feels like spying,' Cara said. 'I mean, Tom's just upstairs. I could go and knock on his door and ask him anything ... oh!' Some of Tom's paintings were fetching more than Seth Jago's were. All were nude studies. Louise? Was that Louise's body in all of them? Most were studies of the model's back, or sideways on, her head bowed, hair hanging down covering her face.

'Muffin 'ell,' Mae said, making Cara laugh. Knowing the 'f' word was banned, Mae had taken to saying 'muffin 'ell' as a form of expletive sometimes.

'Muffin 'ell indeed, sweetheart,' she laughed.

'I don't mean the naked ladies, Mum,' Mae said. 'I mean the prices. He could be stopping over in Torquay at the Imperial or something with that sort of money behind him and he's, like, here in a B&B. But they're not smutty, are they? We did figurative in art at school and it was, like, well we all know what women look like, right? And then some old bloke came and was a model for a couple of lessons and after a while all the giggling stopped.' Mae was sounding more excited, more animated, and happier than she'd sounded in a long time. She clapped her hands

202

together. 'Oh look! It says there he's not painted anything for a couple of years. I wonder why not? I mean, what's got him started again?'

'Maybe it's being here,' Cara said. 'Less pressure than being in his studio, perhaps?'

'We could ask him in the morning,' Mae said.

'You can if you want,' Cara said. 'But then you'd have to admit we've been doing a bit of spying.'

'Not spying, Mum,' Mae said. 'Safeguarding our well-being, I'd say. What if he'd been like some sophisticated form of the Hines who cleaned us out before? Anyway, that's what Google's for – so we can know stuff, the good and the bad.'

And the good is bringing us closer again, Cara thought.

'Group sigh of relief that he's safe, then,' Cara said. She put her arm around her daughter's shoulders and hugged her to her.

'My first shift in the Boathouse today,' Mae said. 'My first payment to be earned on my heirloom paintings.' She yawned. 'God, what a day! What an eye-opener! All this about my, what, step great-great grandfather, and Tom whatsit up there being famous. Crikey. Okay if I go to bed now, Mum?'

'Of course,' Cara said.

And in the morning she would dig out the painting of her great-grandmother, Emma, that Seth had done and show it to Tom when she had a moment, and if he was around. What, she wondered, would he make of it?

CHAPTER TWENTY-FOUR

A week in and much to her surprise Mae was loving her washing-up job at the Boathouse, not that you could call it washing-up because there were three huge dishwashers. All she had to do was scrape the leftover food into the food waste bin for recycling and stack the dirty dishes. Easy peasy. And then there was the fact the landlord, Scott Matthews, gave her a doggy bag to take home sometimes, saying he'd overbudgeted, taken fish or meat or whatever out of the freezer and couldn't refreeze it. Mae thought he was just being kind because he must know she and her mum didn't have as much money these days as they'd had when her dad was alive, but she said thank you and meant it. It meant her mum wouldn't have to spend so much money on food now she'd been given some. Her mum shared the food with Michelangelo – no, Tom, she must remember to call him Tom because it got her mum fired up when she didn't. He was in his room a lot now, putting the finishing touches to his paintings, so he said. Mae had heard him singing in his room sometimes. He was no Alfie Boe, but he wasn't bad.

'Nearly done, Mae?' Scott Matthews asked, coming into the kitchen.

'Just wiping down,' Mae said.

'You're a good girl, Mae. Reliable. Not like some people.' Scott flung open cupboard doors and grabbed two big bags of flour. 'You couldn't pass me two blocks of lard from the fridge, could you?'

'Sure,' Mae said. She was a lot nearer the fridge than he was. Scott was looking flustered. 'What's up?' she asked.

'That waste of space, Taylor, has phoned in sick again. Hungover more like. So now I've got to get some profiteroles done seeing as they're on tonight's menu. Choux pastry can be a bit of a bugger. Forgive the language.'

Mae laughed. She heard much stronger language than that when she was clearing tables, and coming in or going out through the bar for her shift.

'What's choux pastry when it's at home?' Mae asked.

Scott was reaching for a large saucepan from the high shelves above the worktop and the gas stove that had seven hobs on it.

'Fancy puffy stuff that punters love, in this instance filled with a creamy mixture with chocolate on top.'

Mae watched, mesmerised as Scott half-filled the saucepan with water from the boiling tap, then put the blocks of lard into it.

'Your mum's B&B is doing well, I hear,' Scott said, stirring the saucepan vigorously. 'What with the art festival coming up.'

'Yeah,' Mae said.

She didn't know if she wanted to talk about personal stuff or even if she should, but it would be rude not to respond. She was getting more used to having strangers in the house now. Some of them she hardly noticed at all. They came in – sometimes quite late at night, after she'd gone up to her room to read – and got shown to their rooms, and then they'd often be gone again in the morning, up and out, breakfast eaten, before Mae had even got up. Like dragonflies, Mae thought, hovering for a short while, landing briefly, and then taking off again.

'I'm hoping the art festival will boost trade here a bit as well. If I can get the bleeding staff! Present company excepted, Mae. I don't suppose you could stir that for a minute, could you? If you're not in a rush?'

'Not particularly, no,' Mae said, taking the wooden spoon from him. The lard and water mixture didn't smell great, but she guessed once it had flour in it, then got cooked and loaded with cream and chocolate, it would be okay.

Scott was sieving flour into a large bowl, perhaps a bit too quickly because he was rushing, and a puffy cloud of flour drifted towards Mae.

'Right,' Scott said. 'Flour in next. You can go now. Thanks.'

'No. Can I watch? This looks like … like alchemy.'

The flour was binding the water and lard together rapidly and it seemed just seconds before Scott had a ball of shiny yellow mixture in the saucepan.

'Sure,' Scott said. 'Can you get me a couple of the largest baking trays out of that bottom cupboard? Then oil them. Oil's over there,' he said, pointing to a jug with a long spout on it.

Mae did as she was told, by which time Scott had got a cloth bag of some sort and was spooning some of the shiny yellow gunge into it.

'And now the clever part,' Scott said. 'Piping this lot into balls the same size, so punters don't complain their mates have got bigger profiteroles than they have. They take seconds to cook – if we've done the beating properly.'

Within minutes Scott had filled the two large trays with balls of dough and was putting them in the oven.

'Whipped cream next,' he said, pulling out a large glass bowl and tipping three tubs of double cream into it. He reached for a handheld whisk. 'They'll have to cool a bit once the filling is in before I can put the chocolate on. Want to watch or buzz off? Got that boyfriend of yours to see or something?'

'Bailey?' Mae said.

They were friends, good friends, but not really boyfriend and girlfriend. She was too busy working most of the time.

'If that's his name.'

'Not now, I'm not, no,' Mae said. 'I could do that cream for you.'

'Sure you could,' Scott said, handing her the whisk. 'Hey, Mae, could you do another couple of shifts for me? You're a good little worker. Interested?'

'Yeah, why not? I could do the bar or something for a bit of a change.'

'Sorry, not that. You're underage. I was thinking this sort of stuff: food prep, not just the clearing up of people's lefto-vers. Right,' Scott said as a timer pinged, 'that's the pastry done.'

He grabbed an oven cloth, opened the oven door and brought out a huge tray in each hand.

'Blimey,' Mae said. 'That's magic. Yeah, I could do that.'

'Good. Great. Thanks for your help. But you'd better go now just in case someone from the works department is snooping around, checking I'm not making you work more hours than you're allowed.'

'Okay. What time tomorrow?'

'Half past ten if you can make it. It's all pizzas and fish and chips at lunchtime, but I've made a rod for my own back by insisting it's all homemade so ...' Scott opened the fridge and took out a plate with four pieces of salmon on it and began sliding them into a polystyrene doggy-bag box.

'Here you go, Mae, supper for you and your mum and whoever else might be around in lieu of wages for helping out. That artist still there?'

'Yeah.'

'Oh dear,' Scott laughed. 'You don't sound too thrilled about it! Got his feet under the table, has he?'

'Sort of,' Mae said.

207

'Won't be for much longer though once this art festival thing is over, I shouldn't think. Hang on in there!'

Mae shrugged. There wasn't a lot she could add to that.

'Thanks for the fish,' she said.

'Hang on.'

Scott reached for a dish of tomatoes on the central island and gave two or three a bit of a squeeze.

'And some tomatoes that have gone a bit soft for salads but'll be okay for a fried breakfast for your guests,' Scott said, tipping a dish of tomatoes into a plastic bag. 'I expect you miss your dad.'

'Course I do,' Mae said, wondering where this conversation was going. The landlord was just snooping probably. Trying to find out if her mum and Tom were an item, sleeping together or something. Yuk, perish the thought! 'Anyway, thanks for all this stuff. Mum'll say thanks as well. I'm off now.'

Carrying her bounty in her arms like a baby, Mae walked out of the kitchen into the bar, and came face to face with Josh, standing leaning on the bar with a girl clinging onto his arm, a glass of something fizzy in her hand. Mae had hardly seen him since the night of the sailing incident, only once or twice in the distance, and the once when he'd bought lollies with Alice Morrell, but he was with a different girl now. Well, she was welcome to him as far as Mae was concerned. Josh never had got around to saying thank you for saving his life – not even a bunch of garage flowers or anything. Mae thought he might at least have done that, it was only manners, but no. Nothing.

'Hi,' Josh said.

'Bye!' Mae said and carried on towards the door.

That was the problem with small village living – you couldn't get away from people if you tried.

But she was moving on in other ways, what with just being offered extra hours so she'd earn more and everything. Seeing Josh hadn't caused her one little blip of longing or regret or anything. And her mother was more cheerful about the house now as well. Hmm, Mae had a feeling Tom had something to do with that, and was surprised that just thinking that wasn't making her feel sad and angry any more. Well, who'd have thought it!

CHAPTER TWENTY-FIVE

Since that kiss with Tom the night she'd hung the paintings, Cara had hardly seen him on his own at all. She was beginning to wonder if she'd imagined it all. She had the painting of her great-grandmother, Emma, which she'd unearthed from its hiding place at the back of her wardrobe but not yet found a moment to show him. She'd relived that kiss in daydreaming moments and once or twice in dreams that didn't stop with a kiss ... but was she putting too much hope into what had, perhaps, been a spur-of-the-moment gesture for Tom? He was in his room more, putting finishing touches to his new works, was what he'd told Cara. She'd heard him singing or humming to himself while he worked. His clean bed-linen was left on the landing as arranged and he'd changed his bed, bringing his dirty linen downstairs and putting it through the washer-dryer. He'd also borrowed the vacuum cleaner more than a few times so Cara knew she was unlikely to find his room had turned into some sort of squalid squat when he left. When? Ought she to mention that the next time they had a few minutes alone? There were always other B&B guests – none as troublesome as Miss Horsham had been, thank goodness – around or Mae. And what a surprise that was turning out to be ... Mae not rushing out of the room the second Tom entered it any more. Since she'd come back from her shift at the Boathouse a few nights ago with salmon and tomatoes the landlord had given her, Cara had seen a change in her. Little steps, Cara told herself. Perhaps Tom was giving not just Mae the space to accept him, but she was as well.

Now there was less than a week to opening day, Larracombe had taken on a feeling of *en fête*. The various venues where artists would be showing their work had signs outside with opening times. Tom would be showing in the village hall – just him and not sharing as some artists would be. Owners of some of the larger houses had been approached and asked if they could show-case an artist and Cara had been one of them. She'd declined out of respect to Tom – she didn't want him to think that she preferred others' work over his, not that she'd seen a single thing he'd painted yet, apart from on his website.

Yes, Cara told herself as she cleared up after another full house breakfast session, she'd made the right decision to turn Cove End into a business. She'd had to turn away at least a dozen potential B&B guests because she was full up. Her bank balance was beginning to look healthier and she'd paid Tom back his fifty pounds, which he'd accepted gracefully. If she was honest with herself, Cara was beginning to feel almost happy again. Being a landlady wasn't hard. She'd got herself into a routine of doing breakfast, then rushing round the downstairs rooms with the vacuum and the polish, before doing the bathrooms and putting fresh towels in the guests' rooms if they were stopping more than one night.

She was enjoying having people around her again. Even Mae seemed to have lost her hard edge a little, not that she was around as much as she had been, seeing as she now had two jobs to go to. And then guilt over Mark would kick in for Cara. She'd re-hung the paintings they'd bought back from the pubs, but somehow they looked, to Cara anyway, all wrong without Mark in the house too. It had been a relief when Mae had asked if she could have them in her room instead, and that perhaps they could buy something from the art festival to take their place.

'We'll see,' Cara had told her.

Not that Mae seemed too troubled about the paintings, or even missing her dad, at the moment because she was spending more and more time with Bailey Lucas when she wasn't working. She was with him now, grabbing a coffee at the Lobster Pot before doing her shift in the ice-cream kiosk, so she'd told Cara before bounding off happily.

'Anyone home?'

Ah, Rosie. Cara hadn't seen her since the night she'd clouted Tom, although they'd texted one another a few times.

'In here!' Cara called back.

Rosie came into the breakfast room.

'Well, you're a sight for sore eyes,' Cara told her as they hugged and air-kissed. 'I was beginning to think you were avoiding me.'

'As if,' Rosie said.

'So, give. What's been happening?'

'Sitting on my hands mostly,' Rosie said.

'Eh?'

'Ha ha, got you. You've got no idea what I'm talking about have you?'

'No. Didn't have my brain food for breakfast this morning. You'll have to unravel the riddle.'

Gosh but it was good to see her.

'You first. I know you've had guests because I've been snooping and I've seen comments on your website. Good ones. But none from ...' Rosie stopped talking and pointed a finger up at the ceiling. She waggled her head from side to side. 'Still here?'

'He is,' Cara grinned, totally unable to hide the fact she was glad he was.

'And thereby hangs my reason for not calling before. You know me. I wouldn't have been able to keep my hands off him. And I hope you haven't either!'

212

'Rosie!' Cara said. 'Ssh, keep your voice down.'

'Hah. That tells me you haven't. Got your hands all over him, I mean. Any coffee left in that pot?'

Cara picked it up and gave it a little shake, glad that the conversation was moving on.

'Just about. It might not be that hot though. I'll …'

'Not just yet,' Rosie said, plonking herself down on one of the wicker chairs by the window. She took a newspaper from the huge bag she always carried – a journalist's bag she always called it, although Rosie had never been a journalist, but it was big enough for a laptop and any number of other things. 'The reason for my mission, apart from seeing you and Mr Gorgeous, of course. Have you seen this?'

The *this* in question was a newspaper. Cara didn't have a lot of time for reading newspapers, even if she could now afford them.

Rosie opened the newspaper to the middle and laid it out on the table in front of her – a two-page spread about Tom with photos of some of his paintings.

'Do you have any idea just how big Tom Gasson-Smith is?'

'About six foot two?' Cara joked.

'Very funny. No, I mean, as an artist. Look – it's all over the *Western Morning News* that people are going to flock to this festival just to see him. He's a sort of Jack Vetriano in the way he paints women, except Tom paints them without clothes on.'

'I haven't noticed a trail of women going up my stairs to his room. He's not any bother. He brings his bed-linen and towels down and puts them in the washing machine. He even presses the button.'

'Ooh, a man who can multi-task!' Rosie said with a giggle. 'But I think, here, it's a case of the lady doth protest too much! You've fallen for him, haven't you? And you haven't done anything about it? I've been expecting a text to tell me he's been wining and dining you, and keeping you awake all night, but I haven't had one.'

'I'm not answering that,' Cara said.

Cara was used to Rosie and her forthright way of going about things, but she was overstepping the mark here a bit.

'Ah ha. Sometimes it's what people don't say rather than what they do that tells the real truth. Anyway, domesticity is all very well, but that man is sensuality on legs. And you, Cara Howard, do not have a jealous gene in your entire body, do you?'

'Sometimes,' Cara laughed. 'But as my old Granny Rachel used to say, it's a total waste of brain space, jealousy. Either do something about it if you don't like a situation or get over it. Not that she said "get over it" back then, but you know what I mean.'

'Which is just as well because there's more.' Rosie stabbed a finger at the second page, halfway down.'

'Read it to me,' Cara said. She went over and closed the door of the breakfast room. 'My glasses are in my room.'

'You're a coward, Mrs Howard,' Rosie quipped, laughing at her own joke. 'Seems – according to this although I know you can't believe everything you read in newspapers – his wife will be showing not just her body in his paintings but her pottery as well.'

'He told me he's not showing nudes,' Cara said. 'I know his wife was his muse and I know she's a potter. Ex-wife. Louise. She came down. And she went back the same day. She wanted to share Tom's venue for the festival, but he said she couldn't.'

Did Tom make some sketches of Louise when he went to London? Did she manage to persuade Tom to let her share his festival venue? Was that why he'd been keeping a low profile since his return from London?

Cara felt a bit sick now.

'I've looked her up on Google,' Rosie said. 'On your behalf, seeing as I know you're a saint and never would. Seems she's been a bit of a cougar since the divorce. She's just broken up from some spotty youth from a boy band.'

'I didn't ask you to do that,' Cara said.

'I know, darling,' Rosie said. 'Don't be cross with me. I should get out more. All work and no play is making me a dull girlie at the moment. But I want you to be happy and you haven't been for ages, and in my not-so-humble opinion I think Tom could be the man to do that. And as a bonus, I think you're worth ten of her.'

Rosie's words were coming out faster than the Waltzers at the fair.

'Hah!' Cara said. 'I haven't got her body, that's for sure.'

'Blimey,' Rosie said, mock-wiping a fevered brow with the back of a hand. 'Don't tell me you looked at his website?'

'I did. We both did, Mae and me. We thought they were quite tasteful actually. His paintings.'

'They are. But she's still no match for you. He might be a match for me for a few weeks, but I'd do my usual … take a delicious bite out of him, chew a bit, then spit him out again. I've been in lust hundreds of time, but never in love, and that wouldn't be fair on Tom because my gut feeling is he deserves more than that. And that wouldn't have been fair on you either, so I've stayed away.'

'Very noble of you,' Cara said.

'Could I have a little smile of appreciation with that?' Rosie grinned. She reached for Cara's hand and pulled her across the room. 'Look in there.'

The 'there' in question was an exquisite art-deco mirror in a silver surround that had belonged to Cara's great-grandmother, Emma.

'You're still beautiful,' Rosie told her. 'But you deserve stunning. The stunning that being with a man who adores you, and who you adore in return, gives. You know what I mean, and there's only one word that fits in here – sex.'

'That is a step too far,' Cara said.

'Possibly. But I do have big feet. Sevens,' Rosie said. 'So, I'll plough on. You've been so wrapped up in widowhood and the good memories you have of Mark that ...'

'Stop it! I loved Mark. I didn't love what he was doing to us as a family with his gambling, I won't deny that. And I don't want a lesson on how to run my life, thank you very much!'

Cara put her head in her hands. What was happening to her and Rosie? They'd almost never had a cross word before.

'I know I've neglected you a bit lately,' Cara continued, feeling contrite now. 'But what with the B&B and what happened to Mae and, well, I couldn't have done so much if you hadn't been so generous about the computer and getting me back my ring and, well, everything. I'm sorry. I've not been the friend I should be.'

'You're just the friend you should be for me,' Rosie said. 'You ground me. I'd probably be far more flighty than I am if I didn't have you as a friend and Mae as a goddaughter.'

'Flighty's a good word,' Cara laughed.

'So we're still friends?'

'We are. It's just that it's not easy hearing things we need to be told, perhaps.'

'Had to be done,' Rosie said. 'My guess was you wouldn't have seen that in the newspaper about his ex-wife coming down and the last thing I want is for her to do that and get her claws in Tom again. Seeing as she seems to be between toy boys. I know of women like that.' Rosie made a sexy, pouty face. 'I could be guilty as charged.'

'You're incorrigible.'

'But you love me?'

'When you're not being too bossy.'

'I'll take that as a yes, then,' Rosie said. 'And I'll have that coffee now. And lunch if there's any going.'

'There could be,' Cara said.

'Good. So, I've said my piece. I'm sorry if I made you a bit cross, but I do want you to be happy again and I think Tom is the man to help you. You've got to let him in, Cara.'

'I've opened the door a bit,' Cara said, smiling despite herself. 'We've shared a kiss.'

'Yay!' Rosie said, punching the air. Then she came over all mock- serious. 'Just the one? Why stint yourself?'

Cara sighed.

'Mae is in the equation. She's hated all this B&B stuff and resents Tom being here. Not a father replacement as such but a permanent presence in the house for weeks now. Although ...'

'Although she's getting used to him now. She said.'

'She told you that?' Cara said.

'Yep. I'm her godmother, remember, and I do my bit by checking in now and again to see how she is. And my guess is she told me because there's the mother/daughter thing going on with you and her, and she's shown so much hostility towards Tom that she'll feel she's backing down if she shows she's starting to like him. And my other guess – because I've been around the block a bit – is she told me because she wanted me to tell you. So I am. For the record.' Rosie took a deep breath. 'Phew, that's that off my 36B. You'll be at his exhibition, won't you?'

Cara laughed. So like Rosie to lay her cards down and then get on with the next thing on her mind.

'He hasn't asked me.'

'Cara, stop being so wet! It's a *public* exhibition – *anyone* can go!'

'Right. Okay. I'll go. Now will you stop harassing me? I don't like us arguing.'

'Arguing?' Rosie said, laughing. 'We weren't arguing. We were merely having a mind-clearing discussion. There's a difference.'

'Anything else?'

'Yes. You and Mae mean the whole world to me, orphan that

217

I am. Rosie's eyes pooled up. 'But maudlin on a lovely sunny Sunday I do not do. What's for lunch?'

'I've got some cooked salmon. A bit of salad. Raspberries.'

'Lead me to it,' Rosie said.

The two friends ate lunch in the garden. Cara considered knocking on Tom's door to say he could join them if he wanted to but decided against it. She wondered if he'd heard their voices – especially their raised voices – in the breakfast room.

'That was yum,' Rosie said. 'Thank you. But I'm off now.'

Rosie leapt from her chair and began gathering her used dishes so fast and furious that Cara feared they'd break. But that was Rosie – everything was done at breakneck speed. She could be exhausting at times but also the breath of fresh air that Cara needed. She was seeing her situation with Tom through Rosie's eyes now.

'So,' Rosie said, after she'd stacked the dishes in Cara's dishwasher and rinsed her hands under the kitchen tap, 'you did say Tom was upstairs, didn't you?'

'Yes. And I'm not going to disturb him if that's what you're thinking.' She would think about what Rosie had said but would act on it – or not – in her own time. 'Anyway, I've been doing some sewing. It might be another little string to my bow if …'

'Diversion tactics!' Rosie said. 'You don't fool me! Just ask him out, eh? A date. The worst he can say is no and then you'll know exactly where you are. Wear your sexiest underwear and not something that's been through the wash a million times that you wouldn't even use as drain-wiping rags. Anyway, think about what I've said – Queen Victoria would never have married Prince Albert if she'd had to wait for him to pop the question!'

CHAPTER TWENTY-SIX

'I see that bloke stopping at yours has got a solo exhibition in the village hall,' Bailey said. 'Big name that he is and all.'

Bailey had met Mae after her shift at the pub and they were now sitting on the harbour wall sharing an ice-cream. They'd become good friends but, well, Mae didn't really want a romance like she'd had with Josh – it was all too painful when it went wrong and she didn't think she could face that sort of thing for a while. But Bailey was all right. He didn't try things on with her. And he hadn't minded when she went silent on him thinking about her dad and stuff – didn't take it personally.

'Has he?' Mae said, affecting nonchalance.

'I think you know he has,' Bailey said. 'That or you've been walking about with your eyes shut for weeks because there are posters everywhere. Seen any of his work yet? Nudes and that. I looked on the internet.'

'Yeah, I know what he paints. It's not porn, you know.'

Mae took a bite of her ice-cream rather than the usual lick, swallowing it more quickly than she'd intended and it took her breath away.

'Ah, so you're warming to him,' Bailey said.

Mae began to choke, so Bailey hit her on the back to help stop the coughing. When she got her breath back a bit, she expected Bailey to take his hand away but he didn't, he left it there – a gentle warmth between her shoulder blades. Mae thought about wriggling away from him but decided not to … she sort of liked it, like he was protecting her.

'What do you mean … warming to him?' she asked.

'You haven't slagged him off lately. You know, moaned about him filling up the kitchen with his size twelves or whatever they are.'

'Yeah, I know I used to go on a bit. Sorry.'

'Better out than in, all that angst. What with the stuff about your dad and that. He …' Bailey stopped talking to bat away a seagull that kept swooping at them, trying to steal their ice-creams. 'Bugger off. That's not directed at you, by the way, Mae. Anyway, back to this artist chap …'

'Do we have to? He'll be going soon anyway.'

'How's your mum going to feel about that?'

Mae felt herself stiffen at the unexpected question.

'I dunno, she hasn't said.'

'Maybe ask her, then?' Bailey said.

'Hey, are you turning into a matchmaker or something?' Mae said, licking frantically at her ice-cream now as it began to melt more quickly.

'Nope. Could be that psychology course I took, though,' Bailey said. 'I only took it to get out of physics, which I'm not going to ever understand if I live to be a hundred. Makes you see things differently does psychology.'

'What sort of things?' Mae said. Bailey's hand was still in the small of her back – it made her shiver thinking about it, but if she expected Bailey to take his hand away, he didn't; he merely rubbed her back gently, soothingly, as though she was in some sort of pain or discomfort and much to Mae's surprise she was enjoying that feeling.

'Things like sometimes we have to give people space to be

themselves and think things through for themselves and not go rushing in, even when rushing in might be what *we* want. Things like it can be better to just be there, stand back a little from the action as it were, and wait for that person to come to you.'

This was a new Bailey from the cocky Bailey who'd confronted her and Josh in Meg Smythson's shop. She liked this new Bailey – just being there after she'd finished her shift, buying her a coffee, not wanting anything else from her?

'And is that person who's been standing back, waiting, you? And is that person you've been waiting for, me?'

'Could be,' Bailey said. He threw the end of his cornet to the gull that was inching closer along the harbour wall again. His hand moved from the middle of Mae's back to her shoulder. Gently he pulled her towards him, and Mae let herself be pulled.

'Thanks, you know, for being such a good psychology student,' Mae said, a lump in her throat. 'What's the next stage?'

She turned to look up at Bailey.

'The good psychology student needs to know if it's okay to kiss the person he's been wanting to kiss for weeks and weeks but didn't because the timing might have been all wrong, and ...'

'Oh, shut up, you!' Mae laughed. 'And just kiss me.'

'God, I thought you'd never ask,' Bailey said as his lips very sweetly brushed Mae's.

'Tom?' Cara said. He'd just come down the stairs and was heading for the front door, a framed painting – painted side towards him – tucked under each arm. 'Can I have a word?'

'Ah yes, sorry about the banging earlier,' he said. He patted the paintings. 'Framing. I'm not the best at picture framing, but they can't go in the exhibition unframed. I should have said. So sorry if it disturbed you, and ...'

'It didn't,' Cara said. 'Honestly.'

She was nervous now. She'd had almost a week now to think

about what Rosie had said, and she'd come to the conclusion she was more than falling for Tom – she'd fallen hook, line and sinker, and there was a multitude of butterflies dancing a tattoo in her stomach just looking at him. He had a smear of white paint on his left cheek and it was all Cara could do not to reach up and wipe it off for him.

'So, did you want something?' Tom said. He seemed to be stuck there now like a rabbit caught in headlights.

'Um, yes,' Cara said. 'I was, um, wondering if, well, now I can ... I was wondering if I could buy you dinner tonight? You must be getting fed up with leftovers and well, I fancy something I haven't had to cook myself. So ...'

Crikey, that was harder than she'd expected it would be. A woman never makes the first move was what her mother had always said, although Rosie had told her different.

'Buy me dinner?' Tom said. 'I doubt it would be any better than all the delicious things you've been leaving for me while I've been beavering away, but ...' Tom jiggled the paintings under his arms.

'Of course, if it's not convenient ... well, I thought I'd ask, you know, before ... well, before the art festival is over.'

'It hasn't started yet!' Tom said. 'Are you trying to get rid of me?' He did a perfect impression of a sad emoji, and Cara laughed.

'Of course not. Only we haven't talked about that ... you know, the art festival and what's going to happen when it's over and when you're go ...' Cara gulped. She really, really didn't want to finish the sentence – when you're going to leave. So she didn't. 'I've got something to show you,' she said instead. 'I've been meaning to for ages. The painting my step great-grandfather did of Emma.'

'Seth Jago?' Tom said.

'Yes, him.'

'A person could have two step great-grandfathers,' Tom said with a grin. 'Just checking! But I really, really, really do have to get these down to the hall and then come back for some more before, oh, six o' clock or something. So ...'

'Forget dinner, then?' Cara said.

'No. That's the best offer I've had in a long while and one I'm not going to pass up. Where did you have in mind?'

'The Beachcomber.'

'Perfect,' Tom said. 'Can I meet you there, say, about half past seven?'

'Perfect,' Cara said.

'I'll scrub up a bit,' Tom said. 'I expect I've got blobs of paint everywhere and ...'

'Only on your cheek.' Cara held out a forefinger towards Tom. 'Lick,' she said, 'and I'll wipe it off for you.'

Tom licked, long and slow and Cara practically melted with the intimacy of it as she transferred her moist fingertip to Tom's cheek and wiped off the paint.

'If I didn't have my arms full of paintings, I'd thank you in the best way I know how. A hug. But seeing as I have, how about this on account?' He pursed his lips in a kiss gesture so Cara reached over on tiptoe and put her lips to his; the most chaste of kisses but for Cara that second kiss had been a long time coming. She had a feeling from now on it wasn't going to be the last.

And then the door opened and Mae came in. Cara froze. Tom almost dropped the paintings but just managed to scrabble them back under his armpits again.

'Well, well, well,' Mae said, grinning broadly, which made Cara think all her birthdays and Christmases might have come at once to see Mae pleased her mother was kissing the B&B guest she'd been so hostile towards for so long. 'Am I interrupting something?'

'No, Mum, of course I don't mind you going out for a meal with Tom,' Mae said. 'Honestly. It's nice he's asked.'

'He didn't ask. I asked him.'

'Way hey!' Mae said. 'My mum getting into the twenty-first century! And did you kiss him first, too?'

'Whoa!' Cara giggled. 'Not so fast! Tom suggested it.'

'An offer you couldn't refuse?'

Cara felt herself blush. This was a strange conversation to be having with her daughter, having been caught kissing someone Mae perhaps might not have expected her to be kissing, and wasn't it usually the other way around – mothers butting in on their daughters having a sneaky kiss?

'And you don't mind that either? That I was kissing Tom, or he me, like I said?'

'Not any more,' Mae said.

'So, what's changed?'

Mae shrugged, and Cara wondered if she'd asked that question just a bit too soon.

'Everything. Nothing. This summer being a funny old summer in so many ways? Tom turning up; that stupid, stupid thing with Josh; my frock getting wrecked; the paintings being in the pubs? Bailey.'

'Bailey?'

'Yeah,' Mae said, a grin spreading across her face, forming the dimples in her cheek Cara hadn't seen for far too long. 'You're not the only one who got a kiss today, you know.'

'You and Bailey?'

Mae nodded.

'Like mother, like daughter. He suggested it and I took him up on it. Down on the harbour in full view of a tripper boat full of wildlife watchers just back from a cliff-hugging cruise and a few dozen gulls. It was so sweet and gentle … which might be too much information!'

No, no not at all, Cara wanted to say but wasn't going to.

'Well, we're full of surprises today, darling,' Cara said. 'I've got another one for you.'

224

She reached for Mae's hand and pulled her towards the snug.

'Oh!' Mae said as she took in Cara's remake of her much-loved black and white fifties frock. 'I didn't know you were making this. When have you had the time?'

'Between room changeovers. While I was waiting for guests to leave and others to arrive. I couldn't really go anywhere so it's been good to have a project. A secret. At night if I couldn't sleep, I came down and did some hand-sewing a few times. What do you think?'

'It's almost the same. How … where … oh God, it's gorgeous. Can I try it on?'

'Of course,' Cara said, but already Mae was slipping off one frock and slipping into the new one. It was a perfect fit.

'Thank you, thank you, thank you,' Mae said, hugging her mother, kissing her cheek, tears flowing, all at the same time. Then she stood on a chair so she could see all of her in the mirror over the sideboard. 'It's not the one Dad bought me and really it was time to let that go really. This is the one *you* got me and … oh Mum, I'm sorry I've been a bit of a cow at times, a right bitch really. I was either whinging about stuff – like the B&B and Tom being here – or I was going all silent on you. I did that to Bailey too, the silent treatment, but he explained it all to me. I said sorry to him as well. Just now, before the kiss and all that. Well, not the all that cos I'm still a virgin in case you were wondering ….' Mae jumped down off the chair and began hugging and kissing Cara and crying all over again. 'Happy tears, Mum,' she said. 'Happy tears.'

It was like a dam bursting, all Mae's emotion coming out, all the confessions, all the love Cara had known was there all along – she'd just had to be patient and wait for her daughter to come back to her. Cara thought her heart might burst with the joy of it. Well, that and Tom's kiss.

'What paintings is Tom putting in the village hall?' Mae asked, plonking herself down on the sofa now, as though she'd exhausted herself telling Cara what she had.

'I don't know. He didn't show me. He was just going out when …'

'When you brazenly flaunted yourself in front of him? And, being a perfect gentleman, he thanked you in the only acceptable way – by suggesting you kiss him?'

'Something like that,' Cara giggled.

'Yeah,' Mae said, suddenly serious again. 'I wonder what his paintings are going to be like, though? I know his website's full of nudes but, well, I don't think he's so stupid as to think Larracombe will fall at his feet if that's all he's exhibiting. I mean, we're women and we know what women look like and, well, I don't know that I'd want a nude painting of me on the wall over the fireplace or wherever. Or of you? Even if, like, you've kept your figure and that.'

'I'll take that as a compliment,' Cara laughed.

'Meant as one,' Mae said. She leapt up off the sofa and did a twirl in her new frock. 'God, but this is gorgeous. Bailey asked if I was going to see Tom's work. Part of me wants to, but part of me's scared. Someone in the pub at lunchtime said there are a couple of TV crews coming to opening day. One's going to be at the village hall 'cos Tom's the most famous artist here and, well, what do you think? Are you scared what we might see?'

'Not scared, Mae,' Cara said. 'Inquisitive maybe. And we could be in for a surprise. I don't know. I hope so.'

'Me too,' Mae said. 'I might wear this or I might not. It's a sort of memory of Dad, but it's also the reality of you for making it.'

'That's a lovely way of putting it,' Cara said. 'But Tom will be back for some more paintings shortly and I wouldn't want him to overhear us talking about him …'

'Hey!' Mae interrupted. She came to stand in front of Cara and put her hands on her mother's shoulders, and looked her straight in the eye. 'Sorry, you know, for butting in but I've just had a thought. You're not too old to have another baby, are you?'

'Now that's a question I wasn't expecting! We'll cross that bridge when we come to it, shall we? It was just a kiss, sweetheart.'

'Yeah,' Mae said, hugging Cara all over again. 'And we all know where kisses can lead, don't we?'

Indeed we do, Cara thought, as she heard the front door open and Tom's footfalls across the parquet floor – how quickly she'd become used to the sound of Tom's footfalls, distinct from any other guest's.

'Shh,' she said, putting a finger to her lips and whispering. 'We don't want him to hear us.'

Tom was already at the Beachcomber when Cara arrived. He'd bagged one of the alcoves and beckoned Cara over the second she stepped inside. She hurried over to meet him with almost indecent haste.

'Thanks …'

'You …'

They both began to speak at once.

'Ladies first,' Tom laughed.

'Thanks for bagging the alcove,' Cara said.

The place was filling up now. Cara saw Josh Maynard come in, a young girl hanging onto his arm; they both looked rather the worse for alcohol already and Cara breathed a sigh of relief that Mae had seen his true colours. As though sensing Cara looking at him, Josh looked over and waved a hand – nervously Cara thought – in greeting, but didn't smile. Cara gave a little nod of acknowledgement but didn't wave.

'Who's that?' Tom said, raising an eyebrow in Josh's direction. Josh and his girlfriend had climbed onto bar stools waiting to order drinks. 'Not that I'm jealous or anything!'

'No need to be,' Cara laughed. 'I don't know I could cope with a toy boy! He's an old boyfriend of Mae's. The one she was

227

with the night you arrived when she was late back from a sailing trip.'

'No loss I'd say,' Tom said. 'I've had supper in here a fair few times since stopping at Cove End and I haven't seen him with the same girl twice yet!'

'He's always had a bit of a reputation. Mae had to learn the hard way.' Cara gave a little shiver remembering that night, even though it seemed such a long time ago now.

'So,' Tom laughed, 'that's the small talk out of the way. Ah, here's the waitress now with my order. I've taken the liberty of ordering champagne.'

'Champagne?' Cara said as the girl put the bucket on the table. She had two champagne flutes in the other hand, and deftly stood them on the table.

'The very same,' Tom said. He picked up the menu off the table, handed it to Cara and then turned to the waitress. 'Give us five minutes.'

'Sure,' she said and wandered off again.

Tom pulled the cork from the champagne with a very satisfying pop and began to fill the glasses.

'What are we celebrating?' Cara said. It was she who had invited Tom to supper and she couldn't help wondering if she would be expected to pay for the champagne.

'Lots of things,' Tom said. 'Shall we order and then I'll tell you?'

'Hmm,' Cara said. She scanned the menu, which was small but interesting. 'Salmon with watercress sauce, I think. You? Remember it's my treat.'

'Ah yes, so it is, but the champagne's on me.'

So that was that little issue out of the way, Cara thought with a touch of relief.

'Sea bass for me,' Tom said. He called the waitress over and placed their orders.

'So, the celebration?' Cara said, sipping her champagne. It was gorgeous – Moët & Chandon, nothing but the best. Already it was going to Cara's head, making her feel light-headed, giddy with … what? The romance of sharing a meal with Tom? But there was apprehension too, that it might all be over before it had really begun once the art festival finished.

'Ah yes. Well, for me the number one celebration is that Mae didn't come at me all guns blazing and scratch my eyes out when she caught us kissing. Number two is my paintings are now all hung in the village hall ready for the opening tomorrow. I didn't think I was going to make it because number three is I took a big risk changing my subjects and part of me is dead scared people who know me for my life studies won't like the new works, but that's a risk I'll take. And number four is I want to thank you for being the perfect landlady. There were so many times when I wanted to stay chatting to you over breakfast or when I got back from doing some sketches, but knew if I did I wouldn't want to leave and go back to my lonely garret to paint.'

'I'll drink to one of those,' Cara said. 'That Mae didn't scratch your eyes out.'

Tom reached for Cara's hand across the table.

'I've been treading on eggshells over Mae. The last thing I wanted was to upset her by, well, beginning a relationship with her mother. That's if that's what you want and … God but I'm sounding like a lovesick teenager and not the almost middle-aged man that I am!'

'We've made a start,' Cara said. 'Two kisses.'

Their food arrived and the nervous moment for Tom was over: Cara had let him know she was thinking along the same lines as he was. They began to eat, mostly in silence except for Tom asking if Cara wanted her glass refilled. She did.

'Crikey, this is really good,' Tom said. 'Have a taste.' He speared a piece of sea bass on the end of his fork and held it towards Cara. 'Open wide.'

Such an intimate gesture and something she and Mark had

never done, not that they'd eaten out much since Mae had been born. Was Mark always going to enter her thoughts at inappropriate moments, as now? Cara supposed he would and there were lots of memories of Mark that she would treasure, but all the same she gave her head a little shake to banish him from her thoughts while she had someone she was falling more in love with by the minute.

'The salmon's pretty good, too,' Cara said. She returned the compliment with a chunk of lightly smoked River Dart salmon on the end of her fork. She wondered if, perhaps, she ought to be asking Tom what subjects he'd been painting but decided not to. She had a feeling he wanted his work to be a surprise.

'My treat next time,' Tom said. 'That's if you don't mind me stopping on when the art festival's over. Just 'til I decide the next step.'

So, he wanted there to be a next time but he was planning on leaving at some stage, then?

'You'll go back to London?' Cara knew her words sounded flatter than coca cola left in a glass overnight. Louise was in London.

Tom shrugged.

'I ought to,' he said. 'But I don't want to. I suppose what I'm trying to say and making a total hash of it is I've come to really like it here. I'd keep a *pied-a-terre* in London because that's where the major exhibitions are and I'd need to show my face for those, but I was wondering if ... if I'm rushing you by asking if you fancied London for a weekend now and again.'

'I would,' Cara said. 'I'd love to.' She'd finished her meal and placed her cutlery neatly side by side across the plate. Thoughts of London – visiting art galleries, Liberty's, Covent Garden, Oxford Street, doing the tourist bit with a tour of all the famous landmarks, and choosing which restaurant to eat in from all the hundreds there were to choose from – flooded through her head. Tom could rush her as much as he liked.

'Mae, too, if she wants to,' Tom said.

Cara clapped a hand to her mouth – she hadn't given Mae a thought there for a second, but Tom obviously had, and that realisation wrapped itself around Cara's heart like cashmere. Tom was saying, in his way, that he knew Mae would always be a priority in Cara's life and that he was fine with that.

'Of course,' Cara said, swallowing hard, touched almost to tears at Tom's thoughtfulness. 'Thank you. Pudding?'

Cara wouldn't be able to eat another thing but she knew Tom was fond of a pudding, especially her signature panna cotta with passion fruit, which she'd often left for him in the fridge.

'Um, well, no thanks. Not that I'm not grateful you've asked but ...'

'Coffee back home?' Cara jumped in quickly. She hoped Tom wasn't going to tell her something she didn't want to hear. 'I've got something to show you actually,' she went on. I meant to show you before but the opportunity didn't present itself. It's ...'

'Don't tell me!' Tom said. 'I love surprises!'

Tom reached out a hand and put two fingers to Cara's lips, holding them there, and Cara made little kissy noises against his skin.

'Okay,' she said. 'I'll just get the bill.'

'It's all lies!' Tom said when he'd finished reading the piece about the art festival and how Louise would be showing her work. 'Why didn't you show me this before?'

Cara hadn't seen Tom angry before. His anger was sharpening his features, making his eyes as dark as coal.

'I left it on the kitchen table thinking, perhaps, you'd pick up the paper and flick through and see it. I didn't want you to think, oh God, I don't know what it was I didn't want you to think ... that I was jealous or something. If Louise is still a big part of your life, then I'm thinking I should back off...

'She's not. I didn't know she'd gone to the newspapers. Honestly. I'm left wondering, though, why you've shown me now? After we had such a lovely evening.'

'There didn't seem to be a right time,' Cara said, standing firm but feeling like jelly inside. 'I assumed – wrongly I know now – that you would have seen it and I was wondering why you hadn't told me she was sharing your venue.'

'I didn't tell you because she most definitely isn't. You do believe that, don't you?'

'I want to,' Cara said. 'I believe *you*, but if Louise has arranged it with the organisers ...'

'She hadn't up until a few hours ago when I was hanging my pictures and three members of the committee were there helping. Her name never cropped up. I think it would have if they'd agreed she could share my space. There were no tables up for pottery to be placed on either. So ... I'd say that's a definite no.'

'Perhaps she'll be at another venue?'

'I can't do anything about that if she is,' Tom said. 'She's a bona fide artist, fairly well known in her field.'

'I see,' Cara said.

Cara could also see that the absent but ever-present Louise was spoiling their lovely evening – hers and Tom's.

'Look, Cara,' Tom said. He folded the newspaper back up, walked over to the recycling box Cara kept in an alcove by the back door and threw it in. 'That's exactly what I think of that little story. And I'm sorry if I got angry, but it wasn't at you.'

'I know,' Cara said. 'I wish I hadn't shown you now. It's spoiled everything.'

Tom reached for Cara's hands and held them between his own.

'It hasn't spoiled what we had over dinner tonight. Not for me anyway. I haven't told you before, but when Louise pitched up and we met for dinner in the village she asked if there was

232

anyone in my life. And I said yes, there was. I wasn't entirely truthful. *You* were in my life because I was stopping in your home, but that wasn't what Louise meant by her question and I knew it. She got mad at me then. The upshot is Louise doesn't want me – never did really with all the affairs she had, some of which I knew about but chose to ignore because, well, she was still my muse and we were making money, and I'm not very proud of that now. But she also doesn't want anyone else to have me. Going to the newspaper with a load of lies – and possibly wishful thinking on her part – was an act of revenge. She's done it before. So ...' Tom sighed deeply. 'We might not have a smooth ride of it for a while with Louise but we've begun this journey, you and me, and it will be wonderful if we can continue together. And now if you've got a cork in a drawer somewhere you can stick it in my mouth. I've probably said more than enough.'

'A cork?' Cara said. She didn't know whether to laugh or cry. Her hands were still held firmly between Tom's, and she knew she was shaking slightly, a mixture of apprehension that she'd so badly timed showing him the newspaper cutting but also the fact Tom wanted a future with her. 'No, I don't have a cork, but I'm glad you've told me what you have. Coffee or a nightcap?'

'Coffee, please,' Tom said. He yawned. 'I don't think I've ever spoken as many sentences in a row as I did just now. I need something to revive me.'

'Coffee it is, then,' Cara said. 'In the sitting room?'

'Perfect,' Tom said. He plonked a kiss on Cara's forehead. 'Wake me up if I'm asleep by the time you bring it in.'

But Tom wasn't asleep when she went in with two coffees on a tray. Tom was staring at the painting of her great-grandmother, Emma. In it Emma was wearing a blouse that had seen better days – it was frayed on the collar – and her auburn curls were dishevelled. Her face, thin and milky white, hinted at some sadness, but her eyes held the artist's with something like fire in them.

'I don't believe this,' Tom said.

'Believe what?'

'What a painting! I've never seen a portrait of Seth Jago's before, and I don't think the art world has either. Sometimes there are moments in life when an artist thinks, "I wish I'd painted that" and this is one of them.' Tom held the painting out at arm's length. 'I thought I'd fallen asleep and woken up in a dream when I saw it.'

'It's no dream. It's for real. Family legend has it that he painted it from memory. It was the moment he fell in love with her. I know she'd been made homeless and Seth's scoundrel of a father had something to do with that, but no more. Well, no more except that Seth married her eventually.'

'She looks very young in this painting,' Tom said. 'About the same age Mae is now, I'd say.'

'I've always thought it was so romantic, that story.'

'It's full of soul,' Tom said.

He propped the painting against the sofa cushions, studying it in silence for what seemed, to Cara, like ages.

'You sounded surprised,' Cara said. 'When you saw it.'

'Yeah, I said I like surprises, didn't I?'

'You did. But not the one I gave you with the newspaper cutting?'

'This more that makes up for it as surprises go, Cara. It ranks up there with the best of them,' Tom said. 'But now I think – much against my instincts and because I've just heard the toilet flush, which means Mae is upstairs and I don't think it would be right of me to, well, I think you know what my instincts are about moving us on from those two kisses – I'm going to say goodnight.' He reached for Cara and drew her to him, kissing her long and slow, and utterly sensuously before pulling back to smile into her face, his eyes so bright that Cara could see her

234

reflection in them. 'And you're not the only one who can spring a surprise. Just wait until you see my star exhibit – you aren't going to believe your eyes!'

CHAPTER TWENTY-SEVEN

'I can't believe the exhibition has come around so fast,' Mae said. She was helping Cara make topping for bruschetta because her mother had decided they would have a little party after the private view. 'And sometimes I can't believe that Tom's painted enough paintings to fill the village hall in the short time he's been here. How many, do you know?'

'He hasn't said. All I know is he's changed genre or subject or whatever it is artists call the style they paint in.'

'No nudes, then?' Mae said. Not that it would bother her if there were any because Bailey had explained about how an artist only sees the body as a body, the contours and the skin colour, every blemish if there are any, hair and nails and all the other things. It's not, Bailey had said, that he got a hard-on when he did a life class, even though the model was young and perfect, and possibly in some other circumstance he might have fancied her. All he'd been concerned about was capturing her on paper the best he could.

'I don't think so.'

Mae tipped olive oil into the chopped sun-dried tomatoes and gave it all a good stir. She reached for the pot of basil, tore off a handful, placing it on the chopping board, going at it in best

Jamie Oliver fashion. Scott Matthews in the Boathouse had shown her how to do that.

'When Tom first arrived, me and Josh saw him quite a few times standing on the headland looking out to sea. Once it was quite late, the sun almost gone but not quite. And another time when we walked over to Oyster Cove early one morning, he was sitting on the beach, totally alone. We walked quite close to him but he didn't seem to notice because he was so wrapped up in his drawing.'

Mae didn't really want to bring Josh into the conversation but that's how it had been. Josh had made fun of Tom, calling him a loner or something, and saying art wasn't much of a career, was it? Just for a moment, Mae wondered if Josh might be at the exhibition, and if he might have changed his opinion of art as a career, seeing as everyone in the village seemed to know just how big a name in the art world Tom was.

'You didn't say,' her mother said.

'Yeah, well,' Mae said. She was feeling a bit embarrassed now. 'I didn't like Tom then, did I?'

'But you like him now?'

'I like him better. He hasn't tried to … oh, I don't know how to say this … but he hasn't tried to be my best friend or something, buying me sweets or whatever, so I like him because he likes you.'

Mae gave the bruschetta topping a final mix.

'And I imagine if he had, you'd have told him in no uncertain terms you weren't for buying off!' her mother laughed.

'Probably!' Mae laughed. 'What's next?'

'Just the baby new potatoes to peel and cut in half,' her mum told her. 'They should be cool enough. I thought a cream cheese and paprika filling, scoop out a bit of potato and fill the hole with it.'

'I'll do it. The filling,' Mae said. She went to the fridge for the tub of cream cheese and found the paprika in the spice drawer.

'You know what, Mum,' she said. 'I wouldn't mind catering for a career. Cheffing or something. I've enjoyed my time in the pub. Scott – that's the landlord – let me do some prepping sometimes. Some of the sauces that go with the steaks and fish and that. And he let me have a go at choux pastry when one of the kitchen hands didn't turn up for his duty. Profiteroles are very popular as a dessert, so he said. I didn't mess up anyway, even though he said it's not the easiest pastry to make.'

'You didn't say.'

'Echo, echo,' Mae laughed. 'You said that just now. But a girl doesn't tell her mother everything, you know.'

'Of course she doesn't,' her mum said, putting an arm around Mae's shoulder and giving it a squeeze. 'But I'm glad you're telling me now. And I'm glad that we're talking and doing things together and not dancing round one another like we were for a while when …'

'When we were both struggling to make sense of what happened with Dad and you kept the secret about his gambling a bit too long and I was trying to hang onto being Dad's little princess a bit too long when I was growing up and, oh heck, Mum, that wasn't too easy either, the stuff with Josh and not seeing Bailey for the kind person he is, and hating Tom because, well, he isn't Dad. And Rosie being so bossy with me sometimes.'

Mae tipped cream cheese into a bowl and sprinkled paprika on it.

'Only because she loves you.'

'Yeah, I know,' Mae said. 'Who'd have thought that taking in a few B&B guests could, well, help me grow up a bit is what I'm trying to say.' Mae held her mother's gaze and saw that her eyes were glassy with tears. 'No, no, don't say anything. I'm on the brink myself and we'll ruin these fillings if we drip all over them and, oh God, Mum, I love you.'

'Oh, Mae …' her mum said with a gulp. 'I love you too. So much.' She held out her arms towards Mae.

Mae put down the mixing bowl and threw herself into her mother's arms and they stood like that for a few moments, rocking and hugging.

'I don't know where this new and confident daughter who has such profound thoughts has come from but it's making me so happy, I think I might burst. Your dad would be so proud.'

'Yeah,' Mae said. 'He'd be proud of you too. The way you've made a success of this B&B lark even though I resisted a bit.'

'A bit?' her mum laughed.

'A lot then. Sorry. But not just that, there's your dressmaking and stuff.' Mae began to pull from her mother's embrace. 'Hey! I've had an idea. We could turn our dining room into a restaurant – we never use it. We could go for something high-end, foodie. Keep it small. Pop up restaurant style. Not just for B&B guests but the public too. I could do a course …'

'You could. And you can start by making profiteroles for later. I hadn't thought of dessert.'

'I don't think there's time for that,' Mae said. 'Have we got lard?'

'Lard?'

'Yeah, you know, beef fat. Dripping.'

Cara knew what lard was, but not that you made choux pastry with it.

'Er, no.'

'Another time, then,' Mae said. 'How many are coming back anyway? There's an awful lot of stuff here already.'

'You and me, Rosie, Tom, Bailey if he wants to come. Tom asked if he could bring his agent, Claire, and her husband because she'll be down from London, and there might be a handful of people there who've bought his work before … fans, I suppose … and he said if there were, it might be nice to invite them along. Say, a dozen or so?'

'Could I ask Bailey's sister and her boyfriend? She's got the night off and Bailey said because she wants to go to the exhibition.'

'Of course you can. The more the merrier.'

For a few minutes Mae and her mother carried on putting the finishing touches to fillings, peeling the last of the potatoes together and cutting them in half. Yes, she wouldn't mind doing this for a living ... there was something pleasing about making simple things like a potato look good. Taste good too.

'Like Bailey,' Mae said, 'his sister's good at art but hasn't done anything with it up to now. This art festival has made a lot of people think, hasn't it? Changed them?'

'Pointed them in the direction they didn't know they needed to go maybe?' her mum said.

'Yeah, and that's another thing,' Mae said. She wiped her hands down the sides of her apron and took it off. 'The frocks, Mum. I love them and always will but, well, I wore them for Dad really. We used to watch all those old black and white movies together. Remember?'

'I remember,' her mum said.

'You make that sound a bit sad.' Mae realised now that perhaps she and her dad had excluded her mum from their little bubble of old films watching. 'They aren't your thing, are they, old black and white movies?'

'Not really. But it was something you and your dad shared so that was fine with me.'

'Yeah, I know that now. But back to the frocks ... I don't know that I want to wear them all the time any more. I wore them for Dad and kept on wearing them after he died because it made him feel closer. I know he'll always be close, but maybe it's time to wear stuff for me. I know you've only just made me a new one and I'll keep it – I'll keep them all because there'll be times like school proms and parties and stuff when it'll be fun to wear them, but ...'

Mae shrugged her shoulders. But what else could she wear to the exhibition? She only had her school uniform and some ancient sports' gear.

240

'I don't suppose I could borrow a pair of your jeans? And a top of some sort? One of your lacy strappy ones?'

'Now there's a question I never thought I'd hear from my fifteen-year-old daughter! Of course you can. But I can do better than that. I've been squirreling away stuff I thought you might like to wear sometime. Only last week I found some Levi's in the Animals in Distress charity shop that I'm pretty sure have never been worn and that will fit you. Come on, let's go and find them. Tom wants you and me there half an hour before the others turn up, remember?'

'Yeah,' Mae said. 'He told me twice.'

Mae wondered why, but when Tom had told her, he'd had a silly grin on his face as though he had some delicious secret – something she'd be pleased about.

'And me,' her mum said.

'Probably early-onset dementia or something,' Mae said with as straight a face as she could manage.

'Mae, that's …'

'Only joking!' Mae said. Honestly, her mum was so easy to wind up!

'And I'm a bit on edge wondering what we're going to see. I'm beginning to feel a bit anxious now. Anyway, we can't stand here chatting much longer. Rosie will be here soon and I've still to get myself tidied up a bit, turn the sow's ear that's my cooking gear into the silk purse required of a private view.'

'From where I'm standing, Mum,' Mae said, grinning broadly, 'Tom wouldn't notice if you turned up in a bin bag. He's besotted.' She began to run for the door, but stopped to turn round and look back. 'But why take the risk?'

CHAPTER TWENTY-EIGHT

'Cara?' Rosie said. 'You okay? You look sort of spacey?'

Rosie had just pitched up – early – for the private view, looking like she'd stepped from the front page of *Vogue* in a black and white striped off-the-shoulder dress with an asymmetric hem, and heels so high Cara feared she'd snap an ankle on the pebbled pathway up to the village hall.

'Who wouldn't after the conversation I've just had with my daughter?'

'Oh God, what now?' Rosie said. 'I saw her rushing off down the road just now as I drove up. I hardly recognised her for a moment, actually. Jeans? Mae? And a top I think I bought you for your last birthday. Something cataclysmic must have happened to get her out of her period frocks. Not that Josh-waste-of-space back on the scene?'

'Nothing like,' Cara said. 'Sit down. I'll tell you. And before you tell me it's far, far, too early to be drinking Prosecco, I'm having one. I need it. And you can have one too. You can stop the night because there aren't any guests in. Only Tom.'

'And he's graduated to live-in lover?'

'Not, um, yet,' Cara said.

'That's my girl. Ever cautious,' Rosie giggled. 'But he might.'

'He might. And that's all I'm saying,' Cara said. 'My lips on that subject from now on are sealed!' She took the Prosecco from the fridge, and found two glasses. Deftly she took out the cork and began to fill the glasses.

'Are you sure you haven't downed a bottle already? Your cheeks are all pink and you're sort of sparkly. You look great, by the way. Chartreuse is a colour only a redhead like you can wear, and if you weren't my best friend I'd hate you for it because it's my fave colour, but it makes me look like a cadaver.'

'I'll take that back-handed compliment, thank you,' Cara laughed.

She was glad she'd chosen that particular dress now. Cut on the bias with a petticoat neckline and a frilled hem that stopped just above her ankles, it made her feel younger, sexier, slimmer. And comfortable.

'If it's not a post-coital glow you've got, then it's something. And I want some.'

'The glow or the Prosecco?'

'Both.' Rosie held out a perfectly manicured hand – the nail polish the colour and gloss of a London taxi in the rain – for the glass Cara was handing to her. 'God but it's good to see you looking so … stunning wouldn't be too strong a word to use. You sure you've not been on the bottle already?' She reached out and with the back of her hand and touched it to Cara's cheek. 'Yep, you're hot! We must live in hope that Tom thinks so too when he sees you …'

'Stop it! And no, this is the first today. There'll be more later, but this is a little celebration. I'm glad you're early because I wouldn't have wanted to celebrate alone.'

'Quite right too,' Rosie said. 'Never drink alone is my motto. To which end, I've got this little white velour bear called Blanco I prop up in a chair if ever I feel the need for, er, a little celebration.'

'You don't?'

'I do. And stop hedging. What are we celebrating?'

'Mae. Me and Mae. I've got my daughter back. You wouldn't believe what she was telling me just now. Just spilling out of her it was, like the bubbles that just spilled out of this bottle.'

'I won't believe it if you don't tell me, sweetie,' Rosie said.

So Cara did, gulping back tears of emotion and joy every now and then. She told Rosie everything. Topping up their glasses when they'd drunk them down halfway. Dutch courage.

'Seems prepping food is as good as therapy, then?' Rosie said. 'And cheaper. And I have to commend you for your fortitude in fighting the waterfall that was threatening to tumble over – it would have wrecked your mascara. And bloodshot is so not a good look. Where's Mae gone anyway?'

'To Bailey's. She's gone to invite him and his sister and her boyfriend back later.'

'Christ!' Rosie said. 'How much do they eat? I mean, there's you and me, Tom, and four of Mae and her gang, but there's enough stuff here for a Downing Street drinks' party.'

'I'm just hoping it'll be enough. Tom's agent and her husband are coming, and some other arty people from London and possibly some people who collect Tom's work ...'

'Some single ones, I hope. Of the male variety. Someone to give me the glow that you've got, and if you think I believe it's totally down to the fact you and Mae have stopped being at one another's throats, then you're living in cloud cuckoo land! And what's more ...'

Cara picked up a prawn-stuffed canapé.

'Open wide,' she said. 'I think only eating is going to stop your nonsense!'

And with that she ran from the room in search of her bag and a cardigan for later in case they were later back than expected. Cara had never been to a private viewing before, or an art exhibition for that matter, despite having collected art, because she'd always bought from galleries before. Like Mae had said so very recently … the art exhibition was changing so many people in so many ways.

Who'd have thought it!

'Mae?' Bailey said as he opened his front door to her knock.

'I know. Bit of a shock, isn't it? But it's me.'

'Is something wrong? You said to meet me at the hall. You've not changed your mind or something?'

Bailey looked concerned, like he was going to be given the brush-off or something, although most people did that by text these days.

'Nope,' Mae said. 'Mind's as good as it ever was. It's my clothes I've changed. Can I come in?'

Mae had never been to Bailey's house – a small terraced cottage at a right-angle to the harbour, with just one window beside the small front door and two bedroom windows and a dormer above. The contrast between how small it was and her own, large home up on the hill was a bit of a surprise. How did they all fit in – Bailey and his parents and his sister, Xia?

'Course,' Bailey said. He leaned in to kiss Mae and she could smell the fragrance he used … or it could be aftershave, although she didn't think Bailey had started shaving yet.

He ushered her inside. 'Excuse the smell of fish. Some holidaymaker came into the pub with mackerel they'd caught on a fishing trip but couldn't take back to their hotel. So Xia brought some home.'

'Smells good to me,' Mae said. She leaned towards Bailey who had grabbed hold of her hand to draw her into the house.

'Who is it, Bailey?' Mae heard Mrs Lucas call.

'Mae,' Bailey shouted back.

His mother came bustling out. Mae had only ever seen her at school events a couple of times, but she was younger and prettier than she'd remembered, probably the same age as her own mum but not so stylishly dressed. Not that that mattered.

245

'Hello, lovie,' she said. 'Bailey's told me all about you.'

Mae liked the use of the term 'lovie' that Devonians used – from Mrs Lucas's lips it sounded almost like a caress.

'Oh, has he?' Mae said.

'The good bits, of course,' Mrs Lucas said. 'Don't fret. Do you want a cup of tea, lovie?'

She looked genuinely pleased that Mae had turned up.

'No thanks,' Mae said. 'I've got to be down at the hall in, oh God, ten minutes or something, but I wanted to ask if Xia and her boyfriend would like to come back to ours after. Mum's having a bit of a "do" for Tom. You know, the artist who's been stopping. We live at Cove End.'

'I know where you live, lovie,' Mrs Lucas said. 'Lovely house it is. And busy as a B&B, so I've heard. Well good for your mum, I say. And I'm sure Xia would love to. She's in the shower at the moment – I expect you can hear it jumping off its chocks up there, she's been in there so long!'

Mrs Lucas was beginning to sound as nervous about Mae being in her hallway as Mae was about being there. So many people knew so much about her, what had happened with her dad, and it must be as awkward for them as it was for her. Mrs Lucas wasn't judging her though, she could tell.

'Mum! You're rabbiting,' Bailey said. 'And is that fish burning I can smell?'

'Oh, lawks, it could be,' Mrs Lucas said, turning to run back to the kitchen.

On impulse Mae followed, dragging Bailey with her.

The Lucas kitchen was small but quirkily laid out with open shelves on the walls, and curtains on the bottom cupboards instead of doors.

'Just caught it!' Mrs Lucas said, pulling the pan from the flame.

'Sorry, that was my fault, just turning up,' Mae said. She inhaled the distinctive aroma of pan-friend mackerel fillets. She'd always

246

loved fish. Well, you couldn't live in Larracombe and not like fish!

'Gooseberry sauce goes well with mackerel,' Mae said. 'And I know it sounds all wrong because it's for Christmas, but cranberry jelly's not bad either.'

Where was all this stuff coming from? Jamie Oliver cookery programmes and Scott at the Beachcomber were her sum total of culinary advice. But she'd tried both and liked it. Before today she didn't think she'd have dared give advice to someone who must have cooked hundreds of meals for her family.

'Well, the jelly I can do,' Mrs Lucas said, reaching for a jar on one of the open shelves. 'Me and the resident hero have got a lot to eat up now seeing as Bailey and Xia will be up at yours later.'

The resident hero? Mr Lucas presumably? What a fabulous expression!

'You could come as well if you want, Mrs Lucas,' Mae said. 'Save the mackerel for another day. Mum's made, like, mountains of stuff. And there'll be fizz. Only Prosecco but ...'

'There's posh!' Mrs Lucas laughed. 'But not this time, lovie. Some other time.'

'Mae?' Bailey said, anxiously now. 'Isn't there some place you have to be?'

'Yeah, yeah. Sorry.' Mae glanced at the clock on the kitchen wall. She only had about ten minutes to get there now ... she could make it if she ran.

'Bye, Mrs Lucas,' Mae said as Bailey practically dragged her to the door.

'Nothing like your posh place, is it?' he said.

'Don't!' Mae said. 'It's your home, and it's lovely. I like your mum.'

Mae liked that Mrs Lucas had given her children unusual names. If ever she had a child, she'd make sure to give him, or her, an unusual name, something to make her child feel special,

247

different in a good way. And besides, Bailey's dad was still at home and what would Mae give to be able to say 'Mum and Dad' again in the same sentence.

'She goes on a bit sometimes,' Bailey said. 'She knows about your dad but like I said, we don't blab in this family. Anyway, I'm keeping you. Got to get myself into something smarter for later. It's starting to feel a bit grown up, all this art private viewing stuff and coming to yours afterwards. You look great by the way.'

Bailey ran a hand up and down Mae's arm and it made her tingle in a way his touch hadn't before, not like that anyway. Perhaps she was growing up a bit as well, wanting more than hand-holding and a few kisses with Bailey.

'Thanks for the compliment,' Mae said. 'I thought it was time to embrace the twenty-first century. D'you know this is the first pair of jeans I've ever owned. Well, loaned, because they're Mum's.'

'You didn't have to do it for me, Mae, you know that,' Bailey said. 'Okay, I won't lie and say I haven't I've had a bit of stick for being seen out with you in the fancy frocks, but Mum said it was only jealousy and to ignore it.'

'Best way,' Mae said. 'But I'll put one on for the school prom … if you'll be my escort?'

The prom wasn't until November – months away yet – but she hoped she'd still be going out with Bailey then. She'd let him know as much anyway.

'That's a date,' Bailey said. 'Old-fashioned word "date" but it's kind of appropriate, eh?'

Mae smiled but couldn't think of a thing to say. The conversation seemed to have run its course, but no doubt it would flow easily enough again once the exhibition was over and they were back at Cove End discussing it.

'Right, I'm off,' Mae said. 'See you in … whatever.'

She turned and ran down the hill.

CHAPTER TWENTY-NINE

'Darling, I don't think I can,' Cara said. 'I'm getting cold feet.'

Mae, looking so young and fresh and flushed with a sort of dog-rose glow about her cheeks, had an arm linked through Cara's and was almost dragging her towards the village hall. There was a huge sign across the door.

TOM GASSON-SMITH – INTERNATIONALLY RENOWNED ARTIST

Just Tom. No mention of Louise. Cara breathed a sigh of relief.

'Mum, you have to. Tom went on and on about how I had to get you there, so I asked him what it was worth and he said, possibly a tablet – a Dell. They're the best.'

'Mae, Tom is *not* going to buy you an expensive tablet. Or any tablet for that matter. If anyone buys you a tablet, it will be me.'

'Whoever comes up with the readies first,' Mae said with a grin. 'But we'd better go in. And before Rosie arrives. You know what she's like – she'll get all hyper-excited being in the same room as a famous artist and everything.'

She leaned against Cara's shoulder and Cara rather liked this new turn of events, with Mae less snippy. Happier. She'd even stopped calling Tom, Michelangelo.

'You look good in jeans, Mae,' Cara said, still not quite believing that Mae was wearing her first-ever pair of jeans. 'I would have bought them for you before, only …'

'Delaying tactics,' Mae butted in. 'Stop it, Mum. What I'm wearing is not the issue here today, okay?'

'Okay,' Cara said, knowing she'd been trying to hold off the moment. She must have had hundreds of imagined scenarios about what Tom's paintings would be of, and why he said she was going to get a surprise, but she had a feeling she hadn't thought of whatever it was actually going to be.

'Well, we're here,' Mae said, as arm-in-arm, mother and daughter arrived at the door of the village hall.

Cara took her arm from Mae's and pushed open the door. She took a deep, steadying breath. How stupid to be so nervous about looking at a few paintings.

'But there's no one here,' Cara said as she and Mae, hand-in-hand, closed the door of the hall behind them.

'Only me,' Tom said, suddenly appearing from behind the stage curtain. 'Thanks for coming, Cara.'

'What about me?' Mae asked, mock-outraged. She gripped even tighter to Cara's hand.

'Both of you, of course.' Tom jumped off the stage and walked towards them. 'The whole package. I'll just drop the latch to stop the world and his wife coming in for a moment,' Tom said, skirting round Cara and Mae to do so. 'Come on.' He grabbed Cara's free hand and drew her towards a row of paintings. In silence, they stood – the three of them – in a row looking at Tom's work. All seascapes. All huge. Oils. The sea filled each frame, dancing with colour. From a distance the sea appeared to be turquoise, or deep navy, but up close Cara could see there were many colours in each dab of paint, colours you wouldn't associate with the sea, like pink, orange and brown. There was very little foreground in any of them, just a few stems of mauve thrift, or a gull disappearing out of the corner of the painting.

And very little sky either, just a thin ribbon of it at the top of each painting – the pearly grey of dawn, or the raspberry ripple of sunset. The prices were eye-watering – nothing was less than three thousand pounds. Cara would have loved to buy one, but she'd need another three or four seasons at Cove End to be able to afford one at those prices.

More seascapes hung on the opposite wall, but this time they were all watercolours. The sea didn't dominate in them either. Sometimes a yacht filled the frame with just a border of sea around it, or a massive expanse of sand with a child's sandcastle and a discarded flip-flop with the sea in the distance at low tide.

'Blimey, you're good, Tom,' Mae said. 'Bailey is going to love these. He's like, good at art, but not that good.'

'Thanks, Mae,' Tom said. 'I wasn't good when I started, just had a love of it. The more I painted, the more I studied the masters and other – often amateur – artists, the better I got at it. Bailey will too if he's got the passion.'

'Yeah,' Mae said. 'But they're not cheap, are they? I mean … what?' Mae pointed to a study of a fishing boat lying at anchor, in a sea that was almost the blood-red of sunset, tipped slightly to port. 'Eighteen hundred pounds and it's, what, no bigger than A3!'

'Mae!' Cara said.

'Well if the prices do nothing but inspire Bailey to pursue his craft then they'll have served a purpose!' Tom laughed.

'I'm sorry …' Cara began. She thought Mae had lost all her snippiness around Tom, but obviously she hadn't.

'Don't be,' Tom said. 'I've had harsher art critics than that! Anyway, now you've seen what I've been doing in the weeks I've been holed up in your dormer bedroom, come and see these.'

In the middle of the room were two easels, both had paintings on them but were covered with sheets – Cara's best top sheets, she realised now. Tom must have borrowed them.

'Is this why you've asked us to come a bit early?' Cara asked.

Her stomach was in knots now and blood was pulsing past her ears with nerves. She gripped more tightly onto Tom's hand.

'You're going to have to let me go for a second, Cara,' Tom said. 'I'm in danger of having the blood supply cut off the way you're gripping.'

'Sorry, but ...' Cara began as she released Tom's hand.

'Give me a hand with the sheet, Mae, can you?' Tom said. He turned to Cara. 'I'll bring your sheets back, I promise. And I'll put them through the washing-machine. I might even come over all domestic and get the iron out. Right, Mae, on the count of three, pull the sheet your side up and over very gently. One, two, three.'

'Oh my God!' Mae said, once the painting was revealed. 'That's me.'

'Phew!' Tom laughed. 'My credibility as an artist is intact if you recognise yourself from behind!'

'But when?' Cara said. 'When did you paint that?'

Cara had seen Mae like that, rushing off down the path dressed in one of her beloved frocks, so many times – she knew the back view of her daughter as well as she knew the front. In the painting Mae was wearing one of her frocks, the turquoise one with the white polka dots. It stopped mid-calf showing off Mae's slim ankles, and Mae was in the foreground, filling the frame. Tom had captured the crazy paving of the path that led down to the front gate, a few bluish/purple campanulas creeping out of the gaps on the edges of the painting. The B&B sign could just be seen – slightly out of focus – in the distance, swinging rather lopsidedly from a gatepost. Mae's glossy hair was catching the sunlight almost like it was on fire.

'Very early on in my stay. I didn't really know either of you then, but when I looked out of the window, wondering if the view down over the town towards the sea would make a good painting, Mae came rushing out. Her energy was palpable. In my mind's eye, I saw her rushing to the life she was going to make for herself. I loved the youth and freshness about her and the fact she wasn't – isn't – afraid to go against what her peer group does. So …'

'Stop,' Mae said. 'You're embarrassing me now.'

Cara turned to look at her daughter and yes, there were pink patches on her cheeks.

'Well, it's all true,' Tom said. 'I've always got a camera handy so I took a quick snap and then used artistic licence to make it look as though I'd been standing at the front door and not two floors above you.'

'Right,' Mae said. She took a few steps forward and had her nose almost up against the canvas now. She pointed to a sticker on the bottom left-hand corner of the frame. 'What does NFS mean?'

'Not for sale,' Cara and Tom said as one.

There had been more than a few paintings over the years that Cara had admired and would have liked to have bought, which had carried NFS stickers; paintings close to the artists' hearts no doubt.

'But it's for you, Mae,' Tom said.

'Oh, but we can't …' Cara began.

Tom put up a hand to stop her.

'For Mae, Cara. That one's for you.' He reached out to tap a finger on the top of the canvas still shrouded in Cara's best three-hundred-thread Egyptian cotton sheet. 'Want to see?'

'Yes,' Cara said, her voice a whisper. Her heart began to hammer terrifyingly fast in her chest now. What was under there? Had he used more artistic licence and being a figurative artist had superimposed her face onto someone else's naked body? 'No.'

'As Jeremy Paxman would say on *University Challenge* … I'll take your first answer! Can you help take the sheet off, Mae, please?'

Cara closed her eyes, screwed them up tight.

'On the count of three,' Mae said, as though she was now an expert at revealing artworks. 'One, two, three.'

There was a little pause, a moment of complete silence when all Cara could hear was the loud tick of the clock on the wall behind her and then Mae said, 'Like, wow!'

Cara, still with her eyes screwed shut so tightly she was beginning to get a pain across her forehead, tried to read the meaning behind those two, small words. Not shock. Not horror. Something like admiration. Awe.

Tom placed a hand, very gently, in the centre of Cara's back and said, 'You can open your eyes now. Mae hasn't gone screaming and running from the room with shock now has she?'

'No.' Cara opened her eyes. 'Argh!' Cara placed both hands across her mouth. She couldn't quite believe what she was seeing. It was, undoubtedly, a head and shoulders portrait of her. Her hair was a tumble of uncombed curls, she had no make-up on, and the collar of her old raincoat was up on one side where she'd not done up the top button properly. Tom had captured her in the moment of relief that Mae was safe after the sailing incident. She ought, she thought, to not like being reminded of that one little bit, but Tom hadn't known then what the situation was that night, the night he'd arrived and alarmed her in the semi-darkness by taking a flash photograph of her. There was an NFS sticker on this painting too.

'Blimey, Mum,' Mae said. 'He's made you look beautiful.' She ducked sideways out of reach anticipating, perhaps, that Cara might give her a playful smack for her cheek. 'Only joking!'

'She *is* beautiful, Mae,' Tom said.

'Right, if this is going to get all soppy,' Mae said with a theatrical yawn, 'I'm out of here. I need to see Bailey. I want to tell him about the painting of me before everyone else sees it.'

'So you're okay about it being on display to the public?' Tom said.

'Yeah. Why not?'

'And you, Cara?' Tom said. 'It doesn't have to be. I can put it up on the stage behind the curtain. No problem.'

'If Mae's fine with it, then so am I,' Cara said.

'I didn't mean my painting of Mae. I meant the one of you.'

'I'll leave you two to fight it out,' Mae said, then ran for the door.

'Five minutes,' Tom said. 'I …'

Cara put a finger up to his lips.

'Don't say anything. I'm still in shock. I look just like the painting that Seth Jago did of my great-grandmother, don't I? I'd never thought of that before, not that I've ever looked at that painting very much. And I can't believe you've reproduced the subject almost exactly, when you only saw Emma's portrait a day or so ago.'

'Ah yes, I was going to come to that. This is going to have to be quick because, as Mae said, we've only got five minutes to opening time and the local TV crew will be here and my agent and then I might not get a chance to speak to you 'til we're back at Cove End. But … that story you told me about Seth falling in love with Emma the second he saw her in that raggedy blouse and looking so thin after she'd been so ill, and how the fire in her gave her a sort of glow, do you remember?'

'I remember.'

'Well, it feels almost impossible for me to believe it myself now, but that was the first painting I did up there in my garret. That was my "Seth" moment. I didn't know what had happened to you that night, only that something had. You looked frightened and yet determined at the same time. You had that battered old raincoat on and you hadn't done up the buttons properly so one collar was higher than the other and I loved that. I guessed you'd put it on a hurry and possibly because it was giving you comfort in a way you weren't getting from anywhere else. My heart missed a beat or five, I can tell you …'

'Five?' Cara said.

'Maybe I underexaggerate,' Tom laughed. 'Seven. I counted. And I knew beyond doubt when it kicked back in again that I had fallen in love with you at first sight. An old sceptic like me who's never watched a romantic comedy, or read a romantic novel, and who would have given his life savings – not a lot, I have to say, despite the price tags on my paintings – to argue that falling in love at first sight was impossible. I had no idea how things were for you – married, single, divorced, straight, gay ... although I never considered widowed – but I knew in that moment, however you felt about me, I'd never change those feelings for you. They'd forever be in my heart.'

'That's quite the loveliest thing anyone has ever said to me.' Cara reached out to run a finger along the NFS sign – *'Forever in my Heart* – NFS' it read.

'All true,' Tom said.

'It was a slower burn for me,' Cara said. 'A bit like rubbing two sticks together to make a flame and having to hold a piece of cotton wool over it to get it to ignite. But slowly it came. Warming. Burning sometimes. I can't imagine not having you in my life now.'

She turned and folded herself into Tom's arms.

'And that's the loveliest thing anyone has ever said to me,' Tom said. 'I love you, Cara.'

'I love ...'

But Cara didn't get to finish the sentence because there was a bang on the door and she heard Rosie shout, 'Make yourselves decent in there! We're coming in!'

Oh well, it didn't matter. Tom would have got the gist of what she was going to say, and they'd have plenty of time in the future to say it. And there were still two full days of the art festival to go yet. A frisson of pure delight shimmied up Cara's back and across her shoulders that she was now very much part of it.

'Mum,' Mae said when they were back at Cove End. 'I hope you don't mind, but I've invited one of the artists to supper.'

'Sure,' Cara said. At that moment she would have said yes to anything, she was so happy. Cara had been introduced to Tom's agent and her husband – Claire and Martin – and she'd stood watching mesmerised as Tom had done a TV interview as though he did it every day. At least half a dozen patrons had come up to say hello and be introduced too, and within an hour every painting had been sold. It was then that Tom had suggested she might like to go and look at some of the other venues where artwork was on display. Not just paintings and drawings, but ceramics too. Even some woodwork. In the lifeboat station, wall space had been shared by three artists and Cara particularly liked the work of one of them – Janey Cooper – which was largely studies of stones and shells, and birds with wisps of seaweed, sort of semi-abstracted, but the canvases almost came alive. Cara had bought one. She had it now, wrapped in brown paper, under her arm. She and Mae were first back at the house and it was going to be a rush to get everything laid out on time.

'Great,' Mae said. 'Bailey and Xia will be here in a minute with Ben. They said they'd do all the washing up. Great, eh?'

'Great,' Cara agreed. The guest list was expanding rapidly because Rosie had been chatted up by one of Tom's patrons – Luke something or other – and she'd asked if she could bring him along as her Plus One. Cara didn't think anyone would mind if they were running a bit late, but it would be best if they ate tonight and not at breakfast time tomorrow. 'We'd better get on, though.'

'Yeah. What've you bought?'

'Janey Cooper. From the lifeboat station.'

'No!' Mae said. 'Really?'

'Really.'

'Wow! Meant to be! That's who I've invited! She runs art classes over in Hollacombe. A place called Strand House. Bailey's booked himself in.'

Cara unwrapped the painting. It was small but exquisite. Her first purchase of what she hoped would turn into a new collection.

'Bailey will be well taught, I think,' Cara said.

'Won't he just,' Mae said. 'All he's got to do now is save up the readies to pay for it. Xia said she could get him something in the pub.'

'Good. Things are always sweeter, I think, if you have to work for them a bit, not just get things handed to you on a plate.'

Cara walked across the kitchen and propped her new painting on the windowsill, well out of harm's way from any cooking or drinks that might get spilled.

'Like you with your B&B,' Mae said.

'Just like *our* B&B, darling,' Cara told her. 'Anyway, can you get on toasting the bruschetta and I'll un-cling the fillings? Thank goodness there are pizzas in the freezer because I think we're going to need them.'

There'd be time to defrost some chipolatas and get them in the oven with some oil and honey, and maybe a few sesame seeds if she had some – back-up if everyone was starving. Some venues had offered nibbles and wine, although Tom's hadn't. Perhaps he hadn't liked to ask Cara if she'd take on that job. Well, next time she'd ask. Next time. What a delicious thought that was! 'A glass of wine?'

'Mother!' Mae said, mock-shocked. 'I'm underage!'

'Not in your own home, you're not,' Cara said, 'but you can always say no.'

'Yeah, like I did with Josh. I was good at that, wasn't I?'

'You were. So is that yes or no to my offer? I'm having one anyway, bad influence that I am!'

How good it felt to be having this banter with Mae. How good it felt that Mae was bringing up her uncomfortable recent past but yet moving on with it. Just like she was.

'Just a little one,' Mae said. 'While we work.'

Cara poured them both a small glass of Viognier – a visiting present from Rosie – and they set to work for fifteen minutes or so, mostly in silence, although Mae was humming something under her breath Cara didn't recognise. And how good that felt, to see and hear Mae being happy again. A sort of peace had descended on them, on the house.

And then that peace was shattered as Rosie came flying into the kitchen, rosy with too much gratis wine at all the events she'd been to at a guess, dragging Luke something-or-other with her.

'This is Luke,' Rosie said. 'Luke, this is the bestest most beautiful friend in the world, Cara. And Mae – that's M A E, not M A Y, for when you're writing birthday and Christmas cards – who's the bestest most beautiful goddaughter a woman could ever have, even though she doesn't always listen to my pearls of wisdom.'

Cara burst out laughing. Talk about moving fast if she was already seeing Luke as someone permanent in her life who'd be putting his name to birthday and Christmas cards! Perhaps Rosie had fallen in love at last, not just in lust? But that was Rosie, who was looking totally beautiful and glamorous and high-end, with Luke a very good match for her, in Cara's opinion, in what could only be designer jeans and shirt and loafers.

'Very wise at times, I'd say, Mae,' Luke said, his eyes still on Rosie and there was something in those chocolate Minstrel eyes of his that told Cara he was as smitten with Rosie at first sight as Tom had told her he'd been with her. Perhaps it was something in the air around here? Perhaps it was art itself that was enhancing all their lives? She'd try and remember to ask Tom later what he thought.

And then, as though just thinking about him had conjured him up, there he was with his agent, Claire, and her husband whose name Cara had forgotten for a moment because seeing Tom seemed to have robbed her of rational thought. Cara's turn for her heart to stop for a few seconds ... one, two, three ...

before it kicked in again seeing Tom. Tom had been telling porkies saying his had stopped for seven seconds, but it made a good story. She'd try to remember to tell Rosie in the morning.

'I'll do the drinks, shall I?' Tom said. 'I know where just about everything is around here now.' He plonked a kiss on Cara's forehead.

'Please,' she said.

'How many are we?'

'No idea. But there are more than enough glasses, and hopefully enough wine.'

'Ah, I've pre-empted you there,' Claire said, revealing a bottle of wine hanging from each hand. 'We both have.'

Her husband revealed his haul – two bottles in each hand – and swung them up onto the kitchen island.

The doorbell rang then.

'I'll get it. Then I'll do the drinks,' Tom said and ran to answer it.

'Got his feet under the table, then?' Rosie quipped with a nod at Tom's retreating back. 'And his legs?'

'I hope so,' Cara quipped back. 'Rather lovely legs, don't you think?'

'I wouldn't know!' Rosie said. 'Anyway, I'm not looking any more.' She plonked a very noisy kiss on Luke's cheek.

Tom was back in seconds to stand in the kitchen doorway and say, 'Nine more. Patrons and partners. Shall I show them in the sitting room? Followed by the drinks, of course.'

But he went off to do it anyway without waiting for an answer.

Mae shouted across the chitchat in the room that the bruschettas were done, the pizzas were in the oven, the sausages were just about to take their place and could everyone get out of her hair and follow Tom so she could 'get on'.

Cara had a sudden vision of Mae's future, running her own busy restaurant as chef patron of her own kitchen shouting 'Pass' and loving every second of it.

They all disappeared, only to be replaced by Bailey, Xia and Ben, with Janey Cooper in tow. Oh, and someone else. A man, Janey's man?

'I hope you don't mind, Cara,' Janey said, 'but I quite forgot to tell Mae and Bailey that James would be coming later to meet me.'

'Of course not,' Cara said.

'We've brought our own welcome with us,' Janey said. She had something in a plastic bag swinging from one hand.

Oh God, not more wine.

'Lovely,' Cara said. 'Thank you.'

'They'll need defrosting, but my guess is by the time we've eaten our way through that lot they will be.'

'Not wine then?' Cara laughed.

'Nope. Profiteroles. Two dozen. We just caught the corner shop before it closed.'

'That was going to be my call,' Mae said. 'Profiteroles. But I didn't have time.'

'If you're ever strapped for some readies,' Tom said to Cara when everyone had either left or gone upstairs to bed, 'you could always be an events manager. That was superb!'

He and Cara were sitting on the sofa, Tom's arm around her shoulder, his hand dangling over her upper arm. When he spoke, turning his head to look at her, she could feel his warm breath on the side of her neck, ruffling the hair behind her ear a little. Tickling. Cara couldn't ever remember feeling more cosy or comfortable. She was in no hurry to move. Not yet.

'Thanks,' Cara said, 'but I think it was the people who made it. I kept stopping to look around the room and couldn't quite believe that most of them had been total strangers to one another before tonight.'

'There was that, but when artists and art lovers get together, there's always more than a bit of common ground and it makes things easier. I'll stick my head above the parapet again and say it was still you being the king pin, as it were, that brought it all together.'

Cara snuggled up to Tom a bit more – how safe he made her feel. At the beginning of the summer she hadn't been looking for 'safe', or a new man in her life for that matter, because she'd been intent on making a new life for herself. And Mae, of course. She knew now she was more than capable of that but, oh, how much sweeter it was to share, as she was sharing now with Tom, as they did a 'debrief'.

'And Mae,' Cara said. 'Mae helped. More than. Did she tell you Bailey's booked to do a painting course with Janey Cooper over at Hollacombe?'

'No. Bailey did. And Janey. I've not seen her work before, but she's good. I introduced her to Claire because I know how useful it can be to have an agent and they were getting on like the proverbial house on fire the last time I looked. Janey said they've exchanged numbers.'

'Networking,' Cara said. 'Sharing info and the like. I've not seen it in action before.' She wondered if there might be some sort of networking site for B&B landladies that she could join – if only to put out warnings about people like the Hines who had almost ended Cara's business venture before it had begun.

'Ah, yes,' Tom said. 'I've got one more snippet of info. Which you may or may not want to hear.'

He grimaced slightly.

'Louise?' Cara said.

'The very same.'

'So tell.'

'She's sacked Claire as her agent. It came as a bit of a shock. Anyway, she's gone off to New York apparently.'

'A perfect end to a perfect evening, I'd say,' Cara said, smiling, doing her best to keep 'smug-satisfied' from her voice but knowing she'd failed miserably.

'Me too.'

As the party had wrapped itself noisily around her, Cara had glanced across the room and seen Tom and Claire talking earnestly. She'd wondered then what it might have been about but guessed now what it might have been.

She'd turned her attention to the slightly surreal scene being acted out in her own sitting room, with everyone having made an effort to dress, well, in an arty fashion so they stood out, but not in an ostentatious way. Well, apart from Rosie, but she was never going to change, and thank goodness for that. Cara had heard her giggling earlier as she said a very noisy, kissy-kissy, goodnight to Luke on the doorstep. Cara had said he could stop the night too if Rosie wanted him to, but she'd held up her hands in mock-horror and said she didn't do sex on the first date, but if the offer was still open tomorrow she'd take Cara up on it.

'So Claire's swapped Louise for Janey?' Cara said. She knew writers had agents, but she'd had no idea artists did too.

'She has,' Tom said. 'It's a myth that artists starve in their garrets waiting for recognition! They have to get out there and sell themselves these days, or pay a fee for someone to do it for them.'

'You might have starved in yours,' Cara said, pointing to the ceiling where Tom's room was overhead, 'had I not taken pity on you and left food parcels!'

'And very delicious it all was, too,' Tom said. 'The way to a man's heart is through his stomach and all that.' He leaned in to kiss Cara, very noisily, on the cheek.

'No other way?' Cara quipped.

'Might be,' Tom said with a grin. With his free hand he tapped his heart. 'And I laid that on the line, didn't I, when I did that painting of you? Seth Jago did, too, when he painted Emma. A man – or a woman for that matter – can paint with emotion, but he can't always paint emotion ... there's a difference.'

'Explain,' Cara said. There was still an awful lot for her to learn about art. And about Tom.

'Like I said down at the exhibition, it was love at first sight for me. Okay, I'll be honest here because it came with a bit of lust and desire thrown in – I'm a man for heaven's sake!'

'I've noticed. The man bit,' Cara said, snuggling in further. Soon they would have to move from this position. Soon they would need to talk about the elephant in the room, which was where they would sleep tonight – together or separately. Should she be the one to suggest he join her in her room? Or would Tom make the first move? Or would they just sort of gravitate upstairs, arms wrapped round one another, reluctant to pull apart and go wherever their feet and their hearts took them? Being a Rosie must be so much easier in this sort of situation, but that was why their friendship had lasted and was as good as it was, because they were such different people and respected one another for it.

'And I noticed,' Tom said, 'how very womanly you looked that night, how very desirable. And yet how vulnerable. I'm still noticing.'

Is that what Tom had seen? Someone desirable? She glanced back at him.

'Noticing? Noticing what?'

That I want you to make love to me, and I want to make love to you right back?

'That you're not vulnerable any more. Am I right?'

'Not like I was then, no,' Cara said. 'So much has happened this summer and it's not quite over yet.'

Cara could list it all: getting back her ring, and her paintings, Rosie giving her a computer and paying for her to have a website made, Mae with her first broken romance and now a new one, and the new chapter in their mother/daughter relationship. All those things had been gifted her in a way. The only thing she'd been pro-active with was setting up Cove End as a B&B ... and now possibly a small bistro restaurant with Mae's input. But to say all that would be self-indulgent at that moment.

'It's been a pretty good summer for me, too,' Tom said. 'And not just the readies now in my bank account, and the commissions that have come in on the back of the private view. I expect there'll be more of those over the next two days. Claire wants me to put on an exhibition in London by Christmas ... always a good time of year to sell paintings, Christmas. Talking of Christmas ... do you have plans?'

Tom had lowered his voice possibly because, like Cara, he'd noticed it had gone very quiet upstairs – no more bathroom noises, no doors shutting, no chatting.

'Christmas?' Cara said. Now there was a question she hadn't been expecting.

'Yep. Christmas. You know, that time of year for trees and tinsel and presents and carols and goodwill to all men and women. The time for turkey and sausage rolls, Buck's Fizz, and Morecombe and Wise on the telly. Know it?'

Tom reached around Cara with his free arm, placing it across her waist and pulling her closer to him.

'I know it,' Cara laughed.

The last couple of Christmases hadn't exactly been joyous occasions for her and Mae although she'd done her best to make a special time of it and Rosie had gone overboard with piles of presents all beautifully wrapped.

'Good,' Tom said. 'Save the date!'

'The date?'

Tom was deliberately talking in riddles and she was deliberately pretending she didn't understand what he was driving at, although she did ... he was expecting her to read between the lines and know that he wanted to still be in her life at Christmas. And possibly to let him know that was what she wanted too.

Cara was beginning to feel slightly drunk on happiness –

happiness and hope for the future, a future with Tom – because that's exactly where she wanted him to be.

'No one had a more memorable birthday, did they, than the chap whose birthday was the twenty-fifth of December.'

'Jesus,' Cara giggled.

'Him as well.'

'You?' Cara spluttered, surprised that while she felt she'd known Tom forever, there really was so much basic stuff she didn't know. 'Your birthday is the twenty-fifth of December?'

'The very day, although I have to say the world makes rather more of His birthday than it does of mine. But I take birthday kisses in advance should there be any going.'

'Well, in that case,' Cara said, turning in his arms to offer up her lips, practically drowning in the glow that spread over her as their mouths connected. One thing she did know about Tom was that he was a very, very good kisser.

'It's a long time 'til Christmas,' Cara said when they eventually pulled apart. 'There are months and months to go yet. But I think I know how we can fill the time.'

'You do?'

'Definitely.'

Cara began to extricate herself from Tom's arms, and stood up.

She held out her hand to him. Tom took it and stood up too. Slowly they walked towards the door and Cara reached out to turn off the lights. But progress was slow, after more kissing that was getting more passionate by the moment, and Cara was in no doubt now that she was taking the right step.

'If anyone's peeping over the banister watching this,' Tom whispered, 'they'd be saying, "Get a room already!" Your place or mine?' he quipped.

'Neither. The other dormer bedroom is free, the bed made up, the hospitality tray ready and waiting for the morning. I've a fancy to see sunrise from that room. I never have.'

'Never?'

'No. I think I must have been waiting for the right moment.'

'And the right moment is now? With me?'

'Oh yes. Most definitely with you ...'

Acknowledgements

When Margaret and Chris Mason go on holiday they generously give me the run of their magnificent home and garden in which to lose myself and dream – there's no greater gift for a writer.

Again, Charlotte and the team at HarperCollins have expertly guided me from pitch to publication – thank you one and all.

Emails to the two Js – Jennie and Jan – must run into thousands now after nine novels. Girls, you lift my spirits and inspire me on a daily basis – what stars you are.

Thursday afternoons – tea and tiffin, twelve writers sharing their work, their hopes, their dreams. I'm humbled to be one of your number, Brixham Writers – you rock!

My family – Roger, James, Elisabeth, Sarah, Alex, and Emily – listen patiently as I witter on sometimes about characters and plots, scenes and cliff-hangers, and all without too much eye-rolling. Thanks, guys – I love you all so very much.

Dear Reader,

Thank you so much for taking the time to read this book – we hope you enjoyed it! If you did, we'd be so appreciative if you left a review.

Here at HQ Digital we are dedicated to publishing fiction that will keep you turning the pages into the early hours. We publish a variety of genres, from heartwarming romance, to thrilling crime and sweeping historical fiction.

To find out more about our books, enter competitions and discover exclusive content, please join our community of readers by following us at:

🐦 *@HQDigitalUK*

f *facebook.com/HQDigitalUK*

Are you a budding writer? We're also looking for authors to join the HQ Digital family! Please submit your manuscript to:

HQDigital@harpercollins.co.uk.

Hope to hear from you soon!

ONE PLACE. MANY STORIES

If you loved *The Little B&B at Cove End*
then turn the page for an exclusive extract from
Summer at 23 The Strand...

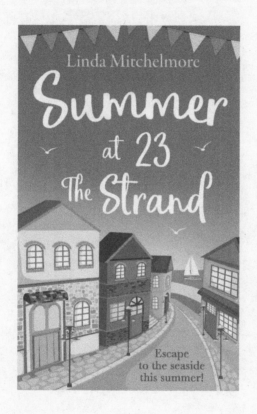

CHAPTER ONE

Early May

Martha

'I'll just check your details.' The clerk behind the desk in the tourist office on the seafront spoke without looking up. Martha, peering out from under the rim of her black straw hat, held her breath. Would the woman detect a lie? A false address? Not a fictitious name as such but not the one the world knew her by? 'So, that's Martha Langford? Eighteen Staplethorpe Avenue, Brighton? Right? From one seaside resort to another, eh?'

'Yes to all that,' Martha said.

'Well, you'll just love it here in Hollacombe, I'm sure. A proper little home from home is how our guests describe Number 23. Here's the key. You'll find your chalet is about five hundred yards to your left as you leave this office. One double bedroom, one sitting room with sofabed cum galley kitchen, one loo with basin and shower. All breakages to be paid for. No barbecues on the wooden deck, I'm afraid, because the chalets are wooden. Fire risk, and all that. To be vacated a fortnight from today by 10 a.m. to give the cleaner time to turn it all around before the next occupants. The key with the luggage-label tag on it to be posted through the letterbox here if we're closed. Any problems—'

'I'll sort them,' Martha interrupted. The last thing she needed was to have to come back here and, possibly, have someone else turn up at Number 23 The Strand to sort out whatever problem she might have. Just standing here, listening to the clerk reciting what she must have recited hundreds of times before, was giving her goose bumps. The sooner she got out of here the better.

'Of course, this could be the last season this particular chalet is let because it's up for sale,' the clerk said as though Martha hadn't spoken. 'It's owned by the local authority at present, as are a couple of others and they need to cut costs, so they're up for sale too. The others are privately owned by locals who keep them for their own use at weekends and in the school holidays, although some do rent them out to holidaymakers. There's not been a lot of interest in Number 23 so far but it's early in the season. Any questions?' The clerk cocked her head to one side questioningly.

'Can't think of any,' Martha said, perhaps a bit too sharply, which is what happens when one's nerves are on end. She didn't want to be rude but she had to go.

Well, Martha thought, as she closed the door of the chalet behind her, what a lovely surprise. She'd glanced at the photos on the website when she'd booked, of course, but she hadn't studied it in much detail. It was bigger than she'd been expecting – more ski chalet than beach hut, perhaps a bit boutique hotel – and just as the lady in the tourist office had said, a little home from home. And so very clean. A nest. Martha felt the welcome of it wrap around her, warm her. The boarded walls were painted a soft shade of yellow, like vanilla custard, with a frieze of stencilled scallop shells in deep turquoise where the walls met the ceiling. Pretty, cotton curtains with blue and yellow sailboats hung at the windows in the double bedroom and living room. The cream, linen-covered sofabed was piled with large and squashy cushions in various shades of yellow and blue, and two small but matching armchairs had biscuit-coloured fleece throws draped over the arms, for colder days perhaps. The duvet on the double bed, covered in a turquoise, jacquard-style pattern, was thick and sumptuous, and the pillows large, plump and inviting.

'All very Eastern Seaboard,' Martha said out loud. 'I love it.'

Some of the tension she'd been carrying with her was beginning to seep away. Yes, she'd made the right decision coming here. It was as though this chalet had been waiting for her. She patted the duvet, her hand almost disappearing in its sumptuousness.

'And I could lie down on you right now,' she laughed, surprising herself with that laugh because she hadn't laughed for weeks now. But she couldn't flop down on it just yet. Martha drew her breath in and then let it all out again slowly, her shoulders dropping as she physically relaxed. Yes, it felt good here. It would give her space and time to rethink what she wanted to do with the rest of her life. But first, she just had to do something with her hair.

Martha had never done a home hair dye before. Ever since she'd been eleven years old and at stage school, her naturally blonde hair had always been professionally cut and coloured. And, of course, for filming she'd often worn wigs. It felt strange, but empowering, to be choosing a new hair colour without others calling the shots. So she'd chosen red; a sort of rosehip red with a bit of gloss to it to cover her natural blonde. The basin in the bijou bathroom – small but perfectly appointed the brochure had said, and so it was – looked as though a murder had been committed as Martha rinsed her hair one last time. Now to dry it. And then cut it. She pulled her hair high over her head and, with eyes closed, chopped straight across. When she opened her eyes again she had about eighteen inches of ponytail in her hand. Shaking her head to loosen her hair, she braved the mirror.

Not bad. Not bad at all. Next came the coloured contact lenses. Martha's eyes were the palest blue, bordering on turquoise, but she reckoned a redhead might have green eyes. So in went the onyx contacts.

'I hardly recognise myself,' Martha said, in a Scottish accent, light years away from her true Home Counties way of speaking. But that was the advantage of being an actress. She could become anyone from anywhere. And she had. Many, many, times. From stage work to period TV dramas, through a six-month stint on a 'soap', to Hollywood. But there was a downside – over the years so many other people had pulled her strings, as it were. So many that she felt she had almost lost the essence of who she was inside. Almost.

Her agent, Ralph Newcombe, had been furious when she'd decided to turn her back on it all.

'You cannot be serious!' he'd raged at her in his office that smelled of whisky and cigarettes, making Martha gag. Or rather making Serena Ross, as she was known to the world, gag. 'You are making me look an utter fool pulling out of this! I've worked my backside off getting you, not the lead role admittedly, but a not insignificant role in a Tom Marchant film. Bets were on that you'd get Best Supporting Actress at the Oscars. And you pull this stunt! I'll be surprised if you ever work again!'

That night, Martha had gone back to the flat the film company had provided and cried and cried and cried. No need for glycerine on her bottom lashes to bring on the tears. And then she'd called Tom and told him she wouldn't be coming back to the set. She'd been flattered by his attention, even though she'd known he was married with two small children – as did the rest of the world. Sitting close to him on breaks, sharing a burger or a salad, a *frisson* of excitement had fizzed through her. His invite to dinner after the day's filming had been tempting. So she'd gone. Just dinner, he'd said. And it had been. Although if she were honest with herself it wouldn't have taken much for their feelings to run over – perhaps not this time they had dinner, but definitely the next. Tom had felt it too.

'Taxi time,' he'd said, leaning across the table to give her hand a squeeze. 'The danger hour approacheth. Two people from out of town with hours to fill till morning.'

Tom had even called the taxi for her, walked with her to the door – just a little behind her with a hand in the small of her back. And that's when she'd been startled by a barrage of camera flashes and saw in rapid fast-forward how it would be if she were to enter a full-blown affair with Tom. She – and he – would be hounded.

Martha, not liking herself very much at that moment for what she'd been on the cusp of, had turned to Tom then.

'The danger hour is too dangerous for me,' she'd said. 'I'm not in the habit of breaking up marriages, despite the magic...'

'...between us,' Tom had finished for her.

Martha didn't think Tom was a serial adulterer, although she was under no illusion that she'd been the first to tempt him. For the two weeks they'd been thrown together, working on *Breaking Ice*, he'd showered her with gifts, in time-honoured Hollywood style – bespoke perfume and a designer handbag, Italian silk scarves and an amethyst pendant on a fine gold chain. She'd worn that pendant on her first – and last – dinner date with Tom. But she'd known in an instant, the camera flashes almost blinding her, that she hadn't been in love with him – merely in lust, feelings heightened and enhanced by the place and the setting and the fabulous clothes. There could be many Toms in the future if she stayed here among the beautiful people with money to spend and lavish lifestyles. Was that what she wanted?

And that was when she'd made her decision to end her contract on *Breaking Ice* and go home, back to the UK. And then... what?

Well, she had a fortnight to work out where her life was going, and a town she didn't know to explore. In front of her, there was the curve of a bay the colour of faded denim, flat as the proverbial pancake at that moment, and the sun was shining. First she'd need to find a supermarket of sorts to buy food, and maybe a bottle of wine, although she knew it was dangerous – very dangerous – to drink alone. Martha placed her four-inch heels in the cupboard in the bedroom, slid her feet into flip-flops, took a deep breath, and went out.

'Can I help you with that?'

A man's voice. A Scottish accent. To answer or not? With one foot on the bottom step of the wooden steps that led up to the deck of 23 The Strand, and her arms full of carrier bags and a lamp she'd picked up in a charity shop, Martha considered her options. If she answered, she'd need to drop the Scottish accent she'd been using for a couple of days and which was becoming second nature now, because this man was likely to ask where in Scotland she came from, and she only knew Edinburgh, Glasgow and Aberdeen, each of which had its own particular accent.

'I can manage, thanks. Only a few more steps,' she said. And then the newspaper that had been on top of one of the bags fell to the floor.

The man picked it up, shifting awkwardly as he rebalanced himself.

'Damned leg,' he said, rubbing a hip. He looked at the photo and the headline on the front page and then at Martha.

ACTRESS SERENA ROSS QUITS BREAKING ICE

The photo was one taken on the steps of the hotel as Tom had guided her to her taxi. There were, Martha knew, more photos of them both inside, cosied up in the restaurant, because she was wiser now and knew that the man in the corner hadn't been taking selfies but had been taking photographs of her and Tom.

'I'll take that,' she said. 'Thanks. The press scraping about in the gutter as per usual, I expect,' she added, with a nod to the front page of the newspaper.

'More than likely,' the man said. 'Don't shoot but... Hugh Fraser. Photographer. Currently on sick leave while my leg heals.'

Oh my God! What sort of a photographer, she wanted to know – paparazzi? – but she was afraid to ask. Her hat had slipped back over her head as she struggled with her bags. If he was paparazzi, would he recognise her? She might have changed her hair colour and be wearing coloured lenses, but her mouth was the same shape. Her nose. Her high cheekbones, for which she was known in the world of acting.

'I'm sorry about your leg,' she said, acting a calmness she didn't feel inside, although it was true she was sorry. 'What happened?'

'You know how, on TV, when you see photographers following a story in the street and they're running backwards and taking photos? Have you ever wondered if they fall over?'

Martha gulped. So he was paparazzi? What on earth was she doing keeping him here, engaging him in conversation?

'Yes, yes, I have.'

'Well, I did. Right over a low wall. Only it was an urban fox I was trying to film without scaring it off. Compound fracture. Hence my stay here for a couple of weeks to strengthen my muscles now the break's been sorted. Running on sand is good for that.'

'Oh!' Martha said, unable to stop the smile that crept to her lips as a cartoon strip of Hugh running backwards and going over the wall played in her head. 'Sorry. It's not funny, I know.'

'That's okay. Every one of my colleagues fell about laughing. And you are?'

'Martha Langford.'

'I'd shake your hand, Martha Langford, if you had one free for me to shake. How about I come over all macho and carry this newspaper up the steps for you?'

And then he did just that, but carefully and with a bit of a limp, Martha noticed.

Hugh took Martha's bags and parcels from her as she scrabbled in her pocket for the chalet key.

'I'm at Number 20.' He waved the newspaper in the direction of his chalet. 'Belongs to my parents, actually. Holiday home of sorts. I'd stop with them in their house back in Exeter but Mum would smother me to death with kindness. Much better I fend for myself a bit, get those muscles working again. Keep an eye open for the next big scoop, as it were.'

Martha shivered. She had no intention of being Hugh's next big scoop.

'Thanks,' she said. 'You know. For your help. Just put my bags on the deck. I can manage now. Things to do. Bye.'

With almost indecent haste she scooped her bags into her arms and grabbed the newspaper from him, pushed the door open with her knee, sidled in behind it and then closed it with a foot.

Hugh seemed like a nice bloke – the sort of bloke she'd be happy to spend time with in normal circumstances, because photographers could be useful to an actress. But her circumstances weren't normal, were they, if the papers were still carrying stories about her quitting *Breaking Ice*? And she wasn't entirely sure she still wanted to be an actress any more anyway. And what was more, she badly needed to get to know herself better before she even thought about making a new relationship with anyone. And could she trust Hugh not to be on his laptop right now letting the world know he knew where Serena Ross was holed up?

Martha kept a low profile for a few days, always on the lookout for Hugh in case he wanted to talk, or asked too many probing questions she didn't want to answer. She'd seen him running a couple of times a day, not fast and rather ungainly, as though he was still carrying pain from his broken leg. She'd also seen him look up at her chalet as he made his way back to his own. But the red sand of the beach and the soft shush as the sea met the shore with a petticoat frill of white foam was calling her. The only thing Martha was missing from her old life at the moment was the gym. There were probably more than a few gyms in the area but she didn't want to join one. Power walking and running could be just as good. She couldn't hide from the world for ever. Or from Hugh. She had to get out there.

Hugh always looked glowing and happy when he got back from a run. Martha badly needed some of that – glowing and happy. But running on the beach was tide-dependent so she bought a tide-table from the kiosk at the end of The Strand that also sold teas, coffees, ice creams and a few beach toys, so she could work out when Hugh might be running and when he might not. She simply couldn't risk, at the moment at least, that he might recognise her, although she had a gut feeling he already had. Only that morning she'd seen him swing his long legs – rather stiffly – over the sandstone wall and drop onto the beach, landing awkwardly, struggling to get his balance the way a duck might on a frozen pond. She ought not to have laughed. Hugh had looked up directly towards her chalet as though he had sensed her watching him. She'd ducked quickly behind the curtain, but the speed of her movement made the fabric flutter. Had he seen?

To run, Martha would need trainers and some leggings and a T-shirt, so she went out to buy everything along with a few groceries. And a newspaper. Back at her chalet she decided to take a mug of coffee and the newspaper down to the beach. She laid a towel on the sand and sat down.

Martha shivered, a double-page feature on the demise of Tom's marriage – TOM MARCHANT'S WIFE FILES FOR DIVORCE – falling open on her lap. Another actress, Amy Stevens, had been cited. Not her. So she'd been right – she hadn't been the first to turn Tom's head. And neither would Amy be the last. Martha felt relief wash over her that she hadn't entered a full-blown affair with Tom and that there had been little between them except animal attraction, a few small gifts and one dinner after filming.

'Was it something I said?'

Hugh. Standing above her on the steps that led to and from the beach. *Could he read the headline from there?*

Martha closed the newspaper with one deft movement. She did not look up.

'No.'

'But you've been avoiding me?'

'If that's what you think,' Martha said with a shrug. 'I like to think I'm thicker-skinned than that.'

Hugh jumped – rather awkwardly it had to be said – down onto the sand and sat beside her without being asked.

'You're not still letting that get to you, are you?' Hugh asked, tapping a finger on the newspaper in Martha's – now shaking – hands.

Oh my God. He knew, didn't he? He knew that, despite the red hair dye, the coloured contacts, the wide-brimmed hat, and her almost exclusion from normal life, she was really Serena Ross.

'You haven't written this, have you?' she asked, waving the newspaper at him. Sometimes it was better to graciously admit defeat than fight a corner she was never going to win. He would know by her answer that she'd guessed he knew.

'No. Of course not. I'm a photographer – wildlife and land-scape mostly – not a fully paid-up member of the paparazzi. But I did recognise you. And I've read that particular newspaper this morning and I see Mr Marchant has moved on.'

'That's not a very flattering remark,' Martha said. He was making it sound as though she were totally dispensable, which, while it might be true in Tom Marchant's case, was doing nothing for her self-esteem.

'I'm not rushing to judge you. You're here for your own reasons and it's not for me to pry.'

'I'm not suggesting you are for one moment but... well... I'm a bit sensitive right now.'

'Yes, I can see how that might be. But if it helps, today's newspaper is tomorrow's fish and chip wrappings, as the saying has it.'

'If only,' Martha said with a mock-groan.

'True. But if you ask me – which I know you're not – you are far, far prettier than his, um, latest squeeze.'

'Well, thank you, kind sir,' Martha said, unable to stop a smile creeping to the corners of her mouth. 'I'll take that as a compliment.'

'Please do.'

Martha felt her smile widen.

'That's better. Cliché alert – you're even prettier when you smile.'

'Thank you again, kind sir.' Martha laughed. 'I know I've not done enough of it lately. But I'll need to go now. My coffee's gone cold and...'

'I could make you another,' Hugh said. He gave Martha a big grin, the strength of it rippling the skin beside his eyes. 'I'm in dire need of a coffee myself after my run. Stay right there,' he went on, wagging a finger playfully at her. 'I'll be right back.'

Before Martha could find breath to reply, Hugh had loped and limped his way back up the steps.

Martha considered simply getting up and going back to her own chalet, because although she didn't think Hugh was a controlling sort of man in any way, she didn't know him well enough to really judge. And it had felt as though it was an order he'd issued just now.

But she stayed. She was safe enough here on a public beach and, as far as she could tell, Hugh didn't have a camera of any sort with him. She folded up the newspaper and put it underneath her beach towel and waited.

Hugh was soon back. He'd put two mugs of black coffee, a

small jug of milk, some tubes of sugar and a packet of Hobnobs on a tray.

'Could you hang on to that while I sit back down?' he asked. 'Only I get a bit of a balance issue now and then from the leg and I wouldn't want to shower you with it.'

'Of course,' Martha said, reaching up to take the tray.

Hugh sat back down and took the tray from her.

'How do you take your poison?'

'Black, no sugar, thanks,' Martha said.

'Ah,' Hugh said, 'we have the same impeccable taste in coffee.'

'Indeed we do,' Martha said, accepting her coffee and holding it to her in both hands. How civilised this was, just yards from their chalets, nothing between them and the horizon except shell-strewn sand and some strings of seaweed left by the tide.

'I hope you don't mind,' Hugh said, 'but I've brought my phone. I don't take it with me when I'm out running in case it falls out of my pocket.' He placed the tray on the sand beside him and took out a top-of-the-range phone from the pocket of his shorts. 'So many interesting things in the sand to take photographs of.'

Martha heard her own sharp intake of breath, like a gunshot in her ears. Of course, people took pictures with phones as well as cameras, and phones could be so slim and so easy to hide. A shiver of unease wriggled between her shoulder blades.

'But no photos of you. Promise,' Hugh said. 'I think I could work out where your thought processes were going there!'

'More than likely.' Martha laughed nervously. She sipped at her coffee – very good coffee she was pleased and surprised to note. But she wanted the focus off her for the moment, so she asked: 'What sort of photographs do you take? And sell, presumably?'

'How long have you got?'

'Until I've finished this coffee?' Martha quipped – gosh, how good that felt, to make a joke.

'Right. Well. Best drink slowly! I do wildlife photography and sell it to book publishers and magazines. Newspapers. I take landscape photographs for the same outlets. Both here and abroad for all of that. Most of that is commissioned but I also sell to photo-banks and agencies, and I have no jurisdiction over where those photos go. When cash flow has been stagnant I've done engagement parties, weddings – both in the UK and exotic beach locations, local theatre productions, that sort of thing. Enough to be going on with?'

'Yes. Thank you,' Martha said. She had a feeling she knew what sort of photographs Hugh might take that went to photo-banks and agencies over which he didn't have, as he'd said, jurisdiction: photos of celebrities being where they ought not to have been, and with people they ought not to have been with. But it was only a feeling – she had no proof.

'And do you know something, Martha?' Hugh went on. 'I've had all-expenses-paid trips to Bali and Bondi Beach, various Greek Island beaches and countless places in Spain, and it's always puzzled me as to why people bother to go all that way when we have perfectly lovely beaches in this country. I mean, look at this one.'

Martha looked. Indeed it did look magnificent with the sun shining, the sea, as she looked out towards Torquay at one side of the bay and Brixham at the other, appeared as though someone had scattered a million diamonds over it. Seagulls dipped and dived on the thermals and a cormorant dived for fish, then reappeared a few seconds later some way from where it had gone down.

'On a day like today, yes,' Martha said. 'I suppose people go abroad for the guaranteed sunshine.'

'Ah!' Hugh said. 'Not always guaranteed, I'm afraid. A friend's wedding I covered in Bali was rained off completely – monsoon didn't come into it! I could set up some wonderful shots here. The bride, barefoot, with her skirt hoisted to her knees, dipping

287

a toe in to test the water for a paddle, with the groom holding her firmly by the waist, his trousers rolled up over his calves, so she doesn't stumble.'

Goodness, what a romantic, Martha thought. Was there a significant woman in his life, she wondered, but wasn't going to ask. They were only ships passing in the night here, weren't they? Hugh was healing and she was, too, in a way.

'I say,' Hugh said, scooping up a handful of sand and shells and letting the sand sift through his fingers. 'Could I borrow a corner of your towel to photograph these? The stripes are sharp and the navy against the white of the shells will be a perfect backdrop.'

'Be my guest,' Martha said, and edged a little further away as Hugh moved towards her, making space for his photoshoot.

'What I'll do,' Hugh said, 'is lay the shells in a line down the navy stripes. See, some of them have little swirls of long-discarded egg cases encrusted on them. And this one has got a frond of seaweed so firmly attached to it it's going to take more than my strength to pull it off.'

'It's like a hat,' Martha said. 'Or a fascinator.'

'Exactly that. And this one is so perfect it's like one half of a pigeon's egg. And just as delicate.' Hugh handed the shell to Martha, placing it gently on her palm when she held out her hand to take it.

'Exquisite,' Martha said. And it was. She knew beaches were always covered in shells from which the living beings had long gone, but she'd never stopped to examine any of them in detail as Hugh was now.

She watched, in silence, as Hugh took photograph after photograph, so absorbed in what he was doing now that he didn't speak either. For Martha it was a comfortable silence.

'I'll photoshop them later,' Hugh said, holding his phone towards Martha. 'But you get the gist.'

Martha was surprised to find Hugh had taken at least twenty

photos of the shells against the backdrop of her beach towel. They were all of the same thing and yet they all looked different.

'I'd buy a card – a postcard or birthday card – with any one of these on it,' she said.

'Now, there's a thought! Never thought of doing cards or postcards. Thanks for the tip.'

Martha had finished her coffee, eaten one of Hugh's Hobnobs, and knew she ought to go. Besides, Hugh seemed to have run out of things to say now they had exhausted the subject of the shells.

And then Hugh surprised her.

'There's a fête on the green tomorrow. Two o'clock. Would you like to come?'

'A fête?' Martha's father had always termed the village fête 'a fête worse than death' but they'd always gone anyway, she and her parents, and bought things they didn't really need or want because they felt sorry for the stall-holders. She hadn't been to a fête in years.

'I know. Very old-fashioned things, but it's for a good cause. They hold two or three during the summer on the green the other side of the promenade and I usually go if I'm in the area. Please say you'll come.'

'I don't think I can,' Martha said. She knew she didn't have a good excuse if Hugh pressed the issue. It was beginning to feel like a date, this invite, and she wasn't ready to date yet.

'It's for a good cause.'

'From my childhood memories of fêtes, they usually are. The church roof or the Scouts' trip to summer camp or somesuch.'

'Neither of those,' Hugh said. 'This one's for the local hospice. It's where my brother spent his last few days.'

Martha hadn't expected that, but the actress in her made her hang on to her composure – a composure she didn't feel inside. Inside she felt crass, and gauche, and uncomfortable, as though Hugh had fed her his final line on purpose to test her reaction.

'I'm very sorry for your loss,' she said. 'But I still can't come. Now, if you'll excuse me...'

She got to her feet and pulled at a corner of her beach towel.

'Of course,' Hugh said, standing up, although it took a second or two for him to get his balance because of his bad leg. 'Thanks for the loan of the beach towel.'

'And for the coffee and biscuits,' Martha responded, pulling the towel towards her.

It was only as she got halfway up the steps that she realised she'd left her newspaper on the sand where it had been underneath the beach towel. Well, she wasn't going back for it now.

But when she got to the door of her chalet and glanced round, she saw Hugh had made it to the top of the steps and was dropping her newspaper in a litter bin. The kindness of his action in getting rid of something about which she had been upset earlier brought a lump to Martha's throat. He really was such a good and kind man, wasn't he? But at the back of her mind was the thought that she couldn't be entirely sure if the invite to the fête had been because she was Martha Langford or... Serena Ross.

Martha tossed and turned all night. She'd been unforgivably rude walking off like that. Hugh had said his brother had died in the hospice and although she didn't know how old Hugh was, his brother couldn't have been very old either. Panic had made her behave the way she had and she was going to have to get over that.

Martha took a mug of tea and a round of toast and marmalade out onto the deck at half past eight the next morning. She took one of the throws and draped it over her knees while she sat at the metal bistro table and waited for Hugh to emerge from his chalet for his morning run.

But there was no Hugh that morning. Martha waited until almost ten o'clock then went in search of him.

'Well, good morning. This is a nice surprise,' Hugh said, opening the door to her knock, as though the fact she'd rebuffed him the day before hadn't happened. He was in checked pyjama bottoms but naked from the waist up. And his feet were bare. His hair was damp and curling every which way as though he was fresh from the shower and she'd knocked and interrupted him just as he was about to put a comb through it.

'I've come to apologise for my appalling behaviour yesterday,' Martha said. 'I meant it when I said I was truly sorry to hear about your brother's death, but I was rude to rush off the way I did without asking you about it. I'm sorry.'

'Apology accepted,' Hugh said. 'After Harris – that was my brother's name, by the way – died there were people who crossed the street to avoid saying anything to me at all.'

'Oh God, that's awful. Sometimes people simply don't know what to say, I suppose, and say nothing rather than say the wrong thing. I've done it myself.'

'It's exactly that,' Hugh said. 'I'd ask you in but this is serious bachelor-pad land at the moment. I'm going to have to give it a thorough going over before I hand it back to my parents.'

Martha tried to peek around him to test the truth of his statement but his not inconsiderable body was blocking her view.

'I can be messy on occasion,' she said. 'As more than a few flatmates have mentioned! But, well, I just came to say I'm truly sorry for how I reacted and if you want to talk to me about Harris, I'll be happy to listen. But I'll go now.'

'Okay. As you see, I'm hours behind. But how do you feel about joining me for a spot of lunch later? The Shoreline does a mean burger, and lots of interesting fish, and salads for the diet-conscious. Do you know it?'

'Give me a rough direction.'

'Halfway between here and the harbour. Keep going in a straight line. You can't miss it. It's got fantastic views.'

'I think I know where you mean.'

'Good. Harris and I used to eat there in the holidays. I could tell you about him.'

'I'd like that, Hugh,' Martha said.

'So would I. So, can I ask you to meet me there?' Hugh asked. 'About one o'clock?'

'Of course,' Martha said. She hadn't planned her day beyond apologising to Hugh, but now she had a lunch date – was it really a date so early in the acquaintance? – she thought she might get into her newly purchased running kit and go for a run. It might help to clear her head. 'I'll look forward to it.'

'Me too, Martha Langford,' Hugh said with a grin.

He was letting her know it was as Martha he was wanting to get to know her, not just because she was also known as Serena Ross, wasn't he? Martha's heart lifted a little.

Martha was early, only about fifteen minutes, but she decided to go on in and find a table.

Oh! Another surprise because there were full-length windows on three sides, the ceiling was very high with Raffles-style fans, and the whole place was filled with light. Outside there was a small balcony along two sides. Tables and chairs were set up outside but Martha decided it wasn't quite warm enough to sit out, although a few people were.

She chose a table for two, by the window facing the sea. The restaurant was built over the road, closed for the summer to traffic, and with the tide high it was as though she was sitting in the prow of a ship. She hadn't expected that – it was almost like being on a cruise in the Mediterranean if she allowed her imagination to run away with her. She picked up the menu. Lots to choose from. Was Hugh going to offer to pay or should she suggest they go Dutch. If they went Dutch it would be easier to say, 'Well, that was nice, but I don't think we have a future together.'

Red snapper or crab? Quinoa salad or pesto pasta?

'Penny for them,' Hugh said.

'They might cost a little bit more than that.' Martha laughed, looking up into his smiling face.

Hugh laid a hand of greeting, briefly, on Martha's shoulder and sat down opposite. 'Thanks for coming.'

'I'm glad to be here and, seeing as I had my first ever run this morning after I left you, I'm rather hungry.'

'Really? The first? Ever?'

'Yep. Although I've been guilty of being a bit of a gym bunny in my time, and daily dance lessons when I was at stage school.'

Talking about this now, it was starting to feel as though it was all in the past for her. Was it? Could it be?

'Did you like it? The run, I mean.'

'I'll let you know tomorrow what opinion my calves have on that,' she said, laughing.

'It gets easier,' Hugh said. 'As most things do.'

And the smile on his face seemed to freeze, and although he was looking at Martha it was as though he was also looking inside himself.

'Do you want to talk about Harris before we eat? You said earlier you used to come here with him so it can't be easy being here with someone who isn't your brother. We could just order a drink and talk? I'm not going to die of hunger if we postpone lunch for a while.'

'I didn't have you down as a mind-reader,' Hugh said. 'But yes, I was thinking about Harris. I imagined for a moment that he was going to come marching in, tell me it was my turn to buy the drinks – he always said that, even though I bought far more rounds than he ever did.'

'And you wish you could be buying that round now?'

A waiter arrived at their table. 'What can I get you?' he asked.

'Just a drink for the moment for me,' Martha said. 'We'll eat later. Okay with that, Hugh?'

'Fine, fine,' Hugh said. 'I'll have a pint of local ale. And you, Martha?'

'Prosecco if you have it,' Martha said.

'We sure do. Won't be a moment.'

293

'That was inordinately kind,' Hugh said. 'To realise I was struggling a bit there. I seemed to have lost all power of thought and speech for a second.'

'We all need a bit of help and understanding sometimes,' Martha said. 'Tell me about Harris.'

'It'll be easier if I show you.' He took out his phone from his jeans pocket. 'I've got hundreds on here. I'll spare you the baby brother photos.' He looked up from scrolling through and smiled at Martha.

'I can probably live without seeing those,' she said, doing her utmost to lighten what was, to Hugh, a difficult moment. 'What did he do?'

'Sports teacher. With a bit of English on the side. Rugby was his game, although he was pretty good at just about everything he tried – tennis, cricket, water sports of every description. Here. That's a good one.'

Hugh handed the phone to Martha, and a good-looking chap, with hair fairer than Hugh's and a big, rugby player's frame, smiled out at her. Despite the physical differences, she could see the likeness between the brothers.

'How did he die?' Martha asked, handing back the phone.

'Leukaemia,' Hugh said. 'He responded to treatment at first and we all held our breath with hope, but then it just stopped working for him and he shrunk before our eyes. It was swift in the end.'

The waiter came back with their drinks then.

'Can you come back in about half an hour, mate?' Hugh said.

'Sure can. Enjoy your drinks.'

'Nice bloke,' Hugh said. 'But I think it's plainer than day that we're not enjoying much at the moment.'

'It can't be easy for you,' Martha said. 'But I'm not sad I'm here. How long ago did Harris die?'

'Just over two years. It's still a bit raw. It's why I try to go to as many of those fêtes as I can and help them raise a bit of money so others can get the care Harris did. Although what I'm going to do with yet another teddy bear won on the tombola I don't know!'

'Offload it to a charity shop?' She was feeling guilty now that she hadn't gone along with Hugh, but there was no point saying so. Hugh just needed to talk. About himself. About Harris.

'I could. But a stupid part of me thinks Harris wants me to have the stupid things. They're tactile. Look… sorry, Martha, I know I'm being less than a thrilling lunch companion. I can be a right miserable sod at times. It's why I've been known to drink myself stupid more often than was good for my liver, although I'm over that bit now. It's why I turned into a bit of a recluse, turned down commissions. And it's why my long-term relationship broke down. Violins time, eh?'

Martha had a feeling that, with this remark, he was subtly letting her know he was unattached at the moment.

'What was she called? Your long-term girlfriend? If you don't mind telling me?'

'No. I don't mind. Abby. Abigail. Losing her was like losing Harris all over again but time has healed me more quickly there. And I realise now she could have been more understanding. Harris had only been gone three months when she walked out. And so, here I am, trying to put all the pieces of my life back together, along with my broken leg. Doing my best to live again. But I'm being a right bloke, aren't I, talking about me all the time?'

'I did ask you to,' Martha said. 'And besides, you must know a fair bit about me if you've ever watched TV or been to the cinema. Or read the newspapers.'

'Yeah, that must suck at times, too, having every bit of your private life splashed across the media.'

'It does. But I don't have to take it any more.' The restaurant was beginning to fill up now and people had come to sit at tables either side of Martha and Hugh. She couldn't risk anyone over-hearing what she was saying. 'Shall we order now?'

'Good idea,' Hugh said.

'And then we can think, perhaps, of something we can do that will put our respective lives back on track.'

Running, it seemed, was the activity that suited them both. Hugh ran on the beach at least three times a day, while Martha preferred to run along the promenade, but only twice a day. If they saw one another in the distance they waved, but Hugh hadn't issued another invite to lunch, or dinner. And Martha wasn't entirely sure she wanted another invite because she still wasn't entirely convinced Hugh wouldn't suddenly send photos of her to some agency. She'd told her parents she was staying with a friend until the hullabaloo had died down, and that she was fine, and would call them soon. Friends texted her and left voicemails but she didn't reply to them either, having told anyone who needed to know the same story she'd told her parents. Sometimes she saw Hugh on the beach, bending to photograph something lying in the sand, or focusing on something out at sea. A couple of times she'd got that feeling a person gets when someone is looking at them and she'd turned to look up at the headland above the chalets, and Hugh had been there. There was a wonder-fully panoramic view of the bay from up there and he'd probably been taking landscape, or seascape, shots. He'd obviously seen her, because he'd waved to her as she turned.

But here was Hugh now, walking towards Martha's chalet where she was sitting on the deck, hat on to shield the low light from her eyes, reading in the late-afternoon sunshine.

He had a bottle of wine in one hand, and two glasses hanging from the fingers of the other.

'I hope you don't mind,' Hugh said, walking up the steps of Number 23. 'But my motto these days is never to drink alone, and I fancied a drink, so I hope I can persuade you to join me.'

'Is the sun below the yardarm?' Martha said, smiling.

'It is somewhere in the world.' Hugh laughed back. He set the bottle and glasses down on the patio table and took a corkscrew from his jeans pocket. 'So, can I pour?'

'You can,' Martha said. 'I might have some nibbles to go with that – some crisps and savoury crackers, and two or three varieties of cheese.'

'Sounds divine,' Hugh said.

Hugh had poured her a very full glass of wine when she got back with the nibbles.

'To you,' Hugh said, handing the wine to her.

'Cheers,' they said as one, chinking glasses.

'I've come to thank you,' Hugh said.

'For what?'

'For having lunch with me the other day. I'd never have been able to go in there had you not been waiting for me. I was hiding behind a pillar waiting for you and watched you go in. But now I've faced my demons and I've been in there alone. Just coffee and cake, but I did it. I sat where we sat having lunch and, really, it was fine.'

'I don't know what to say,' Martha said, cradling her glass in her hands. 'Unless it's that I was happy to join you, and I'm glad you've faced that particular demon.'

'We'll drink to that then,' Hugh said, holding his glass out towards Martha to clink again.

'Onwards for us both!' Martha said, holding her glass high as Hugh reached over to touch it with his. 'I don't know if you've noticed but when I've been running I haven't worn my hat. And my hair's been tied back at the nape of my neck.'

'And no one came up and accused you of anything? Not that anything you may or may not have done is anyone else's business.'

'No. No one. I think there might have been two or three people who recognised me because, when people do, a sort of disbelief that it could be me running towards them, or in the queue for an ice cream, comes over their face like a veil. And then, when I've gone, they whisper to their companion, only often it's louder than a whisper and I catch my name on the breeze... Serena Ross.'

'Be careful who you pretend to be or you might forget who you are.'

'Gosh, that's a very profound statement,' Martha said.

'Not mine, I'm afraid. I'm quoting, only I've forgotten who for the moment. Is that how it's been for you for a while? With the acting name, I mean.'

Martha nodded. 'I see that now. These past few days have been good. Since you showed me the shells on the beach and pointed things out to me, I'm seeing more, if that makes sense.'

'Perfect sense. And 'seeing more' is my cue to come in with a suggestion. My mission here is twofold. There was the chance to share a bottle of wine, of course, but it was also to tell you there's a small boat that does wildlife trips, coast-hugging. It leaves from the harbour early. Would you like to join me? Can you do early?'

'Ah, so you've noticed I don't emerge for my run until after coffee time?'

'I have. Would eight o'clock at the harbour be too early? The carrot here is that there'll more than likely be dolphins off Berry Head.'

'Really?'

'The boat leaving at eight bit, or the dolphins bit?'

'I can do early if I'm going to see dolphins.'

'You're on,' Hugh said. 'My treat.'

Martha was up at six o'clock the next morning. Hugh had said it might be an idea to wear a jacket with a hood if she had one with her, and a scarf, because it was still only May and, while the forecast was good, it could be a lot colder on the water than it was sitting on the decks of their chalets in the shelter of the cliff behind them.

He'd said it in a very non-bossy way as though he really was concerned she might get chilled.

Hugh had said he'd call for her at seven and they could walk over to the harbour. But when she looked out to see if he was on his way she saw he was on the beach, his phone/camera to his eye, back to the sea, photographing the chalets on The Strand.

Why was he doing that? Was he waiting for her to open the door so he could get a shot of her coming out? Was she being paranoid? Whichever, a ripple of unease snaked its way up her spine and out over her shoulders, and she shivered.

But just as Hugh had faced his demons by going into The Shoreline on his own without his brother, so she would have to face the fact that not every lens aimed her way was going to be for evil ends.

Martha reached for her coat, scarf and shoulder bag and went out. Hugh slid his phone back into his pocket and walked to greet her.

'Gorgeous morning for it, Martha,' he said. 'I don't think you'll regret this.'

'I hope not,' Martha said. 'I've usually got pretty good sea legs.' And then she decided to let Hugh know she'd seen him photographing her chalet. 'What were you taking photographs of just now?'

'The chalets. And yours in particular.'

'Why?' Martha said. She didn't know whether she wanted to go and see dolphins any more.

'Because there was a peregrine falcon hovering above it. I think it must have seen a piece of cockle or something a seagull had dropped. I'll show you if you like.'

'Please.'

'We'll need to get going if we're going to catch that boat, though.' Hugh placed an arm under Martha's elbow and steered her round in the direction of the harbour. 'I'll find the best shots and show you as we go along.'

And he did, but still Martha was uneasy.

'Have you ever seen the film *Roman Holiday*?' Martha asked.

'Yep. Dozens of times. It's my mother's favourite. After Harris died she curled up on the couch watching it on a loop for months. I watched with her more times than I can count. So, I think, reading between the lines here, that you're saying I'm not the Gregory Peck character who gets to kiss the iconic Audrey Hepburn character, but that I'm... the photographer?'

'But you haven't taken any photos of me that you're going to present to me, as happened in the film, when my fortnight of escapism here is over?'

'Nope. But then, photographers don't, for the most part, have to sit in a darkroom developing stuff these days. There are no negatives to blackmail people with. Anything unwanted is deleted with a swipe of a finger. 'But back to *Roman Holiday*... Audrey Hepburn's character, Princess Ann, and the journalist, Joe Bradley, as played by Gregory Peck, were never going to get together, were they? Even though they did share just the one kiss,' Hugh went on. 'See how well I know this film!'

'And the Princess Ann character was never going to get it together with the photographer?' Martha smiled.

'Irving Radovich, as played by Eddie Albert. Who never got to kiss Audrey Hepburn, although, as I said, Gregory Peck did. And what a kiss! What fantastic on-screen chemistry those two had, eh? And off-screen for all we know.'

They'd reached the end of the beach now, and would have to get back on to the promenade to make their way to the harbour. Hugh, with his long legs, stepped on to the prom and held a hand out to help Martha up.

Hugh was looking at Martha, a gentle smile playing about his lips. He ran his tongue around them as though they had suddenly gone dry with nerves. She had the feeling he would very much like to kiss her. And much to her surprise, Martha found she wanted very much to kiss him too. In all her twenty-seven years she'd never kissed anyone who hadn't been involved in the world of acting. But would that be wise? Could their worlds knit together happily? Would they?

'Well,' Hugh said, breaking the spell that seemed to have been cast over them both. 'The boat and the dolphins wait for no man. Come on.'

'You weren't joking when you said it was a small boat.' Martha laughed. 'I've been in bigger baths in the States!'

'I'll have to take your word for that!' Hugh grinned.

They were sitting in the stern, just seven other passengers seated onboard. And two crew. *Tea and coffee available on request* was written on a scrap of paper pinned to the cockpit and Martha wondered where it could possibly be made in such a small space – and how, given the boat rocked as the captain spun it round to point out to sea. But then the sea seemed to flatten out as though it had been ironed and they were sailing over a sheet of satin.

'Cormorants,' Hugh said. 'Fairy Cove.'

Just yards out of the harbour and Martha had seen her first cormorant up close, standing on a rock a few yards from the shoreline of a fairy-sized cove. How large they seemed so close up, how glossy and rather elegant-looking with their small heads and slender bodies.

'And the gulls are just waking up in their cliff roosting places,' Hugh said, pointing up at the red sandstone cliff. 'And terns.'

'It's a bit of a day of firsts for me already,' Martha said. 'I mean, do we ever really look at cormorants and seagulls and terns in the normal course of events?' She never had – they were just there, seagulls being a nuisance much of the time, but from the boat they looked as though they'd just come through a washing machine on a white wash, they were so bright in the early-morning light.

'Well, I do,' Hugh laughed. 'They can be my bread and butter, seagulls. Thank God for photo memory cards these days because

301

I can take literally thousands of images and then discard what I don't want. Forgive me if I ignore you for a moment, but there's loads I want to take pictures of.'

'Snap away,' Martha told him.

The captain was giving a running commentary about the area and the wildlife and Martha was happy to let his words wash over her as her eyes drank in the view. Hugh kept standing up to take pictures, then sitting down again, touching her on the arm now and then, gently but briefly, to ask if she was okay, and was she warm enough.

And then, there they were. As the boat rounded Berry Head, there were the dolphins. The captain shut down the throttle so that there was only the shush of the sea and the rumble of the motor as they all stood, as though choreographed, watching the dolphins jump and dive. No one spoke. A woman on the port side put her hands to her mouth and her eyes went wide with wonder as though she couldn't quite believe what she was seeing. Martha tried to count them... seven, eight, nine... but couldn't be sure she wasn't counting the same ones twice. As the boat rocked gently on the current, and everyone seemed to instantly find their sea legs, the dolphins came nearer. Martha had the urge to reach out and touch one, they were so close.

Martha lost track of time. She'd heard how seeing dolphins could be an almost religious experience and now she knew it to be true. Never would she have thought she could see them here, off the Devon coast, and in May, and in the company of a man she'd only just met. They were so free, so joyous, the way they leapt and then disappeared beneath the water again only to surface a few yards further away to make the same manoeuvre all over again. And it was then that Martha knew she had never had that freedom. Her life in acting had been scripted by her mother for the most part. Yes, she'd had a gift for acting – and dancing and singing – but had she only been living the life her mother had wanted for herself? She had spent two-thirds of her life living in what she now realised was a rather cloistered world.

Although it had been Martha who had run out on her acting life, it had taken meeting Hugh to show her the beauty in the real world.

'Thank you for bringing me, Hugh,' she said, sitting back down, quite giddy with emotion now.

'It's been my pleasure.'

The dolphins were moving further away now. Still rising from the water but not as high as they had been.

'I'll hold this experience to me for ever, I think,' Martha said.

'Me too. And we could,' Hugh said, 'make a few more before your fortnight's up. If that's okay with you, Miss Martha Langford.'

There it was again – Hugh's use of her real name, not her stage name. He liked her because of who she was, not what she was.

'We could,' Martha said. 'And I think we should.'

So they did. They still ran each day, but separately, because Martha was never going to be able to keep up, running on sand, with Hugh. But they always met for coffee, at one of the many cafés along the seafront, or back at Martha's chalet, taking their drinks down onto the beach to drink if the tide was out, burying their bare feet in the sand, and letting the sand trickle through their fingers as they talked and shared aspects of their past lives. In the evenings they wandered up into the town to find a restaurant or pub for supper. They even had a hilarious hour in the Penny Arcade playing the gaming machines – winning sometimes, losing sometimes. A bit like life, Martha thought, although she thought she might be on a winning streak now she'd met Hugh.

Hugh had taken Martha's arm in a gallant way and linked it through his to cross roads, but they didn't hold hands. Or kiss.

On Martha's last night, sitting on the deck of 23 The Strand, Hugh uncorked a bottle of champagne he said he'd had cooling in his fridge, along with a plate of deli nibbles Martha had a feeling he'd bought for just such an occasion.

'Glasses out,' Hugh said, indicating the frothing champagne and the need to get it into glasses before it frothed all over the deck.

'Yes, sir!' Martha laughed, holding out the champagne glasses towards him.

When they were filled to the brim, she handed one to Hugh.

'A toast,' he said. 'To you. For helping me with my grief over Harris. So, to you.'

Martha gulped back tears, then took a sip of champagne.

'And to you,' she said, clinking glasses. 'And to legs and hearts that will mend, given time.'

'That too,' Hugh said, tapping Martha's glass again.

'What will you do now?'

'Photography, of course. I've a fancy for photographing the oceans of the world, running on the world's beaches. I've got an idea for a TV series running around in my head – 90 Mile Beach, Bondi Beach. Woolacombe in North Devon, even. It doesn't have to be a big beach or a famous one. The concept is I'd run with a well-known personality and we'd look at the geography and wildlife around us, and put the world to rights as we ran. What do you think?'

I think it's a rotten idea. I want you to stay in my life, not go running off with some random person you might fall in love with on a tropical beach. Was he telling her this was the end of their friendship? Or was he putting the ball in her court, giving her an 'out' if she wanted it?

'Sounds good,' Martha said.

'Once more with feeling,' Hugh laughed.

'Sounds *really, really* good.'

'That's better. A seven out of ten that time. And you?' Hugh asked.

'I've not made any firm plans yet. I quite fancy stage work

again. It's all too easy to iron out mistakes while filming for TV or the cinema. The money would be less but I've got enough to live on for a while. Then again, there's an idea buzzing about in my head like a mosquito that I could train to teach drama. Not at a stage school but in an ordinary comprehensive perhaps.'

'Go for it,' Hugh said. 'You've got a beautiful speaking voice. Well, a beautiful everything actually.'

'That's a lovely thing to hear,' Martha said. 'And?'

'And what?' Hugh swirled the stem of his glass in his fingers. He looked down at the table, up at the sky, out to sea. His eyes settled on Martha for a second and she saw his Adam's apple going up and down.

He was struggling for the right thing to say, wasn't he?

'To our respective futures?' Hugh said eventually.

'I think we both know that isn't what I meant. And I do believe, Hugh, you're blushing.'

Martha prised Hugh's glass gently from him and placed it on the tiny table between them.

'I was taught in drama school that, in the right situation, more emotion, more feeling, more truth can be conveyed by what people *don't* say than by what they do. Action – and conversely inaction – really can speak louder than words sometimes.' Then she cupped Hugh's face in her hands and kissed him. Just a gentle kiss but she let it linger.

'Wow! Is that how they teach you to kiss in stage school?'

'Nope. That one came from the heart.'

And then Hugh kissed her back.

It was that old cliché of fireworks and music playing for Martha.

'And so did that. But back to our futures... I like live theatre,' Hugh said. 'Can I come and watch?'

'Of course. And I've decided a bit of running on the world's beaches is something I'd quite like too.'

'So, we've rewritten the end of *Roman Holiday*.' Hugh kissed her again.

'Get a room already!' someone shouted from the prom.

'Your cabin or mine?' Martha asked as Hugh released her from the kiss.

Martha wrapped the amethyst necklace Tom Marchant had given her in tissue paper and slid it into an envelope. She had no need of it any more but it might be just the thing someone else might love and cherish. On the outside of the envelope she wrote her message:

> *Dear next occupant,*
>
> *I've had the most interesting and wonderful fortnight at 23 The Strand. Life-changing even. I hope you have a wonderful time too. I leave you this gift, which I hope you'll enjoy wearing or will give to someone you think would like it. It might be fun if you could leave some little thing as a welcome gift for the next occupant but that's by no means obligatory.*
>
> *Best wishes*
> *Martha*
> *P.S. Formerly known as Serena Ross*

ONE PLACE. MANY STORIES

If you enjoyed *The Little B&B at Cove End*, then why not try another delightfully uplifting romance from HQ Digital?

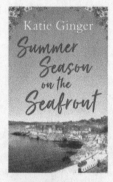